Working With the Ones You Love

Working With the Ones You Love

Strategies for a Sucessful Family Business

Dennis T. Jaffe, Ph.D.

Conari Press
Berkeley, CA

Library of Congress Cataloging in Publication Data

Jaffe, Dennis T.
         Working with the ones you love: strategies for a successful family business /
Dennis T. Jaffe. —1st pbk. ed.
                    p. cm.
         Includes bibliographical references and index.
         ISBN 0-943233-22-4 : $12.95
         1. Family-owned business enterprises—Management. I. Title.
HD62.25.J34 1991
658.02'2—dc20   91-19997
   CIP
Printed in the United States of America on recycled paper

ISBN: 0-943233-22-4
First edition
1 2 3 4 5 6 7 8 9 10

Cover by Andrea Sohn Design. Illustration by Frank Ansley.

Dedication

To my family, my mother and late father, Rhoda and Sidney, my wife, Cynthia, and my sons Oren and Kai, whose unfailing love, support, encouragement, and acceptance make it possible for me to go on the adventures that have made up my life.

Our thinking about growth and decay is dominated by the image of a single life-span, animal or vegetable. Seedling, full flower, and death . . . but for an ever-renewing society, the appropriate image is a total garden, a balanced aquarium or other ecological system. Some things are being born, other things are flourishing, still other things are dying—but the system lives.

-John Gardner

Table of Contents

Acknowledgements

The field of family business research and consultation has emerged dramatically in only the past five years. Like any new, hybrid discipline, it is populated with a great diversity of gadflys, characters, and creative pioneers. Because it lies at the interface of several fields, only those who are willing to look across boundaries and synthesize are able to go on the journey. I've been privileged to meet many of these pioneers, to be nourished by their research and practice, and to work with some of the best. There is a lot from all these people in this book. The best insights come from my contact with them, while the weaker parts are my responsibility alone.

I'd like to thank my partner and wife, Cynthia Scott, for supporting me through the development of this book, and my work in general. I am lucky that she is a family therapist and organization consultant. Her critical perspective, skepticism, and very different family and cultural background have helped me immensely.

For seven exciting years I was affiliated with the Los Angeles Family Institute, which was a meeting place for some wonderful work, ideas, and conversations. Will McWhinney and Robert Carroll first made me aware that such an animal as a "family business" existed, and their explorations provoked my curiosity. I especially benefitted from Will's sharp theoretical formulations. Larry Allman has been my longest-standing colleague and friend in the world of family therapy, and my work with him was my family therapy education. His suggestion that I follow my highest intentions is well taken.

Carol Goodman was a partner and friend during my first research and consulting work, and we collaborated on several family business retreats, and the initial research and interviews with family businesses. Sam Marks invited Carol, Alan Kepner, and I to participate in his Next Generation programs for the furniture industry. Sam's incredible vision, caring, pioneering energy, and dedication inspired us with the importance of this work. Dameron Williams met me through the Chamber of Commerce, and his endless store of stories, his vast network, his careful reading of the literature, his thoughtful critique, and his desire to create a forum for family business in the Bay Area helped this project along.

For the past decade, Saybrook Institute has been my academic home and supported my research. I want to thank my colleagues there, especially President Jules Pagano, who has been a cheerleader for my projects.

David Bork and my colleagues at the Bork Institute for Family Business in Aspen, including Leslie Isaacs, Ann Dapice, Kathy Wiseman,

Sam Lane, Nick Bizony, Elizabeth McGrath, and Tom McMurrain have created a delightful support group sharing ideals, skills, visions, and fun.

Sharon Nelton encouraged my writing, publishing portions of this book in *Nation's Business*. The *McGraw-Hill Business Week Family Business Newsletter* also published several excerpts. Other excerpts were published in the *San Francisco Business Times*, and *Vision/Action*. The bibliography and library of family business materials, compiled by Pat Frishkoff and her staff at Oregon State University, shortened my research by many weeks. They graciously copied many references for me. I have been aided by their bibliography. Nathan Ancell of Ethan Allen Inc. sponsored a research project on succession planning, and the development of a resource guide, some of which has been incorporated into Chapter 8.

Jordan Paul has been a friend and teacher over many years, and his concepts of communication and conflict resolution are so deeply a part of my work that it is hard to write or do anything without assuming them. We have had many talks specifically about family business. John Schoen and Nancy Bowman-Upton, of Baylor University, Pat Frishkoff of Oregon State University, and Steve Pechter of Laventhol & Horwath invited me to conduct seminars and participate in their programs.

The Family Firm Institute is the core professional organization defining and supporting family business research, education, and consultation, bringing together people from the many disciplines of the field. Their journal, *Family Business Review*, and their annual conference, have been a continuing forum for the development of an interdisciplinary perspective on family business.

The concepts in this book derive in large measure from the work of family business consultation pioneers. The first book I read in the field was John Ward's *Keeping the Family Business Healthy*, followed soon by Leon Danco's *Beyond Survival* and David Bork's *Family Business, Risky Business*. The conceptual thinking of these leaders and their important research and observations certainly informed my own work. Models and research by Ivan Lansberg about succession, John Davis about family business structures and development, John Ward about family values and the family council, Gibb Dyer about cultural change and development, and David Bork about family systems models have all influenced me. My concepts about couples in business come from research conducted with Rosabeth Kanter for my doctoral dissertation.

Sandra Dijkstra, agent extraordinaire, had faith in me and this project, when others did not.

Commonweal Healing Center in Bolinas once again provided a haven for me to write and be at peace at a critical point in my writing.

Foreword

You are invited to join in a celebration of family business! It is a celebration that is long overdue. The popular media, with its focus on the soap opera antics of some, would have the public believe that the worst place to work is in a business with members of your family. They even suggest that no good can come from such an environment that is certain to produce disaster.

That simply isn't true! For more than 20 years I have had the privilege of serving families in business. Those businesses range from billion dollar international corporations to "Mom and Pop" operations in which the principals barely eke out a living as they struggle to meet the weekly payroll. The people in those businesses enjoy some of the best work environments to be found anywhere and a greater level of satisfaction than most of the work force. They thrive on their independence, their feelings of accomplishment and the money they earn from their efforts. It is not at all unusual for family members to have more opportunities and more responsibility sooner in their careers—plus more income—than their contemporaries. Further, women in family business have less difficulty "breaking through the glass ceiling" and into the executive suite than their counterparts in the general work force.

There are several reasons we are hearing more about family business these days. After WWII, many veterans were educated via the GI Bill and then started businesses. For the past ten years, those aging entrepreneurs have been transferring control to successors. Also, in the fifties and sixties, workers flocked to large corporations that "guaranteed" security. Now, no longer enamored with the large corporation, workers now seek environments where employers care about them, and in many cases such people have started their own family businesses.

Still another trend that puts family business in the news is the renewal that is taking place in families with names like Ford, Rockefeller, Bronfman, Haas, Morgan, Mars, and Mennen. These successors—who may be 4th, 5th or even 6th generation—are re-affirming the family commitment to maintain the family corporate entity by such actions as creating huge "war chests" of funds to buy back stock from non-family owners or to pay the substantial estate taxes dictated by tax laws.

Since 1970, when I worked with my first family business client, I have had in-depth, long-term involvement with more than 250 families in business. That work has required charting each family's course through every imaginable family business issue including succession between generations, death of the founder, sale of the business, and the complexities of dealing with wealth.

After careful examination of these 250 cases, I found that families who succeed in work and at home share certain qualities or patterns of functioning. These are qualities I have come to think of as Management Principles for Family Business. The family businesses that really worked had some or all of the following qualities in varying degrees:

Shared Values: About people, work, and money.

Shared Power: Across generations, between spouses, among siblings. This is not to be construed as equal power.

Shared Activities for Maintaining Relationships: Families that maintain their sense of humor, demonstrate ability to have fun, and play together are putting "relationship currency" into the family bank so there is a reserve to draw upon during times of disagreement.

Traditions: That which make *this* family special and set it apart from all other families.

Willingness to Learn and Grow: The family that is open to new ideas and approaches is one that, as a group, can solve any problem.

Genuine Caring: Open expression of feelings of concern for other family members.

Mutual Respect: Evidenced by trust between and among family members that is built on a history of keeping one's word.

Assist and Support One Another: Especially at times of grief, loss, pain, and shame.

Privacy: Respect for one another's individual space and for the private space required in each family unit within the extended family.

Well-Defined Interpersonal Boundaries: To keep individuals from getting caught in the middle. Good boundaries keep conflicts between two family members from involving a third person.

To maximize the potential for success, families in business can make a concerted effort to pattern their functioning on these Family Business Management Principles. That is why I am excited to see **Working With The Ones You Love**. It thoroughly embodies these principles. It isn't just a business book, because it is about enriching and building the family that creates the business. If a family reads it and does the exercises, it can learn to apply these principles in developing their business.

Working With The Ones You Love is most exciting because it isn't a book that tells you a bunch of stories about incredible families and businesses, and just leaves you hanging. This is a book you can dig into and work with. Many of the struggles of families in family business that I have seen do not need intensive professional consultation. Rather they need a guide that lets them know what they can do to make things work better.

That is what Dennis Jaffe has done in this workbook. He has created a clear guide to success by taking the best of the literature and experience in family business and adapting it in a self-management format. I can see a family using this workbook for their own growth and development, to overcome the common traps that family businesses fall into, and to build their capacity to follow the key Family Business Management Principles. I am glad to have a place in this effort.

David Bork
Director, The Bork Institute For Family Business
Aspen, Colorado

Introduction

If you work in a family business, you probably regard it as a tremendous gift and an incredible challenge. Every day you work with people you love and trust on things that matter to you. You keep the fruits of your labor, and you have control over your future. Sometimes it's a lot of fun. Other times you may feel it is the dumbest, most frustrating decision you've ever made. There are difficulties and conflicts. One of your family members may be the hardest person in the world to work with. Misunderstandings can have grave consequences, and working out relationships with parents and/or children can seem at times to be almost impossible.

While most family business owners would say that the satisfactions greatly outweigh the frustrations, the difficulties sometimes arise almost without warning. Or did you just miss the warnings?

Family businesses have special problems along with the usual business challenges. Every family business founder dreams of passing the business on to his or her heirs. Yet that remains more a dream than a reality. Most family businesses fail. Fewer than a third make it long enough to be passed on, and only half of those make it into the third generation.

Several years ago, I began clipping family business stories from the business press and local newspaper business sections. To my surprise, I found family business profiles almost every day. The coverage focussed as much on the personal dynamics within the family and how they influence the course of the business as on business strategy and financial results. The profiles suggested that the personal style, values, and relationships of the family determined the direction, culture, and success of the business. The clear message was that family businesses have a special aura, that the family permeates the business, and together, family and business create something powerful and special—but also potentially problematic. Yet not one of the hundreds of leadership, excellence, and management books in the last few years has specifically addressed the complexity, qualities, and challenges that family management brings to a business.

My experience comes from a decade of work as a consultant to family businesses in many industries, from small home-based consulting firms operated by a couple (like my own business), to large, publicly traded family empires whose names are household words. In the course of interviews with scores of founders, heirs, and other family business members, I found that the problems of family business, large and small, are frighteningly similar.

In family companies, whether gigantic or tiny, the worlds of work and family are deeply intertwined, and love and business are often in conflict. The family's habits often find their way into the business and family problems are transferred to work. Large and small business families have intergenerational feuds, problems in communication, and difficulty in separating family from business. They struggle with whether to pass on the business to non-family managers or to their children, and to which child.

At each stage of individual, family and business growth, some businesses and families run into trouble. As both a psychologist/family therapist and an organization development consultant, I have combined the insights from these two different disciplines into a hybrid that applies to the unique situations in which family business members find themselves. Drawing upon my consulting, research on family business, and the tales told to me by successful and unsuccessful family business owners and their families, I have developed an approach to solving the special problems of family business. This method will help those who work with people in their family—spouses, parents and children, in-laws and cousins—manage their relationships and overcome predictable growth crises so that their business can thrive, and their love and caring can remain intact, and even grow.

Working With the Ones You Love is a guide for family business members struggling to balance the two worlds of work and family. Other business books deal with financial planning, strategy, and organization development. **Working With the Ones You Love** is about personal relationships and change, at home and work. It is especially for those who seek both greater harmony within the family and more success in business. It will show you how to preserve the special nature of your business, while overcoming the difficulties of working with people you know intimately.

In a family business, you have two relationships with every member of your family who works with you: your business relationship and your personal relationship. Problems arise when you try to transfer aspects of one relationship to the other. You have (or should have) a different relationship with your father and your boss, or your wife and your partner, even if they are the same person.

My purpose here is to explore the consequences of these dual work/ family relationships and help you manage them so that each person achieves closeness, personal satisfaction, and productivity. The book will lead you and your family through every situation where family and business interact. Each chapter looks at a different stage of family businesses and the particular issues that they face as they grow and evolve.

I am proposing that you and your family engage in a long-term process of increased awareness, communication, shared responsibility, future planning, and conflict resolution. The personal concerns in your family and your business needs may vary, but there are certain techniques and tools that you can use to work together. You begin with yourself, and then find ways to involve the other people in the family in this exploration. If you are the first member of your family to pick up this book, you need to see yourself as the leader of this process.

Many families are not used to talking about themselves with one another. The way you work and act as a family may be taken for granted to such an extent that your family may feel it does not merit discussion. That is the way of many, perhaps most, families. However my experience in helping family businesses shows that such an assumption is erroneous and potentially dangerous.

Several factors today make it increasingly difficult for family businesses to continue doing things as they always have. Things are changing fast in the marketplace. All businesses must continually rethink the nature of their business and how they get things done. A family, too, is continually changing; the owner/patriarch who thinks he always knows what is best for his family, or what his spouse and children want, is heading for trouble. In times of change, people need to communicate more and reconsider things that have previously worked just fine.

I make several assumptions about families and business in this book, which I want to make explicit.

First, I believe that every family business needs to take account of more issues then ever before. In particular, everyone needs to be more aware of one another's feelings, goals, and desires. You can't assume anything. You need to be aware not just of how things are going today, but of potential difficulties you may face tomorrow.

Second, I believe communication about differences is better than avoidance or ignorance. The family has to talk about things, especially in times of generational transition, and there usually has to be a lot of talk. You have to share more than just your positions on specific conflict areas. Struggle and give and take come with the territory. People in families who work together have to let each other know about their values, about their personal goals, and about how they see the business and the future. When they come upon differences, they have to be committed enough to each other to stick with the conflict until a resolution is reached. The relationships are important enough for everyone involved to be committed to achieving resolution.

A third assumption is that every family member must take responsibility for making the situation better. You cannot opt out of major family decisions, or withdraw and say that you aren't involved. There are no victims in a family. Every person can make the family and the business a better place to live and work. If you feel that you are a victim, or that there is nothing you can do, look carefully between these covers. Here are several hundred things that you can do, some of which will have impact. This is especially true for people in a family business who traditionally have felt they have little power.

Fourth, the whole family, not just the patriarch or head, must work together to plan and create the future of the family and the business. The future is too complex, and the different people and groups involved are so varied, that one person can't plan alone, and it certainly can't be left to chance. Everyone must be involved, and it's hard work that takes time. There are no short-cuts or quick fixes.

And finally, I believe that conflict needs to be faced openly, and that differences between family members, even of different generations and statuses, can and must be resolved, or they will poison the future.

This book is not just about how to overcome conflict and keep your family intact and your business alive. It is about how to work together to make the family's experience of one other, and of the business, as rewarding as it can be. People want to be in family business for very deep and personally important reasons. The problems may be common, but the rewards are worth it. I offer this book to help you find your own resolutions, and chart your own path.

How to Use This Book

Chances are you are work with family members, are part of a family that owns a business, are thinking about starting one, have escaped from one, work for one, or have some other reason for wanting to make sense out of family business. You may be in the midst of a crisis, either between you and a relative in the business, or just responding to the unexpected demands of keeping the company afloat.

This book is designed so that a family business member, or the business or family as a whole, can use it as a consultant. You can work on your own to learn new ways to resolve a personal issue with your family business. Or you can work together as a family, chapter by chapter, having meetings, building dialogue, clarifying issues, and making plans. These activities will lead you to look more clearly at where you have been and what you need to do next.

Whatever your role in the family or business, you will learn practical strategies, successful techniques, and problem-solving methods to improve personal and business effectiveness. Each chapter contains tools, exercises and techniques to practice. For example, I offer instructions on how to develop a sustaining family philosophy; hold a family meeting; communicate directly; balance dual roles of parent/spouse/child and entrepreneur/colleague/partner/heir; handle succession; develop a management team; and resolve painful and difficult conflicts. The book contains explanations, stories of family businesses, and examples from my consultation of how businesses have approached and resolved crises. Some cases have been disguised, and are presented anonymously to preserve confidences.

At the beginning of each chapter, the major task of that chapter is described. Start your work by reading the chapter through. Then go back and work on specific exercises and tasks.

There are several Reflection Questions in each chapter. These are not simple "yes" or "no" questions, but rather ask you to reflect on some aspect of your family business experience. When you reach one of these, I suggest you take a period of time, perhaps an hour, and think about the question. Be sure to write down your thoughts, memories, and responses, and keep your notes, because you will want to discuss them with your family.

The chapters also contain exercises, discussion topics, and focussed interactions for you and your family. Plan time to do these together. You may want to set aside several evenings, or a whole vacation day, to work on some areas. Family business difficulties can't be resolved by one or two people alone. They demand a total family effort, because everybody is involved. Even if some people appear to be outside of the situation, they may offer key information and help resolve impasses. Everyone has a piece to the puzzle. Even though it may seem time-consuming, if you actually do the exercises together, you will begin to see your family, and your business, in some very new ways that hopefully will help you overcome some of your difficulties and avoid others.

I want to offer you a warning right now: you will come to points in this book where you will want to pull away and say to yourself, "We just can't deal with this issue right now." That is the point where you should redouble your efforts because that is the point of tension where the seeds of later conflict and decay lie.

There are no simple ways to resolve the communication failures or tensions that frustrate the harmony of your family and the success of your business. No matter what your difficulty, there is one long-term solution: your family will have to step back, look at how it does things, and slowly begin to change. That means you will have to talk about things you may never have discussed, and the people who have power in your family and/ or business will have to learn to share some of it with others.

Writing to everyone in a family business is very complex. Founders, sons, daughters, spouses, in-laws, and outside managers have different perspectives. In trying to deal with these multiple stakeholders in the business of family business, I have sometimes geared my writing to specific people. Some chapters, such as Chapter 8 on succession and estate planning, are written primarily to the business owner. Other sections, such as Chapter 6 on growing up in the business, are written more to the sons and daughters who may inherit the business. But even if the chapter is not primarily directed to you, hopefully it will assist in enhancing your understanding of another family member's situation.

I have drawn extensively on case material from my own consulting and from talks with colleagues. To preserve anonymity, I have altered details and used fictitious family names (indicated by quote marks) or fictitious first names.

A note on my conventions about non-sexist language: since there are men and women in all positions of family businesses, I have tried to include both male and female pronouns. However, a vast majority of family businesses today were still founded, and are headed, by men, who are also fathers. Therefore, in some sections I use the terms "he" and even "dad" when referring to the traditional family business patriarch.

1

The Challenge of Family Business: Managing Dual Work-Family Relationships

"A family moves from rags, to riches, to rags, in three generations."

-*Proverb*

It is the easiest and most natural decision in your life. . . yet it is also a walk across a gulf that can have vast consequences for you and your descendants. You are about to, or have already, started a business. You're excited, and you need help. You turn to the people who are closest to you: your spouse, children, other relatives. You know them intimately, and you assume that love will enable you to work together.

Or perhaps you are on the other side of the fence. Your spouse, uncle or cousin has approached you with the most wonderful opportunity. You can join them in their business, which is growing by leaps and bounds. Wouldn't it be wonderful to share the benefits, and work together?

Perhaps you've grown up in the shadow of your father's, or grandfather's, enterprise. As you finish school and contemplate the future, you wonder whether you will continue the tradition, and what that means for your brothers or sisters. What would it be like to work with them, or with dad and mom? What will you do? Are you up to the task?

The journey of family members from home to business is often short, and seems entirely natural. But moving from a close family to an effective working relationship is an enormous transition that is not as simple as it looks. Nonetheless millions of families have made the journey, and many of them consider these dual relationships the most special, the most meaningful, and the most important of their lives.

Tasks for the Chapter

In this chapter you will begin to look at the special structure and qualities of family business, and examine your personal reasons for having one. You will begin to reflect on your own relationship to your family business, and you can convene your family to look at things together. You will all complete and share the Family Business Assessment Inventory to pinpoint your strengths and weaknesses. No matter who you are in your family, as the person who has selected this book, you are placed in the role of leader for this task. You will need to get the rest of your family interested and involved in looking at themselves.

When you create a business, you often want to share it with your family, and pass it on to your heirs. Like a medieval lord, the family business founder almost automatically considers it something important to pass to his or her offspring. It represents the family legacy, the special meaning that is the essence of the family.

There *is* something both powerful and wonderful about working with a close relative. You can trust each other, you know one another well, and you will work hard for one another. Indeed a study by Joyce McLaughlin and Noel Byrne of 60 family businesses found that the major benefit of a family business was the commitment and dependability of relatives.[1]

But developing work relationships between family members is not as easy as it looks—as you may have already found out the hard way. Indeed, in a study, 52 of 59 family businesses reported stress and conflict in some aspect of managing the family-business relationships.[2]

In a family business you have to manage two different types of relationships with the same person—and sometimes those are in conflict. Families are about love, acceptance, and growing up, while businesses are about results and productivity. The business adds pressure and urgency to the universal requirements of every family member: to grow up and become independent, to care for someone even if you disagree, to be fair, and to be accepted and validated. Because of the different tasks and requirements of families and businesses, two brothers, a married couple, or a father and son often find that they can't work together in the same way as they are a family together. What works for a family can stifle a business, and vice versa.

When relatives start a business they invariably make two mistakes. First, they believe that their caring for one another is enough to carry them through the common business start-up problems. Second, they believe that a family business is just like any other business. How wrong they are. Effectively managing dual work/family relationships takes special awareness, careful communication, and extreme effort.

Family involvement adds several layers of complexity to a business. There are often struggles and difficulties within the family who own the business: communication difficulty, rivalries and frustrated expectations, coping with rapid growth, balancing business with family, and passing the business to the next generation.

Healthy family business relations begin with a structure to organize the family, to keep in touch with what each person wants, what the family stands for, and what the family wants from its business. In order to build an effective business, the family must not only develop a business plan and goals, but a system that will insure good communication between them. Family members need to learn to deal with conflict, to hold each other accountable, and to work for clear, shared goals. They need to learn how to handle predictable growth crises of a family along with business cycles. And founders must help their sons and daughters develop the skills to lead the business in new directions. This is a tall order, but one that can be achieved if you start early enough and plan carefully.

Successful family businesses create their own special worlds, a certain style of business culture, and rules for moving from family to business. One classic example is Brown-Foreman distillers, makers of Jack Daniels and Lenox China. Through five generations, the men in the Brown family, led by the eldest sons of the eldest son, have run the business. Both the business and the family are steeped in tradition. The business operates according to tried-and-true principles; their products are perennials that have lasting value and quality. Like many family businesses, Brown-Foreman expects, but does not require, its heirs to enter the business. Its adherence to traditional Southern culture has so far limited the business to men, and tradition also dictates that the oldest son becomes the leader.

But the company policy of "planned nepotism" is not an invitation for any incompetent to rise in the ranks. The business is introduced to growing family members as a challenge to take on if they can. The young heirs, or "nepots" as they call themselves, are expected to prepare well. They are expected to go to good colleges and professional schools. Once they enter the business, the rules change. Family ties are important, but the family agrees that the business comes first. Indeed, the family was split a few years ago over a marketing question about the independence of brand organizations. Brother Martin disagreed with his older brother Lee. The board was consulted to mediate and they went along with Lee, the CEO. Martin resigned from the company. While the business is run by family members, the traditions of the business are tough and results-oriented, very different from the family rules. Family members not in the business are free to take their considerable wealth and do what they want.

This separation of business from family, and the clarity of the rules by which the business operates, are characteristic of successful family businesses. The clear rules and understandings about succession help to limit conflict and competition in an otherwise intensely competitive clan. They fight with the marketplace, not each other.

In order to help you learn to effectively manage the dual work/family relationships you find yourself in, let's first look at some of the unique qualities and structure of all family businesses. By seeing some of the strengths and weaknesses of family businesses as a whole, you can begin to orient yourself to the important issues in your situation.

What is a Family Business?

A family business is any business where more than one member of a family takes on management or active ownership responsibility. You have a family business if you work with someone in your family in a business you both own or which you may someday own. The essence of a family business is that blood, work, and business ownership are held in common.

There are two major types of family businesses: single generational and cross-generational. Single generation family businesses begin when one entrepreneur invites other family members of his or her generation to share in management/ownership of the business, or when two relatives of the same generation start a business. It may be two brothers, or cousins, or a couple. The line is crossed when one relative asks another not just to help out, but to take on major responsibility with the expectation of a share of ownership in the future. Traditionally, many small businesses were started by brothers or male cousins. Today, women are increasingly part of family businesses.

As we will see in Chapter 5, the most frequent new pattern in single-generational businesses is the couple-owned business. This is a family business where a couple not only works together, but where the business is seen as a shared responsibility (if not always equally shared). Large companies like Liz Claiborne and Mrs. Fields are couple-run businesses where the wife has taken the more prominent role. Couples in business together have their own set of problems, mainly around separating work and personal life, and avoiding destructive conflict and competition.

Cross-generational family businesses usually arise later in a business' life cycle, when the founding generation has grown the business to the point where it can accommodate the next generation. Less frequently such businesses are started by pairs, often a father and son. The complexity of cross-generational family businesses stems from two essential tasks: modifying the parent-child relationship into one of peers at work, and preparing the younger generation to take over leadership. Struggles between parent and child, or between different branches of the family, often create pain and drama, and threaten the future of the business—and sometimes the family too. Since both businesses and families have their evolving life cycles, problems arise when the business and family life cycles are not in synch.

Types of Family Work Relationships

In a rough survey of over 200 family businesses, from case accounts and from my own experience, the following family relationships were reported:

Same Generation

Couple	16%
Brothers	27%
Brother/sister	8%
In-laws	18%

Intergenerational

Father/son	34%
Father/daughter	8%
Mother/daughter	5%
Mother/son	1%

Most Business Is Family Business

Family business is as old as society. Ancient kingdoms were actually family businesses. And behind the impersonal facade of many modern world-famous businesses lies the complex, richly textured relationships, visions, dreams, and struggles of a family seeking a form of immortality and security. As a family business moves through the generations, it is shaped by bonds of family loyalty, ambition, and expression, as well as dishonor and deceit. In the tortured succession of the Richards and Henrys of Shakespeare's plays, multi-generational corporate families such as the Rothschilds and Duponts, and on television in the machinations of JR and Bobby Ewing, and Alexis and Blake Carrington, family dramas play out while the company may be held hostage, waiting for the outcome.

Today the basic economic and social building block of the United States is neither the individual worker nor entrepreneur, nor impersonal corporations, but rather the families that create, control, and operate businesses. Over 90% of all U.S. businesses—over half the GNP and 175 of the Fortune 500—are family businesses. And they employ between 40 and 50 million people! Most of the mega-companies of today started as family businesses, and many of them have remained so through several generations.

Currently the most prevalent new form of business in the United States is the micro-business with only one or two employees, most commonly operated by a couple or family starting in their home. New jobs and new wealth come from these entrepreneurial start-ups, some of which may grow quickly to become the next Wal-Mart, the Gap, Apple Computer, and other new members of the Fortune 500. A majority of these new ventures involve two or more family members working together, with the founders dreaming of passing their fortune to their heirs.

Entrepreneurs may start companies, but wealth flows in families. So for a child of business owners, the family business is his or her major career option. In addition, as companies shed layers of managers, many "surplus" mid-life employees decide to start their own business, often with a spouse or relative.

Half the *US News 100*—the largest fortunes and controlling ownership of companies—are families, and 35 of the 100 hold top management in the companies they own. In addition, many families not in top management have special classes of stock that keep them in control of businesses they founded. For example, though it holds only a small percentage of the total, the Ford family has a special class of stock that enables it to make the critical decisions that control the future of the auto company that bears its name. Similarly, the Weyerhauser family has been involved in top management as well as partial ownership of its paper products company for five generations.

In response to the takeover wars of the past few years, more family businesses, such as Levi-Strauss, have taken their companies private in leveraged buyouts, joining other large private family concerns such as Hallmark, Bechtel, Mars Candy, Estee Lauder, the Newhouse news chain, and the Reichmann real estate holdings. Often the buyouts were motivated by the family's desire to maintain its traditional values and pursue long-term strategies. By taking their companies off the market, these families maintain their autonomy. Smaller family businesses mimic these methods to maintain ownership and control, and to keep their stamp on their businesses.

Family businesses are not just different from other businesses. There is also evidence that they are more effective. A study by *US News and World Report* in 1986 found that of the 47 largest family companies, 31 outperformed the Dow-Jones index! Of the excellent companies cited in Peters' and Waterman's bestseller *In Search of Excellence*, nearly half are family firms, yet this reality is never explored in accounting for their results. James O'Toole, Professor at USC and author of *Vanguard Management*, notes, "If you start looking around at well-run companies that have been around for a long time, you often find they are the work of a single individual or family."[3]

What is the source of this greater effectiveness? The answer lies in the ways that families run businesses differently and the special qualities a family can bring to a business. When a company takes the name of the family of a founder who then passes ownership and control to his or her heirs, the business and the family are identified as one by the public. The family's values, what it stands for, lie behind the name on the door. The family is often a very active part of the community.

In addition family businesses tend to have what Peters and Waterman call "strong cultures," corporate behaviors based on an explicit set of values concerning the way to do business. These values often include emphasis on quality, loyalty to employees, long-term goals, and closeness to the customer, all of which are linked with excellence. Family businesses have a sense of continuity and connection to their history, and as they often note, their businesses are run for more than just profit. While other businesses frequently share these qualities, they are clearly associated with family business.

Family businesses are special: the people who own them care deeply for each other. These caring relationships are passed on to employees. Traditionally, a family business builds family spirit among all employees. Many employees of such businesses are deeply dedicated and feel identified with the first family. They feel the caring and respect from the top that Tom Peters notes is the single most important aspect of company excellence. That caring also extends to customers. A study by University of California professor Amy Lyman[4] found that family businesses were more involved in customer service, and more concerned about creating strong and positive relationships with customers, than comparable non-family businesses.

Many of the most unique, exciting, and people-oriented companies listed in *The 100 Best Companies to Work for In America* are family owned. There is W.L. Gore, The Olga Company, and Herman Miller, each of which sees its employees as "associates," and accords them respect, job security, and responsibility without respect to their level in the hierarchy. Levi Strauss, Johnson Wax, and Hallmark have very responsive family owners, who are approachable and care for employees.

It isn't hard to figure out why family businesses hold these values. Unlike public companies that often are run for short-run financial goals, where the management team is always at the mercy of a "what have you done lately" message from the board, the family business offers the CEO tremendous job security. Family business CEOs last four or five times longer than CEOs of public companies, an average of 24 years. Like kings or queens, they only leave when they die, or quit, or the company goes out of business. Their personal policies are more likely to reward and value long-term commitment on the part of their employees.

The Power of a Family Business

The most important reason for the prevalence and success of family business is that family closeness and understanding is a powerful resource in the business world. Family members have a shared history and sense of identity. They know each other deeply, are aware of one others' abilities and weaknesses, and know what they stand for. Family members trust and care for each other, are loyal to each other, and feel deeply committed to each others' welfare and future. Often they have a special shorthand language, and can talk quickly, share information, and get things done efficiently. And finally, family members have an already established hierarchy, so they know who to defer to, where they stand, and how to divide up tasks according to different status and abilities.

Looking at these qualities of family relationships, you can see how each one can be of great value when transferred to a business setting. The presence of these family qualities in a business makes for a highly trusting, deeply bonded, and effective work team. Family business may have a competitive advantage here because such bonds are more difficult to come by in co-workers. In a new business, success comes more easily when the founders have profound trust in each other and the ability to forge working bonds quickly. Unfortunately, such qualities can also lead to conflict or difficulty, if they become extreme.

Qualities of Family Business Cultures

As diverse in size and type as family businesses are, certain common qualities mark both large and small family businesses:

Quality Focus

Pride in product, family name, customers.

Paternalism

Taking care of workers, knowing what's best. Strongly non-union. Employees are well paid, treated fairly, consistently, with no layoffs. Asks high level of commitment and loyalty from employees.

Family Metaphors
Informal bonds, community sense, "family feeling," loyalty, and commitment to employees.
Stability; Long-term Focus
Stick to their core business, stay clearly in focus. Maintain brand and customer loyalty via quality and consistency, for long-term returns.
Difficulty Changing
Confidence in their way of doing things. Suspicion of new ways.
Personalist Cultures
Personal relations with key people are important. Employees need to fit in. Highly political environment. Power stems from relationships, who you are close to.

As the above list indicates, there is also a downside to family businesses. Traditionally, they are bastions where blood rather than competence reigns supreme, tradition overrules innovation, and pleasing the family is more important than running an effective operation. The term "closely-held" can be more than a tax category for the family business; it often describes a psychological penchant for holding on to the past and ignoring the need for change and sharing control. For every excellent family company, you can probably name one where incompetent relatives have destroyed profits, where family welfare takes precedence over quality work, where byzantine politics make decisions difficult, and where pursuing family feuds is more important than making the business profitable. Obsolete patriarchy, feudalism, and deep and destructive isolation from changes in the global marketplace, are occupational hazards that plague family businesses.

The Family Behind the Business

At 97, C.M. "Pops" Yeager still has lunch every Thursday at the Yaeger's Carriage House he started with four generations of his key managers: son Herb, now 69, Herb's daughters Sherry and Linda, Sherry's husband, and Sherry's daughter, Melinda. Sometimes even Melinda's seven-year-old daughter Shannon helps out after school. Working in the store is a labor of love for everyone. For nearly 40 years, the family's home has been as much in its stores as in its household. Like many family businesses, the store has a solid reputation and great loyalty among its employees. The store itself is like a family. It has been the Yaeger's living room, and their children's playroom for three generations.

The history of the business is like the random growth of many other small family businesses. Pops had a number of stores and other ventures, but they didn't really grow until son Herb came in to help him form the Carriage House as a cross-generational partnership. In a way, the business had to grow then, because it suddenly had to support two families. Years later, Herb's daughter Sherry entered the business when her first marriage ended and she decided to take a year off from teaching. Her sister also came to help out temporarily. Both have stayed ever since. After Sherry remarried, her new husband began to help out after work in order to spend time with her. Soon he too was hooked. After a year or so of this, Herb asked if he was willing to leave his printing job and take on the management of a new store. Today, Sherry's daughter Melinda, who has worked in the business for nearly a decade, has just taken over management of their new warehouse and office facility.

Like most other family businesses, you couldn't understand Yaeger's Carriage House without knowing the Yaeger family. Yet most management training views a company in isolation, detached from the vision, values, struggles, and multiple goals that come from the founders. That won't work for family business, where the issues can't be understood or resolved without taking the family reality into account: is the business run to make a profit, or to provide a place for the founders' children to work and grow? Is the son's ego or the business' future more important? Is the family tradition of no layoffs and support for employees, some of whom have been with the company for generations themselves, more important than the bottom line? Can the two be made compatible?

A family business cannot be understood without understanding the family that created it. Giving your name to a company, dedicating your life to it, and passing it on to your children are some of the most important things a person can do in a life. To understand the business, you must look at the values, shared meanings, aspirations, and personal style of the family.

Building a business is a long-term investment for a family. Whether conscious of this or not, the family sees the business as the most important form of family expression and as a bank for the family future. The business is founded in "sweat equity," the value derived from many years of family members working for usually lower than market returns. The family business is run for the future and the next generation, not just for quarterly profits.

The business is often the main pursuit of the family, and it continues over generations. In many families, the business is also the major source of meaning for the family. Children grow up seeing the business as the deepest, most important reality for their family. It's what the family stands for. Their inheritance is not just the business itself, but the loyalty to its vision, and the desire to perpetuate the family's meaning. Many plays and movies have been created about the torment that a family member experiences trying to respect family values, maintain family honor, keep its good name alive, and complete the work of parents, while also feeling a pull to pursue his or her own unique sense of personal identity.

Unlike public corporations, family businesses can be run with a variety of goals that run counter to or alongside the profit motive. The family business is operated for family as well as business purposes. It can be used to maintain the comfort and security of the family by having relatives on the payroll, by being a source of cash for paying personal expenses, for perks like vacations and cars, or for tax savings on insurance. A well-designed family business can reach a stage when it can finance a fairly lavish personal lifestyle for the family. The only problem with this arrangement, from a business perspective, is that the founders may be taking cash out of the business which may be needed for its future development. In such cases, the family's immediate needs run counter to business needs.

Family concerns deeply affect all manner of business decisions. Even firing a long-term employee can be a family issue. In one company the recent poor performance of a woman was complicated by the fact that she had worked for the business for years, and was a close friend of the wife of the owner. The company was known in the community as one that respected its employees. The family decided that the woman could not be fired. But the wife and others offered to help her with her problems. The woman turned out to be under family stress, and after a few months her performance improved. She now tells everyone she meets about how the business was willing to stick by her in her difficulty. This is what can be special about family business.

Using the business to serve the family drives consultants, and sometimes employees, crazy. It represents a blurring of boundaries between family and business. However, this is perfectly reasonable if the business is **designed** to serve the family needs, as many businesses are. The real question is: do these things weaken the business to the point where its very ability to survive, to give comfort and security to the family in the future, is in jeopardy?

Why Family Business?

Why do families want to be in business together? Several researchers have asked that question, and their responses suggest that the advantages far outweigh the difficulties:

- The business is a special extension of their closeness and the fun they have together.
- It is a way for the family to do something meaningful, important, and public.
- The business provides economic security for everyone, more than they could have working separately.
- They have more freedom, creativity, and autonomy in their work and lives.
- They are known in the community, and that gives them pride and status.
- Women have special opportunities for responsibility and management in the business, which they often don't have elsewhere.
- And finally, people enter the business to please their parents and fulfill their desires concerning the family future.

Reflection Question

Why do you have a family business? Ask the founders why they started it and why other family members participate. Reflect on the benefits of the business to you and your family.

What Does Your Family Business Mean to You?

You can begin to explore the issues in your family business by starting with yourself. You have no choice about being in your family, but you have to make a choice about whether **you** want to be part of the family business. Your family also has to decide if it wants to own, maintain, or leave the business. These are not easy choices, and they are usually made more than once. How will you make those choices, and what do you need to make them?

In a way, your relationship to your family's business says a lot about who you are, your values, and what you will pursue in your life. Yet too often the decision to be part of the business is made impulsively, precipitously, or for confused reasons. Similarly, because the business is run by and partly for the family, family needs may take precedence over business realities. The family may make choices and not really understand the damage or difficulty it is creating for the business.

Families who are involved in business need to be much clearer about what they want from the business, and how they want to run it. They need to look at the needs and wants of every family member and make some very difficult, sometimes painful, choices. Often they'd rather avoid them and just drift.

Begin work on your family and your business with yourself. How are you connected to the family business, and what do you want from it? If you have been the founder or key manager of the business for a while, you may want to take time to reflect on where you are going and what you want from your family in the future. If you are a young heir or non-participant, you may want to look ahead and think about how you want to participate in the business. The best way to start is by setting aside some time, to reflect on some of the issues and questions raised in this book.

Exercise: Your Stake in Your Family Business

Take a few moments right now to reflect on what you get, or might get, from your family business. Spend some time writing your response to each question:

1. What is most important to you about having a family business?

2. Why did you decide to go into the business (or why did you decide not to)? Could your decision change?

3. What are the most important rewards the business offers you?

4. What personal sacrifices have you made for the business?

5. What do you most need to learn to be effective in the business?

You might then spend an evening with the other members of your family in order to share each person's responses to these questions.

The Family Business Cast of Characters

The key business roles in a family business are often an extension of family ones. Each person's position in the family has consequences for what they do and what they want at work. Let's meet some of the typical players in family business in caricature. We'll return to them in various chapters and to the issues they raise and the concerns they have. For now, how many of these characters can you see in your family and business? Who plays each of these roles in your family business?

The Older Generation

Founder/Patriarch: A dinosaur, a breed that is fast dying out. Hard to reach, hard to teach. Won't listen to new ideas, and hard to get to let go.

Spouse/Matriarch: The emotional leader, often the power behind the throne. Takes care of the children, and acts as go-between from father to children. Often was a co-founder of the business, with strong ideas about the future. Especially important in times of succession.

First Couple: A modern phenomena: an executive team that goes home and gets in bed together. Powerful and mysterious, warm and demanding, sensitive and visionary, a combination of qualities that makes for a powerful and supportive company.

Grandpa/Grandma: Myths about them and about founding the business, or its predecessor, are the basis for the values, ideals, and some of the legends, of the business. They stand for tradition. They are larger than life.

The Next Generation

First Son: The heir apparent, the second generation leader, whom everyone is measured against. His faults are the family's secret, and the business' distress.

Rebel, Black Sheep: The child who rejects the family style, defining a new way, often in opposition to the business. May eventually come back to rescue the business.

Uninvolved Outsider: The child who stays away from the business, but who is a confidante of everyone, with an outside/inside perspective that is often critical in tough periods and crises.

In-law: A talented son or daughter who marries into the business, enlarging its talent pool, but creating unexpected rivalries and tensions, activating ambivalence or joy in the founding generation. Never really feels accepted, always trying to prove him or herself. A very uncertain, difficult role.

The Other Son/Daughter: The person from the "other" side of the family who is also in line for succession. When two families own a business this person can create difficulty, ambiguity, or conflict.

The Wrong Spouse: Anyone who marries into the family.

The Outsiders
Loyal Retainer: Like Tom in *The Godfather*, almost a member of the family. Shares the joys, shoulders tough problems, adds to the talent, but steps aside for the chosen heir, and does not ask for equity.

Mentor: The substitute for Dad who trains the son or daughter.

First Friend: The person Father or heir turns to for good, clear, unbiased advice.

Resolving Difficulties in a Family Business

There are many prevalent family dynamics that can add pain and difficulty to work relationships: family members often have blind spots when it comes to one another; they try too hard to protect each other; they may fight over family issues in the business; and they transfer dysfunctional habits and qualities from their personal relationships to the business. Some common areas where families in business experience difficulties include:

Communication: People can't say certain things to people, or don't know how to talk about painful, controversial, or difficult issues. The family can avoid certain topics that in other business circumstances people would be willing to confront.

Fairness: Family members expect and need love, acceptance, and support from one another, as well as a share of the family wealth. Resolving questions about what is fair and just to everyone can be demanding. Everyone expects some modicum of equality. When some family members have different roles in the business because of special abilities, contributions, or opportunities, while others do not participate at all, this introduces an element of inequality which strains the family's desire to be fair.

Accountability: People in a business need to be accountable for certain results. But growing up together in a family, it is difficult to make such demands of siblings, children, or spouse. Family business members find it difficult to ask each other to produce; they also hesitate to evaluate one other.

Succession Planning: The family is an arrangement for producing adults who form the next generation. The business has the same need. But older members sometimes find it difficult to let go and be succeeded by their children. Until a crisis results, they often prefer to avoid thinking about the future. The children/heirs may be ready to take over before their parents are ready to go.

Exercise: Looking at Your Work/Family Relationships

As you will see throughout this book, the business relationship you have with another member of your family has different rules than your personal relationship. These new rules and expectations must be made explicit and explored. Often when you feel a conflict, it is because you are using family rules or expectations in a business situation. Let's begin with a self-assessment exercise to look at your own dual relationships with other family members.

*List each person in your family with whom you also have a working relationship. Divide a sheet of paper in half. On one side write **Family** and the other **Work**. On each side of the paper, write down what you expect from and do with the person in that area of your relationship. For example, think about what you expect from your brother as your brother. You might want him to listen to you, lend you money, help you out, and be on your side. Now think about your working relationship with him. You may expect him to do his job, help the business develop, and work to develop the company for the future.*

After you have written equal lists of what is expected in each area, complete the exercise by noting the most important areas where your personal and work relationships are different.

Family Business Continuity

Today many family businesses, facing new competitive pressures, share a common crisis: will family heirs or outside management take the business into the second generation, or will it, like most family businesses, close down, sell out or fold up? It seems difficult and rare for a family business to grow and thrive across generations. The average life span of a family business is 23 years. John Ward at Loyola University conducted a study of 200 family businesses that were in existence in 1924. By 1984, 78% of them were gone. Three percent of them had skyrocketed to bigness, while fully 80% of those still alive were the same size 60 years later.

Most family businesses fail! According to Ward, only 39% reach the second generation and only 15% reach the third generation. There are several reasons for this high attrition rate:

• **The business is a one-trick pony.** The founder exploits a market or designs a product that is a one-time affair. While the rewards extend for many years, the business never gets its second act together so that, by the time the children grow up, there is very little to inherit.

• **Denial of the need to change.** Many family business owners spend their later careers denying the need to change. They do not innovate or adapt their basic style to respond to new realities.

• **Initial energy and dedication flags.** The business founder has not trained or created a second generation with new energy and ideas. The whole business ages together.

• **Family needs overwhelm business realities.** The family desire to take care of everyone, to take money out of the business, or to act out old rivalries takes precedence over the need to operate a business.

• **Families don't know how to communicate, confront issues.** Sometimes one conflict, difference, or issue creates a schism that makes it impossible to do business. The employees are forced to take sides and productivity declines.

• **The family runs business like a family: ad hoc, random.** A family business can grow quickly. The makeshift procedures developed at the start tend to become institutionalized as the "way we do things." This lack of sound structure is touted as a business tradition, rather than as a bad habit to be overcome. Organizational weakness eventually pulls the whole business down with it.

• **Home and work roles are in conflict.** People treat each other like they do at home, meaning they either argue ritualistically or don't create ways of working together that are appropriate to a business. People are supported for who they are, or how nice they are, rather than whether or not they produce.

If not addressed, each of these problems can destroy your business. How can the business be preserved? You need to look at your family business as both a business and a family. This means applying two different sets of standards to one institution. Look over the list, and ask yourself which of them might apply to your business. To what degree are you running a family business that is family first, or family only? If you flag more than three of the factors on the list, you will need to build a greater awareness of business needs into your family business.

Building a Healthy Family Business

Your family business has certain vital signs that indicate health. While every business and family is unique, there are certain signs that point to areas of tension or difficulty. It is hard to have an unhealthy family and a healthy business, or vice versa. Certain qualities are key to maintaining healthy family and business systems. They are interrelated, just as family and business are interrelated. This section contains an assessment tool that you can use as a quick check on where you are as a family and a business.

The **FAMILY BUSINESS ASSESSMENT INVENTORY** will help you look at the key parts of your family and business. It has six sections, each of which relates to one aspect of a healthy family business. Each member of your family, and perhaps key non-family business managers, should complete the Inventory. All the scores should then be collected and assembled on the scoring sheet. The Inventory is a tool for your exploration; it does not have right or wrong answers. Every family and every business has its own unique way of working—there are no scores that in themselves indicate danger. However, if several people all indicate low scores in one or more areas, then you have cause for concern. Another area to focus on is where people have widely different scores on a particular topic. If one person feels, that communication is fine, while others feel it isn't, that in itself is something to communicate about.

Working with the Inventory involves the whole family and initiates the process of working together to improve your business. Each member of the family, both in and out of the business, should fill it out independently. There are spaces for each family member to record their scores on each scale. Since the Inventory pinpoints areas of strength and weakness, each person should look at his or her score and select one or two specific areas where he or she needs work.

Everyone's scores should then be averaged for a group score. The space on the right column of the scoring grid allows you to record the difference between the highest and lowest score on that scale among all the members of the family. In any scale where there are score differences between people of more than three, family members should explore the reasons for their dissimilar perceptions. In this way, family members can compare each others' responses, as well as define areas where everyone agrees further work is needed. This is the first step in your family's exploration of its relationships and the business.

THE FAMILY BUSINESS ASSESSMENT INVENTORY

For each question below, circle the number that most nearly describes how strongly you agree or disagree with the statement:

3 = Strongly Agree   2 = Agree Somewhat
1 = Disagree Somewhat   0 = Strongly Disagree

Scale 1: MISSION/PLANNING

1. People know what our business stands for.   3 2 1 0
2. We have a business plan that is evaluated
    and updated regularly.   3 2 1 0
3. There is a written succession plan
    for the next generation of the business.   3 2 1 0
4. As our business grows, our profit has
    risen as well.   3 2 1 0
5. We share our dreams and visions for the future,
    and know what each family member wants.   3 2 1 0

Scale 1 TOTAL (Add all circled numbers together):   _____

Scale 2: COMMUNICATION/CONFLICT RESOLUTION

1. Our family meets several times a year to talk
    about how things are going.   3 2 1 0
2. There are no deep conflicts in our family which
    have caused family members to cut themselves off
    from each other.   3 2 1 0
3. Our family openly expresses differences of opinion.   3 2 1 0
4. We are able to resolve our major conflicts
    and differences.   3 2 1 0
5. We have a clear process for making different
    types of decision.   3 2 1 0

Scale 2 TOTAL (Add all circled numbers together):   _____

Scale 3: BUSINESS PARTICIPATION

1. We evaluate clearly and objectively the performance
    of family members in the business.   3 2 1 0
2. Women participate in the business with
    equal opportunities.   3 2 1 0
3. Family members feel they are treated fairly

in business-related matters. 3 2 1 0
4. Family employees know where they stand in
the business, including limits and opportunities. 3 2 1 0
5. Family members in the business have
clear responsibilities and roles. 3 2 1 0

Scale 3 TOTAL (Add all circled numbers together): _____

Scale 4: OUTSIDE ADVICE
1. The head of the business doesn't have to be
involved in everything, or control everything. 3 2 1 0
2. The business is able to hire and retain
non-family managers in responsible positions. 3 2 1 0
3. We listen to and consider new ideas from our
younger generation and outside managers. 3 2 1 0
4. We share our planning with non-family managers. 3 2 1 0
5. Outside advisors meet with us regularly
and have been willing to give us "bad news." 3 2 1 0

Scale 4 TOTAL (Add all circled numbers together): _____

Scale 5: GENERATIONAL CONTINUITY
1. Offspring have been able to learn about
the business from their parents. 3 2 1 0
2. There has been some discussion and planning
for the possible roles of heirs as they enter
the business. 3 2 1 0
3. Heirs have had a chance to work elsewhere. 3 2 1 0
4. Offspring feel that plans for the division
of the business are fair. 3 2 1 0
5. Offspring have opportunity to influence
the future of the business. 3 2 1 0

Scale 5 TOTAL (Add all circled numbers together): _____

Scale 6: OUTSIDE THE BUSINESS
1. The family spends time together relaxing
in non-business activities together. 3 2 1 0
2. Our family is active in the community. 3 2 1 0
3. Everyone in the family is actively involved

in fitness and caring for their health.   3 2 1 0

4. Family members in the business have outside
   hobbies or interests.   3 2 1 0

5. We encourage each person in the family to
   discover his or her own way.   3 2 1 0

Scale 6 TOTAL (Add all circled numbers together):   _____

Scoring and Using the Inventory

Fill in the scores of each member of the family who completes the inventory below. Then take the average of all the scores, and calculate the difference between the two family members with the highest and lowest scores. Some scales may not be relevant to your family business.

	Founder	Spouse	Heir	Heir	Relative	Average	Difference Between Highest & Lowest
Name:	_____	_____	_____	_____	_____		
Scale #1:	_____	_____	_____	_____	_____	_____	_____
Scale #2:	_____	_____	_____	_____	_____	_____	_____
Scale #3:	_____	_____	_____	_____	_____	_____	_____
Scale #4:	_____	_____	_____	_____	_____	_____	_____
Scale #5:	_____	_____	_____	_____	_____	_____	_____
Scale #6:	_____	_____	_____	_____	_____	_____	_____

Your score on each scale can be between 0 and 15. A score below 5 on any scale indicates that you perceive some difficulty in that area. Scores between 6 and 10 on a scale indicate some strain in that area. Scores over 11 indicate you perceive your family business as doing very well in that area.

Working with Your Family to Grow Your Business

You have begun to explore your personal relationship to your family business, and you have gotten your family together to complete the Inventory. For many families, this represents a very new activity. Chances are you learned some valuable things. Now is the time to continue the growth process by turning your collective attention to any problem areas you may have found.

Each area in the Inventory is covered in detail in one or more chapters that follow. If your score indicates that you have some conflict or difficulty in that area, you should specifically consult the exercises and explanations in that chapter:

1. Mission/Planning: Chapter 4.
2. Communication/Conflict Resolution: Chapters 2 and 3.
3. Business Participation: Chapters 5 and 6.
4. Outside Advice: Chapters 7 and 8.
5. Generational Continuity: Chapters 6 and 7.
6. Family Members Outside the Business: Chapters 2 and 3.

Notes:

1. McLaughlin, Joyce and Byrne, Noel. "Family Business: The Family's View."
2. Rosenblatt, Paul C., de Mik, Leni, Anderson, Roxanne, and Johnson, Patricia. *The Family in Business.*
3. Prokesch, Steven. "Rediscovering Family Values." *New York Times,* June 10, 1986, first article of a series.
4. Presented at Family Firm Institute Research Day, October, 1989, Davis, California.

2

Your Family Organization: How Family Patterns Mold the Business

"However frail and perforated our families may have become, however they may annoy and retard us, they remain the first of the givens of our lives. The more we try to deny or elude them, the likelier we are to repeat their same mistakes. The first thing we have to do is to stop such efforts. Instead we must come to terms with our families, laughing with them peaceably on occasion if we can manage to, accepting them as the flawed mortals they are, or were, if we cannot."
-Jane Howard, Families

"In a family firm, the strands of the family system are so tightly interwoven with those of the business system that they cannot be distinguished without seriously disrupting one or both systems."
-Elaine Kepner, "The Family and the Firm: A Coevolutionary Perspective."

Family businesses are organized and run in weird ways—a lot like families. Without knowing the family, it's impossible to really understand its business. Things that just don't make sense from a business point of view begin to take on meaning when the family's needs and style are known. Until a few years ago, organization consultants looking at family business would observe the confusion and blurred boundaries, only to conclude that the only way to make a "family business" into a "business" was to get the family members out. This is not necessarily good advice. One family business, responding to such counsel, asked a score of family members to leave a three-generation business. While the business indeed became more "rational," and hired professional managers, it declined. The consensus was that with the family leaving, the "soul" had gone as well.

Every family business mimics the style of the family that creates it. Lying behind the business, in its shadow, are the relationships and needs of a family. Indeed many of the frustrations, conflicts, difficulties, misunderstandings, and confusions in a family business have their roots in the ways of the family.

When two people from a family decide to work together, they continue to relate in the ways they always have. If Henry is the people person and Stan is the detail man, they naturally create a division of labor where Henry will find his way to sales and Stan to operations and finance. If Henry is the big brother and Stan always has deferred to him, the pattern is likely to continue. If their family values honesty and hard work, and trusts people to do their best, the business will reflect these values. If everybody in the family talks at once, and disagreements are argued until one person prevails, that will be how the business resolves problems.

For many businesses, this continuity is fine. In fact, the business was probably formed to capitalize on the trust and good feelings family members had together, and the unique talents that different relatives might contribute. But the transfer of family patterns into the business is also the source of problems. What if Henry and Stan have always been rivals for their father's attention and they waste energy in a battle for the attention of their CEO father who refuses to take sides or end the conflict? What if the family values getting along over making hard choices, or distrusts people outside the family? Things that work for a family may not work best for the business.

Your family has a structure, rules, even an organization chart that can be mapped just as a business can. In fact your family pattern and organization forms the background of your business. Some family styles make the transition to work styles just fine, but others cause difficulty. Your "family" organization may be fine for the first stages of the business. Years later it can become a liability due to new business demands or fast growth. Your family style may eventually keep your business from taking advantage of new possibilities and growing to its fullest expression.

Because of this basic truth, before you try to strengthen your business, you need to look at your family. The family contains the spirit, the energy, and the commitment that led to the creation of the business, and it also may contain deep-rooted dynamics that can, especially over time, undermine the business.

Tasks for the Chapter

Many seemingly "business" problems stem from the family origins of your business. In this chapter you will discover, explore, make explicit, and question the ways of your family, your "family culture" as it were. You will reflect on your family's patterns, history, needs, style, and relationships to realize how deeply they impact on the business. When you acknowledge and discuss these patterns in your family, you can decide to modify or change that pattern at work.

The exercises and reflection questions are open-ended. They invite individuals and families to go beyond specific differences and issues, to look at who they are, what they stand for, and what each person wants. The best way to complete the work of this chapter is for everyone first to work on each reflection question alone. Then take several evenings or a day to share what you've done. Because this is about family dynamics, I urge you to work on the exercises in this chapter together, gathering all members of the immediate or extended family.

While this may feel like the long way around, I find that a family business is so complex, and the relationships so difficult, that the family needs to spend a great deal of time unraveling them. In order to resolve issues and questions about the business, you need to start with a deep, shared understanding of who you are as a family.

Business is a Continuation of Family

A family business is frequently put together and grows without much thought. At the start, you conceived of a product, made it, and sold it at a profit. There wasn't much to organize. A generation ago, almost all small businesses worked this way. In a less complex world, this worked fine for a small stable business. But today's demands for fast growth and changing business conditions, coupled with the emerging needs of individual family members and the eroding effects of time, give new importance to discovering the family dynamics behind the business' structure.

Let's take a common example of two brothers starting a store. The store is so successful that other family members get recruited to work there. Mother starts to keep the books. Uncle Abe starts helping out with deliveries in his spare time and then is asked to run the warehouse full time. Systems are improvised. As the business grows, everyone is provided for. But nothing remains the same for long. Eventually a crisis intervenes. It may be a business recession, a conflict between Abe and one of the brothers, the opening of a second store and the question of which brother will have to relocate to manage it, or whose children will work in the store. The change creates a crisis, which the emotional resources of the family are not able to solve. Both the business and the family suffer.

My first family business consultation taught me the lesson that family history often holds the key to resolving business issues. I was called in by Mel, who inherited a thriving manufacturing business from his father, Forbes, who had died several years before. Forbes and Mel had enjoyed a wonderful, close relationship. They worked side by side and their strengths meshed, with Mel's engineering expertise combining perfectly with Forbes' great customer relations skills. Together, they built the business into quite a success. As time went on and the nature of their business had become more technical, Forbes had been comfortable letting Mel take over more and more responsibility.

But now Mel had a difficult problem. He wanted his business to grow into the third generation but his two sons, Jerry and Dan, ages 24 and 26, were not getting along. They each joined the business at management level after college. Although they had always gotten along well "for brothers," they were not working harmoniously together. Dan joined the business four years before Jerry, and he and Mel were close. It wasn't quite the relationship Mel had with his father, but he was happy to pass on what he knew to Dan. Dan was, like him, an engineer, interested in the technical side of the business.

When Jerry, with a marketing degree, entered the business, everybody thought he was a natural for sales. He started working with the sales manager and before long he represented the company to department stores and other customers. He was doing great, Mel felt. But Jerry didn't

feel great. He kept getting into fights with Dan, blaming him for quality problems and not producing orders quickly enough. In one angry confrontation, he stalked out, threatening to quit. "Sales drive this company," he screamed, "not manufacturing." If they couldn't ship defect-free products, they were sunk.

I interviewed the trio and some of the other key managers. The conflict was clear, but I couldn't understand why they couldn't just talk it out and come to some resolution. Then I spoke to Mel's wife, Jane. She wasn't part of the company, yet everyone talked about how important she was. Jerry talked to her when he was most upset. She would then talk to Mel. After trying to work with Mel, Jerry and Dan for several weeks without resolution, I spent a long evening with all of them at Mel's home, with Jane present. The whole conversation shifted! I saw that in addition to the management structure, I needed to understand the family structure. Each son had a special relationship with one parent, which created two coalitions within the family. Mel and Dan had always been very close, as had Jane and Jerry. Jerry felt he was less important to his father and that he could never prove his value to him. He didn't feel that his success at sales meant anything to Mel. When he talked to Jane, and Jane talked to Mel, Mel became defensive; he didn't know why Jerry should be complaining to Jane.

Then Mel told a story about the company that shocked everyone. He said, "You know, all this fighting reminds me of Dad and his brother. In fact, Dad didn't really start the business. It was started by his brother, who was two years older." After a few years Mel's father expanded the business and conflict with his brother grew. Finally his brother quit to form his own smaller company in the same industry, which he ran until he died. Soon after the breakup, Mel joined the company, taking over many of his uncle's functions, and working very closely with his dad. The two brothers were never close again.

Nobody in the family knew that story, nor why their grandfather and great uncle weren't close. But as we talked, Mel came to see that he might be feeling some parallels between his sons and his father and uncle. He was concerned that there would be a similar rift in this generation.

Learning about the founding of the business was a powerful event for Dan and Jerry. They didn't want to have a split. Mel began to see that some of his actions, especially spending so much time with Dan, had the unintentional effect of maintaining an old family pattern that left Jerry feeling ignored. He also saw that he inadvertently encouraged competition between the brothers. Jane came to see that her talks with Jerry may have encouraged him not to deal more directly with his father and brother.

Many changes took place in the business, all relating to conscious attempts to shift family relationship patterns. Mel began to encourage both Dan and Jerry to learn more about the other's work. Jane stopped mediating between Jerry and Mel. Dan and Jerry saw that their fights were about Dad's approval, not about business issues. Each of these changes reduced both family and business tension.

As the above example shows, many family businesses are an extension of the family. That's why, for example, none of the offices has closed doors. Or why there is no organizational chart. Or why Dad makes decisions from his house even though he is retired and his son is president. Or why people go to Mother to get Father to change his mind. Or why only family members get to see the books. Or why Mark's wife, who is a secretary, is at all the business meetings. There is no business reason for any of these facts—but the family has its reasons. These have to do with the history and style of the family, its personal traditions, needs, and patterns.

Your business takes on the feel of your family. The energy level of employees, the amount of joking or seriousness, how personal employees are with one another, whether people will interrupt and disagree, even the type of furniture, come from the style of the first family. One of the largest and most successful savings and loans in the country, World Savings, was founded by a couple, Herbert and Marion Sandler. In a visit to the headquarters, I put my cup of coffee on a desk. An officer told me, "No, Mrs. Sandler doesn't want cups on the desks." As this story demonstrates, in addition to taking on the fiscal and management style of the Sandlers, the company has taken on some of their personal values as well. The corporate office is in some ways an extension of their living room. While this certainly happens in non-family companies, when a family is in charge, the style of the business is even more transparently derived from the family's style.

Key family patterns have a way of being repeated in the business. The Bank of America was founded during the Depression by A.P. Giannini, who had a vision of a people's bank, financing small businesses and agriculture. He virtually invented branch banking. In time he retired and was succeeded by his son. However, within a few years his son became critically ill and Giannini was forced once again to find a successor. He did—himself. He ran the bank again for several years, until handing management over to a new successor, Tom Clausen. Years later, Clausen surprised the banking community by naming San Armacost as his successor and retiring to run the World Bank. When the trustees decided that Armacost had to go, they waffled for several years and rejected several candidates before finally naming a successor—Tom Clausen! The return of the father was repeated.

A family legacy can even skip a few generations. Many years ago when I taught at USC, Alan Miller was a student there, receiving a Ph.D. in clinical psychology. In 1986, I was reading a Los Angeles business magazine and there was Alan, receiving an award for entrepreneur of the year. His achievement: while working full time at another job, he had started The Original New York Seltzer Company that in two years had grown to a $100 million a year business. He started the company when his son Randy was graduating from high school, to help him "find a career opportunity"; now Randy is president. The irony is that Alan's grandfather had been in the seltzer business years before in New York and his father had sent Alan to California to get him as far from the business as he could. Yet the legacy and the desire to work with his son were more powerful than geography.

Interlocking Systems

How can you begin to unravel the complexity of your family structure? First, you need to begin to differentiate the family from the business. If you are involved in a family business, you hold membership in one, two, or three groups, each of which has a different perspective. In effect you are part of three overlapping, interlocking systems. Each of these systems contains a group of people, who have distinct interests, locations, needs, and styles of operating:

FAMILY SYSTEM
Membership: Personal family, children and spouses.
Emotion-based, oriented toward security, nurture, fun, and growth. Inward focus on its members.

BUSINESS SYSTEM
Membership: Employees, managers and customers.
Task-oriented, demands productivity from its members. Outward focus on its customers.

OWNERSHIP SYSTEM
Membership: All shareholders, family and non-family.
Owns the business. Oversees and creates policy. Hires top management. Helps create and manage the plan for moving the business into the future as a vital institution.

Membership in these three groups overlaps. You can be a member of any one, or all three. These three systems are interrelated and support each other to a certain degree. Problems arise when it is unclear which system takes precedence. For example, is the business designed to serve the family's needs or does the business come first? Different answers to that question lead to different financial, employment, and strategic business decisions. Also, when two people who simultaneously belong to different systems talk to one another, it is sometimes not clear from which system's perspective they are speaking. For example, when a father who owns a business berates his son in a business meeting for not being prepared, is he acting as a father, as a business owner concerned about competence of management, or as a boss talking to his vice-president?

Looking at the three systems as three interlocking circles, there are several possible overlaps. The middle space, labeled FBO, includes people who are owners, managers, and family members. This includes the business founders and the heirs who have been given ownership shares. Because they have three perspectives, the members of this group may get particularly confused in their relationships and the boundaries between family, business, and ownership decisions may be especially unclear.

The area labelled FB consists of family members who also work in the business, but don't own shares. They may be sons or daughters who expect one day to become owners. FO indicates family members who own parts of the business, but don't work in it. This includes passive shareholders, perhaps children or spouses who inherit parts of the business. Their interests obviously differ from family members who work in the business. BO refers to employees who also own stock in the business.

Each of these groups has a unique perspective on the business. Each wants different things. For example, family members not working in the business may be concerned with the time family managers spend working and may resent the lost companionship, while business owners who aren't involved in day to day operations may want their values or wishes taken into account by management. Understanding the dynamics of a family business begins with defining the membership of each of these spaces.

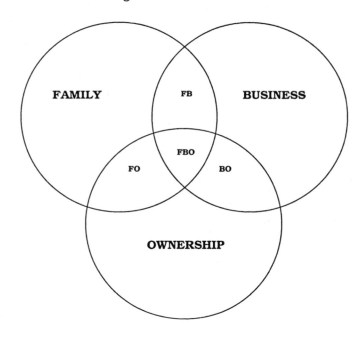

Each different position in family and/or business impacts on personal relationships. In planning the future of your business, the role of family members who are not managers but own shares is crucial. For example, many spouses feel left out or excluded, and indeed many family businesses explicitly exclude them from management or ownership roles. They may then seek influence indirectly. Wives of founders often feel the business is their husband's mistress, and divorce can not only tear apart a family, but can force a sale or other business decisions that would not otherwise be made. Each of these issues needs to be mediated and resolved.

Exercise: Filling in Your Family and Business Systems

Take a census of the members of your family, the owners of the family business, and the key business managers. Make a copy of the circle diagram and write their names in the appropriate space, indicating their single, dual, or triple memberships. Start with yourself.

Then, looking at the list, try to define some of the key interests, needs, and expectations of the group of people in each of the areas. See what each group has in common, and how they differ from each other.

Having a Family and Having a Business

When the family is in business, these different systems may conflict or be at cross-purposes. For example, a business decision may be made to support family desires. Up to a point, this can work. But sometimes the business consequences create disaster, or a sound business decision has profound repercussions on the family.

One night I received an emergency call: Jay, the son of a business founder had to see me immediately. He was very upset. He had to fire his brother the next day and he couldn't. The story was this. His family business had been bought by a large conglomerate two years before. It became a division of the larger company, while retaining the family name. He remained as president, and his younger brother Kevin kept his job. For 12 years Kevin had worked in the business. He didn't know very much and wasn't very good at his job. But the rule in his family was that "everybody helped everybody," and as the eldest, Jay was responsible for his younger brother. The family "helped" Kevin originally by giving him a job, and not expecting very much. This went on for years until the sale.

When his father died, Jay was told to be sure to take care of Kevin. His mother repeated the request, letting him know that she would never speak to him again if he fired Kevin. Unfortunately the new owners were not so patient with this arrangement and gave Jay an ultimatum: fire Kevin or both of them would be out and the family name would be removed from the company. Jay was stuck. He couldn't meet the needs of the business and be loyal to his family. Either way, the business decision would create pain and dissension in the family.

We talked about whether there were other options. I asked how Kevin felt about the situation. Did he like being "carried" by the business? Jay's response was typical of those in family business conflicts. He didn't know if Kevin knew, or what his feelings about the situation were. I wondered whether Kevin might already know and feel he couldn't talk about it with Jay. I suggested Jay share his dilemma with Kevin. We called him, and he came in.

The talk was long and cathartic. Kevin indeed knew and felt terrible about the situation. He knew he should have left years ago, but felt he couldn't disappoint the family. Also, he didn't think he could earn nearly as much in another job. So he stayed, but his motivation and self-esteem both diminished. He had long ago stopped caring. Hearing his brother's dilemma, Kevin decided he would resign and called his mother to say he was quitting to go out on his own. In the years since, Kevin has grown up through a succession of jobs, finally starting a small craft business of his own. He earns nearly what he did in the family business, but is his own boss and feels much better about himself.

These difficult situations, where family needs lead to bad business decisions, are commonplace. As Kevin found, what the family does to help each other may not really help in the long run. Wouldn't it have been more helpful for Kevin to grow up sooner, by working outside the family business? Wouldn't he have profited from someone telling him he wasn't performing, rather than just letting him drift along? Family business members need to explore these issues when they plan and develop their businesses.

If properly designed, the family business can certainly provide resources to support family needs. It can be a family employment agency if it can avoid being a family welfare agency. It can offer family members an opportunity to work together, as long as they are required to do real work. It can give the family a proud name in the community, as long as it attends to its business' growth and development needs. There doesn't have to be constant conflict. However, the family and the business are very different types of systems and their differences need to be respected.

The family is an **emotional support system**, a private retreat designed to protect its members and help them grow. The business is out in the world and must meet the challenge of the marketplace and **produce tangible results**. We can contrast the differences between the two systems as follows:

Family	Business
Raise adults	Make profits
People caring	People producing
Unconditional acceptance	Performance demands
Generational authority	Role authority
Expressive, emotional bonds	Rational bonds
Blood ties forever	Temporary relationships
Informal relationships	Formal relationships
Generational time frame	Limited time frame

What happens when you try to blend these two systems? Sometimes adding the qualities of one to the other can be beneficial. A company that cares about its employees, for example, that fosters informal relationships and adopts a long-term time frame, can develop a very effective work environment. But when a family business contains too much paternalistic authority, informal relationships, and family loyalty, it can become a stifling and oppressive place. The goal of the effective family business is to take on the positive qualities of a family, while limiting the possible negative effects of family on business—and vice versa.

To better understand how to do this, we need to more closely examine the tasks of a family. Every family must come to grips with human needs in five areas. The way a family faces or avoids each of these needs can create health or pathology, conflict or harmony, in its members. The presence of a business further complicates the family's efforts to meet these needs for each person and creates the potential for conflict. A business also needs to address these needs to a lesser degree, though they are not its primary focus.

Intimacy: In a close family, people care about each other deeply and see their well-being as intertwined. They offer each other the unconditional emotional support that builds a sense of self-esteem as each member sees him or herself as invaluable to the family. Family members not only feel close and loving, but they also come to know each other deeply, because they share aspirations, desires, and feelings. Unfortunately the demands of business performance can strain caring and intimacy.

Dependency: People in families trust each other to take care of them and look out for their welfare. Indeed allowing other people to take care of you, and trusting that they will always come through, rarely happens outside of families. Dependency has a very different meaning and function in a business. Trust, commitment, and loyalty are important, but they are conditional and much more limited.

Power: Every family has its own hierarchy of power. At first the parents makes decisions, and are responsible. As children grow, power shifts and moves around. Or power may remain uncomfortably concentrated in one place. In contrast, a business needs to place power in the hands of the people who have the ability for success, and who possess the requisite skills. Family power structures may not be relevant to the business.

Independence: The family creates a container for growing up. When children become adults, they leave the family to make it on their own, usually to create their own new family. Thus the family must teach its children to stand on their own. It must impart a sense of competence and uniqueness, and foster personal identity. But stepping into a business formed by one's parents makes it difficult to grow up and develop a personal identity. A family business keeps people tied together, sometimes making it difficult to foster independence.

Growth: Individuals and families grow through a series of stages. People mature, change, and die. The family must always cope with new challenges, and no matter how it tries to keep things the same, it will always be forced to change. A family business has its own developmental demands and cycles, which are superimposed on the family. They may not be in sync with the family cycles.

Reflection Question

Take a few moments and think about how your family manages the tasks of intimacy, dependency, power, independence, and growth. What did your family do to help you meet each of these needs at different stages of your life? Is there one area where your family communicated a negative or mixed message? Was it not OK to grow up, or depend on each other, or have power?

Now think about how each of these areas is expressed or defined in your family business. In which of them does it fall short?

Closeness or Independence?

As the above list indicates, every family has two major tasks, which in some ways are opposite to each other. The family needs to maintain closeness, connection, and togetherness, and also to enable children to grow up to adulthood and independence. A family business can often maintain and promote closeness, but it has limitations in promoting independence. Children who enter the family business may find their childhood artificially extended, since they maintain their dependency on their parents for their livelihood, and remain under their leadership and influence far into adulthood. In many ways, the business is a continuation of the family, with Dad and often Mom watching over the children.

The struggle for the second to "n"th generation heirs is how to find a personal identity, feel a sense of separateness and competency, and exist outside the pale of the family name, money, and structure. Many family business heirs feel they are being offered a Faustian bargain: achieve security, even wealth, comfort and status, but in return, forfeit the ability to discover themselves. The sense of obligation to continue a family tradition sometimes drowns out voices that suggest alternatives.

Business families often make a fetish of how close and connected they are. It is one of their central values. Closeness is a deep need, and the acceptance and connection of a family can be the central experience in a person's life. But it is a double-edged sword, like most family virtues: too much closeness and sharing cuts off opportunities and experiences of independent identity and differentiation. It can also stifle a business, prevent change and development, and discourage talented non-family employees.

Family theorists have developed the concept of **enmeshment** to denote a family that is too closely interconnected. Enmeshment is different from intimacy and closeness. It is not simply feeling close, or knowing each family member deeply. Rather, enmeshment arises when family members have too few boundaries and too little separateness. It is intimacy when people are concerned about each other, and want to know what is happening in each other's lives. It becomes enmeshment when people feel they must share everything that is happening in their lives, that everybody must think, feel, and want the same things, and that a family member needs no sphere of personal privacy or time away from the family. An intimate family can still allow privacy, closed doors, and some personal life. An enmeshed family cannot tolerate much separateness without feeling hurt or rejected.

I once visited a deeply enmeshed family business. The parents, two sons, and daughter-in-law all worked together. Their offices were within ten feet of each other, and their doors were never closed. There were no job descriptions; everybody always knew what everyone else was doing. In addition, they spent most lunches and weekend time together. Not doing things with the family was discouraged. They even had a vacation home they went to together.

How is this a problem? First, the job roles were so confused that it took hours, and more than one person, to get anything done. Employees had no idea whom to go to for what. The business was slow to react and never changed. Like the family who ran it, the business was barely organized. It was poised for a fall during a market shift, or from increased competition. Personally the sons were not doing well. Neither of them really had learned much more than their parents, who had a very old-fashioned way of running the business. Because they spent so much time together, they never got any outside input. Both of them were treated like children. Their salaries were unspecified, and it was almost as if they were children on an allowance, rather than employed adults. The father controlled the finances, and neither son's family could really plan for his future or think about leaving the business.

The crisis came when business growth stalled. The business could no longer support all three families, and the daughter-in-law who worked in the business began to feel that her family needed more money, and put pressure on her husband to leave, something he felt he couldn't do. This crisis eventually challenged the enmeshed assumptions the family maintained, forced them to develop more separateness, which in turn created drastic change in the business and the roles of family members within it.

In most families, when children grow up, they grow away, and their private life becomes more separate from parents. When they work together, parents frequently know more, perhaps too much, about their private lives. Some single sons and daughters feel their parents are watching over them as if they are teenagers. So one of the struggles for sons and daughters in family business is to keep some of their lives separate.

Whether they work together or not, every family should have areas that are shared and those that are private. If an extended family works together all day, it might be a good idea for individual couples to socialize outside the family on some weekends.

A family is joined by a web of obligations, legacies, and expectations that are passed from one generation to another. One of the prime obligations is to the family business. If the business has been visible and successful, then the business may be the vehicle for the family's reputation and immortality. Heirs also inherit a sense of deep commitment and obligation to continue the business.

Many families tell their children, directly or indirectly, that they need to keep the family name alive. Most children do that by having children of their own. But a business is the child of the whole family. Continuing the business in a traditional way can be a burden on an heir, who is faced with a changing business climate or the desire to do something completely different. When the business seems no longer viable, and an heir must consider selling it to a larger competitor, the founding parents can feel a deep sense of hurt and betrayal. The heir can feel conflicted, guilty, or disloyal. It is important for every business family to look clearly at the hidden messages of obligation they pass on to their children. If they have been unspoken, it might help everyone to discuss them. If sons or daughters feel bound by them and in conflict about their bondage, they need to be free to share this dilemma with the rest of the family.

Reflection Question

Think about the obligations and ties you have to your family. What do you feel that you owe your family, your parents? What have you been told are the important obligations of a member of your family? How are you obligated to the business? How do you maintain your separateness and privacy?

If there are areas where you feel that family obligation, or pressure, conflicts with your inner sense of what you would like to do, or if you feel pulled or conflicted by these obligations, you might think of ways to share this dilemma with other family members.

Hierarchy: The Family Power Structure

A family is not a free form, do-what-you-want organization, although it may seem that way to an outsider and feel that way to its members. In fact, every family is more predictably and tightly organized than we may realize. However, the organization of a family is not the same as a business'. Its structure is somewhat more hidden. Unraveling and describing your family's structure can be a liberating experience which offers a chance not only to examine your family dynamics, but to see whether your business structure mimics it. Like my clients Mel, Jane, Dan, and Jerry, you may discover that family patterns are negatively influencing the business. Such knowledge is the key to change.

A family is organized around a hierarchy of generations. Every family relationship has a reality according to age status. Grandparents, parents, and children have different roles, expectations and levels of authority by virtue of being a member of a particular generation. Children come into the world completely dependent on their parents and no matter how old they are, their feelings toward their parents are influenced by their childhood relations to them. Even within generations, activities, roles, and statuses are organized around age authority. To children, even the difference of a few years is very consequential. So when related people come into the business as adults, age history and status may be invisible, but the influences of the age hierarchy are always there.

When the family hierarchy gets transferred to business, it can cause problems. The oldest brother, while head of the siblings of a family, may not always be the best business leader. In a classic article, Harvard Business School Professor Louis Barnes[1] reports on the effects of incongruent hierarchies, where the business hierarchy did not follow the family status structure. He found, for example, that when a younger sibling had greater power in the business than an older one, there was more stress because the two relations had different levels of authority within the family and the business. Often a younger sibling knows how to take direction from an older one, but the opposite is highly stressful, and can lead to conflict and struggle: "I won't take orders from my little brother." The sections that follow will look at some of the core elements of family structure and how they affect the business.

Avoiding Boundary Confusion

Family business relationships also have "boundaries" that separate different subgroups and activities. Recall the overlapping circles pictured earlier in the chapter, differentiating the various stakeholder groups. Each of these groups have a boundary which separates the members of that subgroup from the others. When these boundaries are crossed, trouble can ensue.

For instance, after Sunday dinner the men in one family who work together would repair to the den for a business discussion. The women in the family felt a boundary that limited them from participating. One day, a new wife, a Stanford MBA, challenged that norm by going with the men. The others were angry and aghast, feeling that she didn't respect them, and they tried to get her into line. It took quite a while before they were willing to change—she had violated an unspoken boundary rule.

When boundaries are confused, conflict and uncertainty results. For example, confusion may result when a non-business family member is covertly consulted on business decisions. This can happen when Father retires but still retains majority ownership, or when a sister and brother transfer their sibling rivalry into competition in management. Competing for who can influence the most employees, or who is better liked, can be destructive to the business. It's also a problem when a family offers Son a job because they want Father to keep his eye on him, to help him with his drug problem.

Let's take a closer look at a typical problem concerning the confusion of family and business boundaries. Mom and Dad start a business in the family home, with Mom as the first employee, and Dad working another job during the day and coming home at night to start the new business. Mom is the cheerleader, the person who has faith in the new venture, and helps get it off the ground. The whole business is built on the "sweat equity" of Mom and Dad working together over endless evenings and weekends. For years they don't take vacations and reinvest every penny.

Over time the business begins to differentiate from the family. It moves to an office and Mom gives up her role in the business to pursue other interests. Dad comes to be seen as the entrepreneur, the creator of the business, while Mom's crucial role is seemingly forgotten. But in Mom's memory and inside the family, her pivotal role remains.

This is where family and business boundaries get confused. Even though she's not technically involved in the business anymore, she still feels an important part of it. After all she started it. Therefore when she sees a family need that can be met by the business, she doesn't hesitate to draw on it. Since she sees the business as an extension of her family, she feels comfortable asking for a job for her son, or her niece.

Now her perception may not be shared by Dad, who is president, and her prerogatives are definitely resented by employees who are asked to do her favors. They wonder why she has the authority to tell them what to do. To further complicate matters, Mom may begin to resent the fact that her husband gets all the credit for the business. After all, she was the one who had the idea, was the one who supported him during the first years.

Chances are Mom still remains an owner of the business. When Dad unexpectedly passes away, she inherits majority ownership. She suddenly is in charge, but without sufficient information to do the job correctly. Without her knowing it, Dad has been shielding her from recent business difficulties by giving her an edited version of reality. She needs to make all kinds of decisions, including those concerning the roles of family members. In particular she must choose between her two children for leadership without really knowing what's best. And she's been out of the business for so long that she can't even rely on non-family help from employees. Poor Mom, poor children, poor business.

As the example shows, one of the most common violators of boundaries is the entrepreneur's wife. By virtue of her marriage and often early work in the business, she is one of the owners of the business. She often stands to inherit outright majority ownership in the business. Yet, she is not in management of the business. However, she may be the power behind the throne, like Rosalyn Carter, conferring with her husband about decisions and having ample opportunity to influence them. Or more like Nancy Reagan, she may actively intervene in management decisions, sometimes without her husband's direct knowledge. The wife is an owner and a key person, but not a manager. Her authority is clear, though not legitimate. She may ask a manager to give a job to her son-in-law or a family friend. But that person may not be the best person for the job, or may not be highly motivated. The non-family manager or employee is put in a difficult bind. What can the manager do? How can he or she risk antagonizing her? Who can he or she talk to about the conflict?

Boundary conflicts also arise with other family members who are owners of the business. As owners, especially if they control significant shares and are on the board of directors, they certainly have some rights to participate and be informed about business decisions, even to question some of them. But they should not have direct authority to make operational or personnel decisions, or to come in and use employees or business resources for their personal use. Not only are there tax and legal difficulties here, but the effect of the family using the business as an extension of itself has grave demoralizing effects on all employees, both inside and outside the family.

Appropriate family boundaries often don't work in business. For example, in a family, parents often try to protect their children from harm, conflict, or struggle—the boundary here is between parents and children. But while it might be appropriate for a father to take care of a young daughter, when she has worked in the business for ten years and he excludes her from his meetings with his banker, telling her to "trust him," he is observing an old family boundary which probably is not appropriate to the business.

Here is a classic nepotism scenario that is as old as organized society. A mother approaches her brother who runs a business, saying it really would be good if her son could get a job in the business. Many people would say that's what family businesses are for. But the real issue is not nepotism, but how decisions are made and by whom. In this case, what would happen if her brother is the owner of a trio of hardware stores and his son manages one of them? The son is told that his cousin will begin working there. That may present several problems. First, the son might feel undermined in his authority. Second, his employees would see that his father made decisions in the store. Third, a new position would have to be created, and the people already working there would have to make room. Cousin would be filling a position outside of procedures, interviews, and qualifications. This would probably undermine employee morale. Employees would wonder how high this cousin would be going in the organization.

The problem is more severe between Father and Son. Father has given his son authority and responsibility, but makes decisions for him. Son feels like he is still at home under the benevolent authority of his parents. The business reality makes him angry at his father, who had said he would let him run the store as he saw fit. In response, Son begins to share fewer of his own decisions, leaving Father to feel that his son does not trust him, which indeed is true. The distrust between Father and Son in turn becomes a family battle, where Mother accuses Son of not being sensitive to Father's needs, and Aunt and Cousin are upset about Cousin's role in the business. Business decisions and family decisions have become one, and both family relations and business suffer.

For a family business to operate effectively as a business, there needs to be clear boundaries between family and business. But what can be done when one family member becomes upset about decisions and conversations that move freely across boundaries between business and family? Many people feel there is nothing they can do except get angry or keep silent. Yet there are definite and usually effective steps that a person can take to try to reduce boundary conflict. When a decision, action, or conversation takes place that one person feels is an inappropriate transfer from one sphere to another, this person needs to point it out to the other family members involved.

For example, in the above situation, the son could have said to his father, "I'd like to make the position available to Cousin Roger. But I've already listed the job and we have applicants. It would be upsetting to my people to just move him in. Why don't you have Roger come down and fill out an application? He can be interviewed by Jerry, who is in charge of hiring. I think he'd be very qualified for the job." There still might be some pressure to hire Roger, but at least it would be from the store manager, and exercised in the proper place.

If Father told Son that he had to hire Roger because it would upset Auntie if he didn't, there are still ways to proceed. Son could say, "I understand that Auntie means well, and maybe we can hire Roger, but I'd like to talk to her about this. I feel a little undermined in my own job, and I'd like it if we could both discuss the situation." Then Father, Son, and Aunt could have a family talk about their expectations and rules about her role in the business. They could talk about how her desires to employ other family members affected the workplace and the business. Perhaps together they could discuss the issue of who makes business decisions and about hiring family members, and come up with a set of agreed-upon guidelines for this practice. Now, some family members may need more than a single conversation before they see the light, and they may get more than a little defensive in the conversation, but the key is to pursue the issue, not give up or avoid it.

Your Family and Your Feelings

Every family has a characteristic way it handles difficult emotions such as anger, disappointment, hurt, and sadness. Some families are highly dramatic, yelling and screaming as they criticize and confront one another. Certain styles are ethnic, such as the taciturnity of a Swedish family or the parallel conversations of a Jewish family. Your family may disapprove of talking directly about feelings, or may prefer that you talk about them privately. You may have a family where Father is never disagreed with. In the Saudi royal family, for instance, which runs perhaps the world's largest family business, the Crown Prince is absolutely quiet in the presence of the King, even though, when doing business outside the palace, he is assertive and voluble. Some families express disappointment or rivalry quietly or indirectly. Your family's style of handling feelings will be reflected in your business behavior.

The problems in a family, in a business, and even in yourself, come about largely through ineffective ways of managing issues of emotion. Many families have indirect ways of handling feelings. They show unhappiness in subtle ways, or by withdrawing. People avoid talking to people about upsetting things, so certain topics become taboo. Before we turn to some of the consequences of the lack of direct emotional communication, let's identify how you and your family currently interact on an emotional level.

Exercise: How Your Family Handles Feelings

Think about how the members of your family handle their feelings. What happens when you, your parents, siblings, or cousins get upset, angry, or threatened? Are you even aware of the feeling? What do you do about it? Do you express the feeling to a different person, or do you change the feeling before you share it? Do you express a different feeling to a different person, or nothing to anybody? What happens to the feeling?

As we've seen, the family is a little world with many complex tensions and loyalties between people, many of them unspoken. For instance, a younger son feels slighted by his father, and continually turns to his mother for solace, who is herself feeling distant from her husband. She becomes closer to her son, and protective of him in discussions with her husband, who is increasingly critical of him. This three-way pattern of interaction is called a triangle.

Triangles are common in families, and in all social systems, as a way of handling difficult feelings. When there is tension between two people, as in the above family, between father and son, and husband and wife, people often do not resolve the issue directly. Notice the son did not come and talk to his father, or the wife to her husband, about their feelings. Instead the son talked to his mother. In turn, the mother did not talk to her husband about her feelings, but about how he was treating the son.

Such patterns are perfectly normal. For instance, many people talk to a friend about their frustration with their boss or their wife. A family triangle becomes a problem when bringing in the third person keeps the original pair from settling their differences. In the above example, the triangle became destructive when the son and father become more estranged because the son shared his hurt only with his mother.

Family triangles particularly stymie family businesses when the third member of a triangle is not in the business. The most frequent third person in a family business triangle is the mother. She is often the counselor for sons having trouble with the father, or the person who protects her husband from bad news. That's why, as crazy as it may sound, you need to bring **all** family members into business discussions. Because family businesses so commonly involve outside family members in business issues, they are part of them already.

You can perceive the existence of a triangle when two people talk about a situation that involves a third person without that person being present. When two parents talk about how to deal with a problem with their child, or adult child, a triangle is managing their feelings. The third part of a triangle can also be a thing, such as the business itself. Two people who always talk about business issues or about sports, are using the external topic to manage the close feelings between them.

The resolution of issues in triangular relationships comes about when the two people who are having difficulty communicating get together to talk about it. This can be done with or without the third person. Sometimes the third member of the triangle can help the other two finally deal with their rivalries. At other times, the third person unconsciously wants the triangle to continue. In the above family triangle, if the father and son get together, then the wife/mother will have to talk directly about her feelings to her husband. She may not be as ready as her son.

Exercise: Identifying Triangles

Think about the various triangles that exist in your family. There are probably triangles involving relatives in all branches of your family. List the most common ones. What issues do your triangles keep you from addressing directly? Share your list with the others in your family. The next chapter and those that follow will provide specific suggestions to build more effective communication about feelings to avoid triangularization.

Confusing Family and Business: Dueling Triangles

In January 1986, a meeting in Sam Sebastiani's home signalled the climax of several years of pain and conflict in one of the country's premier wine families. Sam had been president of the family winery since the death of his father, August, in 1980. That same year he met and married Vicki, who worked in marketing for the winery. Sam's younger brother Don, a California state legislator with whom he had been in conflict since the death of his father, was at the meeting as well. Sam had asked the winery for an employment contract. To his shock, Don was there to tell him that their mother, Sylvia, who owned all the stock, had named Don chairman of the board. He fired Sam as president, with no severance pay.

The issues behind the scenes had been building for several years, and provide a classic example of how family triangles can get mixed up in business. Sam had always been the heir apparent to his stern, demanding, powerful father, August. Like many second generation sons, he was hard-working, dedicated, serious, and single-minded about his inheritance. Don was seen as too young to be a contender, so after several years in the wine business, he entered politics. He was a controversial legislator, and because of the family name, the public had begun to take their anger at him out on the winery.

Critical family events had a hand in the drama. During the final year of his father's life, Sam courted and married Vicki, who was not Italian, nor very close to other members of the family. To complicate matters, at the time of August's death, the winery was entering hard times. Powerful competitors had entered the market, and the costs of modernization led them to experience their first losses in the initial years of Sam's tenure.

All these events worried Sylvia, who had inherited ownership of the business.

Let us explore some of the family rules that may have been broken. First, the winery was not turning a profit in Sam's first years. Second, Sam and Vicki, who gave lavish parties, had a very high profile in the community. Vicki began to be seen as the first lady of the family, which Sylvia was not used to. But the biggest problem was that Sam had not created a working relationship with his mother. She owned the winery, and kept asking him to spend more time with her, sharing information. Seeing her request in early family terms, he refused to go to her house, feeling that he was being asked to become a child again. However, she was also the owner of the winery and resented being treated that way by an employee. As she became more upset over his attitude, she began to talk more to Don than Sam.

Thus there were several family triangles. Sylvia talked to Don, not Sam, about her differences and worries. Sam talked to Vicki, not Sylvia, about his. The third triangle was between Sam and Don, with Sylvia caught in the middle. Sam had become more and more angry at Don's controversial public reputation, which drew hostility toward the family name. Sam wrote Don that he wanted to see him defeated in the next election. The brothers tried to resolve their differences and spoke about selling the winery, which neither wanted. The situation was created because, in effect, nobody was talking to the right person about the right issues. The final action—firing Sam—was the outcome of playing out a family drama within the family business.

However, the results have not been so bad. Don quit politics, and has been helpful as a non-management member of the family board. An effective outside manager, following Sam's strategy, led a dramatic turn-around at the winery. And Sam and Vicki, after they got over their pain and anger, have started a new winery venture. While having very little cash, Sam found that the personal trust of customers and suppliers helped him get started until his first vintage began to win awards. He appears to have used the crisis to further his own differentiation from his family, and has grown stronger, more confident and mature. Like his father, he has started a winery from scratch. Both he and Don are continuing the family legacy, each on his own terms.

What can be learned from this story? The most striking lesson is that everyone in that family was probably deeply hurt and relations have not been healed since the rift. The outcome may have been the same, but imagine the possible difference if the whole family could have gotten together and discussed face to face its values, its sense of the family legacy, the hurt feelings, and conflicts. Maybe the brothers could have achieved peace and the estrangement could have been lessened.

Family Rules and Myths

Every family has regular patterns. While rarely explicit, they are so consistent that they can be described as a series of family "rules" that govern behavior. The rules cover proper behavior, expression of conflict and emotion, what can be talked about, who has more and less power and precedence, and prescribed roles for different people. They are rules in the sense that, if someone acts differently, the family disapproves and tries to get them back in line. The best way to see these rules in action is to think of the first time you visit the family of your prospective spouse. You thought you knew your future husband or wife, but nothing he or she said could really prepare you for the family.

Remember the scene in *Annie Hall* where half the screen showed Woody Allen visiting Annie's quiet, almost stilted WASP family while the other half showed her visiting his boisterous, emotional, Jewish parents? Each family had its rules, and the newcomer found out about them either by violating them or feeling uncomfortable.

Family rules are not usually a problem for the family on a personal level. However, when they become part of the business, they need to be evaluated according to a different standard: do these patterns help the business get the job done. Many family patterns can have a dysfunctional effect on business. For example, the most common family norms are that everyone will be close, nobody will disagree, or at least will keep disagreements to him or herself. In a business, differences and disagreements are necessary. Developing a strategy, looking critically at decisions, and evaluating effectiveness cannot happen without sharing disagreements. That particular family rule just won't work in a business.

Violating a family rule can have painful and difficult consequences for both a family and a business. Consider this situation: a brother and an older sister worked together. The family rule was that the brother, being male, would be the business heir. However, everybody soon realized that the sister had some rare talents. She was an attorney and earned the respect of the employees. But the family rule also prevented discussing this issue, which was, after all, settled. This created distress for the sister, who felt it was unfair, and pressure on the brother, who knew he was not doing as well as Sis. The whole business became paralyzed because the issue could not be discussed. Finally, in great pain, the daughter took an offer from a law firm. The business suffered from her loss, and several key employees quit in frustration.

The most problematic family rules concern hidden behavior and what must not be noticed. Every family has certain types of behavior it would rather not know about and ways it denies unpleasant or painful reality. Often it copes with such activity by simply not talking about it. This may be one person's misbehavior through drinking, sexual activity, forbidden relationships, or legal improprieties. For example, one person's excessive drinking may be ignored. However, this is a problem because such denial actively supports the negative behavior. When a person is not noticed doing something, there is little pressure or incentive to stop. It may even become a problem for other family members, since the frequency of the behavior, in the absence of pressure or help to change, may escalate. People who drink but are not noticed may drink even more because they feel isolated and unnoticed by others.

Not facing reality can have destructive consequences, as for example, when a family does not confront the drinking of its members. If negative behavior is not attended to it tends to repeat itself in the next generation. For example, in one family business the younger son quit college and worked for his father, while his older brother went to business school and worked for a larger business. The younger son was, like his father, an intuitive worker with a feel for the shop work in the business. But he had a problem with self-esteem, and felt in the shadow of his older brother, who he knew would return and take over the business in a few years. He was also dependent on drugs and alcohol, to the distress of the family. The family focussed its efforts on getting him to quit, but without any real conviction. In fact, like many families, they tended to bail him out and make excuses for his behavior, rather than confront him. In addition, his generous salary and perks supported his habits.

The hidden problem was that Dad drank every day, but his wife ignored it and no one else talked about it. Furthermore Dad was very depressed, knowing that he needed to retire soon, feeling that he didn't have the skills to build the business further, but not knowing what else to do. He and his wife also had communication problems in their marriage, and he avoided talking to her.

As long as they felt that their son had the problem, the family got nowhere. In fact, the son's problems were a triangular diversion for the parents from these other pressing issues. The crisis came when the older son joined the business. The younger son fell apart, and entered a family-oriented treatment program. As part of his recovery, the family was forced to notice Dad's problems, and deal with the rivalry between the sons, and between the sons and Dad. Dad faced up to his drinking problem and the way that his son was mirroring his own denied behavior.

Often denied family patterns cause grave problems for the business. In one company, the alcohol problem of the founder was denied by his wife and his son, even though his erratic behavior was paralyzing the company. In response, many key managers also become depressed, frustrated, and dysfunctional, creating an alcoholic family business.

Exercise: Mapping Your Family Rules

Describe your family rules in the following areas:
What makes for a close family.
How we act when we're together.
What we never do.
How we behave in public.
What we never discuss.
What we consider important.
How we treat our elders.
How close family members should be.
What is private and what is shared.
Who gets to interrupt others.
How we deal with differences of opinion.
What we do when we're upset.
What women should do.
What men should do.
What we do when we are hurt or upset.

When you have completed your list, share it with other family members. Where are there differences of opinion? There will be some very striking differences in the way people see these patterns, especially across generations. Each person and each generation, lives in a different world. See if together you can come up with a description of your family. But don't expect to be able to come to agreement on every one.

Now look at each item on the list in relation to your business. Which ones make sense for the family, but might be questioned in relation to work? You might find that you may hold an assumption for the family, but modify it for the business. That kind of flexibility is sometimes needed to maintain a thriving business as well as a harmonious family.

Every family also has its own set of unspoken assumptions about how relationships should work, what people owe each other, how the family operates, what is important, and what the family is for; these define the family's mythology. These myths may be repeated to children as they grow up, or they may be assumed without explicit discussion. Often they are about the business. They suggest ways that the business ought to run, and they often foreclose discussion in the family and among employees about whether they are the best ways for the business to operate. There will be, for example, a family myth about the purpose of the business. These myths, assumptions, and expectations may be invisible to the employees, but the family is aware of them and business behavior can only be understood when the family mythology is understood.

Examples of common family myths that may be transferred into the business include:

- The business will always take care of all family members.
- The business will make us respectable.
- Everyone in the family is treated equally, in or out of the business.
- The leader of the business is the leader of the family.
- Our business success proves we've overcome our immigrant heritage.
- Leaving the business is as bad as leaving the family.
- The sons shouldn't have a feud that divides the family and the business like their grandparents'.
- Every son or daughter has a job waiting in the business.
- The business should never be sold.
- Never disagree with father, who is responsible for creating this wonderful business.
- The family agrees on everything.
- The secret of our business success is our ability to _____ (fill in your family's answer).
- Since we're so successful, we don't need to change.
- Women (or in-laws) don't belong in the business.
- The business can support everyone in the family.

Some of the above examples will be familiar to you and should lead you to begin a list of the ones held by your own family. Family mythology can become a major obstacle to growth and development. Too often a family denies the reality of change, rather than openly questioning or modifying a myth. You may not want, or be able, to challenge and redefine your family mythology in a single sitting. But you need to explore this level of your family reality in order to be free to develop your business.

Exercise: Defining Your Family Mythology

One of the most important activities for any family, especially one in business, is to make their myths and assumptions explicit. Each person should bring their list of proposed myths to a family meeting. Write them all on a large sheet of paper, and see which ones people can agree on. For each family myth, list some of its positive and negative effects on your business. You can expect some lively discussion and some surprises. Then, when the shared list is complete, try to rank order them in order of importance to the family. Some of them will have to do with the core values of the family, its meaning, what it stands for. Others, upon reflection, will be seen to have outgrown their usefulness, or may be questionable. These are the ones that need to be explored deeply. The Family Council, described in Chapter 4, is a good vehicle for this exploration.

Family myths often lead to misunderstandings and conflict, as we will see in the next chapter. Many myths are assumptions that individuals, especially offspring, make about what they can expect and what is fair in the family. But each person may interpret them differently. The differences will be the basis of their actions, and will lead to conflict unless they are made explicit and resolved. For example, heirs may expect that inheritances will be equal. If a father decided to give a larger share to a son in the business, or a parent does something special for another brother or sister, deep feelings of betrayal can result. There is no hurt deeper than the sense that a family member has betrayed a core family myth or value.

The pressure of business choices, and the new demands of change, make it more difficult for a family to maintain its mythology. Many family members don't know how to begin to talk about this reality, so they just act, without sharing their intentions or reasoning. I have worked with many business families where misunderstandings, even anger, resulted because one family member didn't know how to talk about such matters.

Playing Family Roles

People in families also develop what are termed "roles," the customary ways that a person acts in relation to others. As in a drama, people in families play certain regular roles with each other. There are general roles, such as mother, father, daughter, son, that have certain expectations, rights, and obligations. Then there are the special parts each of us plays in our particular family drama. A child, whether through personality or inheritance, develops a reputation which becomes his or her expected role. "John's the scholar, and Mike's the wild one," may denote the childhood roles played by two brothers. These roles usually stem from real events, such as behavior when one is a child or adolescent. However the downside of these roles is that they tend to linger, becoming more of a limit than an expectation. It's hard, for example, for a wild son to demonstrate that he has grown to be responsible in the business.

In a family, each child takes on very specific roles. Some aspects of family roles can be traced to birth order. The oldest child has his or her parents all to himself, and consequently usually develops a great deal of independence and self-initiative. Older children are used to doing things on their own, and since they begin their lives without sibling companionship, may turn out to be more introverted. A younger child enters a social world, with an older sibling who is more than willing to tell him or her what to do and how to do it. Therefore a younger child often develops into a more sociable person, more able to fit in and get along. The youngest child gets lots of attention, and may not have as many demands or expectations placed on him or her. A middle child, almost by definition, is the mediator, the person in between. He or she is often concerned with peace-keeping, with helping the older and younger siblings to get along.

Family roles can constrain everyone. One couple who founded an import business came to me in distress. They told me that their son was going to inherit their business. I asked when he would be gaining control. They laughed, and told me that he had been in charge since he was three. He had pushed his two sisters out of the business; they felt that he was a tyrant in many ways. His family role continued to create pain for all parties.

In another family, one with two brothers, the older son had the role of "hyper-responsible" child. He was always helpful, available, and ready to pitch in. He acutely felt the burden of helping his father run the business, and became his alter ego. Inwardly, he felt pressured, even over-burdened by always having to be responsible, mature, and helpful. Everyone said that he didn't have a selfish bone in his body, but the burden of being a family saint was tiring. This was especially true given the fact that his younger brother was just the opposite. He was irresponsible and wild, spending family money, and continually getting bailed out of trouble by his mother. He felt he could never be as virtuous as his brother, so why try?

The problem was that the early patterns became solidified, even exaggerated, into "expected" family roles. Nobody would notice if Younger Brother did something helpful, and Older Brother wouldn't think of doing anything irresponsible because it would hurt his parents. Interestingly, Older Brother came to me. He was getting burned out, and wanted some separateness from the business, but didn't feel he could take it.

How could this extreme example of opposite roles be modified? The solution seems strange, but it worked. The two brothers were each asked to try to act like the other. Older Brother needed to learn to be selfish, take time off, and have some fun. His brother would teach him. And Younger Brother was given a responsible position in the business, where he actually did have the talents and training to handle it. In a situation where he felt that he could perform and was not under his brother or father's thumb, he delighted in showing he could succeed. Over two years, each brother stepped out from their family roles, to adopt more balanced lives. And each brother felt liberated in the process.

How can you outgrow such fixed roles that develop inside the family? There are no easy answers for these lifelong dilemmas. Having a business just gives them greater urgency, as they cannot be solved by distance. But recognizing that they exist and defining what they are for your family is an important step.

Here's an example of how awareness of roles helped change the situation. Two brothers created a business. One brother had two sons, Brian and Tony, and the other had a son, Ted, and a daughter, Helen. All four entered the business. The family was traditional, and Brian was expected to take over the business. When his father died suddenly, Brian assumed the presidency. But he was more of a technician than a good leader. Employees felt he was distant and unapproachable, quite the opposite of his father. On the other side of the family, there was Helen, who was very talented, and Ted, who had perhaps the most natural leadership ability. Their father was aging, and wanted to retire. As the generational shift occurred, the company's products began to suffer from increased competition and a maturing market. Brian was anxious about the business problems and began to withdraw from the others. Helen became angry, and began to badmouth him to employees. Ted tried to smooth things over and work behind the scenes.

Everyone acted out of their family roles in a business crisis that demanded innovation. Finally, the four cousins got together and looked at their family history. Their fathers' arrangement that the family hierarchy continue in the business was not acceptable to them. Helen was angry at not being granted leadership, and Ted was uncertain how to use his ability to do what he saw was needed. The group looked at how they were playing their family roles and decided to make some changes. First, they decided to allocate jobs to fit their real abilities. Helen was made operations manager, and Ted became CEO. The four decided to operate the business with a board of directors of four equals making major policy decisions. They let go of family roles, to create roles that fit the business needs.

Reflection Question

Think of your own family, and how birth order and temperament led to your family role. Were you the helpful older son, the bratty kid sister, the quiet provoker who always sent your brother crying to your parents, or the one who always got into trouble yourself?

Then remember what you noticed as a child, how you paid attention to other people, what you thought was important and interesting, and your style of relating to others. Were you a helper, a doer, an avoider, a dreamer? Try to describe your family role as clearly as you can.

Now think of your role in the family business. Not just when you relate to other family members, but your area of responsibility, how you manage others, what you stand for, what you attend to, and what concerns you.

Now compare the two descriptions, and write down some of the ways that your work pattern parallels your family pattern. For example, I have noticed that children who take on the helper role in their families often become professional helpers—therapists, doctors, nurses, etc.

You might do this exercise for all the other members of your family, comparing their roles today with their early roles. Many patterns and styles of interaction are set by our childhood experience.

If you are in a family business, you automatically play two roles with some of your relatives, a business role and a family role. Even though they involve the same people, the roles involve different expectations and behavior. Stew Leonard, owner of a successful dairy store in Connecticut, recalls an incident when his younger son was starting to work for him. He was coming late, not showing up some days, and generally not doing very well. Finally the other employees had enough. Stew took his son's paycheck, and left a message to meet him at home. His son came in and they sat down together in the hot tub. Stew began, "As your boss, I have to let you know that you're fired." He handed him his final paycheck. Then, he put his arm around his son, and added, "As your dad, I'm really sorry to hear you've lost your job. How can I be helpful to you?" Needless to say, his son has straightened up, and now manages a newly-opened store.

As this story demonstrates, being able to recognize the dual roles and consciously switch from one to the other can help foster healthy family/ work relationships.

Reflection Question

How can you balance the different realities of being a family member and an employer, or co-worker? Think about how your behavior, your needs, and the expectations on you change as you move from one world to the other. How do you play the different roles? Does your family role limit you at work?

Life Cycles and the Family Business

Neither families nor businesses are static. While the family and the business contain many enduring structures that resist change, each system also experiences continual change and evolution. Psychologist Elaine Kepner characterized family and business as "coevolving systems."[2] Every individual, the family as a whole, and the business are all continuously growing and changing, as is each individual's relationship to the business.

The growth of the individual is biological, as people move from infancy, through childhood, and into maturity. There is also a psychological dimension, as family members of all ages develop their capacities and take on various life tasks. There are slow changes, as well as crises and sudden shifts, such as when a child leaves home or there is a serious illness.

Shakespeare wrote about the seven ages of man, and the history of psychology is dotted with typologies of life stages. The most noted model of life development comes from psychoanalyst Erik Erikson. He suggests that every person's major life purpose is to develop a unique sense of personal identity. Identity is created by completing certain major life tasks that include developing skills, having intimate relationships, raising children, and achieving something important in one's work. In young adulthood a person is concerned with leaving home, falling in love, and learning about his or her ability to work. Adulthood finds us hopefully achieving career success and family intimacy.

In *The Seasons of a Man's Life*, psychologist Daniel Levinson notes that around age 40, men often go through a mid-life crisis that seems almost like a second adolescence, when they doubt their abilities and achievements, and question their commitments. Then the struggle subsides and a new maturity signals the end to this crisis. In this "generative" period a man is concerned about his legacy, as he becomes more introspective and available as a mentor to the next generation.

Each of these life stages corresponds to stages in one's work career. The talents, fears, needs, and goals of a teenager, a young adult, and a middle-ager are very different. Therefore, their interest in the family business, and what they need from their involvement there, shifts. A 40-year-old will want a different role, salary, and relationship to the business than a 20-year-old. Similarly, the focus of a couple changes when they have children, when their children grow, and when their parents die. At times they may have more or less energy to devote to business.

Families too have life stages. There is young love, the formation of the family, children, youth, children leaving home, and post-childrearing stages. Increasingly, family life cycles today also include divorce, remarriages, second families, and blended families. There are mid-life young parents, and mid-life grandparents. You can even be both at once! These family events take place in the midst not only of each individual's personal development process, but of the business' process as well.

Businesses have life cycles like individuals and families. They are born, reach childhood, adolescence, and hopefully middle age, and even die. Each business has its own organic growth cycle, but several general stages can be identified in most business' lives. At each stage, as in personal development, there is a crisis that can lead a successful resolution or actually threaten the future.

1. Founding or Failure: Tremendous vision and energy is needed to get a business off the ground. The founder may have to do everything, and not have much time for family. This is the stage where one puts in "sweat equity," and usually doesn't have much income to take out. The business is precarious and may not survive.

2. Fast Development or Steady Growth: The business is finally launched. People can draw salaries, and they no longer wonder about short-term survival. Now they have to get organized and begin to define how they will work together. Sometimes a business takes off quickly, with high energy excitement and overwhelming demands. Then the pressure is on to get it all done, and to achieve results continually. Fast development speeds up the demands on the family members in the business and forces them to move outside themselves to find key employees to make the business grow.

3. Maturation or Development: If the business continues to grow, sooner or later things will level off. Over time, the business needs to develop clear roles, and if it has grown to near 100 employees, it will need to develop professional management. The founder will have to begin to transmit what he or she knows to potential successors. In many businesses, this is where the children get old enough to participate. The business begins to face questions about its long-term viability. Every business must continually develop through innovation or face decline.

4. Decline or Renewal: Sooner or later the magic ends, and the business faces either an external shift or internal erosion. The founders are tired and want to rest, and the business is no longer fresh and exciting. To avoid stagnation new blood must be brought in from the family or outside it, who can take the business to new places, develop new products, and take new initiatives. If the business is not renewed, it will likely die. The problem is that many businesses do not attend to the need for renewal until it is too late, and there is a crisis. The business must be passed to the next generation when it is vital and strong, rather than when it has fallen apart. Otherwise the next generation is forced to create a new business, rather than inherit one.

Chapters 5 through 9 explore in depth each of these developmental stages. What is significant to note here is that at any given time you are at the intersection of three life cycles—individual, family and business.

Family and individual changes impact on the business, and vice versa. If a family member has a crisis, the effects reverberate in the other systems. Imagine what happens when a family has its first child, if Mother or Father are operating a business together. Work roles have to shift, and the business may have to bring in more money to cover childcare expenses. The strain may make one spouse want to withdraw from the business.

Such changes do not usually happen gracefully or gradually. As Lynn Hoffman notes:

"Families are notable examples of entities that change through leaps. The individuals making up a family are growing (at least partly) according to an internal biological design, but the larger groupings within the family, the subsystems, and the generations must endure major shifts in relation to each other. The task of the family is to produce and train new sets of humans to be independent, form new families, and repeat the process, as the old set loses power, declines and dies. Family life is a multi-generational changing of the guard. And although this process is at times a smooth one, like the transactions of political parties in a democracy, it is more often fraught with danger and disruption. Most families do not leap to new integrations with ease, and the 'transformations'... are by no means self-assured.[3]"

I would argue that the same is true for businesses and the intersections of families and businesses. As an individual, the family, or the business, goes through a sudden shift or transition, the other people, or the other systems, may be forced to play catch-up, as they are faced with uncomfortable, unfamiliar, and perhaps even scary situations. They may even resist the change in the other system, which is the genesis of some of the common family business difficulties.

At any moment in time, each person, family and business are at a certain period in their own developmental cycle, and you can actually map yourself along each cycle. Creating a family and business lifeline can clarify the different cycles in yourself, your family and your business.

Be aware that developmental stages alternate periods of calmness— plateaus—with periods of stress and conflict. Within each of your cycles, reflect on whether you are in a calm or conflicted period of development. For example, you may have a new baby, or may be intensely questioning what you are doing in your personal life. Or your home life may be calm, and your business may be in a crisis/transition period. If you are experiencing transition or conflict in more than one cycle at once, you will probably be experiencing tremendous distress.

Exercise: Where are You in Your Growth Cycles?

Use the biggest sheet of paper you can find. Work together as a family to get the chronology straight. Start with the coming together of the family that started the business, or any other marker event in your family. Go back at least one generation. First list the significant personal, family, and business events by date in a horizontal line. Note at what stage of development you are right now personally, in your family, and in your business. Next, looking at the other members of your family, note the stages of personal development for each of them. This will be your worksheet.

Then, using different color pens (one for each person, one for family events, and one for business events) fill in periods and dates along this horizontal line. Mark today at a point about 3/4 of the way across the page. Positive events move toward the top of the page, negative events toward the bottom. You will end up with several zigzagging lines. See sample below.

Sample Lifeline

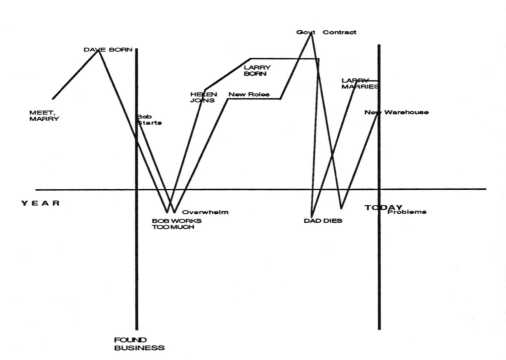

As we've been exploring, the family behind the business is a complex and often confusing and difficult animal. It breaths energy into the business and creates a lot of patterns that affect the business. Many businesses run into trouble because family relationships are transferred without reflection into the business. Things go fine for a while, until there is a crisis. Then things fall apart, in the family or the business. Sharing, looking at oneself and the whole family as suggested in this chapter, is a form of preventive medicine. Each family that has a business must look at its personal relations and family structure to identify family patterns that have been brought into the business that may not serve the business well. The next chapter goes more deeply into methods for building communication, and resolving family conflicts that spill over into the business.

Notes:

1. Barnes, Louis. "Incongruent Hierarchies: Daughters and Younger Sons as Company CEOs." *Family Business Review*, Vol. 1: No. 1, 1988.
2. Elaine Kepner. "The Family and the Firm: A Coevolutionary Perspective." *Organizational Dynamics*, Summer 1983.
3. Hoffman, Lynn. *Foundations of Family Therapy*, page 160.

3

Getting Things Straight: Clear Communication and Conflict Resolution

"Some relationships work better than others. We all know people with whom we feel comfortable, secure, able to talk through a problem, and confident. With others we feel uncomfortable, frustrated, and mistrustful. We rarely understand why some relationships work well and others don't. We tend to accept the quality of a relationship as inevitable: 'That's the way it is. We just don't get along.' We blame problems on the other person and assume that there is little we can do to improve the way we interact.

"Although it takes two to have a relationship, it takes only one to change its quality. Just as we react to others, they react to us. By changing our behavior, we will change the way they react."

-*Roger Fisher and Scott Brown*, Getting Together

One of the most public family feuds in recent years was played out by the Bingham family of Louisville. The patriarch, Barry Sr., tried to resolve a feud between his son Barry Jr., manager of the family's newspaper and media business, and daughter Sallie, an owner who had been forced off the board of directors. Their conflict stemmed from old family feelings and went on for several years, ultimately forcing the sale of the business. The struggle has inspired several books, including one written by Sallie herself, and many of the intra-family messages in the feud were sent via letters to the editor in the family newspaper. The consensus of observers is that there were several ways that the feud could have been resolved short of a sale.

Barry Bingham Sr. was the third-generation heir who built the family newspaper holdings into a lucrative and well-respected empire. He, his wife Mary, and their three sons and two daughters led a storybook life of privilege. But their children's lives were marked by tragedy. The eldest son, Worth, talented, gregarious, and aggressive like his father, was expected to be the successor. His younger brother, Barry Jr., was devoted to him. But Worth's life was cut short by an accident in 1966, just two years after another accident killed his younger brother, Jonathan. In 1971, Barry Jr. was asked by his father to take over the family newspapers. That same year he contracted cancer, which was treated and went into remission.

Barry Jr. presided over a difficult era of declining profits in the newspaper business. While he was shyer than Worth and less prepared to be a business leader, Barry did a creditable job, although he was seen by many as aloof and demanding. In 1977 his sisters, Sallie and Eleanor, moved back to Louisville, and conflict began to erupt. Sallie felt like an outsider. Although close to her father, she had felt excluded from the strong bond between Barry Jr. and Worth when she was growing up. Barry Jr. and Sallie had not had much contact in many years, and were never close. She had been successful as a writer, but her marriage had recently broken up, and she returned to Louisville seeking support from her family.

Barry Sr., who owned a majority of the business, put his two daughters on the board of directors. They were delighted, although it appears that Sallie was also somewhat disappointed at not being asked to take a management job at the newspaper. Her feelings grew, although conflicts did not really get discussed by the family or at board meetings. The family had a long history of not being able to disagree or express conflict. However, Barry Jr. knew about their dissatisfaction, because both his mother and Sallie wrote letters to the editor disagreeing with political stands the paper took. Evidently Sallie was upset that the business did not offer daughters the same job opportunities as sons, and expressed these feelings as political disagreements in the letters.

In 1983 the conflict came into the open. Barry Jr. asked his father to request that Sallie and Eleanor resign from the board. Sallie refused. Then she demanded that the family buy out her shares of stock or she would sell them to an outsider. Increasingly Barry Jr. felt his family had lost faith in his management, although they never told him directly. He tried to work out several arrangements with Sallie and with Eleanor, who wanted to trade her stock for ownership of the TV station so she could run that. The major battle was over the value of Sallie's stock, and how much the company would pay to buy her shares. Barry Jr. stood firm in offering her a lower price than she wanted, and the two were unable to compromise.

Never expressing it openly, Barry Sr. felt deeply torn, and didn't know what to do. Although close with his wife, he wasn't able to bring his son and daughter together to look at the issues. He told the pair that if they couldn't come to an agreement he would sell the papers, but he was never active in getting the two to talk. In the conflict, Sallie cut off contact with her mother, and then with her father. This hurt Barry Sr. Suddenly, without discussing it with anyone but Mary, he announced that he had decided to sell the entire business to Gannett. Barry Jr. felt betrayed.

Everybody made a lot of money in the sale, but nobody was happy. The parents were estranged from their children, and the sons from the daughters. The family name was taken from the newspapers, where they had a proud tradition of liberal political and community involvement, and the wounds are so great that it is unlikely, particularly with Barry Sr.'s recent death, that the family can ever feel comfortable together again. Yet the sale was made to resolve a conflict.

What went wrong? Barry Jr. and Sallie each blame the other, while it is clear that either party could have forged a compromise. But by the end, neither one felt they could "give in," even when the sale was announced. Observers regret that Barry Sr. never got Sallie and Barry together to resolve their issues, and never asked them to reflect on the family tradition of service. To reach a compromise, Barry Sr. also might have gotten together with his children individually, trying to listen and discover what each really wanted.

The Binghams faced a classic family business conflict: the different perspectives, needs, and rights of passive owners in a family business, as opposed to the family members who run the businesses. And they transferred family difficulty and sibling rivalry (who was listened to, who was respected by Dad, who had more power) into a struggle over the future of the business. Both the business and the family lost.

It appears that the whole tragedy came about because the family didn't have a way to get people to sit down and talk about family issues. Instead feelings got played out in stock valuation, in newspaper columns, and in board meetings. The principals never got together over a dinner table, or in their homes, to explore the deep feelings of rivalry between Barry and Sallie. Clearly Sallie never felt recognized by her parents and Barry Jr. never felt supported by them. By the close of the drama, each person was willing to lose everything rather than compromise. Such is the case in most family feuds. In a feud, people are more concerned that the other person not get something, rather than trying to get what they want.

It would appear that Binghams never learned to communicate or to face conflict. This is not an uncommon problem. Often families avoid or deny conflict, until it erupts into painful and sometimes unresolvable schisms. This deficiency can cripple or even destroy a family business because conflict is a reality of business life. The Binghams and many others had to sell their businesses because they did not know how to talk about their feelings, hurts, differences, and change. But by learning clear and direct family communication and conflict resolution, you can avoid such pitfalls.

Tasks for the Chapter

In this chapter, you will learn how to talk with the members of your family business who create the most difficulty and distress for you. You will learn some techniques for getting behind the problem, for clarifying issues, and for understanding what is "really" going on. You'll find ways to get the attention of family members who are not eager to talk about something, and how to separate the "family" from the "business" aspect of conflicts. You will learn how to hold problem-solving meetings with particular family members to discuss difficult issues before they become "family feuds."

Many techniques and examples of family communication difficulties will be presented. There are exercises for family members who do not feel heard, for people who are feeling anger or hurt, for people who want to reconsider family or business traditions, and for those who wish to resolve value and policy differences. Special focus will be on communicating with people who "won't listen." While the exercises focus on communication between family members, they are equally applicable to difficulties between outside managers and family members.

Why is Communication So Difficult?

From the outside, it seems so easy to resolve many of the difficulties of families in business. Yet many families will stop at nothing to avoid discussion of controversial issues. Why are communication and conflict resolution so especially difficult for family business?

The reason is that in a family business, you can't just have a talk about business differences. Family members do not merely face differences of opinion, feelings, or conflicts over policies. They bring with them not just the issue at hand, but a history of expectations, assumptions, hurts, and unfulfilled desires as ghosts in the conversation. For example in a business setting when a CEO father asks his accountant daughter to get him a cup of coffee, he is not just making a simple request. He is also sending a signal about the terms of the relationship and their history. He assumes that he has the right to ask her and that she will obey. But what if she were to reply, "No Dad, why don't you ask one of the other vice-presidents?," or "That's a job for your secretary"? Then they would be arguing over the rules of their relationship. She would be calling upon the assumptions of a work relationship, while he assumes the family relationship is still in effect. You can imagine the arguments at home and over lunch that might ensue, and how other family members—his wife, his son, and his other daughter—might take sides! Often in order to avoid conflict, women who find themselves in this situation choose to say nothing, but their resentment builds and may come out in covert ways.

Now consider that this same daughter wants her father to consider a new form of accounting, or that a brother-in-law is arguing with the boss' son about responsibility. In each case they are struggling not just with the issue, but with their history together, and the nature of their relationship. Resolving conflicts in family business means not just finding good compromises to deep business or personal issues, but understanding that every family conversation deals with the reality of the family and business history. All the baggage family relationships carry gets in the way of sharing and resolving differences. It would be great if when children or other family members come to work, they could start their relationship with family members afresh. But this just can't happen.

Reflection Question

Think about your work relationships with family members, especially the ones you disagree with or fight with. For each person, ask yourself what expectations, needs, assumptions, habits, or frustrations you carry into the current relationship from your family history together. You might have a talk with the other person and ask him or her what he or she brings from the past.

Sources of Conflict

Despite the rich variety of conflicts and communication difficulties that arise in family business, there are actually a very few issues that create them. As you can see, they are all interrelated and cluster around the dual relationship of family member and business associate. Knowing about these common issues can help you identify what is going on in your family business when there's a problem. If you are having a family conflict, you should go through this list and ask yourself whether some of these feelings lie below the surface.

1. Violation of one's sense of fairness or justice.

Everybody grows up with a sense of what is fair and to be expected from the business and the family. Such common assumptions as "every child gets treated equally" are articles of faith. But often these can be interpreted differently. But equal treatment, particularly in a business setting, becomes a problem due to different talents, activities, and circumstances.

For instance a family that wants to treat children equally has a problem when one child is running the business in such a way that its profits increase manyfold. As a key manager, he or she has a right to ask for a hefty share of the profits, but as a child in the family, his or her share may have been determined at birth. In addition, the brother who is a doctor may see the whole situation differently from his home three states away, and spouses may have their own perspectives. Father and Mother, of course, have their own views: they may need income for their retirement so they want to reward the child who is succeeding, but they may also want all the kids to be happy and feel good about their inheritance. And the parents even may disagree with one another about what's fair. So even the simplest principle of the family can be sorely tested over the years.

What is fair and just extends to how you are treated when you are hurt. For example, Fred hired Joe, his contractor brother-in-law, to build an office for the family business. Fred felt the work was not done up to standards, but didn't feel he could confront Joe. So he kept quiet. When the time came to build a second office, he gave the contract to another builder, offending Joe. The sister/spouse felt caught in the middle. Who should talk to whom? Is Joe really aware that he disappointed Fred, and might he have put in the additional work if asked? Or will he get angry and defensive, and accuse Fred of presuming on their relationship to get extra work done? Should Fred apologize or change his behavior? What is fair in this situation? Many family conflicts in business stem from balancing family notions of fairness.

2. Feeling unacknowledged.

This problem arises in family business when you don't feel that your contribution, talent, or ability is noticed by others, especially parents. They may be critical, or they may ignore your achievements. Your parents may have trouble seeing you as grown, or seeing the value of your work. They may not reward your contribution with the kind of salary or job that fits your value, or they may give your older sibling more attention. This situation is very common in companies, where many non-family employees also feel unacknowledged. People in general are very reticent about noticing positive things that others do and we often go around feeling unappreciated or "ripped off."

The conflict becomes even more difficult in a family business, because you may not feel acknowledged or even loved as a person by your relative, and then transfer that personal feeling to the business. I once knew a young man who felt ignored and unappreciated by his father. He decided to work in the family business so his father finally would notice him. As his father continued to be negative and critical, over time the son gave up trying to do a good job.

3. Feeling powerless.

Closely related to feeling unappreciated, a sense of powerlessness arises when you feel you don't have any impact on other family members. They won't listen to your advice nor heed your ideas and judgments. This is a common problem caused by family roles. A family member can be a professional, with tremendous competency, but the family role of "Little Brother or Sister," or simply "Son or Daughter" can prevent that ability from being recognized. Often, for instance, when a sibling comes from working in another business to the family business, he or she can see certain problems in the business that Father or Older Brother find it difficult to acknowledge because the advice is coming from Younger Brother or Sister.

This situation often arises when you have outside professional experience or have performed well in the business, and your father cannot see you as anything but an irresponsible child. This makes some children work even harder, if fruitlessly, while it leads others to just give up. The challenge is to separate the real business issue, such as a needed shift of strategy, new product, or market pressure, from the family's emotional issue. The business suffers when a family role prevents the consideration of a business need.

4. Confusion of family and business roles.

Family members talk to each other without being aware of what role they are taking, and, as we saw in Chapter 2, often transfer family roles into the business. Remember the daughter/manager who was asked by her father/boss to get him coffee? That's a classic example of role confusion.

Myths about Conflict and Communication

Most family business conflicts are resolvable. However we are often limited in coming to a resolution by some common myths about conflict and communication, such as:

1. Since he or she won't change there is nothing I can do.

This attitude is probably the biggest roadblock to resolution. It puts the blame on the other person, rather than where it belongs—between you and the other person. By giving up before you start, you lose any chance to try new ways to resolve the problem. By focussing on the other person, you lose the possibility of modifying your own choices in the situation. Conflict resolution begins with you. What can *you* do to create a positive climate for the other person to work on the problem?

2. He or she just doesn't care or doesn't want to do anything.

You usually think this when someone is not doing what you want. It assumes the other person knows your wants and needs, which he or she usually doesn't. Before assuming the other person's disinterest in you, you might try to air your concerns more clearly and ask the other person where he or she stands. Rather than make assumptions, talk to the other person about yourself and about what he or she wants, feels, and needs.

3. Conflict is bad and wrong if people love each other.

This is a very common myth. But the truth is we don't always agree with people we love, and, in fact, we don't usually have conflicts with people we don't care about. Many families attempt to avoid conflict at all costs, or assume that there is something wrong if two people disagree. They believe that if they talk about a problem, it will get worse, or out of control, or hurt somebody. Yet, if you don't acknowledge a conflict, it doesn't go away. It just remains below the surface, building up. When it finally explodes, it is usually worse for having been avoided for so long. Then everybody's worst fears come true.

4. Feelings have no place in business relationships.

You'd be surprised how many people think this. Actually, of course, all relationships are about feelings of love, caring, and respect. In addition, every family business conflict has an emotional component that must be addressed along with the practical issue at stake. People in families are not rational beings, and they need leeway to discuss the emotional side of issues, such as wanting to be accepted, or feeling hurt or ignored. Every family relationship can generate tremendous feelings. While feelings can be put aside when decisions are made, they need to be acknowledged first.

Self Defeating Responses to Conflict

Family business disagreements often grow out of proportion due to ineffective and counterproductive responses by family members. We are usually raised with a very small repertoire of problem-solving methods, and don't know what to do when these methods fail. Conflict management theorists Jordan and Margaret Paul, in a workbook on family conflict resolution[1], observe that family members tend to respond to disagreements in three typical but self-defeating, non-productive ways. Assuming erroneously that they can't deal directly with the other person, they either try to control or coerce the other, withdraw into apathy or defeat, or try to manipulate indirectly. None of these strategies really brings about a resolution.

Strategy One: Controlling or Coercing the Other.

Using threats, withdrawal of emotional support, and other punishments, some family members try to force the others to do what they want. For example, one son stopped talking to his mother when he had a business dispute with his father. Another brother threatened to quit or sue.

Many parents routinely talk about disinheriting their children if they do not do as they wish. Often they have no real intention to follow through, which hurts their credibility. When people feel there's no other way to get what they want, they may resort to threats.

Often value differences become control issues, leading to fruitless conflict, because the real issues are not brought to the surface. Many parents want to help their children by controlling their decisions. It is hard for parents to see a child, even an adult child, make a decision they feel will be "harmful." Other family members go along without really wanting to. Their feelings build up. The child ends up feeling controlled and coerced, and may undermine or rebel.

When a business is involved, the parental pressure may be to make a career choice to enter the business, or to do something else that the family values. Parents always find it hard to let go of expectations of their children. This reality came to me personally. I had been working with a family business where the parents were very controlling of their children, from picking their schools, to getting them jobs in banks. I came home and my teen-age son Oren, who goes to a school that requires community service, excitedly told me that he had found the perfect place to do his service work: working with a community group to build a downtown ballpark in San Francisco! Now Oren comes from a long-line of community activists and socially responsible family members, and, for whatever reasons, this was not our idea of what the community most needed. There were talks between his parents and our contemporaries about what to do, automatically taking the form "Should we let him do it?" Our initial response, like those of many other parents, was to pressure him to do what we felt was right. Ultimately, we simply decided to let him know that we respected his decision, but it certainly wasn't the decision any of us would have made. He changed his mind. I learned from this how easily parents' sense of what is good for their children can shift into coercion or pressure.

Our culture is very supportive of coercion, threats, and bluster. Unfortunately, when you force someone to do something, you often get their agreement at the cost of the relationship. People feel more estranged, less trusting, and less willing to share information when they are coerced. In families, anger at coercive tactics can lead over time to feuds or total breaks of relationships.

Strategy Two: Withdrawing into Apathy.

Giving up diminishes your self-esteem, and is an admission that you have no influence over the other person or the situation. Both assumptions are wrong, and have drastic consequences. They lead you to lose positive energy and commitment, often over a relationship or business that means a great deal to you. This stance is a dead end—there is nowhere you can go from here.

Feeling defeated is different from strategic withdrawal or making a positive decision to let go. The question is whether you move on to another focus of interest and seek out other opportunities, or keep feeling upset, hurt, or limited by a situation where you didn't get what you want. Are you able to let go, or are you consumed by bitterness?

Strategy Three: Manipulating Indirectly.

Early in life, when they can't reach their goals or get what they want from siblings or parents, children learn to do it indirectly. The child who goes to the other parent to ask for money, the son who, after being told no, sneaks out and does what he wants anyway, or the wife who gets sick to avoid a social engagement are all getting what they want indirectly.

Indeed many self-help tomes and business bibles are manuals of how to manipulate people to get what you want subversively. This may be helpful in more distant business dealings, but when you try to get people close to you to do things indirectly, you lose some important things. First, the issue cannot be talked about openly. Second, communication about what you really want isn't taking place. And finally, you are not treating the other person with respect and honesty. All of these costs are intangible, while the immediate benefit of manipulation may be experienced today. However, like the other strategies, manipulation caries more costs than benefits as a long-term way of managing family/business relationships.

Redesigning Relationships for Communication

Whenever I talk to family business members, they almost uniformly report their most pressing concern is "communication." What they usually mean is that they have trouble getting another family member to do what they want. They want to "communicate" to the other why he or she should do something. More often than not, the concern for communication is really about control. The story of family business and indeed of many families is about the efforts of some members to get the others to do something. Parents want their children to behave in a certain way, and children, especially when they follow parents into their business, want to have impact on parents. Often they have different ideas about what to do, but, unfortunately, only a single business to operate.

In general, people want to force others to change as a last resort. In most situations, they really want the other person to sit down and listen. Only after they don't feel heard and respected do they get into battles over control and lose the possibility of compromise.

The primary communication issue in family businesses is the difficulty family members—spouses, parents, children, siblings—have really hearing one other. They have been together so long that they often stop listening, thinking they "know" the other. But effective communication is about really listening to the other members of your family and allowing them to remain different, even respecting their differences.

Problems in communication can't be resolved in a five-minute chat or even with a formal, "Let's sit down and work this out." Often communication problems have built up over a long time, and they are usually broader than just resolving one difference. Communication is not just applying a series of techniques to a conversation, but implies a set of attitudes about the other person and the relationship. Good communication means a good relationship. A good relationship is one where people

- Have basic respect for each other;
- Take time to listen to and learn about each other;
- Allow each other to be different;
- Consider preserving the relationship to be more important than any particular issue.

When a relationship contains these elements, there is no dispute that cannot be resolved. Without the above elements, it is unlikely that even minor differences can be bridged. While it can't be measured or seen, the most important thing to bring to improving a relationship is the attitude that the relationship, and the other person, is important to you.

People often look at this list and say, "Well, I act that way with **him**, but he doesn't reciprocate." That attitude is self-defeating, and leaves you waiting for the other to improve the relationship. The other person would probably say the same thing about you! To redesign a relationship for good communication, you need to begin with yourself. You help create the environment for the other person, and there are more ways to change that environment than you probably have considered. A person who appears to "resist" open communication can be drawn out, involved, or persuaded to open up under the right conditions.

The place to begin to build communication is with yourself. First you need to conduct a self-exploration of what you want to achieve through communication, and then you have to do a critical analysis of your strategies. Many of us spend a lot of time and energy thinking about how we wish the other person would be, rather than on what we want, or what we may be doing to keep the other person from talking to us.

For example, a son wanted to know more about his father's incredible ability to make financial deals. He felt cut out, as if his father didn't trust him enough to teach him. He kept demanding to be included and even got angry at his father, arguing with him about business policy. But when the son stopped focusing on what his father was doing and looked at his own behavior, he saw that he was afraid of not measuring up to his dad's ability. So he created situations for his father to exclude him, and picked self-defeating arguments. A change was able to occur when he let his father know that he felt distrusted and that he greatly valued his father's expertise. Previously his father had seen him as a know-it-all, not willing to listen. The father never felt valued or appreciated by his son.

Like so many communication cutoffs, in this one each person felt the other did not value him. When the truth was communicated, the situation got much better. Here the key was that the son looked first to changing his own behavior to improve the situation.

The second step to improving communication with a family member is to know the other person better. You can't resolve a conflict without knowing the other person. So if your son, daughter, or brother-in-law is the difficult person in your family business for you, you need to specifically work on that relationship, not avoid it. Put aside the issue at hand, what you want from the other, and try to focus on learning about the person as someone you care about and appreciate. Often when you learn more about someone you can understand why he or she is stubborn about a certain issue.

For example, many business founders seem closed to new ideas, set in their ways, and unwilling to compromise with their raring-to-go heirs entering the business. One son couldn't understand why his parents, who founded a retail store 20 years before, weren't willing to invest in advertising, open a new store, or initiate an inventory control system. He felt angry and superior to their small-business mentality. They dug in. Then he began to listen to them. He heard stories he had heard before, but never really listened to, about their childhood poverty, their feelings about debt, and their concerns about cash for retirement. He understood that they didn't want to lose what they had or forfeit control of their business. They needed security, while he needed challenge and risk. The solution to this conflict was simple: working with his own advisors, he offered to buy the business from his parents at extremely generous terms that included their managing the flagship store for another five years. Once he heard what was really at stake, he could provide what they both needed.

Seek out the person. Let him or her know that you want to improve your relationship. But then tell the person that since the conflict seems so difficult to each of you, you first just want to spend some time together. Have dinner, spend an evening or a day. Your goal is to talk about what really is important to you, and for each of you to get to know the other better, to develop the trust and understanding which are necessary for real conflict resolution. Sometimes I've seen people begin to work better together just because they feel closer, even though they never really resolved their "issue." As they learn to value the relationship as a whole, the problem becomes less important.

A case in point: a brother and brother-in-law had several angry confrontations. Then an opportunity came for the two of them to take a trip to work with a factory that was in grave crisis. Spending two days together, and working closely together, increased their appreciation of one another's skills and commitment to the business. When they came back to their core issues two weeks later, there was a significant shift in how they felt. They had affirmed their relationship, and they saw that each was deeply committed to the success of the company.

In your conversations, focus especially on your shared and different family histories. If the person comes from another family or another part of your family, try to understand their perspective before you share yours. For instance, Jim felt that his brother-in-law, Will, was after his job. But then they spent some time together and Jim learned that his brother-in-law was in the middle of a family of five very competitive boys. No wonder he had to fight to assert himself! This awareness allowed Jim to see that what he took as a personal attack was just Will's style of survival.

You should be open to learning about yourself, reconsidering your positions, and getting a new perspective on your conflict. If you are willing to step back from your position, your example may have the same effect on your antagonist.

One key quality of effective dialogue is persistence. It takes time for one person to change, and by persisting in your desire to work on the relationship, you can keep the process going. I am continually amazed how family members talk about how important something is to them, but then give up after a few minutes of conversation. Persevere!

You also want to look at all the areas you agree on. A conflict becomes less critical when you and another person discover you agree on 90%. You should share your basic assumptions about the business, and talk about what you want from it. You should talk about what you want from the business, and from your relationship.

You also need to look closely at what you want to get from the other person. Your initial response will probably be that you want the person to stop doing the thing that upset you or to do something you want done. How is that likely to happen? Let's say you're upset about your father putting you down. You may threaten him by saying, "If you put me down again, I'll quit." Or you may do to him what he did to you, putting him down for putting you down. What's wrong with these aggressive responses is that they do not have the total result you want. Looking behind your feelings, you probably want more than for him to stop due to your pressure. Rather you want him to stop or change because he really understands how his behavior has affected you. It is sometimes more important to have the other person understand how you feel than to have a behavior change.

Exercise: It May Not Be All His or Her Problem

Consider a person in your family business with whom you have difficulty communicating, or with whom you would like to have a more open relationship. Begin by looking at yourself in this relationship. Take time to consider, and write your responses, to the following:

1. *What do I want from this other person?*
2. *What is the particular issue between us?*
3. *What conflicts have we had, and what has happened to them?*
4. *What issues, topics, or feelings do we avoid discussing?*
5. *What do I feel that this other person does not understand about me?*
6. *What do I most appreciate and value about the other person?*
7. *What am I most afraid will happen if I really let the other person know what I feel?*
8. *What issues are at stake or lie behind the issue we differ on? (These can be family history, old feelings, or things that you want from the other that may not directly apply to the current issue.)*
9. *What would I be willing to give up in order to have a deeper relationship with this other person? Be specific.*
10. *What do I do when I talk to this person that may make him or her less willing to communicate with me? How do I turn off or tune out?*
11. *Am I really willing to listen to what the other person has to say, rather than just wanting him or her to do what I want? What makes it difficult for me to listen to the other person?*

This self-exploration is a very powerful way to prepare for a talk with a person in your family who is difficult for you. Instead of thinking about how you will make the other do something, you shift your focus to yourself. By reflecting, you may come to see the other person, yourself, and your relationship differently. You may end up with a very different message to communicate to the other, or may discover some blocks within yourself that make it hard for you to really communicate.

How to Send Your Message

While communication in families can be intense, upsetting, and difficult, you can learn to communicate effectively and clearly. After you have explored yourself and learned more about the other person, the next step in building effective communication is to begin a dialogue. While this seems self-evident, in fact the way that you start can either open a channel or cause yet another breakdown.

Starting with the most obvious, communication involves two people: a sender and a receiver. Communication difficulties can arise on either end. The sender, the person who has something that needs to be said, may not let the other know what he or she is feeling, or may not send the message directly or clearly. The receiver may not want to hear the message or may misunderstand it. As the sender, you need to make sure you send a clear message, and as the receiver, that the message is clearly understood.

Communication problems start with the sender. Assuming we know what someone else will say is mistake number one. We often think we know how other family members will act when we make a decision. We either assume the worst and it happens, or we assume that things will succeed easily, and get angry and frustrated when they don't. The problem is created when we do not share what we're thinking and assuming. A business patriarch can be shocked when his foresight isn't appreciated, or when his spouse is furious at him. "How can she misunderstand me so thoroughly," he says to himself. Or even worse, he decides that there is a certain way that the person affected by the decision "ought" to act. Unfortunately, even the ones we love continually surprise us. To communicate you must be willing to be surprised, and open to what happens next. People's feelings certainly do not travel along the most rational or reasonable paths, and the only way to find out is to ask, not assume.

Many communication short-circuits stem from your not letting the other person know how you feel. Thinking that he or she knows, or telling yourself that they should know, won't change the situation. It will just leave you feeling superior and frustrated. Or you may assume that the other person won't listen to you or that you can't say how you feel. Often people who assume these things are upset about something another family member has done, feel something is wrong or unfair, and want to be heard. Usually the person with such feelings is younger, or feels less powerful than the other, such as a younger sister vis-a-vis her brother, or a son (now grown up but still feeling like a child) trying to talk to his parents.

In this situation, the person who is upset dreads the actual or possible reaction. He or she assumes "I don't have a right to say this," or "Saying this will only make things worse," or "If I confront him he'll just yell or put me down." Assumptions like these are erroneous, and stop you from initiating communication. If you are upset you need to decide that you will tell the person, no matter what.

Receivers can throw roadblocks in your way. With a variety of tactics, the person you are trying to communicate with may let you know that he or she does not want to hear what you have to say. Many family members interrupt, argue, change the subject, deny what is being said, or use other means to seemingly reject the information. They are defensive at first. "You shouldn't feel that way," "I didn't mean it," or "That's not so," they say. This is the time when many senders back down. They say to themselves, "See, he didn't listen." And they stop trying.

But what would happen if you decided to press on? In one family discussion, two sons were talking to their father about how they felt that he always put them down. His defensive response was that they were wrong and shouldn't feel that way! One son would not accept the impasse. He noticed that his father was feeling blamed, and added, "Dad, I don't want to criticize you. I know you don't intend to be hurtful. But you need to see that even if you don't mean it, what you do makes me feel discounted." He went on to tell his father what he was doing that hurt him.

This is effective communication. The son noted that his father might be feeling blamed, and let him know that it wasn't so. Then he talked about how his father's behavior affected him, the son. Then he explained his message once again. While Dad did not initially understand, eventually he saw what was happening, and agreed to stop criticizing his sons in front of other managers. Many communication channels could open if one of the participants does not take an initial negative response as the end of the story. Persistence signals that the issue is important more than your saying it does.

One of the major ways that communication is short-circuited is by blaming others. You feel angry so you tell the other person "You made me angry." What happens next? The other person looks within, and sees that he or she did not *intend* to make you feel angry or upset. So he or she gets defensive, or argues with you that he or she didn't make you angry, and a fruitless cycle begins.

How can you avoid such battles? A simple but powerful technique for effective communication in all relationships, family or business, is sending what are termed "I" messages. This is a way of communicating upset feelings in which you do not blame the other person for making you feel that way. In an "I" message, you say what happened, what you feel, and what you want from the other. By saying how you feel and what you want, you take responsibility for the process and reduce defensiveness in the other person.

For example, your father keeps checking up on your work, and you feel he doesn't trust you. Rather than blame him for not trusting you, you might say, "When you check up on me every day, I feel like you do not trust me, and I get upset because I feel you still think I am an irresponsible teenager." Then you might ask him to consider acting differently. This works because you haven't blamed Dad for making you feel anything. You've told him that you feel a certain way, what he does that makes you feel that way, and offered a suggestion of how to act differently.

Planning out your communication in advance can be helpful; anticipating the response and devising your counter-response may keep you from getting flustered. It might also be helpful first to talk to another family member or friend about the situation, and then actually practice saying your "I" message to him or her. In workshops, I find that people who are initially afraid or reticent about saying something ease their difficulty with such practice.

The use of "I" messages is not a magic tonic that heals communication, but it is a good starting point for initiating a conversation about a difficult topic. Your relative may at first respond defensively, but if you persist, maybe even repeat your message, you will find that your patience and persistence is rewarded.

Exercise: Communicating Difficult Feelings

Think of some of the things at work, or in your family, that upset you. These may be ways, at work, that family members still see you in your family role, or ways that you feel not respected or allowed to grow. Write these down.

For each situation, think of how you could initiate a conversation with the relevant person using an "I" message. The "I" message contains four elements:

- *What the person did that upset you;*
- *How it made you feel;*
- *What happened to you as a result; and*
- *What you want to happen or be different.*

Write down your "I" message, and plan what you will do if the person reacts defensively.

As the receiver of a message, you should acknowledge hearing what the other person is saying, and *then* respond with how you feel. Before you react, you need to be certain that you understand what the other person has said. It is often best to keep the focus on the other for a while, and try to understand him or her, before shifting to your reaction. It's helpful in these situations to repeat back what you think the person has said to be sure you understand. For example, "What I hear you saying is that when I disagree with you, you feel I don't love you."

This is not to say you can't express your emotional reaction. If you feel hurt, angry, or misunderstood by what you are hearing from another family member, you need to communicate that. But you need to separate your response, which is something *you* need to explore, from the other person's intention, which is often very different. For example, you may feel hurt or belittled, while the other person does not intend to hurt you. Many communication difficulties arise because of our natural tendency to confuse our response with the sender's intentions. In fact, intentions are almost always very different, and need to be carefully communicated.

Resolving Conflict with a Difficult Family Member

As we've seen, the major key to healing family business conflicts is for individual pairs of people to build their relationships and communicate clearly. However there are some people in your family (or in your life) that you may feel were placed on this earth to make your life difficult. They are often in your closest family, and it may seem that no matter what you do, you can't communicate or get the relationship to change.

If you've followed the above suggestions and working together as a pair isn't helpful, your next recourse is to bring in a third party. It may be another family member, or an outside facilitator. The third party is not an arbitrator or judge—he or she isn't there to decide who's right. Rather, the third party should have as a goal to observe how the two of you aren't communicating, and help you actually do it better. The mediator may ask each of you to state the other person's position or feelings, or to clarify what you want. The mediator will also watch to make sure that the two of you do not slip into a repetitious, self-defeating pattern of conversation.

Exercise: Walk in His or Her Shoes

One exercise that can be very powerful is literally to step into the other person's shoes. Studies of negotiation have found that empathy, the ability to see the other person's point of view, is the key quality to effective resolution. Here is a way to try to get into the shoes of the most difficult person in your family.

Find a place where you will not be disturbed and arrange to spend some time in reflection. Sit quietly for a few moments, and then imagine a situation with the person who is difficult for you. Imagine what that person does and how you feel when you are with him or her. In your mind's eye, picture that person in detail as vividly as you can produce. Imagine how that person looks, and what he or she does that drives you crazy.

Now, since this is your imagination, and anything is possible, imagine that you can switch places with her (or him), and actually become her. Get into her shoes, her body, and try to see the world with her eyes. What does she feel, what does she see, what is she concerned about? What does she want and why is she upset? Get a sense of why you upset her so, and how she sees you. You may be surprised at how much you can discover.

Now, go back into your own body and look at this person again. From your experience do you see the situation any differently? Can you discover some new ways to respond in a more helpful way?

After doing this exercise, you might spend some time trying to write down what the other person wants, and what makes the person the way he or she is. This may lead you to be able to define more precisely what the person wants, and how you could work with him or her so you both could get more of what you want.

Getting to the Deeper Issues

If family communication could be produced simply by sending and receiving clear messages, family businesses would be much less complicated and difficult places to work. But the problems of family business are usually deeper than that. The inside of a troubled family business is an extension of the inside of a troubled family. Indeed a family business can often become the chessboard where adult family members play out an endless family drama.

The themes of such a drama are universal. They may be about old hurts—a parent may have been neglectful or even abusive, or siblings may have wounded one another. There are dramas of favoritism, where one parent seems to spend more time, give more attention, or lavish more love on one child. And there's dramas of restitution, where children hang around, finally trying to get the love they felt they never had. In all these dramas the business either has to bear the burden of replaying a situation that began years ago, or is used to redress a family wrong. In each, the business is the site where an old wound is supposed to be healed.

The clue that an old drama is being re-enacted is when there's a repetitious conflict in the business—no matter what happens the conflict continues. Take the example of two brothers, or a father and son, who are continually fighting. They never seem to stop fighting, no solution is ever found, but neither one leaves in frustration. That is the tip-off that the fight is about something deeper: nothing changes and neither person is able to leave.

The key to resolving such difficulties is to move from the business to the family reality. Instead of trying to solve the problem with a business solution, look to the family dynamic. The family pattern must be explored. If, for example, a father has been abusive or created difficulty for his sons, it didn't start with the workplace. The sons need to find a way to explore their hurt and anger. They need to confront one another as family members and maybe even consider leaving the business if the situation isn't addressed by the family.

Just shifting from a business to a family frame, to talk about the feelings within the family, can lead to healing. I have seen several families where, once the parents were able to acknowledge that they had done hurtful things, parents and children were able to work together more easily. In another family, as the son got in touch with his feelings of hurt, he began to see that he would continue to be angry at his father if he continued to work in his business. He decided to resign.

Reflection Question

If you find yourself in a negative, repetitive cycle with a family member, find some quiet time to consider the following questions:

- *How are you replaying family roles in your work? Are some of the difficulties carry-overs from your family relationship? What can you do to avoid this? How are the two relationships different for each of you?*
- *How do you avoid each other, perhaps by bringing other people into your conflict?*
- *Are there old hurts and resentments that you can clear up, even forgive each other for?*
- *What are your roles at work, and how do you intersect each other? Can you create buffers or more separateness?*

These questions may help you get beneath the surface of your conflict, so that each of you can begin to look at it differently. These are big questions, and your history has made communication difficult between you. So don't expect to clear it up in one day. Plan to have several talks over a few weeks.

Practicing Forgiveness

Simply getting to the deeper issues of what causes conflict between family members is helpful, but you must take one more step in healing. Families have a long history together. If you have grown up in a family, you have ample opportunity to feel hurt by the behavior of other family members. In healing family hurts that have turned into open conflicts, the key element is for one person to begin the healing by practicing forgiveness. That means looking at the list of hurts, slights, painful events, and affronts that the other person has helped create, and forgiving them. Often a child or sibling will carry pain for a past event many years later, which makes it difficult to relate to that person as he or she is today.

Reflection Question

Think of a relationship with a family member where you are holding hurt feelings, perhaps waiting for the person to apologize or change his or her behavior in some unspecified way. Focus on the pain of the hurt, or your anger at the person. Then imagine starting the relationship again today, letting go of the past feelings.

Practicing forgiveness is easier said than done. It is not something that you can just decide one day to do because if you do, chances are you will just have the negative feelings re-ignited in your next encounter with the person. There are many ways to learn forgiveness, including personal growth workshops, psychotherapy, and talking things over with a third party, such as your spouse.

When you have come to a point where you are ready to stop blaming the other person for hurting you, then you can begin to approach that person to further heal the relationship. Initiate contact with him or her, and say you want to rebuild the relationship. Spend time together, with the agreement that you will try to forget history and talk about what you want from each other right now. Tell him or her how you would like to be treated, and what you can offer. Try to put aside past history, and focus on building a relationship today. This will be difficult at first. Don't be put off if you or the other person relapses into blaming or defensive behavior. It is what you have been used to, and it will take practice to overcome it.

Developmental and Goal Conflict

When a business has stalled decision-making, there is often an underlying conflict between family members about goals and direction. Understanding the causes that lie behind disagreements can often help resolve them.

Irving "Bland" started a successful furniture design business and later was joined by his sons, Terry and Harry. Terry was great with customers and Harry was a great designer. Then, six years later, his youngest son, Alvin, joined the company. Three years later, Alvin was doing nicely in several different areas.

However, as Irving took over the chairman role and turned over the presidency to Terry, conflict began to surface. At first, Terry and Harry, who were family men, were a little critical of Alvin's erratic hours and single life, even though his work was fine. Terry and Harry were in conflict too, in that Harry felt Terry was spending too much time with community activities and not enough time on work. One day Alvin brought in a proposal to diversify into fabrics and drapes, and suggested that he open design boutiques as a sideline. Terry and Harry didn't think Alvin could handle such responsibility. The conflicts were subdued, but the three became more and more irritable and spent a great deal of time arguing.

The resolution came when they stepped back and talked about their personal goals. Terry saw his future in philanthropy and, approaching 42, wanted to give more to the community. Harry was an artist, completely immersed in the operations of the very creative and demanding business. He felt the others were spending too much time in peripheral issues, while he was carrying most of the weight of the business. Alvin, in his early thirties, wanted to get out of his "little brother" role by doing something on his own. He was raring to make his own mark apart from his brothers.

The resolution came when the brothers saw that their arguments were really unresolvable, as none of them was right or wrong. Rather the business, and each of them, had to learn to become more tolerant of their different goals. Together they decided to let Alvin innovate, Terry serve the community, and Harry manage, offering each person respect rather than criticism. While remaining at work together, this second generation differentiated from each other and the family, without splitting the business.

Feedback and Evaluation

One place where "old business" often comes back to haunt family businesses is in giving and getting evaluations. In a business, people need to give each other feedback about how well they are doing. The business needs people not just to be good-intentioned, but to be effective. When family members own a business, it is sometimes difficult to get clear feedback from employees so family members need to learn to tell one another how well they are doing. But family members have a difficult time evaluating each other. Indeed, assessment is one of the most difficult tasks for family members. Such evaluations are deeply tinged with the emotions of their relationships with one another and their family roles and history.

The very concept of evaluation may go against the grain of the family—a family ethic of "Everyone is equal" or "We don't criticize each other" may stand in the way. Some families offer unconditional support: you can't do any wrong. But others give too much criticism, and people grow up on a steady diet of hearing they are no good, or not good enough. Or old rivalries and hurts make it difficult for family members to be objective about work performance. It is especially difficult for parents to evaluate their children, or male siblings to evaluate each other objectively.

Often the evaluation is felt as coming from an historically critical parent. Here's a common example. A father, president of the company, was arguing with his son, the vice-president. The business argument was about what the son should do with a customer. But the emotional intensity of the son's response to his father's critique came from their personal history, not customer relations. The son always felt criticized by the father, and because of this, the father was handicapped in giving him business feedback and evaluation.

Evaluations by siblings or other relatives are also problematic. These family members are often seen as having no legitimacy—why, for example, should an older brother take criticism from a younger sister? The reverse may also cause problems. An older brother may be expected to take care of, not criticize, a younger sister, or a younger brother may not feel right pointing out mistakes to an older brother.

A terribly common situation in a family business is when one family member knows that another's performance is not up to par, but feels prevented from saying anything. Employees may feel that is isn't their place to reprimand, instruct, or offer feedback to the boss' son. In fact no one in the situation feels able to speak. This might be called the "Emperor's New Clothes" effect, where everybody can see the person is not doing well, even the person involved, but the subject cannot be mentioned.

There are many reasons why people might not be doing well. They might not be motivated to work, feeling that the business owes them a living. They may feel that they cannot possibly please the parent/boss, so why try? They may feel angry, unappreciated, underpaid, or feel that in some other way the family has let them down. Or they may not really know that they are not doing well, because they don't have the skills or training for the job. After all, family businesses usually do not conduct aptitude tests, look at resumes, or check relevant experience before hiring family members. The person may be over his or her head in the job and not know where to turn.

In one such business, the younger son, Jeff, was head of a division, and simply didn't have the skills to do the job. He had entered the business after college, without an MBA or any management training, and as the business grew, so did his responsibilities. His older brother, Ted, had experience with a large company, and moved easily and with skill into his responsibilities in the family business. The father assumed that both brothers would be paid the same, and would have similar titles of vice-president. The problem was that Jeff was causing harm to the company because talented managers wouldn't work in his division and it was losing money. Ted felt devalued because of his salary. It turned out that never, in any discussion, had any person in the company, including the father, ever given either son feedback about his work.

It was a difficult subject, and everyone wanted to avoid it. Yet the tensions were growing. Jeff took to blaming Ted for making decisions without him. Ted got pretty angry too, because he felt that the other family members were avoiding him, which they were. As a consultant, I decided that the first order of business was for everybody to get some outside feedback. We selected a common assessment instrument which employees who worked with each brother would fill out anonymously. As expected, the survey came back with many areas marked "needs improvement" for Jeff, as well as some areas of strength. Ted's review also earmarked some areas needing work.

Since the survey was aimed at both of them, neither felt singled out. The results led to the brothers' first candid discussion of ways that they might not be effective in their work. To Ted's surprise, Jeff acknowledged that he had been dimly aware of some of the areas of difficulty, but did not think they were serious enough to warrant change. Now he could see that he needed to attend to them. Each brother began working on a management development plan to develop his skills and both agreed to attend a management training program at a local university. At this workshop the brothers got feedback from others about their management style for a second time. After these experiences they were able to begin to talk about Ted's frustration with Jeff, and how it demoralized and aggravated him. Jeff was able to acknowledge his deficiencies and slowly begin to work on them.

In a family where people are close and know each other very well, and where there are already complex relationships, I find that the evaluation process should be held in the open with all family members who are key managers participating, even if they don't directly supervise one another. There are several reasons for this. First, relatives may feel they are in competition with each other, as indeed they may be for top positions, and so openness will allow everyone to know where he or she stands. Second, the essence of the evaluation will find its way into the family anyway, so I believe it should be via a direct route, rather than by rumor and hearsay. Third, I believe that it enhances trust and respect for people to be able to share their evaluations, and helps to clarify how work and family relationships differ.

There are a variety of techniques family members can use to make evaluation easier:

1. All evaluations should be mutual, with each person giving feedback to the others.

2. Each person should begin with a self-evaluation. The best assessments are usually the ones you make of yourself. A week before the meeting, you should each write down what you feel you do well, what you are not satisfied with, and what you want to learn or change in the coming months. These evaluations should be shared with each other.

3. Positive feedback is more important than negative, in that it affirms the basic value of what the person does. Begin your assessment with what you like, respect, and appreciate about the other person.

4. Instead of talking about performance in terms of good or bad, you might give feedback on what behaviors you would like to see more or less of. For example, "I'd like him to be more available to me and allow me more time to present my ideas."

5. Areas of difficulty should be specific, and related to clearly defined behaviors, not personality critiques.

6. Evaluation should be done regularly, once or twice a year.

7. The final report should focus on what the person wants/needs to learn, with a plan for how to learn, as well as goals for the next period. It should be a commitment to change, along with a plan for how to accomplish that change.

Despite such techniques, family members will always find evaluation difficult. Often, I find that people have worked for many years, and never been told clearly how well they are doing. That is like flying blind, in that you don't know what to learn or how to improve. In order for anyone to grow in a job, there needs to be time when people talk about what they do well and what they need to do better. By starting the assessment process with your first job in a family business, you make it clear that evaluation comes with work.

In-Laws: Finding a Way to Fit In

Special conflicts can also arise over in-laws. People who marry into a family often perceive that they are marrying into the business. They are, but the marriage is limited. Their role in the family can be very circumscribed and, if they step out of that role, they can be subtly punished. Also, different families have different expectations about the participation, ownership, and involvement of in-laws in the family business. Some are welcomed, and others are excluded. Naturally it's helpful to know in advance how the family will react.

In one family the sister's spouse was asked to leave his public service career to help in the business. The underlying reason for the request was that the son was not doing his job, and so the son-in-law found himself in a delicate situation: he was expected to cover for his brother-in-law but not to talk about it. Finally he felt he had to confront the situation. He asked the family to make him general manager, and demand that the son either take more responsibility or leave. Eventually the son became more responsible, and the two evolved a working partnership. But happy endings where in-laws are concerned may not be so common.

An in-law creates an instability in the family. For example, Christine married Vincent, who was as strong-willed and independent as her father Winston. She felt proud when Dad asked Vinnie to quit his work with a large company to enter the family business. The two men in her life were working together. But slowly, things became strained. Winston was not receptive to Vinnie's new ideas, and Vinnie became increasingly frustrated. Both confided in Christine, and she felt deeply torn. Her father was upset because he felt Vinnie was taking advantage of him, and was too reckless, while Vinnie didn't want to be held back. Finally, Christine said that either the two men had to talk, or she would demand that Vinnie quit. They went off for a weekend, and began to work out an explicit set of expectations for the future. Winston agreed to leave the business to Vinnie, and to allow Vinnie to develop a new division. He agreed to retire in five years, when he reached 65, which he put in writing and announced to the other managers. Meanwhile, Vinnie agreed to cool his heels a little and not be so impetuous.

In this situation Vinnie, as an in-law, was being tested. Winston needed to grow closer to him before he could turn the reins over. In addition, it was hard for Winston to deal with a person so much like him as a young man, when now, at this stage of life, Winston wanted to take a more cautious direction.

The role of the in-law in many family businesses is highly ambiguous. Their relationship is conditional, and in an era when divorce is a 50% possibility, the family has a dilemma. What if an in-law inherits ownership, or a leadership role, but the marriage doesn't last? One father had his son-in-law succeed him, and five years later his daughter's marriage ended. His daughter was left with very little ownership in the family business, while he had to continue to work with his ex-son-in-law every day. Father retired prematurely, with a lot of pain and anger.

Problems with in-laws also arise because the spouses of family business members often have only one source of information about the business: their husbands or wives. So they may hear about injustices, unfairness, or conflict from only one side and may respond to their spouses' hurt or anger without knowing the rest of the story. That is why in some families, a family feud or deep hurt arises from the skewed perspective of the in-laws. They do not have the history or the closeness to seek out other family members or to have their own needs recognized. They may have their own ideas of fairness from their own family, and sometimes they are not aware of family rules or expectations in their adopted family. They may feel resentful, hurt, unacknowledged, or marginal, and not know where to go or what to do to change their status.

While the situation of the in-law is always precarious, a family can make things easier by setting rules or expectations. If the family makes it clear whether or not in-laws will share in the business, and what they can expect from the business, then some of the tension and awkwardness of the in-law role can be reduced. The most important thing a family can do is to include their in-laws in family communication processes. While many families are suspicious, or find it hard to trust the spouses of their brothers and sisters, the negative effects of paranoia and confusion caused by the isolation of the in-laws can poison a family.

Avoiding Family Feuds

The most famous and intractable form of family conflict is the family feud. One can't approach the business section of a newspaper or even a TV soap opera without learning about yet another family dynasty derailing over a family squabble. As the Bingham story demonstrates, family feuds are fascinating in their universality and generate a lot of publicity. But the amount of personal pain generated by family feuds and the business disasters they create harm employees, families, and society. It's often hard to really know what a feud is about. With all the intense emotions, and deep divisions, does anyone really know why JR and Bobby Ewing are such rivals? The intensity comes from the way that families transfer personal needs and feelings, such as love, acceptance, and fairness, onto business issues.

Feuds can be flamboyant. The Gucci family in Italy has had a series of schisms that have split their business. At one business meeting Aldo Gucci fired his middle son and business heir, Paolo, when Paolo wanted to market another line of goods with his own initials on them. At another family business meeting, Gucci cousins Maurice and Paolo came to blows and actually spilled blood. The firings and fights have led to a split in the company, and a raft of legal actions, criminal accusations, and lawsuits. What makes things so volatile and intense?

Family feuds are complex, but in looking at many of them, certain elements stand out. The major quality of the many feuds I've helped to mediate is that people are more invested in being right and keeping their distance, than in the painful, difficult, and long-term tasks of sitting down with the rivals and trying to get to the personal roots of the issue in order to forge a compromise. Compromise is seen as weakness, and hurting the other is more important than self-interest.

Usually there are two people who see each other's motives in black and white, and there is no neutral third party to intervene. Those feuding tend to not know how to communicate well, and are not able to accept differences. The key players perceive inequity or unfairness—someone in the family feels wronged by the other. A feud can motivate the principals into high levels of activity and deep dedication to their cause. Interestingly, there is usually a patriarch or matriarch on the scene or in the wings who is distant, stern, demanding, and unclear about his or her intentions.

Often feuds are between children or heirs. Freud taught us that sibling rivalry is universal and inevitable. But feuding families seem to have a knack for igniting such rivalries, or keeping them burning into adulthood. Psychologists hypothesize that feuds may represent transfers of feelings from the parental generation to siblings or other relatives. For example, children may not be able to get angry at their father for remarrying after their mother dies, but they have no trouble fighting with his new wife, his widow after he dies, or with one another based on perceived relations with father or wife.

The seeds of a family feud are planted years in advance. Patriarchs often don't let their children know where they stand on important issues, how they feel about them, or what they want from them. A business owner who won't reveal who he wants to succeed him, or how he feels, can precipitate a nasty fight if he dies before revealing his intentions, or when he finally reveals them. These silent fathers' reasoning is curious: if the children don't know what you expect or where you stand, they will work harder for the business. This is a big mistake, a tactic which only works for a short time. Ultimately uncertainty over parental approval has devastating emotional effects on children, and their insecurity can turn to anger at an innocent bystander when a target presents itself. So the sons/daughters feel they have to win, except they can't really win what they want, which is their parents' approval. Because they never know how their father feels, people raised in such a fashion have fragile self-esteem and often look for external sources of self-worth, such as status symbols, power over others, or money. Look to previous generations for the genesis of a feud even though it may be between two people in a current generation.

Feuds also spark in families that foster a spirit of intense competition between siblings or don't intervene actively in sibling rivalry. Brothers and sisters spend their childhood fighting, but parents usually regulate them. But in families ripe for feuds, parents refuse to take a stand or teach children ways to resolve conflicts productively—and this attitude extends into adulthood. For example, one father fostered conflict in his family business by his own misguided actions. In a dispute, he took each of his sons aside and told him that he was right, but that he shouldn't do anything about it.

Another founder made it clear that his acceptance of his children could best be expressed in business terms. When a child got upset, he would give him or her a better title in the business, or a gift of stock. This led to building rivalry and increasing resentment, both on the part of family members who were passed over, and those who received the meaningless titles. It also made for a very confused business.

Feuds also spark in families where parents try to help one child in secret so that the others won't know, or plant unrealistic expectations in each of their children. There are other behaviors that foster feuding:

- Unrealistic praise of children's abilities and talent, or telling them they can do anything they want.
- Not letting anyone in the business or in the family hurt family members by evaluating them harshly, or pressuring them for performance.
- Parents who change their mind when a child disappoints or disagrees with them.

- Letting every child know there is space for him or her in the business, no matter what. Here the stage is set for a rich feud after the parents die, when the children discover there isn't enough for everybody.
- Not taking a stand. Everyone waffles, especially the older generation.

In pre-feuding families, people don't do the obvious—getting everyone together to clear the air. There are no established pathways for airing or resolving issues. The family has an avoidant style. They deal with pain and conflict by cutting it off. Or they get third parties, like their spouses, to explain their feelings. When things finally get hot enough, it is already too late.

To make matters worse, there are usually no mediating, healing, connecting people to keep the family together. In healthy family businesses often the mother, or an older, non-family business participant, has the trust of everyone, and can get people together to talk. Feuding families have no such mediators—there's nobody with authority to help work out an accommodation, or no one to support one person going into another business.

In effect, most family feuds stem from fantastic or unreal expectations of family members about the business, fostered within an environment where there is no open discussion of conflicts and no sharing of real difficulties. The message is clear. If you want to avoid family feuds, you need to create strong and open relationships in your family business and build leadership in the next generation. In order to do this, you need to plan well in advance, work openly, make your feelings and intentions clear, and collaborate with all of the involved family members. The Family Council, described in the next chapter, is the best vehicle for this.

If a feud erupts, there are still several avenues to healing available. Solutions may involve one party's leaving the business, splitting assets, disengaging through a series of steps, or a reconciliation. But unless a solution is found, disaster is almost always the result. It can't be a secret, because secrecy, distrust, and avoidance are the three evils that created the feud in the first place.

One family member, or someone else everyone trusts, must take on the role of healer. It can be a thankless task at first. All the communication techniques suggested above are helpful, but the person trying to heal things must be prepared for a long-term process. There are few quick shifts. Rather, healing results after several tentative attempts at reconciliation, talks where the issues are not mentioned directly. Then, slowly, the parties begin rebuilding a relationship with a new, positive base. Like any communication change, it only takes one committed, persistent person to initiate the shift.

In a family feud, often two people, or two parts of a family, simply cut off contact with each other. Over time they can even forget what started the split, but the rift remains. People talk about "pride" keeping them apart, or about waiting for the other to end it. What they don't see is that either party can heal the split by reaching out to the other. The initiator may be rebuffed or distrusted at first, until his or her intentions become clear. The key to overcoming a feud is to find an opportunity for the feuding parties to come together and remember what was positive about their relationship.

For instance, the founding couple of the Jefferson Airplane rock group, Grace Slick and Paul Kantner, had been feuding for years over their personal relationship, their drug problems, and the direction of the band. Amid lawsuits and anger, the band broke up and they didn't speak to one another for years. Recently a third member of their group told Grace that he wanted to play a trick on Paul, and he had her come to one of his concerts and join him on stage. In a moment the audience responded, and the two remembered the special partnership they had. The group reformed, over a decade later.

Multiple Family Retreats

One powerful vehicle for building communication, healing conflict, and avoiding feuds in business families is a retreat where several families work together. I have participated in several of these, and they afford a special way to help families deepen communication. One would tend to think that when several families, who don't know each other, get together for a four day workshop, they would be reticent to talk. But the opposite is the case.

The first family business retreat I facilitated was for a group of seven families. The families came together at the urging of Sam Marks, a furniture dealer who had started a group for furniture industry heirs called Next Generation. Sam felt that while it was useful for the younger generation to gather alone, if people representing both generations got together, there would be a unique opportunity for improved communication and sharing.

The seven families at the retreat included founder/entrepreneurs, spouses, couples who worked together, and several sets of sons and daughters. From the first evening, when people spoke about their families and businesses, it was clear that a very special environment was being created. Each person told a story about his or her family that showed us what was most unique and special about it. Everyone felt that, for the first time, they were in a group that could understand and relate to their problems. Each family created family and business time lines and looked at their family expectations and myths. But what was different in the group retreat setting was that they shared their own experience with other family businesses. The conflicts between family and business, and the search for fairness, for understanding and respect, were presented not just within and to one's own family, but with other families as well.

Having other sons, fathers, wives, and daughters present helped people listen to each other. For example, one son was able to explain to another father about what he did that made him difficult to talk to. With this feedback, he was able to listen differently to his own son. Wives who were concerned about their husbands and about the future of the business received support for sharing their concerns. One mother who felt squelched, who felt her husband never took her ideas seriously, got support from the other women in the group to state her positions more forcefully, and she finally got heard. A daughter, after sharing with Sam how she felt that her father did not notice her contribution to the business, was able, with support from the others, to say the same things to her father, who was also at the retreat.

One of the most powerful experiences was sharing within small groups of people who had similar roles in their families. We formed small groups of wife/mothers, founder/entrepreneurs, sons, and daughters. Each group shared their concerns, and drew up a statement of their common issues and perspectives. Then the groups came together and shared their concerns with the whole community. It was incredible how often certain issues were linked to different family roles! For example, there were three younger sons in the workshop. In their group they found out that the role of "younger son" didn't offer a natural leadership position in the business. Therefore, it was more difficult for them to "prove" themselves or discover their own power and independence. In contrast, the three older sons all took fewer risks, and were more sensible and responsible, than their fathers. And they had all been to business school and wanted to modernize their family business!

As the weekend progressed, each of the families developed a deeper level of communication and got through some issues they had been reluctant to face before. The community of families working together was more powerful than any family working alone. The support of peers in the same family situation encouraged people to share what they previously believed impossible to say.

The power of a retreat format for building communication is so great that, as we will see in the next chapter, it is an ideal format for exploring family values, interests, and concerns. We'll look at how the family can use a retreat to build its own family organization, the Family Council, to explore in an ongoing forum the family issues that relate to the business and family future.

Notes:
1. Paul, Jordan and Margaret: *From Conflict to Caring.*

4

The Family Council: How Families Plan for the Business

"The idea of family members working together with the family's generativity, its high rate of saving, high traditions of service, and stewardship of resources are more honored than achieved. Achievement of these values just doesn't happen any more than one just happens to learn to read, win Olympic medals or build a modern industry. Each achievement requires understanding, support and focused effort...."
-Will McWhinney, "Entrepreneurs, Owners and Stewards: The Conduct of a Family Business."

At around two on the first Sunday of every month, the members of the "Rogers" family drive up the hill to the large home of Stanley and Nicole Rogers. Stanley founded "Rogers Manufacturing" after World War II, and it has now grown through acquisitions into a $300 million a year enterprise with several plants. Stan's oldest son, Nick, and middle daughter, Betty, are in the business, and his other two daughters and son are not. Daughter Sara's husband, Jim, has recently been recruited as a plant manager at their largest plant.

Stan is a classic entrepreneur. For many years he ran the business and his family had no role. A decade ago several events changed all that. First, Stan had a heart attack, and it took him several months to recover. Second, after business school, Nick spent several years in another company, but expressed interest in joining the business. To Stan's surprise, daughter Betty, who had a marketing background, also asked to work in the business. Both children wanted to know what they could expect, i.e., how ownership would be passed on to the family. The other children and their spouses, were quietly concerned as well. The uncertainty made it hard for them to plan their futures. What would their inheritance and future be?

Stan faced strategic decisions in the business as well. While revenues were good, his products were in a maturing market. He faced decisions about borrowing for product development and plant modernization. His managers observed Nick's, Betty's and Jim's capability, and wondered how they fit into future plans. Stan didn't want to lose his non-family talent. He felt everybody looking to him, but he didn't have the answers.

Stan and his family began work with a financial consultant, initially about estate and tax planning. But the scope grew. The consultant asked Stan questions he couldn't answer:

- What kind of life do you and your family want to lead in the future?
- What is most important to you and your family?
- Who will own the company?
- What would happen if you died suddenly tomorrow?
- How can you be fair to all family members?
- How much do your wife and heirs know about your business and financial affairs?
- How will you borrow money to reinvest in the company, provide for your retirement, and care for family members not in the business?

Stan had to admit these were questions he hadn't consciously thought about, and, while it turned out they were on his family's mind, he didn't really know what they thought about them either. Like his friends, he did not think about such things, and he regarded it as wrong to talk to his family about them. But the heart attack led him to reconsider—he couldn't keep putting things off.

I helped Stan initiate a series of family meetings. His children and their spouses came together for a two-day retreat at which each person talked about how he or she saw the future, what each wanted, and how each saw the business. It was one of the most moving and powerful events in the family's history. While not a very reticent family, the Rogers had not taken the time to talk deeply about the things that mattered most to them: their caring bonds, their goals and desired futures, and how the business fit into them. They told family stories, shared feelings about values, and talked about some of the uncertainty they felt about inheritance, ownership, and the future. There were some jealous feelings expressed about Jim's joining the company, and whether that meant that he would inherit a share of ownership, while those not in it would not.

The first retreat didn't settle anything, though the family had hoped it would. Rather it opened up a doorway, and led to deeper sharing and the beginning of a planning process for the family. They created a statement of family values and began to explore what they wanted for the future. They found they all shared certain values, and looked at how the business expressed them. They also had a lot of fun. The kids played together, and they had a wonderful barbecue and time to sail on the lake. After the retreat, everyone felt satisfied but unfinished. They decided to keep in regular communication about family and business issues, and to meet monthly in a Family Council.

Both large and small families find that their businesses are only part of the whole picture. Many questions, as Stan learned, can't be answered at business meetings. The whole family is involved—after all, the family usually owns the business. This chapter presents a model for creating a Family Council, consisting of all family members over a certain age, that oversees the family, the business, and their interrelationships.

Tasks for the Chapter

This chapter will give you instructions for planning and convening a Family Council, to guide your family and manage its relation to the business. The Council is a tool for exploring the values, meaning, purpose, and goals of your family, and the ways it operates. You will learn how the Council can become a tool to build deeper communication and help the family realize its dreams. You will learn how to convene and develop a Council as a forum for your own family's growth.

The Need for the Family Council

A Family Council is the organizational and strategic planning arm of a family, where all members meet to decide values, policy, and direction for the future. At the core, the Council is the vehicle to address and explore family concerns that influence the business and the family. It also defines, clarifies, and expresses the family's deepest values, meaning, mission, and legacy. By forming a Council, a family realizes that it is a large, important institution, whose decisions and activities influence not only its immediate members, but also employees and the community.

As we've explored in previous chapters, family businesses create too many complex issues for the family to leave them to random gatherings or the will of a single person. Many disputes that seem like pure business issues can only be resolved by the family. Investing in a new plant, promoting a non-family manager to CEO, selling or splitting the business, all relate to family interests. That is because, while the situation occurs within the business, it concerns issues that have to do with the family's connection to the business. Without a Family Council this process goes on informally and secretly in most family businesses. The Family Council makes these decisions open and explicit.

As we've seen, many families mistakenly feel that the best way to promote harmony is to avoid discussion of upsetting topics: if Billy is feeling upset because he thinks Dad favors Joey, the best way to deal with the situation is to ignore it. But in reality, if it is not discussed, Billy and Joey only get more estranged, while Dad remains ignorant of the unintended rivalry. A Family Council is the most effective forum to discuss such hurts. Very few issues get resolved by ignoring them.

The Council is also an acknowledgement that old-fashioned patriarchy is dead. Father can no longer unilaterally decide everything of importance for the family. The first son doesn't always inherit the business, and values, concerns, and conflicts among family members can't always be anticipated and mediated by the caring autocracy of the founder-patriarch. A Council recognizes that more participation, openness, information sharing, debate, and democracy are needed in today's complex family environment. Like Stan, the founder has to find out what people want. Without active commitment and involvement of all family members, he may risk deeply hurt feelings or mis-communication. Even though Dad may remain "head" of the family, and make the final decisions in some areas, increasingly families need to get everyone together to share information, feelings, and goals.

The business is the engine that serves the deeper needs of the whole family. The business often expresses the personal entrepreneurial dream of the founder or founding couple. A founder creates a business not simply to make money, but as a form of social expression about something he or she believes in. The business grows not just in size, but to a fuller or lesser expression of an idea. That is why a family squabble about the future of a company like Esprit, between the married couple who founded it, is so difficult to resolve. The debate among the two owners was not just about power or profits, but about the soul, the meaning of the company. When that dream passes to others—professional managers, heirs, or public stockholders—will it continue to hold the original founder's vision?

A founder's vision is only one of the stories contained in the family business. The business is also about the family's development, struggles, and successes. It is where the children help out after school, and what the family is known for. It is where sons and daughters dream of working, something that everyone in the family is often excited about. The business can be so much a part of the meaning of the family that all family members need to explore how the business is working for them. As part of the family, even though not part of the management of the business, they have strong opinions and exert influence. Usually they do it indirectly, to spouses in the business, or through others. In a Family Council, this influence comes out in the open.

Every family is judged personally by what its business does in the community. It isn't only having wealth, but what the family does with its wealth, that creates the measure of the family. The business often provides goods or services to the community, and hires people to work there. If the company is unfair to employees, sells shoddy merchandise, pollutes, or does not serve the community, the non-participating family members will hear about it. Children may be confronted in school. The whole family is a part of what the business means to the community.

Every family member has a different experience of the meaning and purpose of the family business. While parents want their children to echo their social and political views, in practice this almost never occurs. Those in the business see it one way, while those waiting in the wings deciding whether to enter the business, or those outside it, see it differently. These differences are not academic. There are points in every family and business where the stakeholders have to make a clear choice—about direction, about inheritance, about succession, or any number of other issues. When the choice has to be made who makes it, and how is it made? How is the input solicited from all those involved, who may not be formal decisionmakers but are deeply affected by the outcome? Some form of organized family gathering is necessary at these pivotal points in time to communicate, to explore differences, to arrive at decisions, and to implement them.

A Family Council also provides the forum for discussion of how the family uses its wealth and provides for all its members. The returns on a business can be generous, even enormous. It can create substantial wealth. It also leads to difficult questions:

- How will that wealth be passed on to the children?
- How can the parents live after retirement?
- What portion of the wealth should be returned to the community, and how should the remainder be invested?
- What values does the family want to express through the power and influence of its investments?
- How should family members who are part of and not part of the business be compensated?
- Should its wealth remain in the business, or should the family's business investment diversify and become more liquid?

As owners of the business, the family has the capacity to put their wealth and influence into the service of a wide variety of social goals. Family business theorist Will McWhinney notes that some families see themselves as stewards of the business, rather than owners.[1] Whereas ownership means simply having control of wealth, stewardship implies that the ownership exists for a broader purpose.

Many families express a social vision through business. Max DePree, son of the founder of Herman Miller, and the late Bill Gore, with his wife Genevieve, saw their respective companies as embodying their beliefs in participatory management. Everyone in each company is an owner, shares in the profits, and, in Herman Miller, is covered by a unique Employee Bill of Rights. McWhinney points out that the opportunity for such stewardship is limited in publicly-traded stock companies, because they are required to maximize stockholders' profit, but are unlimited in closely-held family businesses. (Indeed such economic limitations cause family businesses like Levi Strauss to take their company private.) The Family Council is the place where children learn about their stewardship, and where heirs and relatives can explore the nature of their family values and commitments.

The Nature of the Family Council

A Family Council is a planning tool for growing the family, its individual members, and the business controlled by the family. The Council is not a single meeting, but rather a regular forum for consideration of the complex issues facing a family in business. It's an ongoing process that formalizes informal exchange among family members. Family members share what they believe and what they want from the family and the business.

The key functions of the Council are communication and clarification of policies. Specifically the Family Council is the focal point for developing, sharing and implementing three types of future planning, corresponding to the three complex human systems that are part of it:

Individual Plans: As we've seen, each person in the family is growing, maturing, and continually redefining personal, career, and family goals. Each family member is at a different stage of his or her individual life cycle and needs distinct things from the family and the business. These individual needs can act at cross-purposes. The Council can help individuals discover what they want, by exploring possibilities and options, and help balance the needs of each individual with the family's and business' needs.

Family Plans: The family has its own developmental cycle: it is formed, raises children, matures, plans for retirement. Members are more closely connected at certain stages, more separated and far-flung at others. What are the overall goals of the family for the future, and what resources does it need to achieve them? How are the different branches of the family related, and how do new people enter the family? The family needs to plan to provide for each of its members, look at its basic values, and create a set of family rules about its wealth and participation in the business and other family enterprises.

Business Plans: The ownership of all or most of the business lies within the family. As people retire, and heirs decide whether or not to enter the business, ownership and management control may move from the family to outside managers and owners. The family's business can diversify from one enterprise to many, or one or more family members can take over control or ownership. In order for the business to be free to chart its course, family involvement needs to be clarified, changes need to be explored, and they need to be communicated and implemented in a timely manner.

The Family Council is the perfect vehicle for generating, sorting through, ratifying, and implementing each of these plans. Naturally as new challenges are presented, and as people grow and develop, new questions arise for consideration. Because the three planning entities are all interconnected, each plan affects the others. One son cannot plan his personal future without being part of the family and business plan. He needs to know whether he can expect to inherit a share of the business, whether he can count on the family to support him to start his own business, and when he needs to make a decision.

A Council can take many forms. It can be a formally constituted organization, with minutes, regular meetings, and prescribed decisions. Or it can be a more casual grouping, meeting intensely during a period of transition and informally at other times. Resource people and advisors can be brought in to help. The Council usually meets regularly, most often once a month for an afternoon or evening. It may include a weekend retreat once or twice a year. The retreat format is common when a family is scattered around the country and needs to fly in for meetings. These can be around holidays, but the Council meeting should be separate, an organized affair with records, a charter, and formal procedures.

The Council is a decision-making group. While power is handled differently in different families, most Councils work on a consensus model. Each person has a different role and involvement in the business so a simple majority is often not practical. When the issues concern ownership of the business, they often lie in the hands of one person or a small group. In that case the Council usually advises or suggests policy, but the owners make the final decisions.

The business founder, or head of the family, often has reservations about whether his legitimate authority over business decisions will be undermined, or challenged, by the Council. This is a difficult issue, that takes time to clarify and explore. Creating a Council is a recognition that there needs to be more collaboration in a family than has existed in the past. The Council can be an advisory group. The purpose is to make decisions explicit, to communicate more clearly, and to make processes that are done informally, behind the scenes, clearer to everyone. That should in fact reinforce the authority of the family leader.

I point out to concerned patriarchs that the Council does not take away authority, but rather recognizes that it is already limited. For example, in many family businesses, the wife of the owner, and mother of the heirs, is a power behind the throne. (As one NFL football coach, asked about why he employed his son as an assistant coach, replied to the media, "I didn't hire him because he is my son. I did it because I'm married to his mother.") The Council makes her role more explicit.

Convening a Family Council: Overcoming Resistance

How do you get a Council started? If the founder/owner is committed to the process, everything can proceed smoothly. The family business leader realizes that the time has come to share information and control. He calls a meeting of everyone in the family to start the ball rolling. But it's rarely so simple!

Since it seems so reasonable to have family input and participation in business as well as family issues, why do so few families naturally create a family forum to discuss these things regularly? The most frequently cited reason is the tendency of the family patriarch/business leader to keep such things to himself. Over the years, the entrepreneurial prerogatives of the family leader can harden into a set of attitudes that effectively seals off the patriarch not only from other family members, but from potential crises, personal pain, business shifts, and the need to change.

Three emotional attitudes common to family business patriarchs interfere with their ability to face the future. These attitudes form the core of a series of excuses or refusals to consider forming a Council and opening up decision-making to include others. They are deeply rooted, and must be considered the key obstacles to facing the future effectively:

Denial/Avoidance: It's hard to conceive of your own death or disability when you are healthy and vital. It's hard to take time for the future when the present demands attention. It seems easier to play the odds, and put things off. As a result, business owners don't learn about estate tax laws, make a will, develop successors, or think of "what-if" possibilities. Ignorance helps them deny the possibility of death, and postpone difficult choices about the future. When founders are in a state of denial, they don't look ahead. Since they don't think the problems exist, they get angry at people who say they do. When change, conflict, or crisis finally hits, it can be overwhelming because none of the groundwork has been laid.

Secrecy: Business owners often believe it will hurt other family members to talk about their desires or intentions, or they don't feel it is anyone else's business. They don't think they should share business information, that it is bad luck, or upsetting. Secrecy keeps heirs and managers off balance and fosters either withdrawal or obsessive attention to the patriarch's needs. It can play off one family member against the other, and it can cause them to manipulate one another. The result is that such owners' good intentions are often misunderstood, or create the opposite results.

Distrust: Owners may distrust the motives of advisors, or not know how to find the people they can really trust. They may be accustomed to keeping their own counsel, and doing things on their own. After all, they are entrepreneurs. They make assumptions like "All lawyers are crooks"; or "I can't talk about our affairs to anyone." They use distrust as an excuse not to listen to anyone, and to insulate their ideas and plans from scrutiny by others, including other family members.

All three of these underminers sow the evils they were trying to avoid. By sealing themselves off from reality and not letting others in, owners run the risk of losing vast fortunes, seeing their businesses decline, and the next generation ill prepared for leadership. In the vacuum, nobody in the family knows where he or she stands, and the situation can disintegrate into feuds, recriminations, and backbiting, with everyone trying to curry favor with the throne. The future of the business is threatened as its resiliency is lost, and good managers, inside and outside the family, bail out. In the end, the family does not realize its heritage.

Reflection Question

If you are the business and family leader, think of your own planning for your personal, family, and business future. Your first thought may be, "I've taken care of it," or "I don't need to get into that yet." These are all forms of resistance. Write a list of all the ways that you may avoid, deny, resist, or distrust planning for your future. For each reason write down some of the beneficial and negative results of that behavior. Then ask yourself if you might look at things differently and open up your family and business deliberations.

Because of these attitudes on the part of entrepreneurs, it is often the family heirs, spouses, or in-laws who first feel the need for the Council. They may be concerned or uncertain about the future, or they may want to know more about the business, or where they stand within it. They may be on the verge of making a decision about their personal future, and want to know what they can expect from the business. They may be concerned about a recent business decision and wonder whether it is proper to say something. Many times heirs have been working in the business, and wonder about the future plans of their parent/leader. They don't feel that can ask at work, and aren't sure it is right to bring up at home. So they avoid the issue. Sometimes they try to bring it up and get rebuffed.

The next step is critical. What do you do when you suggest a Council and get a negative response? When Dad resists, saying he doesn't think there is anything to discuss? Too many family members respond by withdrawing, assuming from the response that there is nothing they can do. Not so. At several family business conferences, I've run workshops on how members of the younger generation can influence the older generation to share information, power, and eventual ownership. I find that in most such situations, the younger person gives up much too quickly. It takes persistence to change old habits and attitudes.

In fact, if you want to initiate a Family Council, many strategies are open to you. One is to meet without the owner. One person, no matter how important, should not be allowed to keep a gathering from occurring. Everyone does not have to be there to get started, and if you wait for everybody, you may be short-circuiting your own future. The resisters can be invited to come as observers, or told that they are always welcome, and that what takes place will be shared. If the first meeting goes well, skeptics are usually willing to come to the second one.

A group of siblings of a large and complex family business with many trusts asked the father to initiate meetings so they could understand the trusts and their future. He declined, saying he was too busy. They met themselves, sharing their frustration. Then one daughter wondered if she could invite their lawyer. After all, she felt, he represented them too, and had said he was their advisor. He agreed to come to discuss the meaning of their various trusts. He came for a few meetings, and then they invited another advisor. After about six months of meetings, the father asked if he might come. They said fine, and he hardly remembered he had rejected their first invitation!

You need to act creatively to overcome the resistance of the single holdout. Often that person has concerns or fears about family gatherings that need to be taken into account. One spouse was adamantly opposed to family meetings. When asked about her reasons, she admitted that she was afraid that she would get criticized, and that the meeting would turn into an angry, unproductive argument. Her fears were realistic, and until adequate safeguards could be arrived at, she didn't want meetings.

Another way to get a commitment to the Council is to have other families that have created one share their experience. The best way to convince a resistant member of the older generation is to have a peer take him or her out to dinner and explain how the Council worked for the peer's family. It sometimes helps to enlist the aid of a consultant. At times I have helped a family have their first meetings simply by creating a safe environment, and being there to make sure things stayed on track. One person said I was her "security blanket."

The Initial Family Retreat

The best way to initiate the Council is away from home at a family retreat lasting a few days. Going away underscores the special meaning of the event, and gives family members a place away from everyday pressures and enough time to reflect on their thoughts and feelings. If you try to create a Council at an evening meeting, you run the risk of having volatile issues come up without time to reach resolution, which may be frustrating and upsetting.

Once family members are committed, scheduling the retreat is only the first step. As the convener, you need to do much more than just set a time. People want to know what will happen, and what they are expected to do. They will probably be somewhat anxious or concerned about what can be said, and the possibility of unresolvable conflict. The retreat should not be a presentation by an expert, nor simply a recitation of plans by Dad about the business. It is a participatory gathering. Each individual must prepare, and everybody needs a chance to work on the agenda and ground rules. The more interaction that occurs before the retreat, the more people will be committed to the retreat itself, and prepared to raise key issues.

A Family Council retreat starts with a planning group. Even though you are all a family, the Council is an organization, and the more clear information you can get from each person, the more effective the planning can be. If the family business consists of only a single family of parents and children, the planners can be the whole family. They draw up objectives, and gather information from other family members. They listen to concerns, and ask about issues that need to be addressed. Larger families send around a survey, and collect written responses from each person.

People feel more committed to a group when they feel that their concerns will be addressed, and that they have a say in the direction of the group. Therefore it is important that everyone participates in forming the Council. Otherwise, you run the risk of having something "come up" at the last minute which prevents key people from attending, or having people participate passively or distantly. From the start, the Council should not be perceived as a platform for a powerful family patriarch. In fact, it might be helpful to have the business leader not be the leader and convener of the Council retreat. Probably, the patriarch can be persuaded that he is too busy to lead the group, and some other person can take it on. Sometimes it is helpful for one of the least connected family members to become the convener, which brings him or her more into the family orbit.

Every family member over a certain age should participate. Children from 12 to 16 are often not included, but in my experience, they are often curious about the business and beginning to think about their future. Sometimes members from far away, or those who feel distant, are reluctant to participate. They may feel that the Council is an attempt to force them to be "closer." They need to be reassured that what is being asked for is only their caring and respectful participation in a forum to discuss common issues. If family members know they are meeting twice a year to discuss differences, sometimes incipient feuds or difficulties between two people can be avoided or limited.

Calling the first Council meeting often has the effect of "activating the family network." This means that, as the idea is proposed and family members recall their concerns, hurts, anger, and difficulties, they become both afraid of the power of the gathering, and also hopeful. Just calling a meeting gets the family to begin new behavior—talking to one another about shared concerns. Siblings call one another and get together. Everyone begins to talk about the issues that will come up in the meeting.

Early on in the planning process, the family needs to generate a list of issues, concerns, topics, and questions. They can be written on paper and put up for all to see. One method for setting an agenda is to put up the list of everyone's concerns, and then give everyone five votes for the important issues. They can "spend" their five votes on one topic, or spread them around. After everyone has voted, the topics and concerns will be prioritized. Some of the topics may be similar, and others may fit naturally together. From this list an agenda can be planned. The following exercise may be helpful in generating a list to vote on.

Exercise: Preparing Yourself for a Family Retreat

Before your family meets, you need to spend some time with yourself, assessing your own relationship to the family business, and considering your own needs, options, and choices for the future. This self-assessment should include three major areas:

1. Where am I and what do I want from my work and the family business? What are your major concerns in your life? What do you want and value most for your work? What are your career goals? Do you see yourself working in the business? What is your ideal working environment?

2. How do I see the business and what does it mean to me? What does the business mean to the family? What are the key family values? What do I expect the business and the family to provide me in my future? What issues does the business need to address in the next ten years, that impact on me and the family?

3. What issues do I have with other family members? What concerns are not discussed in our family? What is my greatest fear for the future? What do I expect for my inheritance? What have I not said, or put off saying, to other family members? What do I want to be different in my relations with other family members?

4. How do I see the family's wealth and its legacy? What are the purposes that I want to see my family's wealth put to? What are the meanings of money in my family? How do I want to make use of the resources the family offers? What do we want to stand for and preserve as a family?

Formats for the Retreat

A family retreat takes place over one to four days, at a place away from distractions, where family members can relax, relate informally, and consider the difficult and exciting issues of their future. People come with a clear sense of commitment, even excitement, about sharing the thoughts and feelings that are most important to them.

For the first meeting or two, most families have found it useful to have an outside person as a "facilitator." This person is in charge of the process of the meeting, making sure that the meeting keeps flowing, that every individual gets to contribute, that people listen to each other, that they don't go off on tangents, that one person doesn't monopolize the discussion, that the conversation stays in focus, and that what is said is recorded and preserved. Given that family members have fairly fixed roles and ways of relating, it is clearly difficult for a family member to take on this role, at least at first. As we have already seen, a family has its own blind spots. Sometimes only an outsider can see them and point them out. Having a facilitator takes pressure off any family member from having to be "in charge," especially the person who is head of the family and of the business. The facilitator can ask questions, and even force the family to confront some issues. The facilitator works as a resource person with the family's leader/convener.

While a facilitator is critical in the beginning, generally a family learns to incorporate the facilitator role into itself within a few meetings. I suggest that by the third meeting that a family member take on the role. This job should be rotated. The facilitator takes responsibility for coordinating planning, setting agendas, helping focus and coordinate the meetings, and following up. The facilitator role is a great teacher for growing heirs, and for family members who want to get more involved in the family's business.

Now let's take a closer look at a family retreat. After discussion among themselves and with a facilitator, the family has agreed on a tentative agenda, and everybody has received a copy. The facilitator helps the group focus its discussion, and attend to details. The meeting room contains flip charts, wall space to display notes and ideas, and pillows or chairs arranged in a circle, open in the front. Everyone can see everyone else. The meetings are scheduled for certain times, one session in the morning and a shorter session in the afternoon. There is plenty of free time, and the family might stay for additional vacation days after the retreat.

The Family Council needs to be a safe forum for exchange. Not surprisingly, many families feel that they need clear safeguards to help them be open. First, the recycling of past hurts and blaming of people need to be short-circuited. The focus needs to be on letting go of hurts, and telling each other what they want from one another now and in the future. People need to agree to back off if things are getting upsetting, but to return to the issue as soon as possible. Ground rules about behavior should be set at the start and displayed in writing on the wall. Examples: no interrupting, no sarcasm, etc.

The retreat should provide a safe setting to talk about difficult topics. For instance, a son and son-in-law can explore their rivalry in the business, and the family can help make it less painful or divisive. A slighted daughter can be heard by her father, with others as witnesses to help make sure the pair is communicating. The Council can also offer a legitimate role for a family member outside of the business, who is nonetheless concerned about some aspect of it, to make his or her feelings known. A spouse can talk about something he or she thinks is unfair, or a brother can discuss his feelings of not being supported by the others.

The second ground rule should be that there be no secret agreements between people. All information and issues should be shared openly, without people feeling that there is more to the story. This is sometimes difficult to live up to, but the Council can dissolve very quickly if people don't feel they are getting the full truth. At the same time, the Council meeting has to be kept confidential; issues and information should not be shared beyond the group, except by common consent.

Notes and minutes of the meetings should be kept by rotating scribes, so that people can have a permanent record of what takes place, and agreements that are made can be followed up on. If someone says he or she will do something, it needs to be written down, and the family has to see that it is done.

Much information can be shared in the retreat about estate planning and the organization of the business, but care should be taken that the retreat not be simply an information-sharing meeting, or a presentation by the business owner. Presentations should be kept short and always followed by discussion. Even if an issue is already decided, there can still be feelings, reactions, and even disagreement to share. This can be upsetting, even threatening to the founder. It is hard for a patriarch to sit and listen to his children talk about feelings that what he has done feels unfair, or should be reconsidered. But these feelings can tear up families if not addressed, so the founder should tell himself that it is better to face these things directly than have them create distance and lingering ill will. Sometimes when disagreement is shared, the feelings become less disabling.

Several exercises are useful in helping families conduct retreats:

Interest Group in Center: One process I use in all retreats is to have different interest groups take the floor in the center of the room and, for a period of perhaps 30 minutes, talk about their concerns. Women in the family, relatives outside the business, spouses, sons, or any other relevant group, have a chance to present their unique way of seeing things. Only after the allotted time does the whole group get to respond.

Pair Interviews: In a family where people do many things together in groups, but rarely talk about difficult issues, I have pairs of people who do not have much interaction spend an hour together talking about their individual histories, goals, and feelings. Then each person shares with the whole group what he or she has learned. This helps build family bonds between people who often have little real understanding of each other.

More, Less: One family member sits in the center, and the others tell that person what they want to see more of from him or her, and what they want to see less of. This is a way for family members to share difficult feelings with each other. Always begin with the positive pole, what people want more of. In this exercise you can also share other kinds of information, such as what you appreciate about each other, or want to know more about.

Changing Roles: Two people who are having difficulty with one another spend a period of time where each has to express the other's point of view to the person's satisfaction. This can help resolve many generational and sex role disagreements by building greater understanding between people.

Planning a Picture: The whole family, or smaller groups, are asked to use construction paper and drawing materials to create a mural or picture, that expresses the family values and mission. They are to watch how they work together and after the project's completion, talk about how it was organized. Who did what and how did they interact together?

By the end of the family retreat, the family should have begun to create a series of documents. These may include a Family Business History, Values Credo, Mission Statement, and a Family Charter, as well as lists of key concerns, notes about discussions, topics to be explored in future meetings, and activities to be done in the future. These should be listed and collated at the end of the retreat, and everyone should get a copy as soon as possible. Now we're going to take a closer look at how to create such documents.

The Family Business History

The Family Council cannot just start with today and plan the future. It needs to begin with where it has come from. The past history of the family and the business is the legacy that the family takes into the future. Sharing this history is a powerful and important start to a Family Council, and a good way to begin a family retreat. The oldest generation of the family needs to tell its story to the others.

This may take some prodding. Often the business founders do not want to think about or recall the difficult early days. Founders are so busy that they may not realize how little their children know about the business. Many founders assume there is some sort of genetic memory, so their children "know" about the business. The children in turn don't think to ask, or feel that their curiosity is subtly turned aside.

One of the most profound experiences I have seen in family retreats has been the telling of the family and business history. The parents, or sometimes the grandparents, talk about how and why they formed the business. They can talk on their own, but sometimes the interview can benefit from having an interviewer. This can be a family member or a consultant if you use one. The story should also be recorded on videotape. When founders are old and grandchildren are young, this can be a way of preserving the family heritage. The interviews should be several hours, maybe over a few sessions. They should focus on questions such as: what were their dreams, how did they get started, who was involved, where did their first money come from, what stages the business went through, and how activities that have become traditions were born. These mythic stories often become the everyday reality of a family and a business, but people rarely know the full story of the origins. The point is not to eulogize, idealize or sanitize the story, but to convey its reality.

Telling the story creates a valuable statement of the family's history. The video can be shared with other family members and key managers, and perhaps edited for the whole company. Making the tape and listening to the story is a perfect way to start a family retreat.

Values Inquiry

The initial family retreat is not primarily spent in making decisions or deciding policy. Subsequent Family Council meetings can accomplish this. Rather, the benefit of a long retreat lies in exploring personal values, and deciding how they are to be expressed in the future. At an initial retreat, each family member should have a chance to talk about his or her history and personal concerns, goals, and values.

The essential task of the family's self-examination is to explore its values. Values are the bedrock on which the family and the business evolve. They say what the family and its business stand for. They guide behavior, and offer meaning and purpose to the family and its enterprises. A family that values personal freedom and autonomy, consistency, loyalty, or equality, will transfer those values to its business dealings. Therefore clarifying and spelling out values together can be a deeply moving, personally inspiring activity for the family. If you know your family's values, you can more deeply understand why things are done the way they are in the business.

Many times, the business is a vehicle to express the family values about contribution to the community, about helping others, or about achievement. The process of clarifying these core values can be a deeply meaningful event for the whole family. It can bring family members closer together, as they recall and define together what they stand for.

Some family values are expressed as a credo passed down through the generations, as ideals to live up to. Etched in the granite in Rockefeller Center is the Rockefeller family credo, "Every right implies a responsibility; every opportunity, an obligation; every possession, a duty." The stewardship of the Rockefeller family has been through philanthropy, and their family organization has had to wrestle recently with a significant change: the sale of the Center, the most visible symbol of Rockefeller enterprise, so that later generation heirs can exercise more control over their own legacies. The debate over that step has clearly shaken some family members. The meaning of the family legacy in such a decision was at least as important to their family council in its deliberations as whatever increase the sale may have meant to its already vast wealth.

Conflicts about policy, business decisions, or even personal issues, may actually be rooted in value questions. Coming up with a shared statement of family values, with explicit understandings of how they are acted on, can offer a guide to resolving other issues which cause distress for the family.

Exercise: Your Values Credo

Here is one way to develop a values list at a retreat. Each person begins by writing down the six most important values he or she sees in the family. Then share the lists, with each person talking about how he or she sees that value, and what it means personally. Then you can combine the lists into a single list of core family values.

For each value, every person should mention some of the things family members do which exemplify that value. If the feeling is that the value has been forgotten or slighted, then the group might explore ways to more fully express them.

Working with families and with businesses, my partner and I developed a deck of value cards[2] that denote key personal and business values. We use them in several ways. Sometimes we have individuals select their most and least important values, and share them with family members. Then the family together develops its own list of key values. From the family's list, individuals can look at how far their personal values differ from the family's. These are areas where conflict is likely to occur over policy or decisions. Another activity is to look at key business values and how these differ from core family values.

The purpose of such activities is to open up a shared inquiry in the family about value issues, not to come to any final resolution or forced agreement. It is better to appreciate differences than to enforce conformity. By seeing that areas of conflict are related to the most basic questions about what is right, family members may be able to step back and see that there is no right or wrong, but rather differences that need to be respected.

Vision, Mission and the Family Charter

First there is a dream, a vision, of the family business. It may have begun in the founder's mind, or in talks between brothers or a couple. They wanted to create something. As the business grew, the vision was modified, got larger or shifted focus. Reality changes dreams, just as dreams create realities. Visions are broad, vivid, ideal pictures of possibilities that inspire, provide direction, and create meaning. They start in one person's mind, but if the business is successful, soon they are shared. In times of change, and when new people enter a group, there must be a period where the vision is shared and, often, enlarged to take into account new realities or people.

Visions are not just for large and complex businesses. Every family business has a picture of what people want the business to be. This vision usually incorporates and adds to shared family values, by specifying not only the kind of business the family is in, but how it will do business, where it wants to business to go, and what it wants the business to mean to others. It's not a static picture, but grows and changes with individuals, families, and the business. One generation's vision will not do for the next. The core values and some key elements may remain the same, but visions grow and evolve.

After hearing the family's business history and developing a Values Credo, the initial family retreat can then share personal visions of what people want the family, and the business, to be like in ten or 20 years. This is not a rational business plan or commitment. A vision can be as wild and impractical as you like. By having everybody share their visions, many differences that may be expressed on a policy level become clear. A person who sees the family relaxing together at a special vacation home eventually will have problems with someone who sees the company growing to have 200 franchisees. You don't all have to agree. Two people can pursue slightly different visions, perhaps with core values in common. Visioning is a way of getting people to share what they value most.

Exercise: Generating Your Family Vision

Here's how to create a shared vision. Begin with a few moments of personal reflection, where you generate an inner sense of how you want things to be in the indefinite future. Sit quietly for a few moments, and read the following instructions to yourself. Let your mind wander in response to the questions—don't try to guide it in any particular direction. Accept what your mind presents you with, without judgment or criticism. You will have time later to assess, evaluate, and amend it.

"Imagine your family some time in the indefinite future. Imagine that it has resolved its key problems, and treats everyone with dignity and respect, is open to exchange, and allows each individual to grow and develop to his or her highest abilities. What would your family be like if that were true? Imagine a family gathering, time at home, and conversations with particular people. Draw out your vision in as much detail as you can.

Now imagine your family business at some indefinite time in the future. The family questions about the business have been resolved, and you have taken the role, if any, that is most appropriate to you in the business. Everyone works in harmony, and the business prospers. Employees, customers, and the community all respect the business as a model of its kind. It perfectly expresses the highest values of the family. Imagine the best possible future for the business in as much detail as you can.

After you have reflected on these visions, write down the major elements of each. What are the key qualities of each one? Share your vision with other family members, as the beginning of a discussion of common elements in everyone's vision. When there are differences, explore where they come from.

After people in the family have shared their visions of the future, the next step is to crystallize these visions into a Business Mission Statement, a short statement of the core purposes and values of the business. You may also develop a Family Mission Statement expressing the family purposes and core values. Sometimes both can be combined into a single statement. The discussion of these mission statements may generate some controversy, as competing values and emphases get expressed. In what ways do the business and the family come first? What is more important, profit or everyone's well-being? Some long-simmering differences between family members may come out. For example, the spouse and children of the founder may have different views. In-laws may have completely distinct ideas. Recognize that there may very well be heated controversy.

Good mission statements can't be designed in one meeting. You may come up with notes, or a draft at your first Council meeting during the retreat. Then take a month to think about it, and propose changes. One part may be controversial, and may have to be put off for more discussion.

The mission statement should be short—not more than 100 words, and it should be emotionally moving, or, as my partner says, "give you goosebumps." It should express your deepest, most important purpose. The Business Mission Statement should be shared with employees, as they may have input. Here is a short mission statement that combines the family and business mission:

"Our business is about service—to family, to employees, to customers, and to the community. We want to grow ourselves, and we want our company to grow, in order to provide a secure 'home base' for everyone. A thriving business will create opportunities for growth, community involvement, and fulfillment for everyone, family and employees alike."

The specific ways to implement this mission were the subject of many deliberations. As with any suitable mission statement, it energized the people in the family and helped them feel good about what they were doing.

Formulating your mission is a process, not a slogan to hang on the wall. It can be referred to when there are important decisions to be made. Having the mission publicly available is helpful not just to the family, but to outside employees, customers, and the community as well. It tells them who you are. A good mission statement includes:

• What you want to do and achieve;
• How you want to do that;
• What you value and stand for;
• Principles behind the governance of your company or family;
• Groups that are part of the whole, such as owners, management, employees, customers and public in a business, and in-laws, heirs, etc. in a family.

Drawing from its family and business mission statements, the family next works on defining its philosophy of how it will do business, with specific rules and expectations. This statement of philosophy and expectations is termed the Family Charter. This can be thought of as the constitution governing your family, especially its present and future relations to the business. It defines the policies, expectations, rights, and responsibilities for members of the family. With a clear charter, a family member can securely explore his or her future, knowing what he or she can expect, and ask, from the family and the business.

The Family Charter sets guidelines in areas such as:
1. Family's commitment to the business;
2. Reasons for that commitment;
3. Central family values: how it realizes its commitment;
4. Family priorities, resources, and strengths;
5. Contributions of family members to business;
6. Contributions of business to family members;
7. Expectations and responsibilities of family members;
8. Ground rules for family participation in the business;
9. Distribution of profits and stock;
10. Guidelines for succession and inheritance.

The following is a hypothetical example of a Family Charter. It is a particularly elaborate and detailed Charter that fits a large, complex, third generation business. If your business is smaller, you may not need to create policy in each of the areas detailed by the Chases. The major purpose of the Charter is to make the agreements and decisions of the Family Council clear and explicit.

Naturally, you can't expect to formulate such a document at your first family retreat. But you will do a lot of the groundwork by coming up with a Values Credo and a Mission Statement. They lay the foundation for future meetings where the Charter is hammered out.

The "Chase" Family Charter

The members of the Chase family have been in the jewelry business for 92 years, and we want the benefits of the business, and the values of our family, to be perpetuated in the future. As our family grows, we want to make clear the principles and values that make up our family business relationships.

How We Do Business:

We believe in respect for people, whether they are employees, customers, or the community.

Our family is concerned with preservation of the community, the participation in activities that facilitate community and world peace, harmony, and cooperation. We encourage family members to participate in community activities, and support the identification of the business with causes that we believe in.

We try to foster some of the most important values of our family in our business relationships with employees and customers.

We have a special responsibility to people outside the family who have helped our business to thrive. We regularly offer 10% of our profits to our employees.

Personal Development and Business Opportunities:

Entrepreneurship is part of our family blood and tradition, and we need to encourage and support it within the business. We encourage, support, and offer advice to family members who pursue independent business interests.

Our family offers the opportunity for every member to develop business opportunities. Our family wealth offers a resource pool for the development of good ideas.

We expect family members to be deeply committed to their ideas, to develop the skills and make the commitment to realize their potential.

We want family members to contribute their talents to the development of the business. Our responsibility is to fulfill, in every way possible, the entrepreneurial instincts and needs of individual family members.

If an opportunity or an idea is a good idea for one of us, we all will pursue it. Therefore, we will share business opportunities collectively.

Business Participation:

We encourage all direct descendants of the founders, their spouses, and their children to participate in the business.

The people who participate in the business will be the owners of the business and receive the rewards for their participation. People who run each of our family businesses will have control over those businesses.

Stock Ownership:

We want to clarify and secure the rights of future ownership and participation to all direct descendants of the founders.

Stock in the family holding company will be offered to direct descendants of the founder, according to direct contribution to the major family business, or new business ventures. A family member can cash out of the business, by selling stock back to the family. Non-family members will not be able to purchase stock, and it is not for sale outside the family.

If someone has left the family business, we support that person's right to change his or her mind, and return to an equity position, even if he or she left, or didn't enter, for a long period of time.

Family Council:

We will meet twice a year, and respond directly to each other when we are feeling dissatisfied or upset. Other family members are willing to act as mediators, but we expect family members to try to speak directly to one other about conflicts. We do not want any individuals or factions to feel estranged.

The Ryan Family Retreat

Each family retreat is different. Here is the story of one family's first retreat. The "Ryan" family is large and growing. Sonny and Ellie Ryan have five children, Graham, Eldon, and Colleen, who are part of their large business, and Craig and Susan, who are not, although Henry, Susan's husband, a lawyer, handles the family trust and real estate investments. The group numbers 11, with the parents, heirs and spouses. Graham, Colleen, and Sonny have planned the retreat, gathering input from everyone, and planning the schedule, with me as facilitator.

The retreat has been precipitated by feelings of frustration over how the three siblings in the business work together, and who will be Sonny's successor. Sonny has hinted that he prefers Graham to become president of the company, but he senses that there are difficult feelings and doubts about this. While the others expect that Graham will probably succeed his father, they feel that the decision should not be made so soon. They want to help design their future. In addition, everyone wants to know more about Sonny's plans for his estate, the business future, and about the family trusts and real estate holdings.

Each individual has written a letter to the family, sharing his or her personal, family, and career goals, and some needs, visions and concerns that he or she would like the family to face. All the letters have been shared. After dinner together, the family meets. They have designed a full schedule for three days of work, but they are mainly concerned with building better communication. They are not a family that is very comfortable sharing feelings. People are reluctant to tell others when they are upset, and there is a family rule about politeness and respect.

The first part of the retreat is spent sharing the family and business history. With Sonny and Ellie leading, the family creates the family history. They also fill in a diagram of their family tree, called a Genogram[3], as they talk about how their family moved from England a generation ago. There is a discussion of family values. They come up with a list which provokes some sharp discussion.

One exercise they use is having all the non-blood family members sit in the center of the room and talk about their experience of entering and becoming part of the family. Then the blood family take a turn talking. Each group shares a very different perspective on the family. The blood family feels a sense of nurturing and security, while the in-laws feels more distance and a lack of communication. All of them as a group then talk about how they see the family.

Some of the wives of family members are concerned because they feel the family is so protective and "nice" that they don't really talk. They feel that disagreements are swept under the table. They talk about feeling slighted by Ellie, and about finding it hard to penetrate Sonny's shell of geniality to know what he is really feeling. Everyone talks about how he or she would like to see the family changed. They suggest more one-to-one communication, and letting one another know when they are hurt or disappointed.

The next phase of the meeting involves sharing personal goals. Each person gets 15 minutes to talk personally about him or herself, what he or she would like, and how he or she sees the future. Even though they know each other intimately, this is the first time individuals have addressed the family in this way, sharing personal goals and aspirations. After each person speaks, the others respond. A list of questions or concerns for the family that come out of this process is kept in the front of the room.

The second day the family creates a family vision and Mission Statement. It begins with people imaging how they would like the family to be, in the future, under ideal conditions. What would their best family vision look like? What would they do together? How would they act? What would be different and what would stay the same? They share their visions, writing down the key elements on paper around the walls. Then they do an exercise where, using one post-it note for each value, each person sorts into a pile, from most to least important, his or her own most deeply held values. He or she then does the same for the values that person sees in the family now, and the values each thinks the family should see as most important. Each person's ranked set of values are then stuck on the wall for everyone to see. The discussion moves to how the family expresses, and even sometimes contradicts, its values. People then talk about how they would like the family to be.

The next day, they begin work on a Mission Statement. They select their core values and think about the family in relation to several areas: the community, each other, the business, and the quality of life they want in the future. For each of these areas, they come up with statements of their major purpose and values. After a few hours, they have a working draft.

Next they draft a Family Charter. They make a list of the specific questions, areas, and topics they want the charter to cover. Then they have several presentations. Sonny and Eldon talk about the succession process. Craig talks about the family trusts. Sonny shares his thoughts on his estate plan, which he has not formulated completely yet. In particular, he is not sure about the future ownership of the business. But he is willing to listen to and discuss proposals.

Everyone is concerned about who will own the business in the future. Their concerns are posted in the front of the room. The Family Charter begins with the family mission and values. But then, they need to clarify and specify specific policies. They list areas yet to be resolved, such as how ownership will be determined. By the end of the retreat they feel very close, and that they have made a powerful start.

After the Retreat

The retreat is just a first step in developing a Council as an ongoing entity to help the family realize its dreams and goals, and to help each family member grow. The Council should always be active in the family as the mechanism for the family to act consciously as a coherent, unified organism.

The Council needs a regular structure, with meetings, minutes, decisions recorded, ongoing communication about issues, and roles for individual members. It can call a meeting on a holiday eve, if only to check in and share what's happening, but it needs to have more formal and longer periods for reflection on major choices and decisions. If the family business is large, and involves several branches of the family, the Family

Council takes on even more importance and formality. Indeed, major business families are linked by family holding companies, offices, and councils that are organized around their business interests.

The Council is more than merely a business structure. The meetings I have seen are full of fun. Milestones, achievements, and special events are recognized and ritualized in Council gatherings. People doing exciting projects take time to present their work. Beneficiaries of family largesse report back about what they've been doing. Young people talk about their college and/or professional school projects. These activities affirm what the family values and stands for. If the family supports one member as an artist, or hears about the conservation work of another, it recognizes that these pursuits are as important as being a manager in the family business. When a Council gets to be so meaningful and so much fun for a family, attendance is assured. The foundation of good feeling, trust, shared ritual, and history allow the group to wade into difficult issues and resolve conflicts.

I have seen another byproduct of Family Councils. They form a vehicle for family members to learn management skills and take on business and professional responsibilities. Acting as leader/facilitator in the Council is a leadership role in some families. It can be almost a coming of age when a young family member takes on the role. There are always some family members who are not naturally considered "business" people. They often feel threatened or alienated from some of the family activities, even though they benefit from them. Service in a family office, as part of the Council's activities, can gently bring them greater understanding and appreciation of the commercial world. Helping the Council gather information about a potential real estate purchase or insurance policy, for instance, is one way that younger family members can learn responsibility. Sometimes when a family member has developed a role or style that seems starkly divergent, even estranged from the family, getting him or her involved in some family activity through the Council can build greater connectedness to the family.

If you want to get started forming a Family Council, begin by bringing up the issues in this chapter with your family. Talk about values during dinner, and ask your parents about the history of the business when you visit them. In a family, you don't need an invitation to begin. Over time, the process you initiate can grow into a family retreat, leading to a Family Council, and greater clarity about your family and its relation to its business.

Chapter 5 talks about one special kind of family business: a couple in business together. The following chapters explore three stages of business and family development in sequence: the new generation entering the business, the changing of the guard, and the renewal of the business.

Notes:
1. McWhinney, Will. "Entrepreneurs, Owners and Stewards: The Conduct of a Family Business." *New Management*, July 1988.
2. Available from the HeartWork Group, 764 Ashbury St., San Francisco, CA 94117.
3. For a good account of how the genogram is used with family businesses, see David Bork's *Family Business, Risky Business*.

5

Married to the Business... And Each Other: Two Worlds Of Entrepreneurial Couples

"To be an entrepreneurial couple—copreneurs—is to become personally responsible for your collective future, to let go of the 'security' of two pay checks, to discover who both of you really are and take positive control of your lives. Once you realize the benefits of copreneuring, working alone will never again seem a viable alternative. Copreneuring is an end to separate lives and separate agendas."
   -Frank and Sharan Barnett: Working Together: Entrepreneurial Couples

It's 11 pm, and the "Thompsons" are sprawled on their bed. Their teenage children are doing homework in their rooms. The bed is piled with data for the sales presentation tomorrow. They are arguing over how to present their products, who will speak first, who will handle the account when they get it. They joke about their different styles, and whether a man or a woman can best sell to the attractive single woman who is the chief buyer for this large department store chain. The Thompsons, like perhaps a million of their peers, are the owners and key managers in their family business. Four years ago, Don Thompson did not make partner in a Big Eight accounting firm, and Sarah was frustrated by her marketing job. Instead of finding a new job, Don had an idea for a great gift product and they decided to create their own gift business. Now, after two years of struggle, funding their operation on credit card lines of credit and promises to banks, they have had two successful seasons. After the holiday season, they look forward to their first family vacation since they started.

New businesses started by couples who jointly share ownership, commitment, and responsibility may be the fastest-growing segment of family business. Reliable data is hard to gather, but most experts agree that the numbers are enormous and growing. The Small Business Administration reports a 62% increase from 1980 to 1986 (the last year in which statistics were reported) in jointly-operated start-ups, most of which are couple owned. Sharon Nelton first wrote about couple entrepreneurs[1], and, in a recent book, Sharan and Frank Barnett[2] use the term "copreneurs" to refer to entrepreneurial couples who share top management responsibility for a company.

Copreneurial businesses represent a special category of family business. All types of business can be started by a couple. They include small shops and restaurants, home-based service businesses, and farms, as well as larger, often publicly-traded firms such as Mrs. Fields Cookies, Liz Claiborne, and World Savings. Yet this form of ownership has been almost completely ignored in management books and even in family business literature.

With such diversity of types and sizes, it is surprising that entrepreneurial couples seem to share certain reasons for forming their business, as well as common satisfactions, stresses, and conflicts. This chapter explores the excitement and difficulties that arise from the special situation of a married couple who create a business together. I will present some of the key challenges that copreneurs must resolve in order to not only maintain their relationship, but build a strong business.

Tasks for the Chapter

If you are a member of a couple running a business, this chapter will help you assess your relationship and manage the stresses. It will show you how to plan and carry out a couple retreat where you and your spouse spend some special time reflecting on goals, how the business fits with them, and how you could make your home and work relationships more resilient, effective, and satisfying. This chapter can act as a "sanity check" for you to look at how your relationship is standing up under the stress of business. It will also help you look at the strain of moving your relationship from home to business.

This chapter can also be helpful for couples who work together in a larger family business. While not all the information will apply, many of the problems are the same.

Exploring the unique consequences of an intimate relationship at the top of a business offers insights into the dynamics of other pairs who run businesses. For example, two partners who are long-time friends, or a parent and offspring, face similar pressures as copreneurs. Copreneurial experience can help us understand the increasingly frequent phenomena of shared leadership between siblings or other relatives. It can also shed light on couples who do not share a business, but a profession, such as medicine, or who work for the same company.

This chapter is especially important for me because I am a copreneur. My consulting business, The HeartWork Group, is run in partnership with my wife, Cynthia Scott. I am also the oldest son of copreneurial parents who, from the time I was a child, ran a private school and summer camp from our home. I grew up seeing the business unfold over our dining room table, and my parents collaborating, arguing, dividing roles, and taking few vacations. After none of their three children decided to take over the school, they sold it to a young couple, who have continued the school out of their home.

I thought I was traveling far from the family heritage when I became a professor and consultant. However, I have in fact started two copreneurial home-based businesses. In 1969, my first wife and I started a residential youth crisis center. It was difficult and both personal and business relationships were full of conflict. I resolved never to do it again!

Four years ago, in a new marriage with Cynthia, we found ourselves building a consulting firm from the downstairs flat of our Victorian house. I can see us resolving the developmental crises that are common to other copreneurs. We've had power struggles over who gets credit for what, we've had to adjust to different personality and work styles, we've tried to preserve our personal life from our work, and we've struggled to have more to our relationship than just business.

I did not consciously view either my parents' school or my own consulting as family businesses until a year or two of work with other copreneurs. Then, during a talk, I realized that I was in fact enacting a very strong family legacy. Like my parents, I valued a shared work/life relationship dedicated to service and teaching, with a strong-willed woman, working out of my home. This personal continuity has convinced me that the exploration of family heritage and models of relationship is one important lens for understanding copreneurs.

Why Copreneurship?

There are several reasons why copreneurship has become so popular. This is an era of corporate downsizing and restructuring. Many people who leave the corporate world involuntarily, or semi-voluntarily with early retirement, find themselves at mid-life with a broad range of choices, maturity, talent, energy, and financial resources. They ask themselves if they want to return to the traditional workplace, and answer "no." Instead they decide to create small service businesses, learn skilled crafts, or operate a store or franchise in a small community.

Another reason is that after a decade of instability in intimate relationships and questioning of sex roles at home and in business, people are placing more importance on maintaining and nurturing family relationships. They may feel that a first marriage ended because they were over-involved in work, without enough companionship and sharing. Or they may want to share more with their spouse. While the renewed emphasis on companionship can take the form of de-emphasizing work in favor of home life, some couples decide that they want to combine the two worlds into one. They like working and are dedicated to their careers, but they don't want to separate their careers from their life together.

Many new copreneurs are mid-life baby boomers, who have lived through an era of social experimentation which involved setting up new businesses that reflected their essential values. Such couples establish companies that reflect human as well as profit concerns, incorporating values of caring, respect for people, and ecological consciousness. They move from larger companies—hotels, law firms, department stores, restaurants, newspapers, etc.—to create their own smaller, but more ideal, model. Today, many smaller, specialized, or service-oriented businesses are able to compete very well against larger corporations, while at the same time providing the owners/managers with a more balanced, integrated life.

The industrial age was characterized by the decline of the extended family and village, and the separation and differentiation of home and work worlds, and sex roles. Copreneurship seems to reverse these trends. The personal and the work/public worlds are intertwined and differentiations are diminished. The household unit is also the business unit, and often the household becomes the business site. The family reenters the business sphere—the family, business, and ownership circles become superimposed.

Many copreneurships are home-based. An editorial in *Home Business Line* talks about their special nature:

"Home based business people have a magical mystique about them. We're people who work when we want to. In the privacy and comfort of our homes. Have more time with our families. Run our business without anyone telling us what to do. It sounds like a dream. And to a great degree, it's true.

"Yes, we make our own hours. Or at least we intend to. We often end up working late into the night, on weekends, and on holidays. Yes, we have more time with our families who want our time and attention while we are working. Yes, we can wear whatever we want to in the privacy and comfort of our homes. But we also have to answer our own phones, deal with door-to-door salespeople, and clients who call us outside of business hours."[3]

Like the blurring of the home/office boundaries, differentiations between male and female roles are diminished or modified. Entrepreneurial couples assume a model of shared leadership, with the women usually bringing a similar level of education, professional skills, experience, and motivation to the new venture. While there may be division of labor, there is no hierarchy of greater and lesser authority, but rather an egalitarian sharing of power and status.

This reality sends a very strong message about sexual equality and the different but equally important contributions of women to the organization. Women take many different roles in copreneurial businesses. They may be the designers and spokespersons for the organization, such as Liz Claiborne or Mrs. Fields. Or they may be the internal, nurturing organizational force, taking care of operations and personnel. In either case they make a statement about feminine styles of management, which can be contrasted with the style of their spouses. The couple models respect for difference, and a willingness to be interdependent and work together.

There are other special qualities of a copreneurship. Because a couple is at the helm of the business, there is implicit respect within the business for the realities of family and personal life. Children, spouses, homes, and household demands are real in a copreneurship, whereas in many entrepreneurial businesses they are actively denied to the point where the workplace is treated as the real family. In copreneurial organizations employees are respected for balancing the two, and allowances are made for this. Since the boss may have to rush home to the day-care center, employees also are allowed this privilege.

The desire to gain control over their lives, and work in their own way, is strong in copreneurs, as it is with all entrepreneurs. They are not against work; they simply want to set their own working conditions. "I just am not able to have a boss," is the refrain of many copreneurs.

A Closer Look at Copreneurs

A shared business venture represents a very special decision for couples. Like the choice to be an entrepreneur, it represents a willingness to blaze a new path and take a huge risk. It is often a huge commitment of time, energy, and finances. But becoming copreneurs has even more significance to couples. It represents a special extension of their commitment to each other, their mission as a couple. Creating a business was compared by several copreneurs to having a baby: it is a special celebration of their togetherness that brings with it overwhelming stress, sleepless nights, uncertainty, and has a mind of its own.

McGrath RentCorp, a public company that rents and sells modular offices which expects to do nearly $40 million in business in this, its tenth year, is a good example of a copreneurial business. The company is highly profitable, highly regarded by its customers, has grown at a healthy rate every year, and has a deeply committed, highly motivated group of employees that enjoy their work. The company is run by Joan and Bob McGrath, and represents many of the special qualities that a couple brings to an entrepreneurial business.

Bob started the company after his previous company was sold. He wanted to start a business that was more in keeping with his values and style of work. He had recently begun a relationship with Joan, who had created a course about changing work beliefs called *The Bottom Line*. Their growing relationship involved sharing ideas of how business should be run. They talked about applying these ideas to the new business.

Several months later when the sales manager had back surgery, Joan came in to help. She never left, and now holds the title of executive vice-president. At first, she learned about the business at a seminar, held every day while driving to work with Bob. They came to see that the company could be a unique way to express their own vision of what a workplace could be, and a way to share and grow in their own relationship. McGrath RentCorp. represents a mature expression of each of their lifelong learning, the special contribution they have chosen together to make to the world and each other.

Joan notes that they bring a powerful partnership into the company. "We complement each other. Our combined talents form a powerful synergy. Having us both rounds out the attention we can give to the company that one of us wouldn't have alone."

The McGraths are equal partners, though Bob is president. They each have a clearly defined area of responsibility and respect one another's turf. Bob deals with financial issues, and how the company relates to its market. Joan's role is to pay attention to people, how they feel as well as how they reach the company's goals. They share household responsibilities as well. If there is a problem at home, or with one of their children, either one will respond.

The company has affected Joan and Bob's personal relationship. They both feel that they have grown to respect the others' talents as a result of seeing them used. Their relationship has deepened as together they have been so successful in expressing their vision in the world.

If there is a down side to sharing the company, Joan feels that it is that sometimes their private life gets slighted. They have to make sure to spend time involved in non-business activities. They recently took a long vacation and were curious to see what would happen. After a few days, they just stopped talking business, and it wasn't on their minds until the last day of the vacation. In contrast, in the early days, they wouldn't leave without calling in every day, as if the business were a child. Joan notes that now they have a much more solid middle management team in place, and they feel more comfortable letting go.

The copreneurial business often springs out of something a couple likes to do together. The safari clothing store Banana Republic began when Mel and Pat Ziegler, who worked in magazine merchandising, fantasized about combining their hobbies of art design and travel. They began their store with exotic leisure clothes and a striking catalogue written like a travel adventure story. Smaller businesses I've encountered, such as a legal practice specializing in small business support; a restaurant offering family recipe ethnic food; a picture framing shop; or a bed and breakfast enterprise all reflect the special companionship quality of the mission of many copreneurs.

Couples quickly discover many practical advantages in their two-person start up. The tax and economic advantages of sharing home and office, and the sweat equity from two professionals mean that they are cheaper to start. Also, your spouse is a partner you know you can trust. Given the stress and uncertainty of a start-up, having a dependable partner is very comforting.

While vacations are few and far between in most start-ups, copreneurs are creative in finding ways to combine companionship with business. For couples, a half-day by the pool or sightseeing, a Sunday brunch in bed at a hotel, or a quiet drink or dinner after a business meeting or sale, make business travel and conventions positively pleasant. Since copreneurs work very long hours, it is often only within a business context that they can find time to be together. And these vacations are fully tax-deductible, and reasonable for a start-up business. One woman noted that she and her husband had more fun time together after they started a business, even though there were longer working hours. Being together at work allowed the two to snatch more mini-breaks.

Some copreneurs fall into full partnership in stages. About half the copreneurs I know began gradually, or with only one of the spouses full-time. The other continued his or her career. Then the business grew, an employee quit, or the other spouse became restless in his or her job. "Why don't you join the business," "I need you to help me," or "The store manager quit; can you help out for a few weeks," brings the other spouse into the business. They then find that they work together well, and discover other advantages of shared work. Most couples report that they found it more fun to work together than they expected. And the business seems to thrive on their energized, caring style of work. Temporary arrangements or transition structures become permanent, as the couple redefines the business as a partnership.

Of course there are also problems as such couples evolve their working relationships. There is a natural imbalance when one person works full-time while the other still has another job. Who makes decisions, and who does the work? What if there is a conflict between an outside job and the new business? How do you hold someone accountable who is doing you a favor by helping you out after work? The business demands 100% of your time, and outside responsibilities are hard to sustain. Fortunately for couples, these problems dissipate as the business grows enough to support both people, or there evolves a natural role division, including greater responsibility and authority to the full-time partner.

Difficulties of Copreneurships

A couple who also owns a business is in a very unique situation, even for a family business, and faces special problems. A classic sociological article[4] defined marriage as the creation of a shared conversation in which two people from different backgrounds come together to build a shared reality. This involves some withdrawal and isolation from former friends and relationships. The intimate, private conversations of a couple strengthen and build the stable intimacy of a strong dyad: the couple do not want to submit their private world to the review of others.

What happens when the couple's shared dreams, its private conversation, is brought into a business? Like other entrepreneurs who gamble with their dreams in the court of reality, couples starting a business run a huge risk. They put out their vision in public. This vision includes their mutual assessment of their abilities to make something happen, the assumption of the harmony and strength of their relationship to be able to include other people, and their willingness to put themselves on the line for it. Weaknesses, areas where their mutual perceptions cannot stand up to feedback from others, and denied or unnoticed strains in their relationship will be obvious to bystanders, who include employees, customers, and clients.

Bringing other people into the couple's world creates another area of difficulty. The concerns an outsider may have about intruding upon the private aspects of the couple's life may lead him or her to withhold information that is important to business success. This is especially true about judgments of deficiencies in the behavior of the copreneurs themselves. It's hard to tell someone that her spouse is difficult to get along with, or using poor business judgement. Like entrepreneurs, copreneurs invite others to share their vision, but they also hang a "do not disturb" sign over certain aspects of their personal relationship and certain types of feedback.

In addition, the world of a new or fast-growing business is full of disappointment, frustration, and crisis. These can disappoint a copreneur's expectation, and strain the relationship, especially if one spouse was more identified with the misjudgment. How can you get angry at your partner at five p.m. for losing several thousands of dollars because of a mistake in judgement and then happily go to dinner and to bed? The private relationship has to be hardy enough to stand such a difficult test.

A second threat comes from the business draining their private life. Entrepreneurship is a single-minded pursuit, even a form of obsession. For copreneurs even more than entrepreneurs and other family businesses owners, the business constantly threatens to swallow up the personal. The neat boundary of home and marriage as a refuge does not exist. Worries and struggles cannot be shared with a spouse who is a sympathetic outsider. Rather difficulties are shared from the start. In addition, there's a danger that the couple becomes the business, and has no life outside of it. For example, sex can decline when a couple works together, and indeed, lack of time and energy for sex in professional couples has been termed "the Yuppie disease."

Like other family business members, spouses have two relationships: one as partners and one as spouses. If they treat the two relationships as identical, then boundary problems spill over, and role confusion will result.

At times the personal relationship spills over into the business, as when one spouse comments on or corrects the other's behavior in public (e.g. "Dear, you have a spot on your tie"). Indeed patterns of personal relationships, such as deferring, rescuing, or avoiding certain topics, have business consequences, and must be recognized and dealt with.

Many couples bring unresolved couple issues into the workplace. One wife kept hearing about her husband's difficulty supervising employees in the office. She felt she had to protect him, but her protective behavior insured that he kept re-creating the problem. Another couple had a relationship characterized by very little division of labor. Each person would do a little of everything, but both individuals had trouble checking in or coordinating activities. They simply could not clarify their roles and responsibilities and their business was run on the same ad hoc basis. The pair became confused, overwhelmed, and angry at each other. Role clarification, communication, and handling of conflict needed to be addressed before their business could develop.

Feelings about the business also can spill into the home. The anxiety of cash flow problems or difficult employees can make it hard for the couple to let go. There isn't even an outside person to distract the other.

Added to these problems is the natural tendency for a couple relationship to form a series of triangle coalitions. Couples often "triangle" in other individuals to help them handle tension and anxiety in the relationship. Triangling in other employees or children who work in the business can pressure them to side with one spouse against the other. This is a natural way to handle tension, but it can come at the expense of the couple relationship—and often the parent/child or employee/boss relationships too. These coalitions foster competition or conflict between the copreneurs, and can create anxiety and instability in the business organization as employees feel themselves drawn into the couple's conflict. The best known instance of this was the crisis several years ago at Esprit, where strains in the relationship of the founding couple, who each owned half the business, paralyzed operations.

Many of the above strains echo problems in entrepreneurial business generally: tendency to over-identify, avoidance of feedback, overwork, and employee coalitions. However, some problems seem to be peculiar to copreneurial companies. Specifically there seems to be a vast psychological difference between the "conversation" that a single entrepreneur has with his or her company, and the implicit message given to an organization headed by a couple.

The presence of a couple can activate old emotional responses by employees. In many ways every workplace evokes responses that arise out of one's family heritage, but no relationship is more powerful at evoking emotional responses than an analogue of the parents. Because of the presence at the head of the company of a man and a woman, almost inevitably an otherwise very egalitarian couple evokes childlike behavior in employees. A family is Mom, Dad and the kids. Since the owners are Mom and Dad, employees often feel that the couple are like parents, and, for better or worse, feel treated like children.

Copreneurs themselves may help create such a set-up. Given the situation, they may indeed feel like parents. Often copreneurs find themselves talking about employees like their children and treating them accordingly. This is so common that copreneurs are almost inevitably benevolent, caring, but also paternalistic employers. This is a topic that copreneurs I know feel must be discussed in the business itself, for it is so automatic, yet can be destructive, when employees feel prevented from "growing up," or acting on their own.

Prerequisites for Success

With all the complexity, risk, and uncertainty of the copreneurial venture, perhaps the greatest surprise is that there are relatively few casualties. One would expect a high business failure rate, as one does with any entrepreneurial venture. However, my survey did not uncover many failures. In fact, copreneurs may even be more successful than a corresponding group of entrepreneurs. The special strengths of an effective couple relationship are especially useful to resolving the pressures of starting a company.

My impression is that copreneurs tend to be a hardy bunch with strong personal relationships before going into business. Given the risk and strains of a new venture, plus the added companionship and pressure, a fragile couple wouldn't even try to take this on. The nature of copreneuring scares them off, just as the nature of starting a business scares off many otherwise talented people. There seem to be some prerequisites for success. Here is a list of qualities of successful copreneurs:

- Solid relationship that grows stronger from working together;
- Deep trust and respect for each other's competence;
- Contributions of spouse valued;
- Respect for women and feminine style of expression;
- Shared sense of mission, vision, and values;
- Clear boundaries between work and personal life;
- Good communication skills;
- Stress and disappointment handled without mutual blame;
- Complementary roles.

To have a successful business and personal life, a couple's relationship has to be strong, flexible, egalitarian, and relatively free of deep, basic conflicts. It is helpful if you had positive experiences working together, perhaps planning large events or a project like getting a new house built. If you enjoy working together and are able to exchange ideas in an easy give and take, then you are ready for shared work. One copreneur punned that he so "enjoyed his wife's company," that he began to work with her. There must also be good communication between the two of you. The relationship should not be one where one person habitually bows to the will of the other, or does not feel free to speak up.

Each person should be deeply respectful of the other's abilities. A couple relationship is one of unconditional acceptance, without pressure to produce anything. You are loved and accepted for who you are. In business, you need to produce results—just the intention to do something, or the vision, is nothing if you do not have the relevant skills and drive to achieve the goals. Therefore, each person has to be respectful not only of the other's being, but of his or her ability to come through. Each must value the other's contribution. As one spouse put it, when his spouse was successful, he felt grateful for the "gift" she was giving to the company.

The hardiness of the relationship is tested in many ways by business. Each person has to respect the other for succeeding. One person may be more publicly identified as the spokesperson or leader. This is true even if the couple experiences their relationship as egalitarian. The person in the public eye needs to respect the contribution of the other, and the person in the shadow has to cope with his or her jealousy.

There are several other key qualities that couples need to develop to insure that their personal and business lives succeed. Like other family businesses, these include formulating a clear mission and vision, clearly separating work from personal life, communicating clearly, and developing clear and complementary work roles. Let's look at each in depth vis-a-vis couples.

Shared Mission and Vision

Copreneurs, like all entrepreneurs, are deeply driven by their mission and vision. They are working not only to make money, but to make a statement, and see their business as a form of social expression. Each member of the copreneurial couple must be an entrepreneur. That means the business must be an equal passion for each. A reluctant spouse, who enters with a feeling of obligation or lack of clarity, proves an obstacle to the entrepreneurial spouse. If the commitment is unequal, the less committed spouse soon elects, or descends, to a less central role in the business.

The couple needs a shared vision not only about its business, but about its life. Many copreneurs see their endeavor as marking a certain life stage. They develop the business, then move on. Couples have to agree on the place the business has in their lives and when it's time to leave.

Letting go is difficult, but it may be easier for a couple to move on to other ventures than for a solo entrepreneur. Couples have each other, and take their relationship with them. They have shared talents and experience that can easily be transferred to other ventures. Mike and Jo Fisher founded Fisher Graphics in middle life to gain more independence, and to have something to share with their growing sons. After working together for 11 years, they are ready to move on to the next challenge. Similarly, Liz Claiborne and her husband, Arthur Ortenberg, retired from leadership in their company to pursue their social and charitable interests. And the Zieglers left Banana Republic, which they had sold to the Gap, when their dream of a travel magazine did not win the support of their parent company. In each case, the business was a stage of the couple's growing personal mission.

The vision needs to be clear and vivid. It should include not only what the couple wants to do, but how to do it. The McGraths may not have dreamed of the specific offices they market, but they had a dream of a certain type of workplace and of close, warm, shared work relations. Their vision is of a certain style of work and values.

Shanna Brutoco started a small gallery in her home, selling art objects related to **The Course in Miracles,** a spiritual philosophy. After seeing how customers responded to her special selections, her husband Rinaldo, a venture capitalist/lawyer, joined her to expand it into a catalogue business and public showroom, the Red Rose Gallerie. They see their customers and galleries as educational centers, offering seminars, support groups, and a place to explore new values and personal transition. Like other copreneurs, the opportunity to express their deepest values through the business has strengthened and expanded the meaning and richness of their marriage.

Reflection Question
Think about your values and sense of mission vis-a-vis your business. Have you and your spouse clearly articulated it together? How do you see your business, and your life, in ten years?

Strong Work/Family Boundaries and Balance

The couple manages both a household and a business, and it needs to separate roles and responsibilities in each. This is even more difficult if the business is run out of the house. Part of the management problem is who will pick up the kids, or who is responsible for housework. Finances are often enmeshed as well. Some copreneurs adopt traditional household sex roles and responsibilities, while others consciously share house roles as they share business responsibilities.

There is always spillover between work and personal lives. The most common instances are the ways the partners respond to each other as spouses at work. Everyone who works with copreneurs is familiar with the little ways that their personal lives show in the office. Spouses snap at each other, whisper to one another in meetings, remark on each other's dress, or make inside jokes. This can make employees ill at ease, as they feel they are observing private behavior, which they are. Successful copreneurs have learned to rein in this tendency, or at least to help everyone become comfortable with their behavior.

Successful copreneurs develop ways to maintain personal/work balance. They talk about having two relationships, one at work and one at home. They don't have business meetings in the bedroom, for example, or over dinner. They take non-business vacations where they don't talk about work. They try, with their limited time, to cultivate friends and hobbies. The most successful copreneurs have things they enjoy doing together other than business. They extend the intense sharing of their work relationship to other projects or hobbies. Once they have learned to share, there seems to be no difficulty in sharing non-work projects and time together. They like being together by doing, one couple said.

Exercise: Separating Work and Family

Think about your relationship in relation to your personal time and work time. Divide a piece of paper in half, and on the left write the activities that you do together as a couple and family, and on the right the ones at work. After you have completed your list, draw a line and continue listing activities that you would like to add in each area.

Now share your lists with your spouse. Talk together about how you could expand the personal side of the list, and limit some of the work activities, without the business suffering. Be creative.

Good Communication and Conflict Resolution

Entrepreneurs must be prepared to make mistakes and deal with stress. The copreneur must be able to accept setbacks, disappointments, pressures, and differences of opinion without having them poison the personal relationship. Successful copreneurs know each other well enough to share differences without hostility. One wife told me she knew exactly when and how to bring up an issue with her husband. It was not fear of confrontation, but rather respect for his style and care about their spousal relationship, that made her so careful in this area.

A copreneur cannot blame his or her spouse for setbacks. One of the greatest sources of difficulty and even failure in couple business comes when spouses blame each other for business problems. For example, one wife was continually blaming her husband for some poor tactical decisions. The result was that he avoided making any more decisions. Their business became paralyzed, and their relationship continued to build hostility. This was one of the few copreneurial businesses that I have seen fail due to relationship problems.

The different styles of a couple can lead to conflict. For example, in many copreneurial businesses, one spouse is more people-oriented, while the other is more technical, numbers, and systems-oriented. This would be a classic sex role stereotyping if a significant number of couples did not have these talents reversed. There are tough, hard, numbers-oriented women, and soft, caring men. However, the couple has to value these differences, not fight over them. For example, one couple ran a natural food store, with Wednesday morning staff meetings. The two found themselves continually at odds, with the wife angry at her husband for not caring enough about people. They would leave the meeting and continue at dinner and into bed what they both called "the Wednesday night fights." They eventually tempered their conflict by temporarily switching roles: the wife tried to mind the numbers, and the husband worked with the staff. Each gained an appreciation for the other's position.

Another way to avoid conflict is to define clearly what tasks each partner will achieve and when. The other spouse is then expected to back off and not actively interfere. Each person should be held accountable, but there should be allowance for doing it his or her own way.

In addition, couples who can leave the stresses, worries, and problems of the business at work greatly value that defense mechanism. They come back to the problems the next day, after a rest. A good example of this was revealed in a recent newspaper article about a wife who picketed her husband's office because he would not give her a raise as his office manager. She was serious, and he was stubborn, but she admitted that she left her crusade at the office door. They were not, however, equal partners in their business.

Other copreneurs have a friend whom they talk to about the problems they are facing. As one couple said, "it is difficult to come home and complain about your partner to your spouse, when your spouse is your partner. Sometimes it seems as if the work day just continues at home." Friends do what a traditional spouse does: give an outside perspective. Some couples talk about how, to get some time apart, they regularly go out to dinner with friends and without their spouse. As busy as they are, it seems critical for copreneurs to have other people they can confide in.

Families and relationships often survive by avoiding issues. One person is the peacemaker, or keeps the lid on things. Several copreneurs mentioned that this pattern of not talking about issues led to difficulties when they were in business together. For example, a man who is extremely controlling and overbearing, whose wife had accepted his behavior, ran into difficulty in business. They had to deal with the effect of his behavior on employees, and he had to learn to let go of pressures and trust other people.

Copreneurs, like all successful couples, must learn to check in with each other regularly about potential problems to avoid misunderstandings. Taking a few minutes at the start or end of each day to clear things up and talk about feelings is a successful tool.

Copreneurs also need a conflict resolution process. Many couples have agreed that their businesses are 51-49%, with one person having the deciding vote if there is disagreement. This makes good business sense. Esprit was unable to function as long as Doug and Susie Tompkins each had equal say in management and ownership. Their business conflict escalated as their personal relationship ended. Their creditors finally forced them to put a tie-breaker person on the board and to hire independent management. Finally, the conflict was resolved when she got financing to buy him out. This was the first thing the couple had agreed about in years.

Exercise: Resolving Areas of Disagreement

Think about the areas you and your spouse disagree or feel differently about, at work and in your personal life. Think especially about those in which you think the other will not change, or which you avoid or do not bring up. List the issues and then write what you want or feel, and what you think your spouse wants or feels about each issue.

Now talk about each of the issues on your list. Take them one at a time, with no more than one per session. You both should take time to present your perspective, need, feeling, or desire. The other should just listen, without interrupting. Then begin to explore each issue to see if you can agree on a common ground.

Clear, Differentiated Complementary Roles

Within their shared vision of the business, copreneurs need to have clearly defined, separate roles. The most common arrangement is some form of inside/outside or technical/people division of labor. It is rare for one person to have all the skills to run a business. With copreneurs, there are two chances to get the right mix. That is one source of the power of copreneurships. But this mix can't be utilized unless each spouse needs to respect the other person's turf. If not, one person can undermine the other, creating confusion and difficulty for employees.

An example. The wife of a chef, who ran the dining room of their restaurant, kept hearing complaints from staff, who felt her husband was rude and overbearing. She would cool them down, apologize for him, smooth things over. But she never told her husband so his behavior did not change. Their staff problems got worse and worse. In effect, she was protecting him by depriving him of the information he needed to change. She also was interfering with his supervision of his staff—if she respected his role, she should have told them to go to him. A resolution only came when the entire staff met and began to give the chef feedback, and he learned to listen to their feelings and moderate his temper.

Another couple had difficulty because, when the husband did not do some of the things that were expected of him, his wife did them. He began to be less and less clear about his role, and she became angrier and angrier at him. Finally, he had to leave the business. He had never identified, and taken responsibility for, a clear role, and his wife was never really willing to let go of any responsibility. She was a solo entrepreneur masquerading as a copreneur. Some copreneurships mask relationships where this ultimately turns out to be the case.

While roles have to be clearly defined and complementary, they can also be flexible or changeable. One of the exciting possibilities in a copreneurial business is for each participant to learn new skills and shift roles from time to time. For example, a wife joined her husband, who was a decade older and well-established, in a corporate design agency. After ten years together, he became tired and wanted to take more time off. The agency suffered, and his wife became frustrated because he wasn't doing what he traditionally had done. He felt bad about it too, but just wasn't motivated in the same way any more. They needed to see that she wanted to grow in the business, and he wanted to pull back. When they agreed to change roles, and put her in the central position, both felt more energized.

The Orsborn Group is a small, ten-year-old public relations agency owned by Dan and Carol Orsborn. Originally Carol was president, but subsequently Dan took over and Carol became a senior account representative in order to have more time to raise their two children and promote a book she wrote. When Carol returned, they decided on a joint presidency. While the two have different styles and personalities, they both know how to run the business, so this shared role arrangement can work. This flexibility allows them the freedom to develop personal talents and projects outside the business.

Exercise: Role Clarification

Write down your role in the business, what you do, and what you are responsible for. Now write down your spouse's role. If it is relevant, add the roles of other members of top management of your business.

Now share the lists and discuss how clear you are on your roles and responsibilities. Where are there areas of overlap, and possible conflict?

Divorce

Divorce severs the copreneurs' relationship and thereby poses a grave threat to the business. When a couple separates, the business is in limbo. Who will get custody of the company?

Horror stories abound. One wife who had developed a business with her husband decided to divorce him. The next day the board fired her, so she lost two relationships, not one. Another woman who founded a business asked her new husband to join her when they married. The business thrived, but their relationship did not. Since their separation, he has tried to get control of the company, provoking a nasty series of lawsuits. The wife of the president of Schering, a family business, sat on the board of directors for years with no management role. One day she ended her 30-year marriage and since has tried to get the board to agree to a sale of the company, pitting her in a proxy fight and lawsuit against her former husband. Portia Isaacson Wright has been married five times, and in business with three of her husbands.[5]

There is little that can be done about this unfortunate ending to a relationship. It is very rare for a couple to split and still maintain its working relationship, though a few couples try. For example, the rock group Fleetwood Mac contained two former couples, and their most successful record was about the breakup of their relationships.

The possibility of intervention comes earlier when the marriage is strained and the couple tries to mediate or resolve its issues. A spouse who leaves suddenly and without warning has not been communicating very well. If a couple senses separation as a possibility, perhaps they can try to arrange the orderly disengagement of one from the business.

Partners regularly have complex buy-sell arrangements, which regulate and finance the buy-out in the event of death or disability of one of them, and such an arrangement would be possible for copreneurs. But just as many people feel it is bad luck to arrange a pre-nuptial agreement about a possible divorce, so copreneurs are reluctant to create contingency plans for a failure. However, given that the fate of a business involves more than just the two people in the couple, this attitude is unwise. Just as it is hard to face one's death and plan for succession, so a couple in love cannot imagine the opposite. But it often happens and consequently should be planned for.

The Couple Retreat

Copreneurship has so many pitfalls that the only way to succeed is to be conscious of what one is doing, and talk frequently and at length with your partner about all aspects of business and personal relationships. Communication can be done in bits and pieces, and you may already be communicating well. But copreneurs need to plan their relationships just as owners plan their business. One tool that all copreneurs can use to enhance their effectiveness and communication is to create a special time to look at what they want, where they are, where they are going, and how they want to get there.

A powerful vehicle for this is the couple retreat—one to three days away from home or work where couples look systematically at their life, their relationship and their work, in mutual exploration and problem-solving. This is an adaption of the family retreat, but even if other family members are part of the business, the couple retreat is intended as a renewal process for them alone. The purpose of the retreat is to share more deeply than they can in the pressure of daily life, and to step back and look at their tasks from a broader perspective.

While family business retreats contain many family members, and are often facilitated by a consultant/resource person, couple retreats work better when the couple are alone. I often work with copreneurs to explore the issues and plan their retreats, but they always conduct them on their own. Unless they have a very serious conflict needing mediation, this should suffice.

Before the retreat, take time to reflect on goals, issues, and values concerning your business, family, and life. Think about your family's communication, roles, work/family boundaries. Consider also your personal growth plan, support groups and friendships, family and children, and finances. You can use some of the exercises in earlier chapters to clarify where you are and what you want. Begin by looking at each of these in relation to yourself, without sharing with your spouse yet. Couples often develop a joint reality between them that is so powerful that taking the time on your own before sharing is very important. Define what you want for yourself before you adapt to your spouse.

The retreat should be punctuated with special times for doing things together. You might go to a romantic place near the water or prepare a gourmet meal. Be sure to take quiet time to be together. Sometimes walking quietly can help you get into focus and see pressures in a different way.

The first part of the retreat involves each of you looking at your personal, career, and family goals. What do you want? What are your ultimate goals?—they don't have to be "realistic." Try to listen to your partner not as if you already know what he or she is going to say, but as if you are hearing things for the first time. One technique that is critical: don't interrupt, and take care that you keep the focus on one person at a time. Couples have a tendency to change the subject, ramble, or shift focus without even noticing. If you are the person presenting, your spouse should keep his or her goals to himself or herself until you shift focus. This is critical to success!

After you have shared individual goals, dreams, and visions, then you should take time to develop a shared vision of the personal and family life you seek. Sometimes couples have been so involved in work that they haven't shared their values about children, friends, family, or their life apart from, and after, work. Take time to write down the central elements of each person's dream. Then work to develop a shared vision.

Next look at your key goals and develop clear ways to achieve them. For example, when it comes to having more intimate time, couples have come up with solutions like setting aside one evening a week or one weekend every two months, where they go out or go away or have a special time, when they do not talk about work. They keep that time sacred, just like important business meetings. Or they try to spend a family night with children, where everyone has time to talk about him or herself.

The next phase of the retreat involves creating a vision of your business and how each of you can make it happen. One important topic to cover is what each person does in the business, his or her specific roles and responsibilities. Then look at how the areas overlap, and how they work together. In what areas do your roles lead to possible conflict? Are the conflicts about turf or about how the business will run? You especially need to look to the future of the business and how each of you want to fit into it.

Sometimes copreneurs find that they need to broaden their management team, bring in additional managers, or even begin to withdraw from everyday operations. Think about the next phases of your business, and how you want to participate in it.

After the retreat, you both should have clarity about your plans for enriching the personal, family, and business dimensions of your life. Make sure you have goals and an action plan, and you both check up on them. Don't let things drop! Taking a retreat several times a year is important for your personal and business health as a couple.

Whenever a couple works together, they need to work on the areas presented in this chapter. In addition, they need to attend to the other issues in a family business including bringing in family members, planning for succession, and employee-family relations. In the next chapter, we begin to explore the two generational family business.

Notes:

1. Nelton, Sharon. *In Love and In Business.*
2. Barnett, Frank and Sharan. *Working Together.*
3. Home Business Line, Editorial, Dec., 1987.
4. Berger, Peter, and Kellner, Hansfried. "Marriage and the Social Construction of Reality."
5. Machan, Dyan. "My Partner, My Spouse." *Forbes*, December 14, 1987.

6

A Tough
Act to
Follow:
Growing up
Into a
Family Business

"I must study war, so that my sons may have the liberty to study mathematics and philosophy, navigation, commerce and agriculture, in order to give their children a right to study painting, poetry, music, architecture, and tapestry."
-John Adams, 1780

Marvin and Harold Fagel, son and father, had a close but difficult relationship in the company Marvin's grandfather started.[1] Marvin and his younger brother Mike grew up around Harold's Midway Meat Co., a meat packing business in Chicago. Time with Harold was spent at the plant. Marvin knew he was the heir apparent, and entered the business after college and "boot camp" in the Chicago stockyards. Like many family business fathers, Harold believed he had to be harder on his son than other employees, and had difficulty giving up any authority to his son. He was critical of Marvin, always demanding more of him and almost never praising him. Luckily, Marvin had a good sense of his own abilities and was able to develop even under this oppressive regime. But his father would not let him in on financial information, trading, or other essential aspects of the business. Marvin became frustrated, especially when he experienced a taste of authority on one of his father's infrequent vacations. Finally, he had enough.

One day, a customer made him an offer: to start a new specialty meat business. Marvin was able to talk about his frustration with his father, and asked Harold to stake him in the new venture. Marvin wanted to make his own mistakes, learn, and prove to Harold and himself that he had the stuff to take over. The business was as hard as any small start-up, and Marvin had problems with his partner, whom he eventually bought out. But the business thrived, and surprisingly, so did his relationship with Harold. They were now peers, and were able to collaborate and share the joy and struggle of founding a new business. After a few years, Harold offered him the supreme compliment: he offered to buy him out. Here was a dilemma: was it the time for Marvin to come back? Would Harold offer him real authority now that he had proven himself? Marvin accepted the offer and returned to work with his father, not without some of the same problems, but with Harold's newfound respect and willingness to share control.

While Marvin successfully developed a working relationship with his dad, and earned his independence and self-esteem, other sons and daughters of family business founders find this task more difficult. Too often they don't know how to find the opportunity to grow in a family business, or to have their fathers see them as mature. Being able to work well with Dad and feeling he will be willing to eventually turn over the reins of power is but one of the difficult questions surrounding the decision to enter the family business.

Tasks for the Chapter

This chapter explores coming to terms with the family inheritance and deciding whether or not you should join the business. This is not a one-time decision or an easy one. It can take many years, and involve several trips in and out of the business. There is a great divide between the business needing you, or your relatives wanting you there, and the reality of whether it is a good idea for you or the business over the long-term.

If you are a son or daughter whose family has a business, this chapter will help you decide whether to join the family business. You will look at yourself and the opportunities in the business, and decide if it is right for you. Members of the older generation can use this chapter to look at their hopes, aspirations, and ways of presenting them to their children and heirs. You will explore the best way to invite your children in.

The most consequential decision a family business heir has to make is whether to join the business. Despite this, many sons and daughters make this decision almost unconsciously. They may assume they will join and never give it much thought. Or they fall into it—there may be a crisis and they start to help out. Then they never leave. Or they enter the business because they've lost a job and don't have a clear idea of other alternatives. They find themselves working in the business without a strong sense of why they are there or where they are going. A decade later, when they begin to burn out, they ask themselves, "Why did I do it?"

One heir told me that, when he was vice-president of the family firm, he had stomach pains so severe that he was afraid he had cancer. They were increasingly disabling. Finally he heeded the message and left to pursue a career as a professor. His pains never returned. As this example graphically depicts, you can't just enter the family business by default. You need to make a positive commitment to join, and that decision has to be for the right reasons.

Joining the business is a decision fraught with all kinds of emotional issues for both parents and heirs. For an heir, joining is one way of coming to terms with the family legacy. For the older generation, their children's entry represents continuity, immortality, acceptance, and ultimate validation. But for heirs, siblings, relatives, and in-laws, joining the business represents a double-edged sword: it can provide a form of validation and affirmation that has so far eluded them, and it can also be the setting for continuation of pain, competition, rivalries, and struggles that began, and have their rightful place, only in the family.

For any son or daughter entering the business, the feeling that Dad needs help, that the family is calling upon you, or that you owe it something, leaves many of them with confused, complex, and conflicted motivations. For younger siblings, seeing an older brother or sister enter the business can define their future. It may mean that the possibility of getting close to Father is closed to them (or at least they feel it is), or that they are free of a burden and can pursue their own destiny. Other problems arise when an heir can't do the job, when there's rivalry among siblings ("Daddy always loved you more"), or when an heir brings unresolved issues from childhood to work, such as anger at the father's absence while growing up.

Entering the business can offer the promise of redeeming a relationship with your parents. One daughter, spending a summer interning as her father's secretary, noted that by driving to the office with her father and working near him, she could finally see what he did. It made them closer than ever before. Doris Hurley, whose parents founded Haagen-Dazs Ice Cream Company, notes, "As a child, you don't necessarily understand what is going on when you have parents who are completely dedicated to their business." The resentments she felt as a girl were healed somewhat when she began to work in the company and could finally understand her parents' perspective.[2] However, the need to resolve childhood issues could carry you into the business without your having a genuine career reason for joining.

Growing Up in a Family Business

Personality develops out of the child's struggle to define himself or herself within the setting of the family. The child of a business founder is deeply etched by the demanding presence of the business, its rewards and consequences, and the strong character of the parent who created it.

The primary experience of children growing up in family business is that the business is Number One. Its problems, joys, and reality hover over the household, and children frequently feel neglected or left out. Many of them never feel they have their father's attention, and this void marks their character.

Sibling rivalry has a special dimension for family business heirs. No matter how special, how talented, or how commanding you may be, the most important sibling in your family is the business itself. The world of growing up is forever charged by the business, where Dad (and often Mom) spent time and lavished attention. Sons and daughters alike remember wondering whether they could compete with the business for their parent's attention. The mysterious, intense conversations, the sudden crises, the months when money is a problem, all stem from this overwhelming entity called the business. Now they are considering joining what has been their rival all these years!

Children learn about the family business by watching and listening to their parents. One son heard his father come home every night and rage on about the stupidity of his employees and the aggravation of the business. He never said anything positive about it. After college, when his father invited him to join, the son said, "Are you kidding! After seeing the grief it caused you, I couldn't imagine working there." He never saw the positive side because his father only communicated the stress.

As this story demonstrates, business owners must recognize the messages they give their potential heirs. If their parents had little time for the family, they may regard joining the business as an invitation to do the same. I asked one of my sons if he wanted to go into my business when he grew up, and his response was, "No way, you work too hard." So much for sensitive fathers.

It's never too soon to talk about the business. If possibilities are shared early on, then the topic is legitimate and comfortable. Learning about the family business is really training in business in general. Many heirs value informal family seminars when they go on to other careers. It's important for the business to be a positive possibility, but not become the grand prize, with one winner and many dissatisfied losers. Not wanting to go into the business shouldn't be a defeat for the owner/parent, and not having the right aptitudes or desire shouldn't make a son or daughter feel diminished. Parents should be involved in the exploration of many career options with each child through high school and college. The family business can be a setting for summer jobs and a learning experience about the world of work.

The Marriott family is typical of business families that are successful in getting heirs involved in the business. When he was eight, Bill Marriott started going on business trips with his father. By his teens he was cooking in company restaurants, and his teenage son David has started the same way.

The particulars of your family business will influence your attitudes. I grew up inside my parents' family business. Our house was right in the middle of their school. During breakfast every day, the teaching staff and the bus drivers all came by to get their keys and messages. So instead of feeling deserted by the business, the business was part of my house. Many children of family businesses start helping out very early. One five-year-old I know was given a business card for her birthday, which she proudly gave to her friends. Children can be taught to associate pride and achievement with working in the business, and to understand what their parents are doing there all day. Contrast this with a family where the children never see where their father goes to work, but they hear every day of how the employees are stealing, customers won't pay, and the government takes every penny from him!

But business families can have an opposite set of norms. The business can remain something of a mystery to the household. In many cases entrepreneurs keep control over the business by keeping everything to themselves. They find it hard to share information with anyone. One fifth-generation daughter of a famous "and Sons" public company told me that her father never mentioned business at home. After college, she took a summer job in the company and decided she liked it. Since her two brothers did not elect to join, she will become chairperson when her father retires. She wishes she had learned more about the business while growing up, but girls then were simply not considered relevant. But things have changed. To help prepare for her eventual chairmanship of the business, the company recently hired a woman as CEO!

John Connelly's three sons had a better experience. After his divorce, he took custody of his three teenage sons. Each day at dinner, they would talk about what had happened in his furniture business that day. The boys greatly enjoyed the companionship and learning, which also included many weekends of sailing together. I met the Connellys when they sailed to one of my family business weekend seminars. After college, each son entered one of the family businesses. Steve, the middle son, works with his wife running the family furniture store. His older and younger brothers work in another business recently started by John. John himself plans to retire soon with his new wife, and leave one business to each of his sons.

Growing up in a family business also involves coming to terms with the powerful personality of the founder/owner of the business. The entrepreneur is a person whose vision strives for expression, who is used to having his way, and who has been hugely successful by the time the child comes of age. Dad the founder sets the tone of the household, and defines what is important. Entrepreneurs generally have a hard time listening to anyone, let alone their children. Many heirs note that their relationships with Dad were more lectures than exchanges. They may feel subtle, or more overt, pressure to be a certain way. Frustration of the need for Dad's approval can set up a cycle of endless seeking. Some heirs enter the business thinking that they will finally get approval from their fathers. They rarely get it at that late date, finding instead that the same cycle of invalidation continues. They have to find their own ways to build self-esteem.

In addition, the family's money can be a powerful, even coercive pressure to go along with the family. The threat that the money will be withdrawn, combined with the carrot of continuing wealth and a starting salary more than any 25-year-old could earn on his or her own, moves many heirs into the family business orbit.

Exercise: Images and Memories of the Business

Think back as far as you can. For each decade of your life, write down a list of the pictures, the impressions, the statements by your parents, and your own thoughts and fantasies about the business. Try to generate specific images; remember conversations and your visits there.

After writing down each impression, reflect on what message or conclusion you drew from the event. For example, after your first visit to the manufacturing plant, you may have viewed your father as a magical wizard ruling over a mysterious kingdom. Your conclusion might be something like, "My father is very powerful," or "This is the most exciting and wonderful place I can imagine." These early impressions color your decision to join, and your sense of what the business is. How do you see these impressions affecting you today as you face your decisions about your future inside or outside the family business?

Potential Values Clash

The family values and ways of doing business are a powerful resource for a young person, but joining the business and taking them on can be a painful burden. In many businesses, the family name is on the door and on the product. Heirs are expected to continue the family's tradition, even as they go in new directions. As one family business heir said, "That's my name, and my parents', on the door. People know what we stand for. I can't do anything that might question that. It's a powerful responsibility. Sometimes I wish I could be more anonymous."

The founder has one perspective. The sons and daughters who may inherit the business have another. They are not necessarily entrepreneurs, as their dad (or mom) may have been. For them the business has always been there, and the most important decision they will make in their early adulthood is whether or not to become part of it. If they do enter the business, they often generate a new, sometimes quite different vision, of what the business can be.

Today, a new generation of family business heirs is redefining American business. Many of these "kinpreneurs" elect to move into management positions and eventually become the owner/managers. This generation differs profoundly from their parents, who were children of the Depression, World War II, and the fifties. These baby boomers, coming into awareness in the sixties, bring to work a new set of values and commitment to a new management style. They are experimenters, educated more broadly both in school and in work/life experience. They want to take their businesses into new directions, reflecting new values. They also face a new business climate, with heightened competition and pressure to increase productivity, cut costs, and precisely define strategy on a global scale.

The new family business generation embodies a shift in basic workplace values. Many of the intergenerational battles in family businesses today have, at the core, conflicting values about how to do business. The old and young generations fight the battle over business innovation in every workplace. But in family business the battles can be more personal and more difficult. Some of the qualities of the old and new values are:

In a traditional business:
• Firm was patriarchal, passed on to oldest son;
• Founder worked and kept power until his death;
• Business cycles slower, more predictable;
• Values not in conflict;
• Women in helper roles: men at work/woman at home;
• Issues weren't discussed directly: silence and secrecy.

In today's business:
• Successor can be any son, daughter, in-law, or outsider;
• Succession often occurs in prime of founder's life;
• Business characterized by continual change, pressure;
• Different goals and values for business, work, and life;
• Women are part of home and work, figure actively in management;
• Communication and sharing of values, feelings and issues is key.

These value differences are too often acted out as a battle for control over which way is right or wrong. Neither way is necessarily better, although today the younger generation expresses the newer values more frequently in their business dealings. Fathers' fear of being forgotten and their need to be given credit for their achievements sometimes make it difficult for them to be open to the new perspective. The shift of generations, played against the shift of business practice, can create a difficult conflict, as the feelings from the family are superimposed on the feelings about the business.

Value differences, which are manageable within families as each person grows in a different direction, create conflict in determining the direction of the business. The heir wants to be true to him or herself and his or her emerging values, as well as respect the tradition and legacy of the father. So one of the issues in deciding whether to enter the business is coming to terms with the values expressed by the older generation and seeing whether the potential for expression of yours, if different, is available.

When one social activist son finally joined his father in his business, they had to deal with how important social responsibility would be as a factor in determining what projects to support. In the end, the father deferred to the son, but in other families such value issues are wrenching.

Heirs' Struggle for Identity

Many struggles for personal identity are painful and difficult, but nowhere is this more true than for family business heirs. It has been said that it is nearly impossible for the son or daughter of the founder to develop an independent sense of identity. If you realize anything less than perfection and the now-idealized achievements of Dad, you are a failure. But if the business grows and thrives, people say the whole thing was handed to you. In addition, jealous siblings, in-laws, and relatives hover around, sniping and undercutting your efforts and legitimacy.

An heir of a strong parent has a difficult task. He or she must find some way to be distinguished, and create a separate identity. Often doing this while remaining in the business is impossible. Some heirs create their identity in conflict with their parents. The grandson of R. J. Reynolds put his fortune into a campaign against smoking, and John Robbins, Baskin-Robbins ice cream heir, has become a critic of the processed food industry. Others find different ways to pursue the traditional family goals or values. One of Robert Kennedy's sons took a decade to create an alternate energy company in Massachusetts, before entering the family business of politics, just as President Bush created an oil company in his early years, before following in his political father's footsteps.

Yet the second and third generation members of family businesses often achieve a healthy sense of identity, feel a deep sense of achievement and finally get the "respect" from company and family that Rodney Dangerfield is always lacking. Those that are successful find a way to fulfill themselves, even though they inherit a business and a tradition, because the business they inherit comes complete with a new challenge, or they see a new initiative or select a new task. In short, they create a new business from the old one.

Coping with inheritance of family wealth can be an identity struggle as well. A recent article on "affluenza," the struggle for identity among people born into wealth and status, cites the costs, benefits, and parameters of the struggle to forge an identity out of a cradle of privilege. Some family business heirs have trusts and stock that mean they do not have to work for a living. John Levy, a consultant who works with heirs of family fortunes, has written about how this can infantalize the heir, causing significant psychological distress. Levy describes a syndrome where heirs never feel a sense of their own capacity, a sense of meaningful commitment to something, or an ability to come to terms with who they are and what they want to do. Coupled with that, American culture is highly ambivalent about inherited wealth. It is fine to earn money from your own business, but not to have money from your family. For a youngster, an inheritance can be a burden as well as a gift.[3]

Many wealthy heirs struggle with drugs, confusion, or destructive relationships until they come to terms with their inheritance. In effect, heirs feel deprived of the opportunity to make it themselves, because of the success of parents or grandparents. This phenomena prompted *Fortune* to run a cover article about how some CEOs had decided not to give their children more than a modest inheritance, or to delay the inheritance until they were close to middle age. They wanted their children to be comfortable, but not to take away from them the opportunity to create their own lives.[4]

Psychologist Judy Barber, who specializes in counseling about personal relationships to money, notes that four factors seem to characterize heirs who come to terms with their gifts:

1. They have role models and mentors to whom they can talk about their feelings and dilemmas.

2. They make their own choices about professional advisors. In this way they create their own investment and earning philosophy and methods.

3. They find a support group of peers to share the questions that come up. Networks of inheritors who focus on personal struggles as well as defining a socially responsible personal approach to investment, have been formed around the country, and heirs who are comfortable with their situation often take advantage of these.

4. They discover a purposeful way to contribute to society. They discover that work is not just having a job to make money. There are many ways that they can use their gifts and advantages to make important contributions. One of the ways is by finding a new meaning or reason for commitment to the family business. If they didn't earn their fortunes, at least they can use it well, and consciously.[5]

Discovering Yourself: The Hero's Journey

Since a sense of personal identity is so crucial to every human being, how does a family business heir develop one? In *The Power of Myth*, Joseph Campbell[6] uses the mythic hero's journey as a parable for personal development. The hero's perilous journey is a metaphoric model of the personal challenges an individual must overcome in self-development. In mythology, the young person can't just stay home, grow up, enter Dad's business, marry the girl next door, and find wealth, status, happiness, and fulfillment. Self-development, or any type of growth, can't occur without struggle. Studies of career development of high-level executives at the Center for Creative Leadership show that top managers report a career with strenuous challenges, several tough changes, and a variety of difficult assignments. This often cannot be provided in the family business.

The reason why a family business is usually not a good place to grow and develop is that the hero has to leave home. The hero's journey begins when he (the hero myth is about male development) wakes up to a call, and leaves his family and begins a quest for something important. This quest develops his inner talents. Through the quest, he builds himself; he isn't given a self whole. Like all heroes, the prospective family business heir needs to see himself apart and independent from the family. Unfortunately the family business sometimes does a strange job of short-circuiting personal development by making a seductive offer to the hero to stay at home and not grow.

The experience of those who stay in the business is instructive. First of all, it is hard for them to learn. How does an employee confront or push a person who will be the boss in a few years? As I was given a tour of a gigantic family business, the manager pointed to a young person sitting in a training session: "That's Don H., who will be our CEO in 20 years." The young heir is rarely if ever given a performance review or allowed to earn a paycheck. One son told me, "I would ask people how was I doing, and all I'd ever hear was, 'just fine'." Another family I know had five sons, each of them instantly a vice-president. As near as I could tell, one of them was vice-president in charge of bicycle deliveries at 22.

In order to cope with the emotional pressures of not knowing how they are really doing and being treated as special, heirs often close off the outside world. They fear and avoid feedback or learning. I am amazed at how few family business heirs take management development courses. While middle-managers at most companies take courses regularly to develop additional skills, family business heirs tend to avoid learning. It is almost as if they secretly doubt themselves, and are afraid to test themselves with outside feedback. One younger son, who had always worked for his father, was having a terrible time learning to manage people. He finally went to a course in supervision, and, for the first time in his life, received clear feedback on how he came across to others. He also received some good coaching on how to get better results from others. But in the company neither his father, nor his brother, nor the employees were able to teach him.

There are some special situations where an heir goes directly into the family business, and personal development does occur. But they feature a real challenge to overcome. For example, just as Rick was finishing business school, his father, who owned a furniture store, had a heart attack. Rick and his younger brother came in to help out, and within two years, the father was dead. They were both so young that the manufacturer whose goods they sold fully expected that they would sell the business. But with their mother's support, they decided to keep it. Since they had to learn quickly and on their own, their personal development took place within the family business. They were not struggling against their father, but rather were maintaining his legacy while developing their own identities.

Other family businesses send their children to divisions far away from home for seasoning, as English gentlemen used to be sent to the Continent. Hong Kong business families often send their sons to run businesses in San Francisco. This gives them the opportunity to work in a community that does not know their family, and offers a suitable challenge which enables them to grow.

Estee Lauder is one of the few women business founders of a Fortune 500 company. She has also helped her oldest son develop into her successor. Leonard was able to go on his own "hero's journey" inside the company, because, early on, it was recognized that he had special competencies not shared by his mother/founder. He was an organizer, an internal leader, which the company needed to continue its wildly-successful growth. Internally his achievements and authority are clear and obvious.

The company has had its family difficulties. By the time younger brother Ron entered the company, Leonard was already the heir apparent. Ron complained that, even after several years, when he gave an order people would check it with Leonard. Finally he left the company, and has pursued a political career, most recently spending a great deal of money on a fruitless race for mayor of New York. The consensus is that Ronald is struggling to gain his own identity, separate from brother and mother. However, inheriting close to half the family-owned company should help fund his projects.

The journey to work in another company is a rich seasoning experience for a prospective recruit to the family business. Ideally, you should spend several years in one or two jobs with other companies. As one founder put it, "Let them make their mistakes in other people's businesses." It offers a chance to get away from the family and to be known for your personal achievements. You will not have to deal with people knowing your father or mother, and your work will be evaluated on its merits. For a wealthy person, receiving your own pay check for your own work is a special gift as well. But, most important, serving an apprenticeship at another company enables you to see how another company is run. One small bank owner sends his children to work in larger banks. He wants them to learn how to work in the organization their bank will become, not the one it is.

Other heirs work in professional service or consulting firms. This experience is invaluable. As an accountant or lawyer, you can see many companies and learn skills you will need for management. When you return to the family business, it will be more as a peer, with the experience and ideas that the business may need to grow. When Dad or Mom want to do things the way they've always done them, you can say, "Well, with all due respect, you ought to know that most companies are switching to this inventory system, or marketing this way."

Working for another company is the first stage of your personal development journey. It often involves living away from the family, and may involve the development of intimate relationships, marriage and children. Separation from family of origin seems to be a prerequisite for adulthood. Staying inside the family business is sometimes like a child who never leaves the parents' house.

Every young hero also needs a mentor, an older parent-like teacher who can teach, sponsor, and protect. The mentor relationship combines features of an intimate, family-like bond with the accountability of the workplace. The mentor takes a special liking to the young hero, seeing his talent and raw ability. He or she takes a personal interest in his development, much like a parent. But unlike a parent-child tie, the relationship is two-way. The young person must respond to the tutelage by achieving results, and is expected to support the mentor's work. A mentor teaches about organizational politics, and sponsors a young person for greater responsibility. The young mentee learns about working for an authority figure who is not Dad or Mom. It is very difficult for a parent to be a mentor. The personal baggage children have of looking for approval, or rejecting authority, or simply not listening to someone they have always known, make it difficult for parents to act as mentors.

The young hero-in-training also needs a unique, creative achievement to reach personal identity. At work, this means starting something such as a new product introduction or opening a new division. This is the chance to develop and demonstrate leadership, and teaches skills and tools that will later be called upon in the family company.

Leadership effectiveness is not inherited, and it doesn't come from merely serving time in the family business and learning how to do things. To be an effective leader, you need to overcome significant challenges, have confidence in yourself, and possess the wisdom of personal experience and the ability to listen to others. Just as a soldier can only test his courage in battle, so you can only learn your leadership ability by actually leading. Several types of challenges are important to your development as a leader. You not only need to know how to complete a major project and direct people, but also to admit mistakes and deal with adversity. This can only come through experience.

Self Assessment: Your Development as a Leader

Thinking about your career, write down the activities that you have done or experiences you have had that helped you to develop in these areas. Reflect on what you have learned about yourself from each type of experience:

1. *Receiving negative feedback about my performance;*
2. *Completing a major project;*
3. *Directing a large group of people;*
4. *Dealing with adversity, such as a personal failure;*
5. *Developing key management/leadership skills;*
6. *Negotiating a conflict between two people or groups;*
7. *Admitting a mistake;*
8. *Rising above a personal setback;*
9. *Learning how things are done at other businesses;*
10. *Taking on a project that is above my head.*

Extending the Proper Invitation

Parents also make it difficult for heirs to enter the business. There are lots of reasons. One of the most profound is that founders are often ambivalent about their children succeeding them. Some are downright hostile, like the troubled father in the movie *The Great Santini*, who couldn't accept his son beating him in a one-on-one basketball game. Edsel, the son of Henry Ford, was by all accounts the model son, always trying to please his father and possessing the moderation, taste, intelligence, diligence, and drive that make for a perfect second generation business successor. However, Henry never missed a chance to tell Edsel how poorly he was doing, and undermine his authority in the company. Even when Edsel was president and Henry was ostensibly retired, Henry called the shots. Edsel's tragic death to cancer before he was 50 is attributed by many to the abuse from his dad, whom, to the end, he never confronted. Today there is more legitimacy for the son to rebel, and if Edsel was a child of the sixties or seventies, he might have started his own company, or fought his father more directly. He might not have been so afraid of his father's disapproval, or so impaired by it.

If you are a founder, you should be aware of your assumptions and attitudes about training your children in the family business. Many men of the "old school" believe that they have to be toughest on their sons, that their children have to start at the bottom, that praise will soften their children. If you believe this, ask your children how these assumptions sound to them. From the child's perspective, these attitudes translate into "Why do I have to be punished for being his kid"; "I never know what he thinks of me or whether I'm doing a good job"; "I'm not going to be an office boy in his business when so-and-so will offer me $50,000 to start." Many sons and daughters feel almost brutalized and permanently scarred by the experience of working for a distant and demanding father. They feel constantly on the spot. Even coming to one's parents for a family dinner can lead to a performance evaluation. They may never feel they are good enough to measure up to Father's expectations.

The way a parent invites children to join the business also sets the stage for the future. As we've seen, the family business is powerful, grown-up, and mysterious to young children. So it's helpful to send messages about how your children can fit in. One cartoon I've seen shows a father standing next to a baby carriage, pointing to smoke stacks and saying, "Someday son, this will all be yours!"

However, the message gets more complicated as a child grows older. For example, one father told his children that they could expect nothing from the business that he built. His son Jack told me, "Growing up was crazy. Everybody in school looked at me and told me I was the richest kid in town, while my father said I had nothing. I finally left." Jack went on to work in another family's business, where within five years he became a partner and co-owner. His father is still wondering why Jack didn't stay and join the business. He doesn't understand that the invitation to join was unclear.

The other common situation is where the child feels pressure to join the family business. It is expected, and he or she is supposed to be thrilled at the prospect. Many heirs fit the role nicely. But others feel pressured: they risk a family rift if they say "no," or lose faith with themselves by joining. Some heirs "resolve" this dilemma by picking fights, getting into self-destructive behavior, or screwing up—that way the family will refuse to let them join. But these are indirect methods of communicating which, needless to say, take a sad toll on everyone.

There is always some form of invitation about joining. It may be direct or indirect. Many fathers pride themselves on saying, "The decision to join is the heirs' alone; they can do whatever they want." But the message is rarely that clear and hands-off. There are subtle ways to make parental feelings known. For example, children may hear Dad saying that they have so much talent and ability that they should set their sights above the business. Many women get the impression that not only are they not encouraged to prepare themselves for entering the business, they are not even considered. Indeed it may come as a surprise to Dad, after Daughter has her MBA, to hear that she thinks she has a role in the business.

The invitation is delicate. A founder is proud of what he has done. But an effective invitation has to convey a sense that there is unfinished business, that there is a meaningful role for the heir other than signing checks. But on the other hand, owners shouldn't make extravagant promises they can't keep.

In one family business each son, daughter, and son-in-law received a visit from the founder/owner/CEO. He came to them and began a process of wooing that was almost seductive, trying to coax them away from their corporate and professional jobs. The claims were powerful but vague: you can make more money, I'll give it all to you eventually, we really need your talent, it will be great. There was no duplicity involved, but the invitation appeared to be a mixture of effusive family feeling combined with the business need for executive talent at a time when cash was scarce. His sons were aware that his invitation was slightly unrealistic, but they didn't want to appear ungrateful. Things went fine until they had to face such issues as capital for development and transfer of ownership. Then the lack of explicitness became clear, and the differences led to strain.

Parental pressure can have a tremendous effect on a young person. Rod Correll was the only son of the son and heir of a family leather business. He writes of his decision to join his father:

"While nothing was ever said, I knew that my dad wanted me to come into the firm. For all but two summers during high school and college, I worked in the firm. I was acquainted with the company and the people who worked there. I did not share my dad's view of a tremendous future in the leather industry, but I had no idea what else I wanted to do with my life. Nevertheless, I had a strong feeling that I wanted to make it on my own. I did have one budding idea, not a tremendously strong one, but it was a seed I was starting to nurture. I enjoyed learning, and I thought that teaching might be fun. One day in the summer of my junior year of college, I asked my father what he thought of my becoming a teacher. I still remember the impact of his words, that teachers were wimps and that I would do far better coming into the firm. At that point I was not wed to the idea of a career in education. Nevertheless, his words felt like a door closing. I felt caught in a dilemma. Out of duty, or perhaps dependency, I felt drawn to the firm. Out of an innate need to establish my own identity, I knew I should work elsewhere first."[7]

Rod frames his story as a journey toward personal differentiation from his family and its business. Soon after he entered, his father became ill, and died several years after, leaving him the entire business. As a loyal steward of the family vision, he developed the business amid a fierce economic competitive climate. He found a mentor who bought into the business and became his partner, and then, several years later, bought the business back. After several years, he bowed to an inevitable need for deeper capitalization, and sold the company to a large conglomerate.

Rod became an executive running his company as a division. After a few years, he came into conflict between a cautious parent company and his own entrepreneurialism. At the same time, he remembered his dream of becoming a teacher. After much soul-searching he resigned from the business and entered Yale School of Management. After receiving his degree, he taught, fulfilling his early dream, and is now a consultant and the executive director of the Family Firm Institute, an organization for family business professionals. After serving his apprenticeship within the family business, he was able to go out on his own.

A parent must be particularly aware of the motivations for asking a son or daughter to join. Many parents see the business as a way to salvage or develop their children. They think the business will make them mature, or motivate them to grow. The business is expected to be a therapeutic community. In fact, family businesses often have the opposite effect, for a son or daughter can enter with the feeling that, once again, his or her parents will always take care of him or her. It's hard to motivate a son or daughter to work in the family business if he or she feels pressured to join, or the invitation is presented too obviously as a gift. Offering an outrageously overvalued salary as an incentive, or a car as a "signing bonus," can be de-motivating. Look at your reasons for wanting your offspring in the business, and make sure that your needs intersect with theirs. Why are they joining? What do they need and want at this stage of their life?

Large family businesses evolve their own rules about how to join. They recognize there is not room for everyone to join and that entering the business must be a truly mutual decision. For 13 generations, the Rothschild family, with branches all over Europe, has been a leader in banking and financial services. In dealing with a family of thousands and many heirs seeking to enter the business, the Rothschilds have devised a clear set of rules. To enter the family business, a Rothschild heir must:
1. Be male;
2. Attend college and graduate school in a field relevant to the

business, such as banking, finance, or accounting;
3. Announce the intention to join when graduating from school;
4. Work for five years in a related business;
5. Enter the Rothschild companies under the direct supervision of a relative other than a parent. After five years the supervisor, alone, decides whether he is suitable for a career in the family business.

These rules have kept the field clear for many generations. Some of them, such as working outside the business and not being supervised directly by a parent, are generally agreed to be good rules of thumb for any family business. In fact, the Rothschild companies offer themselves as training grounds for the heirs of other family businesses. This helps them cultivate future customers.

Selling the business to your children may be a hard sell. The two brothers who run Seaman's Furniture, a very successful New York chain, have two sons and two daughters, highly talented business school graduates with many career alternatives. The fathers want their children to succeed them, but know that they have to woo them. They don't do it by soft jobs with no responsibilities; that was the old way, and somewhat ineffective in the long-term. Rather they have taken pains to make the business attractive and to carve out jobs that offer real challenges to lure their children away from their corporate jobs. Their children are critical to helping the company through its leveraged buyout and cash flow crisis.

Deciding About Your Future in the Family Business

Deciding to enter the business involves reflection and consideration. As we've seen, your decision begins early in life, with your impression of the business and the talks with your parents or family members in the business. Hopefully you will not have received an overly idealized or negative set of impressions. You will have spent time helping out after school, and the business will be somewhat familiar territory. You will feel comfortable in the business. By the time you enter college, you should have a general sense of what the business means and offers to you.

Nancy Bowman-Upton of Baylor University Business School noted the most common reasons for children entering the family business:[8]

Make money	67%
Like the business	50%
Good career opportunity	43%
Family influence	40%
Help family	39%

Their reasons are pragmatic: the family business is a good business opportunity. But their decision is tinged with family pressure and obligation. Before entering, you should be sure that your mix of reasons has more to do with it being right for you, and less to a sense of obligation or pressure. The wrong decision can have painful consequences for you and for the business.

When I teach a family business course to college undergraduates, a majority of the students are pondering this very decision. Many have worked in the business for years while growing up, and now, close to their business degree, they are wondering how the family business fits with their career plans. They value having me and other family business heirs to share their feelings with. They often struggle with mixed emotions from childhood. While they see opportunities in the business, they are also afraid of the family hurts that they carry.

The major course assignment is to write a history and profile of the family business. This usually turns out to be a deep and powerful personal experience. First they interview all the key members of the business and family, especially the older generation. They record the history and ask how the business and family evolved. Usually they discover many new facets of the experience, and find their elders pleased and open to participate in the project. Then they explore their own skills, goals, and aspirations. Finally they create a business plan and projection of the business needs and options for the next decade. This picture of the past, present, and future of the business is a good platform for considering their future in or out of the business. I suggest this exercise for you, if you are exploring your family business as a permanent career choice.

If you will be facing this decision, take some time to consider the following issues. Do so even if you think you have made up your mind already. Your first task is to figure out if the family business is right for you. You need to explore issues about it in relation to you personally. You need to assess your inner readiness, needs, and aspirations. This should be done on your own, outside your family. Friends, outside business acquaintances, and mentors can help you. You should try as well as you can to filter out the coercion or seduction of your family.

Start not with whether or not you want to join the business, but with more general questions. Take time to write down your thoughts and to talk with friends.

- What do you want in your life?
- What are your personal and professional goals?
- What are your key values?
- What kind of work experience and career would you like?

• Do you have a secure sense of self-esteem and ability independent of the business and your family?

Next look at your skills, interests, and talents. A good career exploration tool or a trip to a career center or counselor can be very helpful. You are not imprisoned by your talents and career aptitudes, but you need to take note of them. While a good inventory of what you are good at is helpful, the key aspect of career exploration is listening to yourself. For example, I test very high in technical skills and somewhat lower in people areas. I'm also introverted. But the trouble is that I don't like technical tasks, I like public service and working with people. To go in that direction, I faced some hard self-development work.

Now it's time to add the family business to the equation:

• Do you like what the business does?
• What do you want from it?
• Do you feel the business is open to your best creative input?
• Does it offer you challenges and opportunities, or are you only interested in what it can provide you in terms of lifestyle?

The last can be a dangerous discovery.

Now look at the family business in relation to other opportunities. Consider also that the family business is not a closed door and that often the best career path into the family business is one outside it. Perhaps you may eventually want to work with your father or mother, but don't think you can learn about business from them. Find some other mentors and tutors first. Remember that while your family may open the door for you, if you cannot contribute, the business may not be able to keep you without harm.

You also need to think about what you offer the business:

• What skills and talents are needed to develop the business?
• Have you learned what the business needs, particularly to drive the company into the future?
• Do you have basic business and management skills? If not, how will you develop them?
• What can you do that is different from what other family members, especially members of your own generation, already offer?
• What do you need to learn in order to make yourself marketable in the business?

The next phase of your assessment is to talk with your family, especially those who are in the business. The most important person to confer with at this point is the parent or other relative who owns and runs the business. You need to understand the precise nature of the opportunity and the expectations of the invitation. You need to have some clear and sharp conversations about "what if," getting the precise nature of what is expected, offered, and possible. What if your sister or cousin decides to enter the business as well, what if you show real leadership ability, what if father is disabled, what will be the ownership distribution in the family? These issues need to be faced squarely, in several focussed conversations between the owner/founder and the heir. You may not get final answers, but you'll get the current state of the owner's thinking, how he or she will make the decision. You need to get beyond glowing generalities about the business to some clear expectations and possibilities.

Be sure to explore the following questions:

• Is there room for you in the family business?
• Can you work with your father or other family members in the business?
• What are the major struggles you've had with the relative who owns the business?
• Do other family members think it's fair for you to join the business?
• Are your expectations of the future, promotions, responsibilities, and succession shared by the owners?

You need to enter the business with a clear contract, role, and expectations. Your family may be reluctant, even evasive at first, but, if you persist, you can get information to enable you to make a more informed choice. In your personal reflection and conversations with your family, you need to explore the following issues:

• **The nature of the invitation to join.**

What will be expected; how will you fit in the business future? What job are you being offered? What can you expect in the future as both an employee and family member? Can you expect to become an owner? How does ownership relate to employment?

• **Working agreement about entering.**

Precise specification of whom you will work with, standards expected, salary, job role, and career development. How will you be held accountable, and how will you get feedback about your job?

• **Introduction into the business.**

How will your entry be presented to other employees? How will your presence affect the futures and roles of others in the company? How will you be treated differently from other employees?

• **Working relationships with other family members.**

How will you work with the family member who owns the business? How will your relationship with that person have to change? What difficulties might come up working with a family member? How will you work with parents, in-laws, siblings? What do other family members in the business know and think about your entry?

If your brothers, cousins, uncles, or other family members work in the business, you should talk about these issues with them as well. Your entry into the business affects everyone in the family and in the business. I know of one business where each family member had an agreement with the CEO who was their father or uncle. However there was no way that agreement could be honored in full because they contradicted one another. But the cousins didn't know—they didn't talk to one another because their father/uncle told them not to. Only after he died suddenly did they find out he had sold 500% of the whole to them! They were able to avoid a bitter battle, but the pain that was caused by these impractical agreements was deep and lingering.

As a family business member, no matter what your role, age, and experience, your entry into the business is a big decision. Don't do it without thinking and talking about it. While you can't decide the future on every one of the above issues, you can set some expectations, dates, and guidelines for the process. Ideally, these issues have been shared and clarified in a Family Council, and there is a Family Charter that you can consult for guidelines about how the process will unfold. Sometimes the entry of a family member into the business forms an acid test of the viability and durability of family agreements.

As a child of a family business, and as the likely heir of the financial benefits of the business, you have a very special opportunity. You may very well have a secure place in the business and very likely you can become a leader in it. But this goal is not predestined, and it may not be right for you. For one thing, the business may not last long enough. Secondly your siblings and other relatives also have a part to play, and part of your journey may involve learning to share. You need to manage the transition from your family to the family-related workplace by exploring the alternatives, creating a plan for developing yourself inside and outside the business, and making a positive choice to join or not join the business based on your own real needs, talents, and goals, not out of inertia. Hopefully, this chapter has helped clarify some of these issues in such a way that you can make the right choice for you.

Notes:

1. Halbrooks, John. "Handling the Boss When He's Your Dad." *Inc.*, Oct. 1979.
2. Nelton, Sharon. "Shaky about Joining the Family Firm?" *Nation's Business*, November, 1983.
3. Farago, Robert. "Affluenza," *The Robb Report*, January 1987, and John Levy quoted in Peter Ediden, "Drowning in Wealth." *Psychology Today,* April 1989.
4. Kirkland, Richard. "Should You Leave It All to the Children?" *Fortune*, September 29, 1986.
5. Barber, Judy. Presentation at Family Firm Institute conference, Davis, California, October 1989.
6. Campbell, Joseph. *The Power of Myth.*
7. Correll, Rod. "Facing Up to Moving Forward: A Third Generation Successor's Reflections." *Family Business Review,* II:1, Spring 1989.
8. Bowman-Upton, Nancy. Presentation at Baylor University, First Annual Family Business Conference, 1989.

7

Building Working Relationships: Bringing Family Members into the Business

"You love the daylight: do you think your father does not?"
-Eurepides, Alcestis

Brothers David and Leon "White" started a manufacturing business 40 years ago. They came from a close, extended, prosperous Jewish family, newly arrived from Europe. Their sons all grew up in the business, working there as soon as they were able. There was a family rule that "the business was for everyone, and that everyone was expected to work there."

When David's three sons, and Leon's two, finished college and entered the business, the nature of the business started to change. Competitors were emerging, and more specialized manufacturing and marketing tools were needed. As each son entered the business, the ad hoc nature of its organization frustrated him. Cousins and brothers fell all over each other. A younger cousin was expected to teach the business to his elder, just arrived from business school. This caused many problems; family authority structures are generational, so to have lines of authority between siblings or cousins just won't wash. The business was suffocating, not for business reasons, but because it had to be a container for every child in the family.

Tensions appeared between David's traditionalism and Leon's vision. To further complicate matters, Leon's oldest son, Ray, was not very aggressive or farseeing, while David's second son, Andy, had all the skills to be a natural heir to Leon. What you might imagine happened: the two families began to feud. Cousins began to fight and stopped talking to one another: "I won't take orders from him," became the refrain. A personal dispute between Ray and Andy, unrelated to the business, further polarized the two families. As revenues declined for three years, Leon began to consider the unthinkable: sell the business.

What this story points out is that merely deciding to join the family business, if you are an heir, or just inviting all your children in, if you are an owner, will not work. The business must have room for every person it invites, each person must be appropriate for a particular job, and there must be clear lines of authority and succession.

Tasks for the Chapter

This chapter will help show how to manage the process of bringing new family members into a family business. It will show how to make the best transition from being in the family to being in the family business. It will look at how to form the most effective working relationships with those already in the business—parents, siblings, and other relatives. It will detail how to structure the new person's training to maximize success and point out common problem areas, particularly between fathers and children. Even if you have already started working together, the exercises in this chapter may help you strengthen your working relationships and overcome difficulties.

Restructuring Relationships for Success

As we've seen, stepping into the family business can be the most difficult tightrope act a young person will ever face. Entering the family business means that you must create a new relationship with your father, mother, or other relatives who work in the business. This new relationship cannot evolve naturally out of your family relationship. It must have different rules. You must do this even as you maintain the family relationship at gatherings, Sunday dinners, etc. No wonder it's a tightrope act!

If you are a family member already in the business, you too will have to work on your relationship to the new person. You are their dad, uncle, mom, cousin, or aunt. They know you as a lovable creature, and maybe have a very imperfect picture of you as a business person. You have to shift your relationship from family to business. This means getting to know each other a second time. It also means working on aspects of the family role that you may have transferred to the business.

When a family member enters a business to work with a relative, the pair will want to review their current and past relationship, preparatory to defining their new working relationship. They want to exorcise negative thoughts and overcome bad habits. In addition, family members have a few common fears about working together they rarely talk about. These include: "I'm worried that you will expect me to be perfect because I'm your son"; "I'm concerned that you have so many outside interests that you won't be fully committed to the business"; "You always disagree with everything I say"; "I can never get a word in edgewise when I talk to you"; "I want you to see me as an adult, not as your kid." In order to deal effectively with these fears and to establish a new relationship, the two of you should to take inventory of your relationship thus far and articulate your concerns.

Don't let yourselves get too busy to do this exercise when you start working together because the first months of work set the pattern for many later difficulties. You can't predict or foresee the real difficulties so you have to build in enough time to deal with what comes up. If you begin to avoid issues at this early stage, then you will have set the stage for some major difficulties later on. If you've gotten off to a rocky start, you may want to take the time to get your work relationships on a better track.

Exercise: Inventory of Family Relationship History

The pair of you should sit down and talk about your relationship together. Each person shares what you like and value in the other, and why you look forward to working together. Be sure to say what you expect of the other.

Then shift to the difficulties. Each of you have fears and concerns about working with the other. Say these. Make an agreement to check in about these issues at a frequent and regular basis. This should be done away from the office when you have privacy and time to talk.

Guidelines for Owners/Founders

As a founder, it is a special event when your son, daughter, or other relative enters the business. You may be proud of them and want them to show their talent to the employees and the community. After all, they have your genes. Also, no matter what your intentions, the odds are that one of your heirs will succeed you and take the business into the future. You may not know whether they have the required ability and leadership. You should therefore design their early years in the business to help you, and them, make a decision. There is a lot riding on this entry, and it is your job to set the conditions that make it work.

The period when heirs are adolescents and young adults, learning professions and working inside and outside the family business, constitutes the early planning phase for succession, even though it is many years before the actual changing of the guard to the next generation. In this period, no decisions about inheritance and succession need be made. However, the owner ought to spend time with each person in his family and the business, talking about possible futures. Long-term options and possibilities should be evaluated so that each person knows where they stand and can plan a future. The key is to create a family future with the maximum number of options, not to narrow them. The more educated and the more your children's innate talents are developed, the more they learn and grow, the more you teach them, the more options you have for the future business.

When sons or daughters enter the business, there should not be an office party to celebrate their entrance. This just sets them up for failure. The entry is a difficult act. They must first gain acceptance by the other employees. What do they have to offer beyond the family name? What can they do? At this stage your heirs will be tested in various ways. Other employees will want to know what they are like, whether they can be trusted, and if they can understand their needs. It is vital that the heir develop credibility with employees by accomplishing some important task. Employees are now assessing the relative's future leadership potential.

In addition to being sensitive to employees' needs, the founder has to be supportive of the heirs' needs at this stage. The father who carefully monitors their learning experiences, seeing that they receive the right mix of challenge and responsibility, that they rotate through different areas of the business, and that they receive feedback about their performance, is building a base for succession. At this stage, the potential successor is often at an equal level with a non-family manager. The founder should be aware that both people are sizing each other up, competing even, and that they need clarity about your future intentions. Do you expect to see family succession? Will you wait and see? What will be offered to the non-family manager if your son or daughter becomes CEO? Can the manager expect to get a portion of ownership in the company? These are the questions that your people will have as your heir takes a place in management. A competent future leader can lack a clear mandate from the founder, which can cripple his or her attempts to move the company forward.

Rules for Bringing a Family Member Into the Business

The way family members are brought into the business determines how well the relationship develops and sets the stage for the future. While this is uncommon, I find that when a young person enters the family business, creating an explicit contract and working agreement with their parent/CEO, and sometimes all the other family members already in the business, can make the entry process smoother and more effective. There are several critical guidelines. It may be too late for you to implement some of them, but they represent the shared experience of building effective working relationships in a family business.

1. Clear, explicit expectations about what the person will do, his or her role and future. When someone enters a family business, there should be a clear position for him or her and potentials for growth should be clearly delineated. If you are the person entering, you should negotiate as carefully and explicitly as you would on joining any business in which you are considering a career. Don't assume anything. This negotiation is a good way for family members to talk about things they may never have shared.

2. Salary should be based on service to the business and comparable to that of other employees doing the same work. This is a particular problem in family business because it often contradicts a family norm of treating everyone equally. Many families give every family member the same salary. Sometimes this makes sense as, for example, when siblings have similar responsibilities. But that would be a good decision if they were non-family managers as well. If you regard salary as a family right, this can erode your commitment to the business, the morale of other employees, and the continuing health of the business. In my consulting I help people to differentiate different types of money in a family. If a family wants to give its children gifts, it should go ahead. But the business needs a boundary from the family, and shouldn't be used as a bank account or a family charity.

3. If possible, heirs should be supervised by a non-family manager who can become a mentor. The learning and growth process is better if you have a person outside the family who can show the new member the ropes. It should be someone who everyone trusts and who is willing to be a teacher. You should make sure that the arrangement is clear or else rivalry and conflict can be built into this role. This is especially true if the heir is being trained to take over the role of the mentor. Some companies have hired experienced executives for the caretaker/leader/mentor role.

4. The new person should have real responsibility for a clear area of the business and performance should be reviewed regularly. A person only learns by taking responsibility and struggling. It's hard to grow if you have a vague staff assistant role. Many heirs get their start by taking on a difficult project, even having a visible failure that they can learn from. People respect an honest failure, a clear risk, more than they respect a person who hides. One of the greatest occupational disabilities of family business heirs is that everybody is so busy taking care of them that they don't have the chance to get real feedback from anybody. Either inside the family or in the business, you need to have your performance assessed. You can't improve if you don't know how well you are doing.

5. Give siblings different areas of focus. Rotate into different areas of the business. As potential leaders, siblings need to know the business. They meet employees, become familiar with problems, and develop skills by moving into different areas. Heirs of larger businesses should have a fixed series of assignments that take them into disparate areas of the business. In a smaller business, a store or office, you also need to take on different responsibilities. The biggest problem is that people tend to stick with the tasks they are good at. If you have an older sibling who is already in the business, it may be hard to pry him or her loose from the books, or sales, to give you a chance to learn. Don't fall into duplicating your family roles, or doing the same things from your first day.

Parent and Child: Working with Dad or Mom

Like the effective copreneurial couple, the parent/child work relationship runs best when there is a nice complementarity of roles. Marvin Davis, the oil, movie, and deli tycoon much in the media, is joined in business by son John, who does the computer analysis for his deals. John enjoys working behind the scenes with his dad. Some pairs play the good cop/bad cop, or the hard/soft roles. Sons and daughters in this position readily see the benefits: they serve as alter egos and apprentices to master businessmen. In this capacity they can develop their talents and feel good about their contribution to the business. They are not unlike people in other companies who yoke their future to powerful elders.

However, personal satisfaction, business development, personal growth, and family development cannot take place unless the heir entering the business has a positive, mutual relationship with his or her parents in the business. A study of working relationships between fathers and sons and daughters by Ann Patrick Lemay[1] found several factors were related to positive experiences:

1. The relationship must be one of mutual respect and acknowledgement of each person's unique roles in the business;

2. The heir needs to have some clear authority and responsibility within the business, a sense of accomplishment, and active participation in the continuing growth and development of the business;

3. The heir needs to have a sense of equality with the parent, and the pair needs a mechanism to discuss and resolve conflicts;

4. The heir needs training in the skills needed for business success through advanced education and work outside the business.

This study affirms that the process of taking over a family business is most effective when it is gradual. The heir entering the business is able to learn from the father, while having the father's respect for his or her growing competency. The key element in successful relationships is a sense of mutuality. Heirs feel that their father listens to them, takes notice of their accomplishments, and genuinely understands their needs for responsibility and achievement.

Many parent/child business pairs ultimately achieve a sense of mature peership. For example, Georgette Klinger, who started a chain of skin care salons, was joined by her daughter Kathryn. They have come to the point where they respect each other's differences and are able to battle out conflicts. Georgette has learned that she has to give up some of her entrepreneurial control to make room for her daughter's very different personality and perspective.

The evolution from parent and child to a new relationship where two competent, dedicated, respectful people work together, probably takes place in a majority of family businesses. But four factors can intervene to make this process more difficult. By being aware of them, you can hopefully avoid these pitfalls:

• **Conflicts in the entrepreneurial style of the founder.**

Founders have been the head of the business and family for many years. As we've seen they are used to getting their own way, keeping their counsel, and not communicating. They can develop what has been called "entrepreneur's disease," which is a tendency to close off to the contributions, leadership, and ideas of others. This can be difficult and hurtful to a son or daughter who feels cut off from opportunities to learn and contribute. He or she feels that such behavior means distrust or disapproval. Carried to an extreme these attitudes lead to a frustrated and angry adult child, who becomes resentful or withdraws.

• **Difficulty in growing out of dysfunctional family patterns.**

Relations with a father may have been strained when his son or daughter was growing up. I have seen several families where a father has been abusive or very detached, leaving scars in the relationship to his children. Sometimes the pair hopes to put such feelings aside and develop a working relationship, and this can happen if the father is genuinely able to convey respect to his child. There may also be a genuine desire to forgive and try to rebuild a relationship through work. More often, however, the work relationship is unchanged: Dad is withdrawn, uncommunicative about what he wants, angry and sullen, or belligerent. Son or Daughter too play their traditional parts and no one knows how to change or even talk about it.The usual result is for the heir to become apathetic or fatalistic and wait for Dad to go, or for him or her to exit angrily. The only way to improve such a situation is to re-create the relationship with new levels of communication and clarity using the techniques described in Chapter 3.

• **Lack of clarity or expectations about roles and succession.**

Often the invitation is clear, but what it means is not. Sons and daughters have their fantasies, Dad has his own. At first motivation and commitment are high. But the business may demand years of financial sacrifice, and the heir may feel that his or her contribution should be rewarded in this lifetime, like any employee. Or he or she may want to know when Dad will give up the top role, or begin to let go of responsibilities. Like the Queen of England, Dad won't say when or if he will leave, and he resents any discussion of it. He'll retire when he decides to or die in his chair.

This can lead to erosion of the relationship, and bad feelings in the heirs and their families. In one business, after trying to bring the issue up, the son took another job. The father felt hurt and rejected, and cut off the relationship with his son. Neither was able to talk about how the lack of a clear future led to the separation.

• **Clash of needs and/or interests due to differences in life stages.**

While Son or Daughter is struggling to build an identity and career, often Father is dealing with issues of slowing down and letting go. This can lead to trouble. For instance, many sons are frustrated by fathers who they feel are not willing to "bet the store" and take the kind of risks they took when they were younger. But the father has already lived with risk—now he wants to consolidate and move on. Perhaps he wants to harvest the business, and live well for the rest of his life. In other situations, a younger father may be looking forward to many more productive years. He is not ready to be supplanted by his child. In either case, when the pair is not willing to understand their different perspectives, the stage is set of parent/child fights about expansion, marketing, product development, acquisitions, and succession which can be frustrating to both.

John Davis and Renato Tagiuri[2] mapped the developmental stages of fathers and sons and found that certain age matches are more or less harmonious. When a young heir is starting out or finishing graduate school, and his father is in his forties' mid-life crisis, there is likely to be strain in a working relationship. Each individual is facing his own conflict and is less likely to be sympathetic to the other.

The most harmonious relationships occur when the son has reached adulthood, after the mid-twenties, and the father has resolved his mid-life crisis and has reached a point of maturity where he is available as a teacher. While still having many years of active involvement ahead of him, the father is willing to admit to himself that he needs to train a new generation. This stage of harmony lasts until the son reaches middle age. If he isn't given full responsibility for the business by then, he may become frustrated. But if Father is in his mid-fifties, he may not be ready to leave, although Son is more than ready to take over.

Davis and Tagiuri's scheme also clarifies why some older fathers, whose sons are 30 or more years younger, may have an easier time with their sons. They are ready to let go when the sons are ready to take over. Generally, after perhaps a decade of harmonious relationship, the son needs either to take on major responsibility, or move out. Otherwise, he can be like fruit over-ripening on the vine. And while they did not study women in this context, I would assume that the same would be true for daughters.

You can situate your relationship using the chart below. Look at your own age and that of your father, and locate yourselves on the chart. This will suggest whether there is likely to be strain or harmony in your relationship. (Of course, every relationship is unique and so this may not apply in your particular case.)

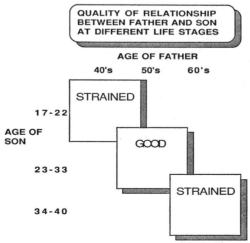

From research on fathers and sons in family business by John Davis, USC, and Renato Tagiuri, Harvard

To maximize the possibility for harmony, you and your father should get together and talk about your aspirations, goals, and concerns at this particular stage of your lives. Also look ahead a decade to your needs at the next life stage. Each of you might share what is most important to you in your life, and your feelings about how the business should run. The purpose of the talk is not to resolve disparities, but rather to understand better your differences. Appreciating differences usually leads two parties to find ways to accommodate them.

For example, one of the most common difference is between the son's willingness and desire to take risks and the father's need for a comfortable, more conservative lifestyle. This difference can be a source of conflict, unless both parties find a way to allow both. In some cases the son buys out the father, securing his income. In others, the son takes over a high risk, high promise part of the business, like opening a new store, or entering a new area.

Leon Danco, the dean of family business consultants, offers this blunt advice: Business fathers need to "understand that the hairs on your chest are numbered and that your primary goal is not to generate more money and sales than anybody else but to perpetuate your business." Heirs, he says, need to "understand your father's drive, recognize his accomplishments, and help him keep his dream alive." This advice recognizes that the delicate relationship of father and child involves the capacity to support each other's sense of self-esteem, and the ability to really listen and see the perspective of the other person.

Networks for the Next Generation

Working in Dad's company can be a difficult and stressful experience. Meeting other people in the same struggle can be supportive and helpful. A dozen years ago, a support group called the SOB's (Sons of Bosses) began in Chicago. It quickly spread around the country. Along with a few daughters, the sons met regularly to share their experiences. It struck a chord: many frustrated and hurting heirs came together and found they had similar experiences. The group was a sounding board for ideas and a place to vent frustration. Many of the members had fathers who would not let go and who turned them into glorified servants. But as they formed a support group, they began to change their response to the founders/fathers' treatment.

Group members were sometimes able to help each other see the ways in which they were diminishing their own power or missing opportunities. Sometimes the group would ask, "So why are you in the business?"

As this group points out, if you feel that you are being disrespected or abused, you may need to confront your father by being willing to leave the business. While the future may be the carrot that Father has dangled over you to make you sacrifice today, the trade-off in both money and respect may not be worth it. Some heirs find that when they leave, their fathers develop the respect for them that eluded them while they were in their shadow.

Gathering heirs into groups is a powerful way to find support for your personal and business growth. I ran several workshops on "Empowering the Younger Generation." Usually everyone in the group has a shared issue: "I have these feelings or concerns, but my dad, who owns the business, doesn't think they are important or legitimate." They then feel frustrated, angry, helpless, and devalued. In the workshop, I teach communication techniques for bringing up this issue, repeatedly, until it is finally addressed by Father.

Such workshops and the meetings of networks like the SOBs give heirs the courage to confront these issues in their families and to make a difference. As one daughter noted, "Now I know it isn't just my dad and me who have trouble communicating. And by talking with others in the same boat, I've gotten ideas on how I can work on resolving our differences of opinion on how the store should run."

As we learned in Chapter 3, it only takes one person to communicate, not two. Once they have gotten over their own fears, heirs can use their love and respect for their fathers to get the issues addressed. It does take time, patience, and persistence.

Often heirs thought the issue was getting Dad to talk about something, but discovered the real issue was that they were not clear about what they wanted for the future. The process of working together to clarify their own futures, to talk about what they needed to learn and possible career alternatives to the family business, was deeply meaningful. Some heirs questions their assumption that it is best to work in the business. One or two people ended up seeing that they needed to tell their fathers that they couldn't stay in the business any longer unless their role was more clearly defined. If the answer was "no," they were willing to leave the business to preserve the relationship. Others needed to confront how they had hidden in the business and not developed their talents and capacities. Several heirs designed a self-learning program to develop their own management and business skills.

The third generation of a family business has its own needs. Sometimes a network or retreat can help a whole generation of a family business define itself. One family business owned several hotels and resorts. Each one was operated independently by a branch of the family—descendants of the founder, who had died a decade before. The family was distant, as each branch lived in a different state and had different philosophies and styles of management. There were also some conflicts over whose business was larger. The younger brother had not been an active part of the business, but he was the chair of the board of the holding company. He was concerned about creating more closeness, and a sense of overall unity in the business. While not close to his brothers and sister, he was the one family member whom everyone trusted, and he wanted to use his role as a trusted outsider to become an organizational healer.

His intervention came when he considered the 28 members of the third generation, in high school and college, who were deciding how to be part of the business. He called a third generation gathering for the summer where they all could come and learn about the business, and talk about future options. He brought in resources for career development, and designed a learning retreat which would become an annual event. Key managers came from each resort to explain its operation and the opportunities that existed. He explained the nature of the business. He then asked each of them to imagine he or she was the new CEO of the business. What would he or she do? The heirs spent time in small groups sharing their responses. The results were powerful and enabled them to begin to consider what it would be like to take a leadership position in the family business.

He hoped that eventually the second generation would participate in the conferences as well, and that the gathering could be at a different resort each summer in order to develop a sense of oneness in the family. The retreat would also work out some rules about how the third generation would participate in the business. One suggestion, which was accepted by his brothers and sister, was that each third generation person be invited to take a first job in the business in some resort other than the one owned by his or her parents. That way each one could develop a special relationship with the aunts and uncles, and learn about the other facets of the business. This intern program would be a first step in working for the business as a career.

Daughters: Fighting Invisibility

If you are a daughter in a family business, you can count on several things. First, you can bet that your father did not tell you that you would inherit the business, or expect you to. But times have changed for women in business. The number of women in management has increased from 14% in 1964 to 33% in 1984! Nowhere is that more evident than in family business. Women are entering as co-founders of new businesses, and, after law or business school (where women make up nearly 1/3 of the graduates) and often a few years at a professional firm or large company, are seeing the unique advantage of the family business.

Unlike her brother, a sister can often see that the family firm probably offers her more of a chance to realize her ambitions. A survey of 91 graduates of a program for women in business offered at the Wharton School found that they perceived their family businesses as holding greater career opportunity for them. After stints at large corporations, female heirs of small and medium-sized family businesses often encounter the "glass ceiling," a barrier to advancement into top management that women are not able to pierce. While able and talented, their horizons are often limited in other companies. From this vantage point they are able to re-assess the opportunities in their family's business. They informed their sometimes traditional, patriarchal fathers that they want in. While this often causes surprise, many fathers have been able to reconsider their attitudes and make room for their daughters. This is often helped by the inability or unavailability of sons. So, for example, we see Christie Hefner moving into the leadership position in her father's almost all male empire at Playboy enterprises.

According to one of the only studies of women in family business, the issues a woman faces are very different from those of her brother. Colette Dumas studied 20 daughters.[3] Like their brothers, discovering a personal sense of identity within the family business was a struggle, but it had different themes. They all noted the tendency to be considered invisible. Even after many years of service, one woman was not even included on the organization chart! Women tended not to be noticed, and were not expected to be assertive in demanding responsibility.

Daughters always begin as "Daddy's little girl." One daughter said, "Even though I've been here a long time, I still have to kiss him every morning. Otherwise he'll be hurt. I don't think he's made the transition to seeing me as an adult." Their developmental issues related to joining the business were different from those of men. They didn't need to prove or assert themselves in quite the same way as their brothers. Instead of becoming a rival to Father, and seeking her own large projects and responsibilities, the daughter more frequently takes on a support role, listening to Father, admiring him, supporting him, encouraging him. She tends to see herself more as a steward than as an entrepreneur. Rather than facing the male need to do something different or make something bigger, women seem to have less difficulty acting as steward to their fathers.

The journey of the daughter, however, has its own perils. She faces two particular rivals. First, she is often seen as a usurper by the father's right-hand man and key outside manager. While that manager might accept a son as successor, the manager and daughter seem to get into a hostile triangular rivalry for Father's attention. The other common triangle is between the father, mother and daughter. By entering the business the daughter gets closer to her father, winning a sort of rivalry with her mother. Several daughters reported having difficulty with their mother when they entered the business.

I speculate that perhaps the easiest succession process would be mother to daughter. Suzette Foley joined her mother and aunt in Sue Mills, a school uniform manufacturing company. "They seemed to have so much fun, and it was just natural to join in," she said. The company, founded by her grandmother, has grown enormously. Her business skills and energy were needed and she was invited to join. Curiously, the husbands of both women executives are entrepreneurs in their own companies. Suzette's entry was especially successful because there was a clear role for her that fit her skills, there were no other siblings or cousins waiting in the wings, and because she had nothing that she needed to "prove" to her mother. The three women wonder if their relationships would be so smooth if they were all men. They are all close and their personal and business lives are quite intertwined.

While sons and daughters were more the focus of attention in the last two chapters, in the next chapter, the main character will once again be the patriarch or founder of the business. The issue is the passage of the business ownership and management to a new generation, and the exit of the founder/CEO from active involvement. This is a long-term process, and is the crisis that sinks a majority of family businesses.

Notes:
1. Lemay, Ann Patrick. Unpublished research report.
2. Davis, John and Tagiuri, Renato. "Influence of Life Stages on Father-Son Work Relationships." *Family Business Review*, 2:1, Spring 1989.
3. Dumas, Collette. "Understanding of Father-Daughter and Father-Son Dyads in Family-Owned Business. " *Family Business Review*, 2:1, Spring 1989.

8

The Succession Era: Building the Next Generation

I stay too long by thee. I wear thee.
Dost thou so hunger for my empty chair
That thou wilt need and vest thee with my honours
Before thy hour be ripe? Oh, foolish youth,
Thou seekest the greatness that will overwhelm thee.
> *- Shakespeare,* Henry IV, Part I,
> *King Henry IV to his son Hal*

Rarely are sons similar to their fathers: most are worse,
and a few are better. . .
> *-Homer (a father)*

Hank, the oldest son of CEO Henry "Dale," is the sales and marketing manager of the family clothes manufacturing business. A few years ago, Glenn, who married Hank's older sister Sara, quit his job with a large company to run their factories. Henry Sr. brought Glenn in when they were having trouble with their factory managers, but didn't consult Hank on his decision. Hank and Glenn were not close, and Hank was somewhat threatened and miffed by his father's action. In the years Glenn worked there, he did a fantastic job of turning the factories around, but Henry had also heard that Glenn was cold and distant, and not well liked. Glenn would counter that hard decisions had to be made and that the other family members were so busy being nice that they weren't taking necessary action. Their relationship was not going well. Each of them would report individually to Henry, who seemed comfortable with that arrangement.

Hank's youngest sister, Kay, is the company's human resources manager. The youngest member of their family, Alan, teaches at a local college. Henry enjoyed working with his family, but, like many an entrepreneur, he kept many things to himself. These included details of the business financing, future plans (he was 72), and his feelings. Family members found it difficult to talk to him about sensitive issues. Their accountant and estate planner devised a plan where he gave a gift of stock to his children every year, but the plan was not very explicit, and the gifts were infrequent. If the company was cash-poor, the gifts don't come. Everybody in the family has some stock. One recent Christmas, he gave large, equal stock gifts to each of his children and a smaller gift to Glenn, who was the only in-law to receive stock.

That was the situation when tragedy struck. Henry died suddenly, and many of his expectations and ideas for the future died with him. His heirs had the ability to run the business, though they were unfamiliar with some financial details. The stock was mostly given to Harriet, Henry's wife, who became the majority owner. But the management structure of the company wasn't clear. Who would run the business? Hank claimed the lead role as the oldest son and longest-tenured family employee. But Glenn felt that his special skills and talents entitled him to the role and believed Henry had intended that.

The rivalry that had simmered between Glenn and Hank broke into the open. They barely spoke to each other, and employees felt they had to take sides. Finally, Kay brought the whole family together. Over a long series of meetings, Hank and Glenn began to talk over their differences, and agreed that they would try a shared leadership structure.

The process was painful, and they are not certain their solution will work. But they know that the company would face difficulty without both of them in management. They all wished that some of the work on their relationship, as well as some clarity about Henry's intentions, could have been accomplished before he was gone. There are still many issues to be resolved about the future ownership of the company, and they have very little guidance in how to arrange future financing. Henry's close-to-the-chest style only added to their grief and strife.

Succession is the eternal problem of every living organism, and every organization. From the Catholic Church to the few remaining monarchies and within every organization and political system, the question of carrying on the vision accounts for more intrigue, bloodshed, and conflict than any other question. Succession sparks wars in organized crime, ignites battles over future policy and direction between competing groups, and sets the direction of nations.

No one is immortal. But while creating a successor in one's own image, or creating an organization that outlives you, gives you a shot at eternity, founders find it hard to let go. The succession issue runs especially deep when the family and business are combined. Blood ties, deep emotions, and business needs combine into a volatile mixture that takes years to resolve. Family bonds, loyalties, legacies, and dreams vie with the desire of the new generation to place its own stamp on the world. Indeed the greatest test for a family business comes when the second generation must take over—fewer than a third survive this transition.

Succession is the key communication test for a family business, in effect, its final exam. It is the most consequential growth step for each member of the family and for the business as a whole. The heirs not only move into power in the business, but they also feel pressure from the environment to move the business in new directions, to revitalize product lines or services, and to deal with new realities.

This chapter outlines the issues and tasks of the succession era, when a family business moves into the next generation: how founders can set the proper expectations; how heirs can convince founders to initiate planning; how to make the decisions with everyone involved; how to balance old loyalties with new realities; how heirs can find out where they stand; and how to make succession work. Successful generational succession in business and family involves consulting with everyone in the family and business, spotting and developing talent, making some hard choices, facing conflicts, and, finally, if you are a founder, learning to let go and allow other people to take care of the business.

Tasks of the Chapter

In this chapter, each family member faces his or her needs and concerns about the future as we explore ways to work with the whole family, business advisors, and employees, to create a plan for the next generation. The dual goals of the family business will be addressed: continuing family connection while setting the stage for renewing the business.

You can use the material in this chapter to create plans for
- *Personal and family future;*
- *Founder's retirement and business succession;*
- *An estate plan for the family future;*
- *Management and ownership transfer in the business.*

Succession can be orderly, taking place in stages over time. It can be quick, sudden and decisive, or it can be conflicted and ugly, leaving scars that never heal. The potential for a Shakespearean tragedy, where things move inexorably to a conclusion where everyone suffers, are nowhere more likely than in family business. Fathers can harbor deep doubts and fears about their child's succession, and sons and daughters can fight with a vicious and unresolvable rivalry. However such conflict is not inevitable. Instead, while strife may be a natural tendency, the behavior of the founder can moderate and regulate conflict rather than cause it to flower.

Today transition is particularly complex because there are so many possible outcomes. The traditional pattern of the oldest son getting the business, which has endured for thousands of years, is at an end. Now the business can be sold, or any child or several can inherit it. Family members have different needs, and the future of the business, the individuals in it, and the family wealth all must be taken into account.

Succession is a delicate balance of timing and communication. While in the past an heir might be willing to wait patiently for 20 or more years to reach control, today the average age of corporate leaders is going down. New entrepreneurs start companies in their twenties, and often retire by 35 to the pasture of venture capitalism. The family business heir who has worked his or her way into demonstrated responsibility, will chafe at the bit if the wait for real authority is much beyond age 40. But most founders/parents aren't ready to retire at 60. So needs may be in conflict.

Moving On: The Hero's Maturity

We began the story of the hero's journey in Chapter 6, in relation to growing up in the business. I focussed on the heir's need to develop an identity by going on a hero's journey toward personal and career development, that might or might not lead into the family's business. The founder/entrepreneur is also a hero, whose quest involves the creation of a business out of nothing. The hero's myth ends when the creative challenge is complete, the business is successful. But this is not the end of the story for the entrepreneur. Let us look at how the heroic leader fares as time passes.

The founder has certainly earned a sense of self-confidence and pride. However, in middle life, his focus has shifted. First, he often wants to take it easier. Now that the business is a going concern, he and his spouse want to relax a little. During this period founders begin to take money out of the company, "harvesting" their investment. They want some of the experiences they have denied themselves. This is fine, except as his products or services mature, or face a slower growing, more competitive market, the funds taken out may be the funds needed to innovate, or develop new initiatives. He may want to retire, to become chairman of the board, but retain his huge salary, even though the business needs to pay his son, the president, and his daughter, the vice-president. What a bind the heirs are placed in, deciding which is more important, the founder or the future. One son quit the business rather than refuse his father's wish, which led to a downward cycle that affected everyone's wealth.

Second, also naturally, the founder's self-confidence leads him to make the mistake of thinking that his experience of the past is the only teacher he needs to face the future. His past experience of marketing will not prepare him to face global competitors, and his hands on knowledge of engineering or finance will not teach him to use computers and information systems. Many founders are comfortable acknowledging they couldn't run the company today that they founded years before. But some can't admit that, and they threaten the business' future and the family's legacy. As the world changes, the founder has less and less desire to go out and learn new things, and certainly less energy for the struggle for a new market or product. That is fine personally, but the business needs to keep a lean and hungry attitude.

Third, and most destructive, the founder plays everything close to his chest. The founder maintains his sense of mastery and power by keeping control. He is doing what he knows how to do, keeping everything in his head. At a time when the business needs to grapple with new challenges, and try new ways, the founder's quirks, his secrecy, denial, and excessive control, can create difficulty for the business.

Sometimes a business founder retains his skill and acumen but it becomes applicable to an ever narrowing arena. One founder, an accountant and a skilled dealmaker, saw only the excitement of acquiring companies, while his sons and key executives were left with the problems of managing them. They needed time to digest all the new companies, and to deal with significant management issues. But all Dad continued to do was make deals, and he looked down on them for their concern with operations. He needed to learn to respect their expertise and not to see himself as the center of the universe.

Emory University management professor Jeffrey Sonnenfeld studied the departures of entrepreneurs and found that the way in which the leader leaves is one of the most important aspects of his legacy.[1] Some leaders leave a strong company poised for a new generation, confident, and able to move ahead. Others keep their hands in, making it difficult to develop new leadership or create change. Sonnenfeld observes four exit styles. Two are characterized by succession conflict, leaving scars in the company and difficulty in developing further: **Monarchs** do not leave until they are carried out, or are forced out by a coup d'etat. **Generals** also leave involuntarily, getting forced out, but they immediately plot to return and rescue the company from the inadequacies of their successors.

In contrast, there are two styles that leave the next generation free to take the company in new directions: **Ambassadors** leave gracefully and serve as mentors to the new generation after retirement. They support and nurture new blood. **Governors** rule for a limited time, then move on to other pursuits after retirement.

Reflection Question

If your father has run the company for a long time, as most family business patriarchs have, how do you see him preparing for his exit? Which one of these styles does he most fit? If you are the founder, which characterizes your style? What are the short and long-term consequences?

Building the Next Generation: The Greatest Challenge

A study by Nancy Bowman-Upton at Baylor University[2] noted these major concerns of entrepreneurs in passing the business to children:

Treating all children fairly	31%
Reaction of non-family employees	22%
Family communication conflict	20%
Estate taxes	20%

The problem is that each of these desires can conflict with the others. For example, a founder may deal with conflict by avoiding talking about differences between his children, and may instead create an estate plan that saves taxes. In trying to treat children fairly at one point in time, he may slight or undermine the heir who wants and needs control of the business. His children in and out of the business may not even agree on what is fair: one may want capital to invest on her own, the other may want to re-invest in the business. Planning for the future involves walking a delicate tightrope and much discussion; you cannot avoid facing some difficult conflicts. A founder who tries to please everyone completely, or who avoids hard choices, courts disaster!

Heirs have different concerns. They have to come to terms not just with their own identity, but with the myth of the founder. "Everybody has heard the story 47 times—the blood, the sweat, the tears, the risk-taking. The folklore that surrounds the founders has to be daunting," says Craig Aronoff, management professor at Kennesaw State College in Georgia.

The successor struggles with many burdens, such as gaining control with a clear mandate to make the changes that are necessary, and dealing with other siblings and people who have legitimate claims on the business. The heir often has unfinished business with his or her parent, and mixes up the need for parental approval with running the business. Very often there is a cash crunch, as when the founder and his family need cash to buy out others, and for retirement, leaving very little for business needs. Often when the successor inherits the business, he or she finds that, while it has been successful in the past, it is in deep trouble, which the founder is unaware of. Letting him know about it is like a slap in the face. All these currents force the chosen successor to be a diplomat as well as a businessperson.

In order to complete their life's work and pass it on to their heirs, owners face a very different challenge from founding the business, but one that is equally exciting and demanding: to implement a workable plan so that the business can last beyond their lifetime and its benefits are passed on to heirs.

Family business founders run a successful business for many years. They meet each challenge as it arises, guide it and help it grow. But the challenge of planning for the future is different than responding to any other crisis for two reasons. First, the future is a challenge that they can't respond to on their own because they won't be there! Second, the future involves not solving a problem, but creating a structure that anticipates the most likely difficulties and develops resources for other people, primarily heirs, to solve problems. This means developing *other people's capacity* to lead, which is different from leading yourself.

The passing of generations involves many transitions, often occurring more or less simultaneously. The founder retires to other interests, leaving day-to-day management. The heirs settle into their own careers, inside and outside the business. The business needs its own renewal. The successors find they cannot rest on the past, but need to redesign the company to stay in business. Which members of the family remain in the business, how they work with non-family managers, and who owns the business, are all part of planning.

Several types of succession need to be accomplished. There is leadership succession, ownership succession, and even succession in family emotional leadership. Each kind has different considerations and a separate process. The key is for the family to meet, spend enough time together to explore what each person wants, and then to create the financial, structural, and legal framework to make the plan work.

Billye Erickson of Capsco Leasing has an exciting plan to develop her next generation, without discouraging her outside managers from seeing a future in the company. She bought her business about a decade ago, and has two sons and two daughters who might inherit the business. She has devised a plan to develop their skills and plan succession, which she would like to see in the next few years, when she reaches 60. Erickson brought together a group of businesspeople she respected to be her advisory board. Each member is paid a nominal amount, but, more importantly, is offered a chance to buy into the company when she arranges a leveraged buy-out at the succession.

In return board members teach the possible successors. Each heir becomes an apprentice to a board member for several months. In order to learn other ways to do things, each heir works as an intern in the board member's business, in addition to working at Capsco. The advisor is asked to give a candid evaluation of the heir's skills. By the time the apprenticeship period is over, Erickson will have a good idea of whom to entrust the business to.

However it's not a winner take all competition. Erickson has defined 14 key positions in the business. Since there are four children, her other key managers know that there is room for them to advance as well. She expects that more than one of her children will stay with the business.

As the above example demonstrates, effective succession includes everyone involved in the family and business. Planning is not an exercise for the patriarch or matriarch to do in isolation. It involves the future of each member of the family and a wide circle of other stakeholders, including relatives, in-laws, employees, customers, and other shareholders. It takes many years, not just a few meetings. The seeds for effective succession are planted years before, in the family messages and the clear expectations given to children and managers.

Because of the dual nature of family businesses, planning entails organizing for both the family's and the business' future. Planning for the family future involves creation of an **Estate Plan** that implements the founder's wishes for how the business and other inheritance will be passed along to family and other heirs. Planning for a business future involves creation of a **Management Succession Plan** that creates continuity by arranging for a new generation of management. The pool of talent needs to be matched with the business needs. The creation of estate and management succession plans is not a short-term project or something that can be put off indefinitely. It is something that you need to begin today, if you are to survive as a business tomorrow. While the two plans are somewhat separate, they are intertwined. The succession decision affects inheritance, and the business ownership affects the chosen business successor. Ideally, both plans are worked on together.

The succession plan and the estate plan are highly interrelated. If one son becomes your designated successor, your other heirs will want to know what they can expect. Therefore it is often strategic to announce your estate and inheritance plan with the succession announcement.

Creating these plans involves three groups, representing the three overlapping systems in the family/business world:

• **The Family Council**

It can be active as a forum for communication, for exploring different needs, and for learning about the family's business affairs so that it can take over when the need arises. Both estate plans and succession plans should be discussed here. The Family Charter probably needs clarification and amendment during the succession process.

• The Board of Directors

This group represents the ownership of the company, and includes not just formal board members, but business advisors, some family members, and perhaps some non-family managers. It becomes very active in generational transitions—charting the direction of the business, mediating conflicts, and taking over in a crisis. It should be active in creating the Management Succession Plan.

• The Management Team

Family and non-family managers need to talk about and implement new directions for the company. This is not a plan the founder can hold in reserve, but an active process that takes place continually. The next chapter will look at the management issues involved in organizational renewal.

One reason not to put off completing these plans is the possibility of sudden death or disability. A wise business is prepared. Here's a simple example: John had two sons and two daughters. Nick was president of the company, and Dan was head of sales/marketing. John died suddenly. Nick succeeded him, but Dan was restless. He didn't want to take orders from his brother. Nick became uncomfortable and didn't know what to do. Both daughters felt things were unfair as well. They wanted some dividends for their own families. Mother felt torn. Conflict resulted.

In the past John had always stepped in and resolved things, but he wasn't there now. Mother and the four children had inherited equal shares of the business. How can Nick buy out the others, or provide for their legitimate needs? How can Nick gain the control he needs to make the critical decisions? Will everyone always be looking over his shoulder and complaining? Some succession! Does he have to convince his mother, brother, and sisters of the wisdom of each decision?

In this situation, at least the two sons knew how to run the business. But what if the owner is the only person who knows the business or has essential information? Who will take over, and how will they learn? Who will teach them? One crucial part of planning is to look at the "what ifs," specifically, what will happen if the founder can no longer run the business.

When a business is owned by two or more partners or stockholders, ownership succession is even more complicated. When there are two partners and one dies, the usual candidate to purchase the business is the surviving partner. They prefer to do this rather than share control and ownership with heirs. Here's why. Two brothers were partners in a retail store. One brother died suddenly. The surviving brother had always got along well with his brother's wife—until his death. Now they clashed over money. She needed money to live on, but the business was strapped. He couldn't pay her and hire a new general manager. So he had to borrow money to buy out her share of the business, creating a burden of debt for the company that ultimately led to its bankruptcy.

The usual mechanism for transfer of the business to a surviving partner is the buy-sell agreement. When the agreement is drawn, the surviving partner agrees in advance to buy the business, and the estate of the deceased or disabled partner agrees to sell the business, for an agreed-upon price. The price is determined at regular intervals or based on a predetermined formula. The agreement is usually funded by life insurance purchased by each partner. When one dies, the other, as beneficiary of the insurance policy, has the funds to pay off the estate for the business.

This avoids one of the most difficult issues when one partner dies: when both worked for the business, the business could afford their two salaries. But after a death, the business must pay to hire another manager. It often is quite a strain to have also to pay the family of the deceased the equivalent of the partner's salary. Often a partnership doesn't earn much profit, or the profit must be reinvested in the business. So with the automatic buy-sell agreement, the funds are made available, and the surviving partner has the funds to continue the business.

When all the partners are of advanced ages, there is a need for more planning. What will happen if both die or can no longer manage? A business needs to plan for every emergency. While financial insurance can be purchased, there also needs to be planning on a personal level for the possibility of disaster. While this can be upsetting, and often poses difficult issues, no business can afford to leave itself without a plan for such risks. The challenge for any business is to be prepared for the crisis that will always come.

Sometimes a crisis forces the issue, but also allows time to plan. Etta Allen was a young mother, and her husband was starting a home heating contracting business. Suddenly he learned he had incurable cancer. What would happen to the family when he was gone, since he had only the fledgling business to leave? They decided that she would learn the business. He taught her before he died, and she become the first woman to get a contractor's license in California. The employees were very supportive while she spent time learning the business and going with her husband to chemotherapy treatment. In the years since, the company has grown manyfold, and she has raised her children and become active in community affairs. She is now preparing to turn the business over to her son. But, she remembers, if she did not have the chance to plan and learn, she would have had no legacy.

Exercise: Founders' Future Planning Assessment

How well is your business facing your family and business future? Take a few minutes and place a check mark in front of the statements that are true for you. Answer from the perspective of the founder—if you are an heir, see how many of these questions you know your father has dealt with. Be tough on yourself: place a question mark in front of things that are partially true or you are uncertain.

_____ 1. *I have designated a successor to take over management of the business.*

_____ 2. *I have a will.*

_____ 3. *My family and heirs are aware of what is in the will and my wishes.*

_____ 4. *I have talked to each family member about his or her future dreams and plans.*

_____ 5. *I have begun the process of shifting my estate to my heirs.*

_____ 6. *My heirs' estate tax will be minimized when I die.*

_____ 7. *If I should die suddenly, everyone knows what to do.*

_____ 8. *If my business partner dies or is disabled, I have arranged to buy his or her share of the business and have funding for the purchase.*

_____ 9. *I have talked to each of my grown children about the business and his or her inheritance.*

_____ 10. *I am facing family conflicts and disagreements and trying to resolve them.*

_____ 11. *My family is able to talk face to face about disagreements.*

_____ 12. *Every one of my children is assured he or she will be treated fairly in my estate plan.*

_____ 13. *My estate plan takes into account differences and needs of each heir.*

_____ 14. *I have talked about succession in management with my employees.*

_____ 15. *My designated successor knows everything he/she needs to run the business if I die suddenly.*

_____ 16. *My family has regular talks about the business and family future.*

_____ *17. I have set my retirement date and made plans.*
_____ *18. I have other interests besides work.*
_____ *19. There is a stock ownership plan to insure focussed control over the business after I die.*
_____ *20. I have a board of directors to guide the business and help me.*

How many can you answer "yes" to? You should have checked 15 or more.

There are several reasons why planning for succession should be initiated as early as possible, maybe many years before the actual transition. First, as we've seen, there is always the possibility of disaster, disability, or death. Just as inventory and buildings are insured, so there must be provision for continuity in the event of the owner's death.

Second, the potential successor must be prepared to seize the reins of the business and establish continuity. That means careful preparation and training. He or she needs time to develop relationships of trust and legitimacy with employees, suppliers, customers, banks, advisers, and the community. The successor does not automatically gain acceptance.

Third, the business must remain vital by renewing itself continually, constantly changing and keeping up with new pressures and shifts in the marketplace. Last year's wisdom is this year's folly. While individuals grow older, even become stale or burned out, the business must maintain active and up-to-date leadership.

Fourth, if the business is to be sold, either to an outside person or to its own managers or a key manager, the prospective buyers need time to prepare to find financing, or to raise the money. They also need to make a good decision about their own future, and the owner needs to be satisfied that the buyers can continue to run the business.

There are severe financial and business consequences for owners who deny the need for estate, tax, and succession planning or who put it off. When legal rules about succession and estates are ignored, decisions about a family future are made by probate court. Tax law often forces owners to choose between keeping control and saving money to pass on to family. If they wait too long to give up control, they may lose the talent of a potential successor (especially a son or daughter) who gets impatient. The tax costs of dying intestate, or trying to avoid estate taxes in the last year of your life, or the first year after it, make Uncle Sam the major beneficiary. Often the business has to be liquidated to pay estate taxes, or an unforeseen disaster can leave owners without the means, or ability, to complete their embryonic buy-out plan.

What makes a business founder begin to contemplate succession in his business and the future of his family? Some begin to shift their priorities and think about slowing down or retiring when they have a close brush with death or someone beloved dies. The loss or close call can be a learning experience, that heightens the perception of what is really important. It reminds them that the family is the treasure, and the business is the gift. It may shift their priorities, as they re-discover the importance of personal relations with spouse, children, and other relatives.

Other founders feel themselves losing their spark or feel pressure from their children who want more responsibility in the business. Or a key manager or child may leave or threaten to. While a critical event often sparks planning, the process of looking into the future should start well before that. However, many founders never plan at all.

Reluctance to Plan

Family business owners are often entrepreneurs who have built their business from concept to visibility, leadership, and success in their community. They are deeply tied to their business, are there every day, and seen as the personification of the business in the community. While some have heirs poised to take over, many have no clear successor, or are not certain who will emerge in the next generation.

This is not peculiar to family business owners. Lack of planning is prevalent even among those whose job it is to draw up estate plans. A survey of wives of American Bar Association lawyers found that nearly a third reported that their husbands had no wills, and nearly two thirds had no wills themselves. Further, a third of those whose husbands had wills didn't know where the wills were kept, and 85% of them had never talked to their husbands about the estate plan! This is a powerful example of denial in a profession whose members should know better.

There are, of course, psychological reasons to deny one's death and avoid succession planning. We all have a tendency to deny death and act as if we are immortal. In addition, founders may be so identified with the business that they are not sure who they are if they leave. They may have no idea how to relax or what else to do. And they may be highly ambivalent about electing a successor. If that person succeeds, they may fear being seen as a failure, while if the successor fails, they have kept their reputation intact, but in fact failed at providing for the future. They may even feel some anger at the next generation, unconsciously resenting their children not having to earn the business.

Father is not the only guilty party when it comes to not planning. Ivan Lansberg of the Yale School of Management uses the term "succession conspiracy," to refer to an implicit agreement by everyone to avoid thinking about the future. The founder avoids planning because he or she can't deal with letting go, the children because they may find out that Father has chosen someone else, the employees because they want their father figure to stay forever, and everybody because they resist change. People hold on to old ways, and to nostalgia for the "good old days" until they create danger for their company future and family frustration.[3]

Giving Up Control

Not planning often relates to owners' reluctance to give up control over the business. So they claim that they don't feel their heirs are quite ready, or that the time isn't right. For such people, it will never be. Some fathers can't leave. One fiftyish CEO son told me that this year his 85-year-old father has finally dropped out of the company's everyday affairs. The reason? He is going on his honeymoon!

Founders find it hard to be open and share control. When starting a business, that is a strength. Over time, it becomes a liability, for other people need to share responsibility for the future. You absolutely cannot insure succession without giving up control. Throughout history monarchs never went quietly—their sons often helped them along. Unlike kings, it is better to decide before you die.

Too many family business founders are possessed by the "lone wolf" syndrome: they feel that everything rests, and always will rest, on their shoulders. Since the problems and pressures are theirs' alone, they don't seek counsel, even distrust it. Spouses and friends feel shut out, which builds distance and estrangement. Offspring may feel guilty even bringing up the issue of succession because they feel they "should" be grateful for the business opportunity Father offers or for their inheritance. But adoration is for children, while mutual respect is more appropriate of adult father/child relationships.

Sometimes fathers need a little push to let go. Rick "Smith," the talented son of the chairman of "Smith Financial," was always the golden boy and heir apparent. He got his MBA and spent three years with a large investment bank in New York. The only question over succession was when. Rick entered the company and began to work alongside his father, who had inherited the business from his father. And there they stayed. Dad, at 50, was not going anywhere, but Rick, itching for authority and wanting to make his mark, was frustrated. They often disagreed, but Rick dutifully bowed to his father, who did things based on his admittedly vast experience. After seven years, a large company offered Rick a division presidency, and, to his surprise, he and his wife found themselves attracted by the offer. He went to his father and said he was going to take the job.

His father could see Rick's reasons. The next week, the board voted to make Rick president of Smith Financial and he didn't leave. He thought things would change, but they didn't. Like many heirs, Rick had responsibility without authority. His father sometimes reversed his decisions, and, a year later, his father was still clearly in charge. What was Rick to do? He felt himself wanting to leave again.

The Smiths needed a family planning process, followed by decisions about how to accomplish the transition. Dad had difficulty listening to Rick. He had waited for his father to retire, and assumed Rick would as well. Also, like many people in his late fifties, he wanted to consolidate the business and insure his own future. His entrepreneurial energy was low, while Rick was wanting to move into new markets, and take advantage of some opportunities he saw. In several talks, Father and Son saw that their differences had to do with their life stages. Father agreed to a more limited role, overseeing investment opportunities with some of his long-term clients. He purchased another small business with his wife, in order to let go without retiring. Rick was finally allowed to run the financial business.

Father's difficulty in giving up control is the cause of much grief and resentment among heirs. They feel that they are not given the opportunity to demonstrate their abilities because their father cannot learn to appreciate and accept the inevitable succession. Ralph, like Rick Smith, entered his family manufacturing business after working for a big accounting firm. He returned at his father's request, with the task of taking over eventually. He felt proud of his father's invitation and great loyalty to his family's heritage. But, quite reasonably, he also felt that his father had an obligation to let him take over. What happened was quite different.

Ralph worked in one division of the company, stepping right into effective leadership and increasing profits fourfold. His father was proud of his achievements, but responded to his requests for more information about finances and a picture of the business as a whole with the statement, "You have enough to do." Ralph felt that Dad wanted to keep all the decisions to himself, not inviting his advice. His feelings were even stronger than many children's because he had learned strategic planning at his old firm and felt that the company needed a good plan for its future. But his father put him off, saying that a plan wasn't really needed for a few years. The cycle continued: Father was positive and seemingly supportive, but never really brought Ralph into overall management. He had no chance to share decision-making, exercise leadership judgment, or be seen as the real successor. Dad was acting out his ambivalence about succession, leaving Ralph in a real bind: how to confront the issue, and get the chance to really prove himself.

This is the dilemma and struggle of many family business succession dramas. The heir has to use effective communication techniques, persistently, to confront the owner's behavior and ask for clarification. The communication exercises in Chapter 3, the family meetings I've suggested in Chapter 4, and the initiative of the younger generation or a concerned spouse are critical to shock the isolated businessman out of his shell and face the future. The resulting "confrontation" meetings can be something like the jarring sessions where a family confronts an alcoholic member: people say to him that he needs to open up and change drastically, or he risks cutting off the people closest to him because they can no longer tolerate the effects of his behavior. Indeed, the owner who can't give up control when the time comes often has a work-addiction that is as all-encompassing as other addictions.

Giving up business control means owners need new outlets for involvement. When a founder leaves management of a company, he cannot go out to pasture. Today, with people active into their seventies and beyond, the business founder has to learn that his career does not end with leaving the business. Many elders have developed new businesses, become venture capitalists and mentors to new businesses and other sons and daughters, or community or political leaders. One founder in his early sixties noticed that many of his peers were also leaving their businesses. He started a support group for business owners starting new careers called Beyond Business.

Allocating Inheritance: Ownership and Management

Before you are gone from the business, however, you must settle several questions about your business' future. First, you need to decide who will run the business. Second, you must decide who will have the controlling ownership. Third, you must decide who will have the financial benefits of the business.

Management, ownership (benefits), and control of the business are each separate issues. If you are a founder, most likely you currently play all three roles—you own and manage your business and reap its financial rewards. Now you need to decide who will take on each of these roles in the business' future. This is a tricky, complex, and often conflicted series of choices.

Most business owners want to pass on the benefits of the business to their heirs and family. This often entails sacrificing or giving up personal control, management, or ownership of the business. Realizing the financial benefits of the business, such as a regular income, sometimes demands a full or partial sale of the company. This is especially true in a small business, where there is not enough income to pay managers and outside business owners.

Family business founders want to sell or leave their business intact, and their heirs usually feel loyalty to insure this task is carried out. If the business is liquidated, it will lose much of its value, both real and symbolic.

One of the business problems in generational succession is ownership dilution. Look at the chart of four generations of ownership at "Griffin" Construction. What would you predict happened by the fourth generation? The business floundered, with many Griffins in management but none firmly in control. The company fell heavily into debt, and the bank ended up with the greatest share of the business. As it lost money, the bank demanded a sale, but buyers couldn't be found. Finally, everyone agreed that Norman Jr. would become CEO. Provisions were made to sell him shares of other family members.

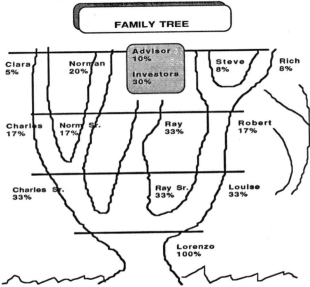

FAMILY TREE

Clara 5%	Norman 20%	Advisor 10% / Investors 30%
Steve 8%	Rich 8%	

| Charles 17% | Norm Sr. 17% | Ray 33% | Robert 17% |

| Charles Sr. 33% | Ray Sr. 33% | Louise 33% |

| Lorenzo 100% |

If each owner has several children, who in turn have several children, after several generations nobody has enough ownership to control the business. Boards of directors containing family members can squabble endlessly, confusing family with business issues, and never agreeing on who will run the business. For example, after about five generations, King Ranch, the largest cattle operation in Texas, covering several counties, is owned by nearly 80 heirs. Over time, they became uncertain of their mission and the strategic direction of the business. Tres Kleberg, one of the owners, has spent many years working within the ownership group, helping build a family council that reconciles the diverse interests of family members and develops strategic options. In the meantime, the business itself has been turned over to non-family management.

Through dilution and loss of vitality and focus, family fortunes tend to dissipate in three generations. But the creation of a trust allows families to maintain a single fortune with many heirs. The essence of a trust is that ownership is held in common, but many people share the benefits (e.g., income) from the trust. The trust keeps the stock of the family firm intact, and the trustee makes the decisions for all beneficiaries. One heir can have control over the family trust, even though one or more generations of heirs can benefit from it.

While the wealth of a family can be distributed to everyone via trusts and buy-out agreements, the business itself should be managed and controlled by one or at most a few relatives. It used to be one son inherited the business, with the others expected to go into other lines of work. Now some businesses contain several family members, from different parts of the family tree. The selection of a successor involves "pruning" the family tree, limiting ownership to the people who will actually control the business. A majority of family feuds and conflicts are about the allocation of ownership between people in and out of the business. One common situation arises when there are two marriages, and the second wife inherits substantial ownership. There may be tensions with children from the first marriage, and even a complete split. She may inherit majority ownership but be the least equipped to use the control wisely.

Families have two separate sets of interests that can conflict with and even battle one other. There are the active owners, who work in and manage the business. They take a fairly long-term view of development and have motivation and incentive to re-invest their profits to grow the business. Often this group contains one or two siblings who become the business' chief executives.

The second group is the passive owners who are not involved in the business. This group may include the semi-retired former owner and his or her spouse, as well as heirs from several branches of the family tree. They are concerned about their future. Some of them may want to take "their money" from the business to invest in their own entrepreneurial schemes.

In a smaller business, one sister, whose three brothers worked in the family hardware store, wanted to sell her stock or be bought out so she could start a home-based design business. At first her brothers resisted, saying that family stock was not to be sold, that she should see her ownership as investment for her future. But finally, after she said, "Why shouldn't I have the same opportunity as you to use the family's wealth to start my business?" the brothers obtained a loan and gave her cash.

The differences between active and passive family business owners can be vast. Each group sees the ownership of the family business as "its" money or inheritance. This can lead to misunderstanding, and, as we have seen in earlier chapters, even to family feuds. The issues are the different meanings that the family wealth has for people: owner/managers may see keeping the business thriving as the meaning of their inheritance. They may even feel it as a burden they didn't seek, but which they "owe" the family. Others may want the freedom that wealth brings to live comfortably. Still others want to pursue the family legacy by starting their own ventures in business or public service. While the pot may be large, it may not support everyone's wishes.

Special strain arises when people have overvalued the family business or when the business is not as liquid as people assumed. What if the business cannot get a loan, or cannot support a buy-out? Or more commonly, what if the active and the passive owners each slip too deeply into the "rightness" of their needs, and are not open to a reasonable compromise? This is likely when the wishes of the founder are not clearly stated, or when certain family members feel wronged or deprived by the family. Then the family wealth is seen as "reparations" or redress for past hurts and wrongs. The complex meanings of family inheritance makes the division of the whole extremely delicate. It is no wonder that many business owners try to avoid making hard choices.

An added pressure when the founder is close to retirement is differing needs for cash. The founder wants to maintain a good income, and deserves it. But the successors may need funds to modernize or develop the business. The pressures to "harvest" the business versus investing in it can cause strain between generations. Some accommodation needs to be reached because, during the generational shift, there is often a great crisis in the company in response to new competitive demands, maturing markets or products, and the need for new products and initiatives. The founder can get angry if there isn't enough for him, and the non-management heirs. This issue is faced in a majority of companies trying to make it into the next generation.

Fairness versus Equality

Another problem in allocating family inheritance and making decisions about ownership and control of the business is the confusion between fairness and equality. Many parents develop the family rule that everything is given to children equally. If one gets a present, all do. If one gets a share of the business, everyone does. Since children are of different ages and have different needs and abilities, the task of defining equality in large and complex families could tax King Solomon. Equality for all can end up being unfair to some, even demoralizing, and dangerous to the business as well. What of the young man who ran a business where majority ownership was held by his two older sisters, who saw him as their adorable baby brother who needed the benefit of their wisdom to thrive? What happens if their wisdom goes against what he learned in business school about prudent management? This is an example of the dilemmas that a policy of absolute equality in division of inheritance can produce.

The patriarch must realize that fairness does not necessarily mean equality. The person who inherits control of the business deserves the fruits of his or her success. If his brother starts a business with family funds, he is not usually expected to share it equally with his brothers and sisters. Effective management of a small business demands that the chief executives have control over business decisions, and have the ability to retain the profits of the business for future development.

Passive owners have different needs. Often one family member needs help and support in getting launched, or is not as successful as the others. Early help can be important to an heir starting a business, or getting a special form of education. One set of parents felt comfortable supporting their commercially unsuccessful but hard-working and critically-acclaimed artist daughter. Doing so expressed one of their family values.

The task of defining fairness is not arbitrary. One of the deepest dilemmas for founders is caused when, with the best of intentions, they create their own definition of fairness. Just as the parents who try to practice equality run aground, so a person who defines fairness without asking the people concerned has set him or herself up for misunderstanding. Defining one family member's concept of fairness is important, but the understanding needs to be shared with family members. Because of different needs and perspectives, everyone will have his or her own ideas of what is fair.

Many patriarchs get stumped by this. They feel caught when their daughter wants one thing that she insists is fair, while their son wants another. They are indeed caught. Resolution comes about when they see that it isn't their problem alone, and it cannot be resolved by saying nice things to each person in private. Their differences need to be explored in the open, and the two parties need to learn about the other's needs and perspective before they can forge a compromise. Often, for example, the siblings have a very incomplete understanding of one another's needs or resources. Once each sibling understands the other's perspective, there's hope for a resolution. This is a place where the Family Council can effectively operate.

Many business owners develop estate plans or plans for transfer of business ownership with their lawyers and accountants alone. The plans are perfectly designed to minimize taxes, but don't resolve or even recognize any of the personal aspects of the transaction. Because they are left out, family members are confused, and misunderstand or reject the process out of hand. Tax considerations are important, but as one accountant observed, if a family is worth $10 million, what is a hundred thousand dollars of extra tax for the purchase of good feeling and ability to realize individual goals? It is not that an accountant doesn't know this; it's just that an accountant does not usually learn about the complex, personal stakes in the family. An estate planner needs to meet with everyone to become familiar with personal goals and needs; the plan needs to arise from personal relationships and out of a shared consensus about what is fair. There's just no other way to do it right.

Reflection Question

Think about what you most value in your life. Not only the people, but the personal values, what you want as your legacy. Get a clear picture of what you want to complete in your life. You may want to write this down. Think about what you want to accomplish in your business, and what you want to leave each member of your family.

Now think about your personal, business, and estate planning. Have you created plans so that the likelihood of your wishes in line with your values, will be carried out? Don't leave something this important to chance!

The Succession Process

New leadership does not emerge by proclamation. It must be developed, nurtured, and installed in a thoughtful way. The transition needs to be well planned and well managed by transition structures that involve everyone. A study by Gibb Dyer[4] at Sloan Management School looked at family businesses that were successful and unsuccessful at managing succession. Businesses that made healthy transitions contained an open, collaborative environment in the business and the family. Everyone was able to talk about issues and was invited to a forum to work on them. They could talk about differences and were willing to take the time to do so. In other words, the families and businesses that had mechanisms which enabled them to talk together about each others' needs and desires, resolve actual and potential conflicts, make changes and course corrections when needed, and who seek the advice of outside board members, thrived and grew through the succession process.

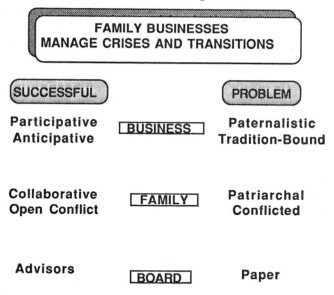

A business must go through several phases before a new generation successfully takes over. The early phases pave the way for the later ones. Neglecting early groundwork makes it more difficult later on. All the phases contain the same imperative: succession planning is not the sole prerogative of the founder. It involves everybody. It begins with the development of potential heirs which was discussed in Chapter 7. If you have set in motion mechanisms for potential heirs to build their reputations and skill in the business and have begun to cultivate a talented cadre of young family and non-family middle management, you are well on your way to creating smooth succession.

There are several tasks yet to do. First, you will want to reflect on the future of the business. Just because you will be leaving doesn't mean you have to turn off your imagination or creativity. But as you bring other people in, you can no longer implement your particular visions without collaboration. You need to share with your heirs, key managers, and advisors. More importantly, you will have to learn, perhaps for the first time, to be open to the different perspectives of your heirs. In their educations and apprenticeships, they may have learned some new, powerful, and even necessary ideas for the business. As they enter your business, take a personal pledge to try to be open to their point of view and not to mold them into a carbon copy of you. You are their teacher and coach, which may demand different management skills and style than the previous entrepreneurial stage of business.

One of the critical tasks is for you to set down and teach what you know and take for granted about the business. Owners carry a lot of informal knowledge in their heads about how the business is run and how to make it thrive; they often intend to tell it all to their successors, but may not get the chance to finish. To avoid disaster, begin a notebook that collects your everyday knowledge about the business. Include procedures, finances, informal relationships, commitments, agreements, obligations, and operations that aren't written down. In the event of death or disability, this information can be critical.

The next task is to conduct a management assessment of the business. What are the skills and talents that are needed for the next generation of leadership? They are certainly different from the skills you needed to start the business. Who are the potential successors who might take over the business? The pool of possible people includes children entering the business, managers who desire more responsibility and have potential to develop the skills to run a business, and possible buyers outside the business. What are the skills of each potential key person? What areas do not seem covered? The owner must assess each candidate and have at least two possibilities. Remember you are not just filling your own slot, but also looking for the whole next generation of management.

There are several ways that succession can be managed that are not mutually exclusive. The owner can designate one or more children as heirs apparent. A non-family manager can be designated, usually a key executive, such as a store manager or a general manager. The entire management group can be built together with the intention that a successor will emerge from the group, or finally, a successor can be recruited from outside the business.

When a potential heir comes into the business, every manager, and even your other offspring, will look at him or her and make assumptions about whether or not he or she will inherit the business. If you say nothing, people will wonder, including your heir. Wouldn't it be better if your intentions were announced to your son or daughter and to the others? Every employee takes the future into account in determining the degree of commitment to the business today. I've seen non-family managers decide to leave a business, or allow themselves to be hired away, because they don't see their future clearly there. Your other sons and daughters may decide to avoid the business if they think things are already settled. You owe it to everyone to be straightforward—otherwise there could be a lot of bad feelings.

William Beaton worked with his two older brothers in a family radio station business. He expected to end up with some ownership, and his father kept telling them that they would all share in it. But like many founders, Father shared neither his plans nor his intentions. After his death, the two older brothers ended up with almost all the stock, and William almost none. His brothers soon fired him, and he sued them. If there had been more shared discussion and planning before Father's death, the succession might have been more harmonious. If the intention was for William to leave the business, or if William was not producing, then his pain might have been less if he had known earlier.

Often business owners feel there will be even more problems if they do not make up their minds early about who is to succeed them. What will it be like for sons to compete against daughters? Are outside managers, sons-in-law, and others under consideration? Competition is part of business, and anyone who participates in sports knows about the exhilarating effects of competition on motivation and energy level. But the key to healthy competition is for people to be competing not against each other, but towards the goals of the team. There is a difference between competing by doing excellent work, and competing by undermining the competitors. Destructive conflict comes most often when nobody is sure what tactics or rules are in force. A powerful owner should set up clear expectations for how and when the succession decision will be made.

Many owners who know how to deal straightforwardly start by letting people know that succession is not a closed question, and that it will be made only after a certain number of years. They then outline ways that potential successors, often including non-family managers, will rotate through key management jobs and be part of a period of business growth and development. In this way succession is tied to demonstrable ability to lead and develop the business rather than who is able to stay closest to Dad.

Selecting a successor may be difficult. You must separate potential from actual achievement. A person may be excellent at a particular job but not have the breadth to become an owner/manager. The choice involves an element of intuitive judgment and risk. Will the person work out? The risk is equally high with a family member or an outsider. Whatever a person's desire to run the business, he or she may not be up to the job. Once the selection is made, it involves a real transfer of control that makes it almost irrevocable. Therefore, the testing and training process is critical.

Sharing thoughts and ideas with all the people involved can be very enlightening and helpful. Many problems stem from founders' fear, old family messages, or just old-fashioned guilt. Many founders think that, if they share such thoughts, they will disappoint or de-motivate people. In fact, the opposite is true. Knowing what is on your mind, other people can share what is on theirs and make you aware of other possibilities. For example, many founders get caught in the dilemma of naming one person successor. When they talk to their sons or daughters, they often find that the heirs are more comfortable with a shared management team, and so what Dad thought was a problem is really not. Many second and third-generation family firms are run by co-presidents, or teams. Just as a couple can share leadership, so can two cousins, or brothers.

If the environment of the business from the first day of work is one where people can talk about these issues, and check in about how they are doing, then the possibility of misunderstanding can be minimized. The palace intrigue of people trying to make others look bad to enhance their own reputations, thrives in an environment of secrecy where an owner does not share his reactions. The problems of brothers or brothers-in-law acting as rivals, or the daughter who is outstripping her brother, or an heir who has serious problems as a manager, need to be faced early. When an owner finds his trust and confidence in a person eroded, the earlier that the issue can be talked about openly, the more likely it will not poison the working environment.

A related fear is that other managers and family members will feel upset, betrayed, or unmotivated if they are not chosen. In fact, very often the people not selected agree with the choice, recognizing they were not right for the job. Moreover in some companies, second place can be a considerable benefit, packaged attractively with stock, profit sharing, and incentive pay. Managing one division or a store, can be attractive for a family member who is not CEO, or for a non-family manager. If a key person leaves, however, because he or she is passed over, it is often better to have that happen sooner than later, so that a second tier of able management can be installed before the actual succession.

Siblings: Conflict or Continuity

Less than half the family businesses in the country have only one potential heir. In most, there are two or more siblings, plus cousins and in-laws who might inherit. The business can also be sold or liquidated. How do families work it out? Some divide up the territory, both psychic and material. Each child develops different talents and goes in separate directions. Some oldest children go out on their own, leaving the business to their younger siblings, while other younger brothers and sisters leave the business when they see their elder becoming the designated successor. But the process of making these decisions is rarely clear. And in many businesses, more than one young family member works in the business and considers the possibility, "this could all be mine." Albert Thomassen quotes a Dutch successor:

"My father wanted to settle the succession with my mother. They don't want to appoint one of the children as successor in advance. So they decide that whoever of their children will prove his worth best will be given general control over the firm. This caused enormous rivalry among me and my two brothers. Eventually an organization expert was called in who guided us through the succession process. My mother actually forced my father to retire from the firm."[5]

Everyone knows an instance where destructive sibling rivalry has poisoned a family company. But looking closely at rivalries reveals that they are actually triangles, and at the head is usually the father. The father sets the competition in motion when he communicates that he is not sure of who will succeed him and that somehow succession is tied to each child's value to him. He may prefer one son or daughter to another, or suggest different things to one or the other.

If rivalry begins, a father can intervene actively to limit it. He can keep the rivals away from each other, and find areas in which each can be effective. And, as we've seen, the founder can set down clearly the rules and expectations for succession, so that the rivalry can remain challenging, not hostile. The key is to find ways to keep the succession battle from being a win/lose affair, to preserve the self-esteem of the person who is not taking over the business.

Ben Bridge Jewelers, a nationwide chain, has had two harmonious successions with siblings working together. Herb Bridge grew up in his father's store, and was given a quarter share of it when he was 18. But he wanted to work on his own. He got an offer to run another store, and told his father he was taking it. His father said, "That's a nice offer, but you can't leave the business, because I am." His father's departure was sudden, but it worked out because Herb and his younger brother Bob were trained and ready. Now each of them has a son who is highly competent and comfortable with the competition for president, because they are very secure in their fathers' love and in self-esteem. Also, the rules are set. Every year, each of them is evaluated by the executive committee of the company, which will make the final decision.[6]

There are several ways to accomodate multiple successors:

1. Shared leadership: The pair or trio forms a leadership group. The example of copreneurs is one model. They can divide up executive functions but make key decisions together.

2. Split the business in two: One part of the business can be spun off or divided in some other way. In one company a division that was primarily a supplier of the other was split off with the daughter getting ownership, and being allowed to solicit outside customers. A variation of this strategy is for one sibling to head a semi-autonomous division or part of the business within the whole.

3. Buying another business: Often the succession conflict is because each heir wants to run a business like Father or Mother did. This can be resolved when each sibling is offered the same prize: financial support for buying or starting his or her own business. Some families have formed family venture pools, where all family members share in a percentage of the profits of each family business. If one sibling inherits the business, the whole family can profit, and other siblings can develop through going out on their own.

4. Taking leadership in other family enterprises: Some families have real estate and stock holdings that are more valuable than the business. While one sibling takes over the company, another can head the family development or trust office, offering the family the opportunity to develop a more diversified business empire.

The important thing is for the founder to discover that there may be more options than he is considering. There should never be a situation where the rivals feel they have entered a winner take all sweepstakes. Yet, sadly, many families believe that message, which creates the potential for the succession era to lead to the estrangement of one of the heirs.

The siblings from related families may form an organization, like the Rockefeller cousins, to represent their own perspective on the business. One family of several sons, daughters, and in-laws, was the fourth generation of a real estate development company currently run by two brothers. The two brothers had been fighting since birth. However, the company was strong, and the pair had complementary skills so that people agreed that neither would have been successful on their own (one was too much of a perfectionist, while the other was too much of an opportunist). A sister also owned a third of the business, though she wasn't involved in management.

Each of the owners had children, who knew each other and expected to have a part of the business, which was organized into a complex network of trusts. But the owners were not making their future intentions clear. The heirs decided to take matters into their own hands. They began to work with a consultant on their own relationships and on their feelings about each other and about the business. After a few months, each member of the group began to treat their father differently. One daughter became more assertive, telling her father that she felt slighted about her role in the business. The oldest son began to be more assertive in making decisions when the brothers were in conflict. He became the mediator. The heirs began to develop their ideas of where the business should go. Finally, the fathers elected to join the process, and by that time, they faced a clear, close and united group of heirs. It was easy to work out the transition to the next generation.

Succession can become a sibling rivalry between children and in-laws or non-family managers. The rivalry in each of these relationships is fueled by lack of awareness of the owner's intention or guidelines, a perception of scarce resources within the business, one person's feeling unacknowledged or unappreciated, and the lack of a model for cooperative relationship and shared leadership.

Sometimes, there are hidden issues that the business and family has not dealt with. For example, a common issue is the lack of competence or commitment of the blood heir and the dilemma this poses for the in-law or non-family manager. By "divine right" the business will pass to the direct heir. The outsider might develop a covert role as the "real" brains of the business, working through the designated successor. The agreement is that the heir will have a more symbolic or less demanding role. The trouble is when the heir does not clearly perceive his or her lack of ability, or doesn't offer reasonable compensation to the key manager. But what if the son does not recognize how much his brother-in-law is contributing, or if the smaller percentage of ownership he has been given is not enough to keep him content? Resentment may build, getting fueled by the added resentment of a sister or other family members. If succession is not settled in such a situation, pressure can be placed covertly on the founder to decide in favor of the outsider, or the business can be paralyzed or hurt because people feel they have to take sides in the conflict. The outsider may try to discredit the heir, or act against the best interests of the business by not doing things that need to be done, or by withdrawing and not caring. In such situations, everybody seems to lose.

A father's ambivalence comes out the strongest at the point of actually turning over the reins. One son notes that waiting for his father nearly made him leave. He vows not to do that to his son. He has told his son, from the time his son enters the business, he will remain five more years, period. Many public companies use a fixed retirement age to create orderly succession. In some families, the wife exerts pressure here. She is often the person who can see the perspective of the heir, and she is ready for more companionship with her husband, but also understands his fears about leaving. She can sometimes effectively mediate the disengagement.

What can be done to facilitate succession conflicts, or help guide the business through this era? Often it is helpful to engage a consultant to help everybody discuss the issues, and come up with a working succession plan. An outside adviser can help the people who find it difficult to communicate, and a founder/owner who doesn't know how to share, open up the channels. The use of communication techniques from Chapter 3, and the active participation of the Family Council, described in Chapter 4, are crucial during the succession era.

Outside Advisers: Support for Transition

It is especially important to amass a good team of advisers during the succession era. The entrepreneur often plays bankers, accountants, lawyers, and consultants against each other, getting advice but not sharing it. Now more than ever, the founder needs advisers that act as a team, and help him make decisions and check the accuracy of his information.

Outside advisers add expertise to that of the owner and fill in if there is a crisis or vacuum. They have skills that an owner cannot have, and an objective perspective that can be invaluable. Advisers can spot new opportunities, offer fresh ideas, and help mediate differences of opinion among owners or between generations. They can take up the slack in a crisis, even taking over management temporarily. There are two categories of outside advisers:

• **Board of Directors.** Especially in a public company, the board of directors exercises a check-and-balance function. Every business should have one, and not just on paper or as a rubber stamp. Too often board members only get together for coffee with the lawyer once or twice a year, and sign the required papers for the owner. Children, spouses, cousins, and friends of the family are often directors, for ceremonial, social, or convenience reasons. The next chapter will explore in detail the need for a board and how to set one up.

• **Professionals.** These include your lawyer, accountant, insurance agent, banker, and other professionals who provide resources that are critical to your survival. You are free to heed or ignore their advice. But when you ignore it, be sure that they know why you are doing it, and that you explore your decision with them. Often the underminers of family business—denial, avoidance, and distrust—operate when advisors tell you things you do not want to hear, for example, that you are delaying certain critical functions to insure business continuity. One business owner I know spent years talking to an adviser about estate plans, but his family has yet to see a plan, and he has yet to make a decision, even on an interim basis.

Use your advisors pro-actively to help you deal with problems before they become crises. However, many business owners regard these people as their personal advisers, not the business'. They counsel him alone, rather than bringing other family members into their deliberations. This is not the best idea—advisers to family businesses should understand that all the involved parties should be privy to their advice. Also advisors should at least occasionally act as a group. Many founders have a divide and conquer strategy, or keep advice to themselves. As we've seen, succession issues are among the most difficult a founder will face. Having support from peers and outsiders the founder trusts is the most effective tool in managing the succession process.

Orderly Succession

One of the most effective succession processes I've seen was in a large food company where three brothers, a brother-in-law, a sister-in-law, and a cousin were all in management. The owner saw each of their contributions and was unsure which one would be the best new CEO. He had a hunch that it might be his son-in-law, but was afraid to name him outright. Also, he wasn't ready to go yet. He began to define a role for himself as chairman of the board, managing the company's move into international markets. But as each of his successors proved themselves competent and committed, he grew more and more restive about how to deal with succession.

As he became less involved in day-to-day management, the six family members and the key non-family manager began to meet as a team. They talked about the evolving direction of the business, including new products, marketing, and the need for new capital. They worked well together, and the patriarch felt confidence in all of them together. Over time he began to consider that the group itself might be able to settle the question of succession. He asked them and to his surprise, they agreed. They came up with a structure over a two-year period to give them each overall familiarity with the business, and a shared process of yearly performance review and discussion of how things were going. Together they began to trust and value the leadership of the brother-in-law, and to feel good about the growth of the business. At the end of the two years, they affirmed the leadership of the brother-in-law, choosing him as successor.

Contrast that process with one in which a father/owner named his oldest son successor without communicating his intentions to either his other son or his key manager. All three had worked well together, with no sense that any decision was near. Father had talked about the decision with his successor, but the others were not part of the deliberations. After the choice, there was a period of distrust and withdrawal by the two others, who found it difficult to remain committed. It wasn't that they disagreed with the choice, but they felt that they didn't have time to prepare for it, and weren't consulted about when the choice would take place, or what the father's criteria were.

A more comfortable succession is one that takes place in stages rather than all at once. Alberto-Culver, the household goods manufacturer, is in the midst of an orderly succession. Last year Leonard Lavin, the 70-year-old chairman, promoted his son-in-law and daughter, Howard and Carol Bernick, to key positions, designating Howard as successor. Leonard had always been a typical entrepreneur, exercising tight control even over the minutest details, which had led many executives to leave the company. A few years ago, Howard, who had recently married Leonard's daughter and joined the company, was put in charge of a committee whose task was to look at what management problems were leading to the company's erosion of market share and profitability. During that same period, Carol was involved in the creation of several new products.

The management committee gave Leonard some bad news: his tight management style was stifling innovation and creating problems. Leonard agreed to let go, and affirmed his confidence in Howard and Carol. Most important in this process is that it has not been a win/lose battle. It involved a hard business decision, but one in a loving and close family. Leonard has not been exiled or sent away. The three have formed an intergenerational management team that is likely to last for a decade or so. After all, Leonard is still one of those business owners who refuses to consider retirement. But he has allowed his management role to shift to make room for the new leadership. He has a new role as scout for fresh markets, while still counseling his successors. They, in turn, have the authority to match their responsibility.

The new generation of the business really begins when the successor is named, or a succession plan is developed. Then the founder must apply his time to finding new avenues for his energy and talent, perhaps a new business venture or source of involvement. As the story of Leonard Lavin shows, the owner often does not leave at once. He or she makes the choice and ushers in a transition period where the owner and successor work together. They gradually shift to the point where the new leader makes the decisions, and the owner begins a phased process of withdrawal from daily operations.

The departing CEO often needs to retain some actual or symbolic role. He may retain a fancy office, a title, and certain critical functions, like stockholder relations or financial development. If his name has been synonymous with the company, he will often continue as a fixture of the customer relations, shareholder meetings, or franchise meetings. But the center has shifted to the new manager. At this point, the key hurdle to be passed is when the new leader makes a decision that the founder/former CEO is not comfortable with. Will he rescind it, undermine it, argue with it, or support it? If you are a founder who has installed a successor, have you passed that milestone?

As we've seen succession is not simply the prerogative of the founder—family, employees, and heirs all need to be brought into the process. In order to avoid painful misunderstandings and destruction of the business, planning for the next generation in the family and the business has to start very early. The legacy of the founder and the achievements of the heirs lie in the balance. The next chapter continues the exploration of generational transitions, looking at the ways that the family business deals with employees and completes its own renewal in terms of direction and management.

Notes:
1. Sonnenfeld, Jeffrey. *The Hero's Farewell.*
2. Bowman-Upton, Nancy. Presentation at Baylor University, First Annual Family Business Conference, 1989.
3. Lansberg, Ivan. "The Succession Conspiracy." *Family Business Review*, Vol 1: No. 2, 1988.
4. Dyer, Gibb. *Cultural Change in Family Firms.*
5. Thomassen, Albert. "Succession in Family Business." Unpublished paper, 1988.
6. Rambeck, Richard. "Succeeding at Succession." *Seattle Business,* May 1989.

9

Employees are Family Too: Renewing the Organization for the Future

"In concept at least, we build organizations to meet our needs as individuals. Our needs—as customers, as employees, as managers, as shareholders, as citizens. But all too often, quietly and slowly, and while we're not really watching, we're trapped by the very thing we've built to serve us. Suddenly we find ourselves enslaved by mindless bureaucracy, by habit, or simply by comfort. People, the only real sources of renewal, stop trying. Customers vanish. The best employees lapse into apathy, or vote with their feet and leave.

"The challenge is a tough one and not unique to corporations. We are commonly trapped by the things we seek: material possessions, fame and glory, the good life. . . .The challenge is never completely solved; it recurs like weeds in a garden. But the challenge is far from impossible. The essence of living, really living, is renewal."

-*Robert Waterman Jr.*, The Renewal Factor

The reason so few family businesses reach the second or third generation has to do with the difficulties of family succession combined with inability to achieve renewal of the basic business. The need for continuous organizational renewal has never been so acute, as the rules of business today change almost yearly. Not only must the founder turn the business over to an heir, but the heir must be up to the new challenges of bringing the business into the future. In order to survive, the business must learn to do things in a new way. In many industries, the business must almost be re-invented every generation. Here is a story of success, and a notable failure.

Chad Frost grew up in Grand Rapids, Michigan, where his father was the third generation to run the Frost manufacturing plant. Chad became an engineer with Textron and didn't expect to return to Michigan. But a combination of frustration with large corporations, the chance to make a real difference, and feeling of responsibility for the family legacy led to his return. The company was losing money and threatened with extinction. Ruben, Chad's father, ran a traditional family business: loyal to his employees, taking care of family members who worked there, while keeping tight control over information, and delegating little.

New competition and higher costs had left the company in a terminal state. After engineering a turnaround at an acquisition for another company, Chad agreed to try to do the same with Frost. But the only way he could do that was to create a total turnaround in the family business culture. He decided this involved getting the family out of the business and building a new spirit with the employees, who had to achieve almost inconceivable productivity gains to keep the company afloat. He needed every employee to be 100% committed to the business.

After 117 years of traditional attitudes, the company was forced to modernize and install self-management teamwork. Ruben and Chad bought out other family members, and got them out of management. They then sold these shares to the employees, who were all put on salary and called "shareholders." The employees were empowered by sharing ownership as well as responsibility. Every "shareholder" learned new skills and, in effect, became an engineer. On a shoestring budget, they modernized the factory themselves and became competitive. The reward for everyone was, within two years, the company became profitable, and began to grow swiftly for the first time in a decade.

Chad is proud of what he has done. While Frost is no longer a "family business," Chad has taken the positive features of the family tradition: excellence of product and concern for employees, and retained them while facilitating the greatest transition the company has ever faced.[1]

Contrast Chad's story with the malaise at Mars, the candy company that is one of the largest privately-held businesses in the U.S. Forrest Sr., who inherited a small offshoot of his father's candy company, built a powerful, innovative, and caring company. Like other large family businesses, he developed strong brand identification, a durable dependable stable product, and a loyal work force. He believed in work democracy, to the point where not only were employees called "associates," but even private offices were taboo. In 1973 he turned management over to his two sons, Forrest Jr. and John. They are fierce rivals. Forrest Jr. is more social, while John is an introverted technician. Instead of pursuing acquisitions, or developing new products, the organization is dying of its traditions. Palace intrigue between adherents of John and Forrest, a bitter divorce, heightened competition, and loss of market share, are taking a toll. Observers say that neither grandson is really up to the task of running the large company. Talented management, once loyal, is starting to defect. Instead of being renewed, the company continues to turn in on itself because the virtues of its family business culture are becoming liabilities.

Family businesses extend way beyond the family. Even a small business forms a community—of employees, professional advisers, and often a network of suppliers, customers, and clients. Keeping the whole enterprise afloat is a task of continuing and increasing difficulty. The initial success of the family business and the growing confidence of the founder often plant seeds for future distress. As the business grows and the founder ages, he or she must be able to change management style and emphasis. What works for the start-up and growth stages of any business, are not the skills that will take the business into the next generation. Family businesses that are successful over long-term have several periods of renewal—major shifts in people, strategy, management structure, and form. Renewal does not simply happen, nor should it wait for a crisis. Major transitions can be anticipated and planned, and mechanisms can be in place to handle the new challenges. As we've seen, the most critical renewal period is the one that takes place after the founder has made his or her contribution, and put a succession plan in place.

In this chapter we look at how a family-owned business can navigate a successful business renewal, cultural shift, and management transformation. We will examine how the family can open itself to the creative advice and fresh air of non-family managers and advisers. A family cannot service all the needs of the business, especially a large business;

therefore, development of committed managers and leadership outside the family, is critical. This chapter shows how to build systems so that bad news can enter the family quickly, and how to respect, retain, and accommodate non-family talent. It covers the design and uses of a non-family board of advisers and building a management team that includes both family and non-family management. By its success, the business can outgrow the family who created it. The key to long-term prosperity is developing a collaborative relationship between family, managers, and advisers.

In the long run, the future for a family business lies in either of two directions. A new generation can take over the helm, bringing it into new directions while continuing the tradition and family legacy. But sometimes no family member has the skills to run the business. While the business can be sold, the other option is for the family to turn operations over to a non-family team of managers.

Tasks for the Chapter

If you are a business founder or heir, you can use this chapter to look at your organization culture and explore how you can use your most valuable resource—your employees, managers, board, and advisers—to help you renew the business and create a positive future. The whole family can reassess its role and style of involvement in the business for the future.

Non-family managers can use this chapter to learn how to work effectively with family owners and managers, to create an organization ready to face its future.

The Culture of Family

"We're all part of the family," is what you hear from family and non-family businesses alike, referring to a culture where people are committed to each other, respect personal needs, and feel close bonds. A business family should create a wonderful place to work for employees, who share a portion of the family feeling.

A great example is Bob and Joan McGrath of McGrath RentCorp, whom we met in Chapter 5. They hold semi-annual staff retreats, take employees out for celebrations of the couple's anniversary, and actively solicit employee input. At one retreat, they put together a book with a series of pictures of each employee, where each worker wrote a page about what it was like to work at McGrath. Their statements included:

- This is like a close family where promises are kept and people are fair. I have an unlimited chance to grow.
- Not a group of superstars, rather a team of champions.
- Demands a high quality of life with the work environment...expect friendship, caring, and love along with the work.

Joan and Bob believe that when you expect the highest standards from people and respect and pay them accordingly, they will respond. Indeed, the company has unequalled sales, growth, and quality in their industry.

Their style of working is more than just treating employees well. The 100 employees are a participatory group that has a hand in major decisions, especially in how the company will accomplish its goals. Each employee is given a scope of responsibility to make decisions and to discover new challenges. Another innovation is that all of their employees come to stockholder meetings. They have a bonus plan and are developing ways to give stock to employees.

Bob has two adult daughters who are not in the business. If either wanted to work for the company, she would have no special privileges because the McGraths feel that would be unfair to the people who have made such a deep commitment to the company. They want every employee to have a future in the company. They see McGrath RentCorp as not only for their personal family, but for the extended family of employees. Indeed their company is so attractive that most of the employees from companies they acquire stay with them.

Another exemplary company is Just Desserts in San Francisco, started by husband and wife team Elliot Hoffman and Gail Horvath. Like other copreneurs, they not only take their own personal and community work seriously, they allow their employees the same latitude. Their benefits policy is among the most extensive for a bakery, and includes special circumstances leave, if needed to work out a personal problem or family crisis. Their profit-sharing plan is generous, and the books are regularly opened to employees.

But there can be a dark side to family work environments for employees. The image of family the company wants to convey is one of caring camaraderie. Yet as the previous chapters have shown, that is not the whole story. The family, after all, is not a democracy, but a generational hierarchy, under the benevolent despotism of Dad and Mom. A family is a place where parents are clearly in charge, taking care of children who are expected to obey the rules. In this light, the sense of "family" in family business has costs as well as benefits. It only has room for one or two grownups!

Family feeling can be costly to the business as well. The paternalistic, "father knows best" climate is fine in a small, relatively stable world, where Dad's experience and dedication can take care of everyone. But what happens when the business grows, demands get overwhelming, and the environment changes? What happens when Dad gets older, and his touch is not so golden?

The major management problems in family business come from the same qualities that employees value about the business—its family-like bonds. A family business attracts employees who have an affinity for the goals, values, and style of the family. In the early stages of the business, people sign on because they are attracted to the charismatic energy of the founder's vision. They are listening to him, rather than to the outside world. Many family businesses are threatened by the development of a bureaucracy of "yes men," who act like feudal lords, always seeking the ear and will of their king. On the positive side, the business becomes an extended family, but the negative side is that the founder has duplicated his blind spots, and avoided hiring people who will confront, push, or question him. The corporate culture can be summed up as an attempt to "please Dad."

Think of a family, where the children have not been allowed to grow up, where everyone is maintained in a childlike state of dependency. The business has grown, but the founders and his "family" have not. The visionary founder often sees himself as a godlike person whose every impulse makes good business sense. Like many entrepreneurs, family business founders tend to hold on too long to their original ideas. Henry Ford, who refused to change his Model T car or even to offer it in colors other than black while his competitors leapt ahead, was similar to other family business founders who are reluctant to tamper with the formula. For a decade after his death, the heirs of Walt Disney lost millions slavishly doing things the way Walt did, rather than watching the marketplace. Their turnaround came when they found an outsider, Michael Eisner, who became the spiritual successor to Walt while bringing new skills and an updated vision. Now the company has grown up very quickly.

Family feelings have other limitations. Family businesses, like families, tend to be supportive places to work. They often have a policy of "no-layoffs," and offer tremendous job security. They are like civil service empires, large bureaucracies where people do what they have traditionally done with the calm security of knowing that they will be taken care of if they continue to do things the way the owner wants. There is nothing wrong with this attitude as long as the environment where the business operates doesn't change. It promotes caring, and sensitivity to the rich tradition of the company. As long as the public continues to buy your clothing, soap, newspapers, or food, and your family brand name is perceived as high quality, the family culture works fine.

But takeovers, global competition, new market tastes and niches, obsolescent factories, new information technologies, and new values about work often make it impossible to maintain a traditional family culture. Just as the family cannot remain the same, the family business cannot remain static. Indeed generational disputes in families are often clashes between the old and new values. The traditional Chinese patriarch who ran a plant store and refused to use an adding machine or copier, and the deli supplier who refused to advertise his specialty products and capitalize on tremendous customer loyalty in order to expand, were both confronted by heirs who pushed them to change. Often a son or daughter has the courage and power to demand change, while the loyal employees, after a lifetime of listening to the founder and being taken care of by him, are less likely to rock the boat.

In the early days, the founder and a small, young, hungry, ambitious group create the company. They are lean and mean, overworked but feeling good about their achievements, and reap the rewards of fast growth. Then growth slows and employees age. Many heirs find themselves in companies where the average age of employees is the age of their fathers! When I asked one company how they oriented new employees, they laughed and told me they hadn't hired anyone in 15 years.

Aging employees are indeed a problem. How do you ask somebody to think about retirement, when the business is his or her life? Especially when the founder has the same problem! The reticence to upset loyal employees impedes family businesses from developing a second tier of managers, trained and ready to enter key roles. Some businesses also exhibit a fear of hiring competent younger people who have the skills to help the business grow. This creates an upside down pyramid structure, where all the employees are on the top. These problems are characteristic of all maturing organizations, where traditional ways have taken it as far as it can go.

In one business the son of the founder faced his father's best friend as head of a division whose success was critical to the business. At 80 he was slowing down somewhat. But the son couldn't bring up retirement with his father's best friend (though his father was long gone), and didn't feel he could train another person for the job. So the business foundered on this weak link. In fact, it turned out that this manager felt he couldn't quit because he didn't want to let his old friend down!

Several damaging habits regarding employees creep into family-managed firms over time:

- People are kept on for their loyalty rather than results;
- People will not confront the founder or each other;
- Focus on internal politics and power struggles rather than the environment;
- Management finds it difficult to let anyone go;
- Oriented toward its past rather than its future;
- No new blood shaking things up;
- No long-range plan for development;
- No innovation of systems or products;
- Company focusses on its existing markets and customers;
- Employees lack abilities to handle new demands.

As this list shows, the family business culture is often characterized by denial of real challenges, and an emphasis on pleasing the boss rather than on achieving results. The focus on the past damages the capacity for facing the future. People feel there is no need for change, because they've always been successful. However, employees do not develop these attitudes on their own. They grow because employees mirror the attitudes of the founder/entrepreneur. After the creative task of building a viable company, the founder often becomes, if not fat and happy, at least so set in his ways that he resists change and innovation.

There is a good reason for such attitudes. The owner feels a deep sense of gratitude toward people who stuck with them when they were struggling. In one company, for example, the bookkeeper who started by helping her friend, the founder's sister, ultimately became controller of the $10 million company. She had no capacity for forecasting, or cost controls, and the company was bleeding money. But people couldn't let her go. They kept trying to get accounting consultants to go around her rather than hiring somebody to supervise her. They did not consider, for example, that there might be other ways to reward her long service, like a bonus or stock, rather than keeping her in a position over her head.

What Do Your People Think?

Like any set of parents, the owner/managers of a family business make many assumptions about how their managers and employees "feel." They look for overt signs of discontent, and are happy or satisfied when they hear none. But to build a strong organization, you need to listen a little harder. Because of the sensitivity of family members, especially the founder, employees may get the message that disagreement, conflict, or difficulty is not appreciated. One sign of a paternalistic environment is that people are supposed to be happy, or keep their feelings to themselves. After all, don't we take good care of people?

Employees may feel resentful of, or have difficulty with, the nepotism of the family. If family heirs and founders continually harvest money from the business, while salaries are slower to go up, and bonuses are nonexistent, feelings will grow. If Dad's second son does not do his job and another manager has to cover for him, or is supposed to be supervised by him, or worse yet, is working under him, that employee will be in a quandary.

Many family executives feel they have the pulse of their business if they just talk to their managers periodically. But they are in danger of hearing what they want rather than what they need to. The non-family manager has quickly learned that survival comes from not making waves, and certainly not from bringing bad news. So a cycle of denial and withholding can go on for years, until the business decays to the point where the marketplace gives the business feedback. You might ask yourself when was the last time that an employee came to you to tell you something you didn't want to hear. If you can't remember, the likelihood is that you are avoiding feedback.

What can be done to bring these issues to the surface? The best choice is for the family to develop a corporate climate where employees feel comfortable dissenting, disagreeing, or bringing bad news. A true/false survey is a quick and accurate way to gather feedback from employees. Just as an assessment tool can alert family members to different feelings and opinions, so an employee survey is one way for difficult issues to surface. Anonymity can be preserved by having people respond in sealed envelopes, and by having an outside person, such as a consultant, collate the responses. In addition to the survey questions, you should have space to invite people to respond to other issues in an open-ended way.

Begin a survey by stating your purpose in doing it. I suggest a statement such as:

"I am concerned that the presence of family members in this company might have some unintended negative effects on morale, or that there may be feelings about family participation in the company that I ought to know about. This survey is a first step in getting those issues addressed. I will be receiving the results of this survey, and will then meet with all of you to discuss what was found and how we can best respond to the issues raised. I make two promises to you: that your confidence in answering this survey will be respected, and that your concerns will be explored and considered fairly. I thank you for your consideration in responding to this survey, and hope that it will be a step in making this a better place for all of us to work."

Some of the questions that could be asked in a true/false survey include:

1. I feel there is less chance for advancement because of family members in the business.
2. I feel that family members are not treated as other employees.
3. (CEO) is not willing to hear opinions he or she may disagree with.
4. I feel my opinions and viewpoints do not count.
5. Salaries and rewards are not reasonable compared to effort.
6. People are promoted more because of personal relations than ability.
7. It is hard to disagree with a family member in the business.
8. I am not sure why certain decisions are made.
9. The owners are taking too much money out of the business.
10. I don't know how the company is doing.
11. Information about the company is not shared very widely.
12. Bad news is not wanted in this company.

The questions can be more specific, according to what you want to know. The purpose is not to bring you the last word about conflicts and difficulties, but to open up a dialogue. After you have received the survey information, the next step is to have a employee meeting. In a small company of under 100 people, it is possible to meet all together, especially if the issues are serious enough. Sharing the survey results can also be helpful. The best strategy in the meeting is to communicate your concerns, the data, and your desire to improve things. Then open the floor to suggestions about what might be done. If the feedback is negative, you don't need to explain yourself at length, present your view, or even apologize. In fact, try to keep quiet as much as possible. Ask questions and dig for clarification, but don't try to answer people at the meeting. Their concerns deserve serious and careful reflection. Take time to prepare a response. Your major purpose at the initial meeting should be to let people know that you are ready to hear their feedback, not talk over it. Your ultimate goal is to resolve issues in ways that respect the family's needs, keep the business strong, and maintain employee motivation.

As I've noted in Chapter 8, the involvement of employees is most critical in the period of planning and implementing succession. Employees are often very attached to the business founder, and while they may be critical of his leadership, they have family-like feelings about his leaving. They need to express those feelings and have their concerns for the future addressed.

Fast Growth: Can the Family Handle It?

A visionary founder, a creative product, loyal employees, committed family members are the man ingredients for business success. Stir the pot with a good economy and years of hard work and sweat equity. The dish at the end is a hardy, profitable, effective business. But with success comes new difficulties. As a business grows, it demands more specialized talent, presents greater complexities, and creates new problems of meeting demand and creating organizational systems. The story of entrepreneurialism is the story of the rise and fall of the entrepreneur. For every entrepreneur like Ken Olsen of Digital Equipment, who has taken 20 years to build his start-up into a true challenger of IBM, and to manage creatively the needs of growth and development, there are others who fall, or get pushed, just after their company succeeds. The story of Steve Jobs, who built Apple into one of the most innovative companies only to be fired by his hand-picked colleague, is one of many about entrepreneurs outstaying their welcome.

An entrepreneur doesn't have to be fired. The marketplace can do it for him, by allowing astounding growth and then showing him that he is not up to the task. After amazing success, toymakers Coleco and Worlds of Wonder each faltered under the pressure of continuing to innovate, getting enough goods to market, and following up their initial success.

The business can grow quickly, but the growth must be managed and controlled. A person who can keep all the data from a $10 million company in his or her head can't repeat the feat when the company reaches $100 million. After growing, the business' ad hoc organization needs to be formalized. There are two choices: the founder and his management team can develop their skills to meet the challenge, or they can hire managers who know how to manage this size organization.

For any business, the transition from entrepreneurship to a professional management team is difficult. After a new business succeeds, there is usually a crisis as the company has to move from the tight control of the lone entrepreneur to build a larger team of competent professionals, with the right skills to handle growth. It's just a little more complex when the entrepreneur is Dad or Mom.

The business that is taking off faces similar issues, but they descend upon it more quickly. The start-up business is loosely organized: everybody helps out and does a little of everything. Then success strikes. Every day new employees come on, who do not have the personal relationships or do not understand the informal structure. Since things are not coordinated and there is no clear structure or plan, everybody works hard, but often act at cross-purposes. Fights break out due to the tension and confusion, and family owners struggle valiantly to create order and get things done. But they don't have time to organize the company, because they are selling, or filling orders, as quickly as they can. The reckoning comes when they can't meet demand, or quality slips, or costs get out of control. A company can slide down as quickly as it grew.

The need for a change is apparent when the task of keeping things running seems overwhelming. There just doesn't seem to be time to get things done, and there isn't. The problem is not in the work, but how it is organized. The ways that the company has run in the past no longer work.

Self-Assessment: Organizational Growing Pains[2]

When a company has outgrown its leadership or organizational structure, UCLA Management Professor Eric Flamholtz suggests that it develops "growing pains," symptoms that the unclear or loosely organized facets of the company can no longer handle the demands made upon them.

How many of these are true of your company? Place one check in the box if this is a problem, two checks if it is a significant problem. When you are done, total the number of checks, counting double checks as 2. Scores above 12 indicate that your management has not kept pace with the demands of the business:

_____ *1. People feel that "there are not enough hours in the day."*
_____ *2. People spend too much time "putting out fires."*
_____ *3. People are not aware of what other people are doing.*
_____ *4. People lack understanding about where the firm is headed.*
_____ *5. There are too few good managers.*
_____ *6. People feel that "I have to do it myself if I want to get it done correctly."*
_____ *7. Most people feel that meetings are a waste of time.*
_____ *8. When plans are made, there is very little follow-up, so things just don't get done.*
_____ *9. Some people feel insecure about their place in the firm.*
_____ *10. The firm continues to grow in sales but not in profits.*

The family can aggravate these company growing pains by its own paternalism and denial. Family members may not have the skills to know what to do, and they may be reluctant to seek expert help. A family afraid to demand accountability from itself will have trouble asking it from employees. The denial of trouble, and the demand that everyone just "try harder" in order to make the company work, can burn out staff and diminish a company's ability to function. The company needs to learn new ways, but the family culture can fear, deny, or limit change.

If your business is feeling some growing pains, if you sense that your management, your father's management, or your products and services, are maturing, or you are on the edge of a generational transition, drastic action is needed. In systems terms, you can't change the system at the level you are in—you need to move the organization to operate on a different level. The business needs to be opened up to fresh air: new blood, new ideas, new energy, new methods.

From Paternalism to Collaboration

The presence of growing pains is a signal that the company needs to move from the loose, personal organization of the entrepreneur to a more carefully managed, clearly structured organization where responsibility is shared among several managers, each with a clear area of responsibility. When you see these warning signs, you need to explore ways to redesign your management team by rethinking your own role and that of each family member. Things can no longer get done by people whose commitment is characterized by uncritical loyalty, or whose talent is not questioned because they are close to the family owners. A major shift in the business structure must take place.

Specifically, looking at family businesses that successfully built cultures that last beyond the founder, we see certain changes as the organization grows and matures:

From	To
Founder is sole power	Shared power
Founder alone knows key information	Open communication
All control with founder	Management team controls
"I know what to do"	"Let's find out the answer"
Founder only trusts himself and family	Trust employees
Founder embodies the business	Organizational identity
Founder operates by personal intuition	Planning & intuition
Single product or service, unchanging	Multiple products
Distrust advice	Seek advice

Loyal employees	Competent employees
Hire people you know	Hire those who can do the job
Tradition: "The way we've always done it."	Vision: "How we'd like to do it"
Certainty	Uncertainty
Stability	Continual change
Management by good intentions	Management by skills

The development of a management team is far more than a change of faces at the top. The new leadership has to take the company in some new directions and develop new ways of doing things. This is not a wholesale rejection of the family's tradition, but it does represent some important value shifts. The old pattern of paternalism and single-handed control needs to give rise to a culture where control is shared and many people participate in creating the company's future. While succession can be from a founder/dictator to a new ruler, more frequently we see family business, and indeed all businesses, shifting to more collective leadership in the second or third generation.

To move successfully into a new generation, a business must be renewed by new structures and directions, as well as new leadership. Organizational renewal is not simply a question of hiring a new CEO or shifting a few boxes in the organization chart. It is a top-to-bottom questioning of everything that has made the business successful. Family business renewal involves three areas: strategic planning, management development, and family involvement.

Strategic Planning: The Crisis of Direction

When the business is maturing, growing fast, or simply facing a leadership transition, it must reassess where it is going and what it needs. As the family grows and a new generation becomes involved, the original mission of the business may be less practical as a long-term direction. At crisis and transition points, the business needs to see where it is, and what opportunities and threats lie ahead. Since the family business has a tendency to turn in on itself, one critical resource is a board of directors or advisors who are outside and independent of the business. When leadership is weak or in conflict, the board can act as a rudder, helping the business discover its direction and making critical decisions about ownership and the future.

Strategic planning is similar to the family planning process of the Family Council, but it involves more expert assessment of where the business is and where it might go. The blind spots of the founder, the inexperience of heirs, and the naivete of outside family members all create the need for another group that can act as a balance for the family and the business. The keys to success are to get outside advice and create a strategic planning process.

Strategic planning involves looking at the environment you are operating in, deciding what business you are in, developing a strategy for how you will operate, setting goals and creating an organization to reach them. The strategic plan is written and developed by many people over time. The best plan is not something written by a consultant or by the leader, but one where everybody has a chance to contribute. While managers and employees should be involved in the planning, the owners and the board of directors should make the major decisions.

The reason for this is that owners have somewhat different interests than managers. As we have seen, in a family business the owners may include family members who do not work in the business, and outside minority stockholders. Owners hire the managers, even if they come from the ownership group, and they oversee their performance.

The owners are represented by a board of directors. In many closely-held companies the board is a ceremonial group consisting of Mother, Dad, and an uncle, cousin, and maybe the oldest son. They are names put on paper in the lawyer's office. But family business consultants like John Ward, Gibb Dyer, and Leon Danco observe that having a figurehead board takes away a valuable resource from a company.[3] The board, when used correctly, is a group of experts, outside the business, who can help the company set policy and oversee the implementation. It is a critical tool for the success of a company, even a tiny mom-and-pop operation. The board can deliver difficult news to a scared or defensive founder/owner. It can act as a bridge between warring ownership groups or family members at odds. It can prepare the way for succession, or mandate or lobby for needed business changes to save the company.

One of the best uses of the board is to mediate family conflicts. Some families use the board to fight family battles. They argue over all manner of personal issues, thereby paralyzing the company. In many family businesses, responses to difficult issues have been delayed by family conflict. Often outside board members can act as a brake to childish family communication. Having an outsider there to say, "Let's get on with it," or "Can't we put this aside," can help the business move while a family is struggling.

The board should meet face to face at least twice a year, and have all financial and business records available before the meeting for their review. As a rule of thumb, you need one outside director for every family member. Board members can be recruited in a variety of ways. Often, they are willing to serve for no fee, if they are community members or respect the business you are in. They are often local professionals. One business owner had an owner of another business on his board, and he served on the other business' board. Sometimes a trusted relative from another business can be a good board member. Choose a board wisely; select individuals with different styles and skills.

The board doesn't have to be formal. Sometimes legal liability makes it difficult for people to serve. Some companies have an advisory board. For example, during a period of economic difficulty when family succession was unclear, Bechtel, one of the largest privately-held businesses, created an advisory board for its president. It helped the company reassess strategy and decide succession.

The board doesn't even have to be a board. One model that has been adopted by many family business leaders is the chief executive network group. The people who are most likely to understand your business situation and be able to give you advice and valuable, if difficult, feedback are other business owners. In a group of peers, people can be candid about their problems, and can confront each other. There are several organizations that bring together chief executives. The two largest are Young President's Organization (YPO), and The Executive Committee (TEC).

The TEC model is to have a group of ten business owners meet together for one full day a month. In effect, the group functions as a board for the ten companies. Each month, each person checks in with the group, and individuals ask for time to deal with problems. After about a year of membership, a TEC member becomes familiar with the issues in each person's organization, can see patterns and similarities across issues, and begins to view his or her organization in context. The other benefit of TEC groups is that they are able to deal with personal or business issues. Sometimes the problems of a family business owner lie on the family/ business boundary; peers are able to deal in either context.

Let's see what a board can do. "Zeller Corp." is a family manufacturing company, started by Cyrus "Zeller." He owns 100%, and his son and daughter who are managers eventually will inherit it. Right now, Cyrus still plans to work for another five to ten years, and he expects to steer the business through some upcoming crises. He knows many other businesspeople in the community, and decides that he wants a more active board. The board now consists of Cyrus, his wife Helen, and his lawyer. Cyrus decides to include three new members, his friend Fred, one of his more important suppliers and an entrepreneur himself, his cousin Nan who has an MBA and has started a successful business, and a friend who runs another business. Cyrus and Fred each decide to serve on the other's board in lieu of compensation. Cyrus feels that he has some unique talents on his board, all people who know what it is to run a business. He plans that they will meet four Saturdays a year, and will end the day with a dinner for them and their spouses.

Why set up board if there isn't a particular crisis or reason? Cyrus feels there are some good reasons. He is concerned that he has become stale and is not recognizing potential problems. He also has some ideas about how Zeller Corp. could grow, and he will be making some risky decisions about expansion, acquisitions, and borrowing. He wants help and advice, direct and not just tailored to what he would like to hear.

He also wants a group that knows the business, in case something should happen to him. He needs Helen to be informed, and he wants people who know the business, and Helen, who would be available in a crisis. In addition he has some problems with his children and is not sure what to do about succession. He has four children, and he isn't sure that the son and daughter in management have the desire or will to take over. While he will make the final decision with them, he wants help from the board. And finally he wants to consider the option of selling the business or turning it over to a professional manager. He feels that the board is the best instrument for him to explore these issues.

The board will not work miracles. In order for it to function, Cyrus has to take time to fill them in and to prepare materials on key decisions and financial data that they get at least two weeks in advance. But he's glad that he has to prepare. It keeps him thinking and on his toes; otherwise he might put these plans off.

Management Development: The Crisis of Ability

Owning a business or starting one does not necessarily qualify you to operate one. As the business grows and develops, the success of the venture depends on the quality and participation of the team of managers and employees. The family must take pains to cultivate and attract good managers, and develop their skills and nurture their contribution to the business.

The key tasks for management development are to develop or hire competent managers and offer them incentives to stay, and create a clearly defined, participatory management team. Let's look at an example.

"Baker Bearings" had been a highly visible part of the community for 40 years as the town's largest employer. Ben Baker had worked with his father, Al, for many years, developing the business. There were many fine managers, especially Carl, chief of factory operations, Len, warehouse and shipping manager, and Harvey, the engineer. They were all old school; that is, they had learned, like Al, by doing. They knew how to keep the factory running and produced quality ball bearings. Ben was highly educated, an engineer who entered the company just after graduate school. He and his father were very close, talking every day, and Ben instinctively knew his father's vision and helped him realize it. This was possible because Al respected Ben's less abrasive style and technical knowledge. The business prospered under their shared leadership.

Four years ago, Al died. Ben continued to run the business as he had, not seeing a major transition. But times were changing. Foreign competitors were offering cheaper bearings of astounding quality. The company received orders by bidding low and because of their reputation for quality service. But profits dissolved. There were also problems in the management team. The major managers were all friends of Al, and Ben never felt he really had the authority to overrule them. They would squabble a lot, and Ben would mediate, but not very effectively. He would settle a problem, but then either not follow through, or the problem would erupt somewhere else.

Things came to a head when Ben hired a young engineer, Tom, to oversee operations and modernize the factory. The others did not accept him, while Ben became more and more dependent on him. While the factory was in crisis, the two would talk for hours about new ideas. Ben felt that the managers weren't acting like a team but didn't know what to do.

In meeting with everyone, I noticed that expectations weren't very clear. The managers were angry not at Ben's authority, but rather his lack of it. He didn't make decisions and carry them out; rather he withdrew and avoided situations. They were frustrated. They felt Tom was competent, but that he and Ben spent too much time together, keeping Tom from really getting involved in working at the plant.

It was clear that Ben was giving his team a double message. He was telling them to participate and develop things, but he wouldn't give them any control. Rather he would listen as if he were a parent and then make a decision. He never thought to empower his employees to take action. Even Tom felt like a child. Talking to Ben, it was clear that he had become like his father, with Tom playing his role as son.

The goal of my intervention was to help Ben share his burden by creating a management cabinet that would run the company. At a retreat we discussed the major issues and created task forces to work on each one. One of the big problems was how to integrate Tom into operations. Instead of being off with Ben, he became chief of engineering, on a peer level with Len, Carl, and the controller.

We worked on the management team's charter. The responsibilities of each person were clarified. Previously weekly meetings had been mostly lectures and real problems were argued about but never resolved. Often meetings were cancelled. A meeting structure was created where major problems were put on an agenda, financial data shared, and one issue discussed each week. Minutes were taken, and decisions and follow-up were monitored. All of these created a layer of organization on what had been mostly ad hoc.

The next innovation was adding structure to the lower levels of the organization. Everything in the company was run like a family: the manager told people what to do. The new structure involved creating teams that would make decisions together and troubleshoot. People received additional training so that they could take on some of the technical tasks that the leaders had been burdened with. The company also had to look at its compensation structure. It wanted employees to make a long-term commitment and so needed to offer good incentives to stay.

The example of Baker Bearings is typical of the changes that family businesses need to make to meet new challenges: shift from a parental figure taking care of things to a team sharing responsibility and offering significant financial rewards for success. It isn't enough to thank people. The currency of the corporate world is sharing profits and ownership. As a family business begins to move from paternalism to collaboration, the compensation system has to be revamped. Profit sharing, gain sharing, and offering of stock are common ways to make sure that people who have been responsible for the company's development are motivated to continue giving. The awareness among long-term employees that the family is harvesting the value of the company, or earning a hugely disproportionate share of the profits, can demoralize them.

Such a transition can't come overnight. People have a difficult time changing. The key to making such change in a company is patience, keeping people involved in sharing the process and helping people learn new skills. In the new situation, much more is expected from each employee. Some people will respond as if a window has been opened. They liked the security of the old culture, but the new challenge is even more exciting. Others will resent the change, feeling things shouldn't have to change, that it's not fair. They will need encouragement, and perhaps a little confrontation. In a major organizational transition, as many as one third of the employees may leave. But this opens the opportunity to recruit new people with better skills.

The hidden resource of the family business is the untapped creativity and initiative of its employees. The traditional family business culture does not ask much from employees. Now, everyone is asked to participate in making decisions and sharing control. This will be a shock for many employees, who have been rewarded for loyalty and conformity.

The shift to participatory management can be exhilarating. Ken Clarke was a management consultant who occasionally helped his mother, June, with organizational problems in her home nursing care business. She started the business out of her home when Ken was a child. As the business grew and faced new regulatory demands, Ken began to spend more time helping her. Finally, a few years ago, he began to work there full time, at first temporarily, then becoming president. As the company grew to become the largest home health agency in Marin County, California, Ken faced the problem of motivating and developing the staff to meet the incredible demands of their jobs. He was a business-man, not a nurse, and he needed the marketing and clinical skills of his staff.

His choice was to make the organization one that was really "owned" by its staff. First he created a powerful incentive bonus for each staff member, based on the growth of the organization. He decided that all profits should go to the employees equally as bonuses to the extent that profits existed. Then he moved to build a new management structure where a team shared decisions and worked together. Over a year, in thoughtful, careful steps, he moved from a benevolent dictatorship to mutual collaboration. The nurses and home health workers on his clinical staff became among the highest paid in the nation, as befits an agency that is tremendously efficient and effective. As the family torch moved to the second generation, Ken built a very different and much larger organiza-tion than the one his mother ran. After family discussion, it was decided that ownership of the business will pass to Ken's daughter, Katy.

Family Involvement: Crisis of Will and Wealth

As the business reaches a new stage of development, a family must reassess its mode of involvement. The basic questions are: does the family have the commitment to take the business where it needs to go and does the family have the ability and skills to take the business where it needs to go? Both questions need to be explored and deliberated as the family plans its involvement in the next stage of the business. There is no reason why the family needs to own or manage the business. It needs to decide if it wants to do that, and not feel that it is trapped and has no choice.

The major tasks concerning family involvement are to evaluate the skills of family managers in each generation, to plan with the needs of the business future in mind, and to settle issues of future ownership and control. If you've established a Family Council, it has set the parameters for family involvement, but the question remains whether the business is best served by that involvement.

During any transition, the relationship of family and business must be reexamined. Does the business come first, or the family? Some families place the business first, and family involvement must be subordinated to business interests. These companies find it easier to decide to shift to professional management, and can recruit managers with the assurance that they are coming to a business, not an extension of the family. Other families have the business to serve their family. They use the business to provide employment and harvest cash from the business when things are going well. This stance may strengthen the family but weaken the business. Employees may resent their looting the business, or feel demoralized or frustrated in getting business needs addressed, and may quit in bitterness. In most cases, the trend will be for a family business that had initially been run for the family to shift in the direction of being run as a business first. This will enable the business to generate the resources that need to be ploughed back into development, and will demonstrate to non-family managers that the business will also serve their interests.

Another question to be settled is the overall direction of the business. Is it to remain independent, or entertain acquisition offers? While any company today is a candidate for acquisition, a family business must define its intentions as clearly as it can. Family members can be involved in management or ownership, both or neither. There are several options:

- Retain management and ownership;
- Retain ownership, hire non-family management;
- Share ownership and management;
- Sell company, stay in management;
- Sell company, leave management, start new ventures.

If suitable family talent is not available to run the business, then the family will often consider a sale rather than a move to non-family management. In that way, the family will be able to take out its investment. This enables individuals in the family to make their own choices about investment opportunities, and offers the family more individuation.

Selling all or part of the company it often difficult, as the business is the family. The business often holds a deep meaning for the family that makes it hard to let go or say goodbye. But if a sale seems the right choice, then the problem becomes finding buyers who can run the company and have the financial means to give the current owners the cash they need and ought to get. The key manager or managers are conceivable buyers of the business. They know customers and the business' potential. Another possible buyer is a competitor or larger company.

One alternative is to sell the business to employees in an Employee Stock Ownership Plan (ESOP). The ESOP is an employee benefit. It creates a market of people with an interest in buying the company, the talent to run it, and the means to fund the purchase. This enables the older generation and non-managing relatives to get some of their investment out of the business, and keeps ownership among people who have a stake in the future growth of the business: employees and managers. It helps resolve the conflict with the needs of the older generation by paying elders to relinquish control to the new generation. It also fights paternalism by sharing leadership and control among a broader group, sometimes everyone in the company.

Studies find that employees who are part of ESOPs are more participatory, and such businesses have a higher rate of growth and profit than comparative non-ESOP companies. ESOPs are only several years old, and are increasing geometrically. They are a growing movement, not just to sell off failing businesses, but in service and other labor intensive industries, like Avis and United Airlines, where commitment and motivation of the work force is critical.

The family can retain ownership but leave management if it determines that the new generation does not have the will or the talent to run the business. Ownership and management are then split, as they are in a public corporation. However this is not always possible or effective in a small business. It usually runs on the owner's "sweat equity," the energy, dedication, and willingness to work long hours. There may not be enough money to pay for good management, to reinvest for the future, and to pay the income desired by the owner/heirs.

All of these choices would be easier if the family spoke with one voice. But in any transition, there are often several competing groups. Some, such as the less involved relatives, want to get their money out of the business, while one or more heirs may want the chance to run the business. If there are major differences of opinion among the family about the business, there may be an opportunity to have one side buy out the other. Instead of perpetuating a destructive battle, sometimes a family can salvage peace by removing the source of the antagonism. The point is that all concerned parties must openly discuss the various options and come to a decision.

Custodian of the Family Legacy

The family business is a rich legacy of family history. As the business moves over several generations from the entrepreneurial stage to second generation stewardship toward professional management, the family does not recede in importance. The family, as owners, are still keeper of the founding mission and meaning of the enterprise. Each generational shift poses the question of how the family legacy will be handled, and how the business can be most successful.

For example, Chris "Dowd" is chair of a small factory, the third generation heir. As chair, he is the custodian of the company, maintaining its reputation as a solid, sensible, if a trifle stodgy and conservative community enterprise. He is carrying out his family's original vision, resisting the expansionist fever that envelops his type of business.

Yet all is not peaceful or simple. Like many family businesses, this one was founded by a patriarch—in this case his grandfather just after the turn of the century—and then divided among the offspring. The company had a complex family split in its last generation. Grandfather Dowd had an older daughter and younger son. The daughter married and her husband, who was well-liked and competent, was the heir apparent. His son, Chris' father, started a promising career at a big city bank.

Suddenly and tragically, the son-in-law was killed in a freak accident. For a few years, the factory was run by stand-ins, as Grandfather continued his management. On his deathbed, he called in Chris' father and asked him to take over. Melodramatic, but a request that couldn't be refused. Chris' father became president, but his sister received half ownership. While daughter owned half, her brother's firm control over operations meant she effectively had no say. Like his father, Chris spent a few years in an urban bank, married, and entered the family firm. Also like his father, he was knowledgeable and competent. As Chris entered his thirties, the stage was set for the transition to his management. Like all things in this family, it was played in muted tones.

Father and son, both strong and able, had different dispositions. Dad remembered the Depression, where companies survived by being stolid and unchangeable. Chris, like most sons, wanted to strike out in new ways. He and Dad bumped heads, but slowly Chris won Dad over. The generational shift happened gradually over nearly 20 years, as Chris' youthful folly mellowed, and his father let go. During that time, Chris looked for ways that he could express his own personal style, building his own identity while in the shadow of his father. Like many second and third generation heirs, he became involved in community service.

When his father died, there were three major shareholders in the family: the father's second wife, Chris, and his sister, all of whom were on the board. It might be predicted that the children would resent their stepmother's control. The recent court battle between the children and new wife of E. Seward Johnson for control over his Johnson & Johnson company fortune is one of many intergenerational battles that can paralyze family businesses. However, Chris liked and respected his stepmother. Differences arose with his sister, although the precise reasons were never clear. For years, the board has been a quiet battleground between the two.

Chris was now chairman of the board. He was not involved in everyday operations, but rather represented the company in the community, and set its overall strategy and policy. This year, another important transition will take place. The board must choose a new president. Chris' candidate is a long-time employee, a good manager. His sister wants someone else, a younger person who has been with the firm only three years. The younger person is less experienced, but more charismatic, aggressive, and talented.

The decisive board meeting began with a discussion of the two candidates. Chris was aware that he had the votes to get his man elected. He also knew that the win would create very hard feelings. Another feeling gnawed at him. He sensed that this was a special moment. Suddenly, unexpectedly, he began to question his assumptions. He intuited that his candidate may not have been the best person to take the company into the future. He stunned everyone on the board when he recommended that the younger man be selected. Afterwards, he talked privately to his candidate, and found that his reservations were shared, and the man would not leave if he were not elevated. In fact, he was made a director of operations, and promoted as well.

Chris was elated and deeply affected. He had agonized and struggled over this choice for several months. He knew his choice was right, and moreover, that it represented a special potential for healing between the two sides of the family. He looked forward to building on that base in the coming years. Chris saw his stewardship as carrying a special obligation. In this case, and earlier with his father, it involved holding back his own personal preferences. But the result was that he felt fuller, more successful than if he had followed his personal need to have his way. This is the special reward of some family business heirs.

Chris has not lacked opportunities to take responsibility or to give in his own unique way. His legacy offers him time to be on several community boards, and to exercise influential leadership in several areas of the community. Here he has his own special work, and pursues his own personal growth. The business is not only for him, but for the family and community.

Looking ahead he sees another transition. Both his children and his sister's are graduating from college. He envisions some of them entering the company. He can only speculate about what will happen, because the next generation has to chart its own course. But he still has a few years to steer and help out.

Dynasties in Public Companies

Many family businesses grow to modest size and then go public to raise capital, to provide cash to family members, to bring in new management talent, or to limit liability. The decision to sell stock and become a public company, while limiting family control and influence, does not end it. Many public companies remain family businesses, with family members firmly in management control, and family heirs being trained as successors. A second generation McDonnell runs McDonnell Douglas, number 34 on the Fortune 500, and a member of the third generation is on his way up. The Busch family has headed Fortune's number 53, Anheuser-Busch, for four generations, and the fifth generation is in place. Weyerhauser, number 66, has George Weyerhauser, fourth generation at the helm, and his nephew heads a division.

The family issues I have been presenting do not end in a public company. Rather they become more complex and the stakes become higher. The disposition of the family's stock holdings to heirs, and the way they are used to influence management, affect the business future.

Edsel and Billy Ford, great grandsons of Henry, announced their frustrations with the non-family management at Ford in a cover story in *Fortune*. They are both fast-track middle managers. The family dimension of their power lies in the 40% of the special class of stock owned by the Ford family that allows them to retain control. Their feelings erupted in public when they were not named to the powerful executive committee of the board of directors. They felt they were being treated as second class board members. Actually, their role represents part of a delicate power sharing. If the whole family, which includes scores of Fords, were behind them, then things would be easier. But the rest of the family is behind management, and, while it wants Edsel and Billy to succeed, does not want to push its weight around. The Ford Family Council will have to thrash out the issue. Meanwhile, Edsel and Billy continue to be middle-managers and sit on the company board. While it is likely that one of them will rise to the top of the company some day, it is by no means assured.

It's not that the family couldn't put them on the top. It's that they wouldn't, at least not yet. As a public company, the family has more interests than just putting their own into power. When a family business goes public, the family has to share its power and influence with other stockholders and management. As long as the family remains a unified block, it can retain power. But when a family feud or a split causes a rift, then the company can be bought up by a canny raider. They often get a good deal by exploiting family squabbles. Moreover if a raider wants the company badly enough to offer a premium price, then a firm can be bought.

Going public dilutes the family interest, but it does not end it. The family that is small, and able to clearly define its interest, can remain in control. When the family gets larger, and begins to put significant portions of its stock into trusts, control is less firm. When a family is large and several generations removed from management, or when only a few heirs remain as managers, then the family begins to define a more distant role towards the business. As at duPont, while the family retains significant shares, its interest in the company is more of an investment. It acts like most public shareholders, pressuring management for a good return, and prodding them for high performance.

The large families behind large family companies form complex extended family organizations. Unlike other families whose blood ties become weaker as they grow apart and pursue separate interests, a family organized around a company or a series of business interests in trusts, has many reasons to remain together. Members gather together regularly not just for fraternal purposes, but to make decisions about business interests. The rules for participation in a large family business and the meaning of ownership and participation usually get more codified and explicit as generations succeed each other.

But even when a family has only a small percentage of ownership of the company it founded, a family member who enters management still has a significant advantage. First, there is the symbolic role of the bearer of the company name. Second, if he or she owns enough stock, he or she can't afford to be alienated. It is hard to fire an employee who has such special advantages. So the role of the family heir even in a public company tends to be highly visible, and very political. Succession is never automatic, and at a public company, there is a highly visible apprenticeship and trial. As in other family businesses, the heir would do well to work outside the family company where he or she can develop in less of a hothouse atmosphere. When the heir shows promise, and enters the company, he or she can take on a series of visible responsibilities, en route to the top. Of course, in a smaller family, owning more of the stock, ascension is more assured. But to run today's large company, an heir needs to have not only the spark and the dedication, but the ability.

Non-family management is much more important as a family firm grows. Some companies, for example Hallmark and Noxcell, have called on an interim, non-family leader when heirs skip a generation or are not ready to assume leadership. The interim manager can be a talented outsider who comes in for a period or a loyal manager who has earned a period of glory. Some growing companies employ an outside manager as a tutor/mentor to the heir. A San Francisco service company I know hired an interim manager to help the company grow and set up a franchise system. The owner was aware that he did not have the skills to accomplish the transition nor did his son. The manager trained the 28-year-old son to take over operations when he left after four productive years. The manager was well rewarded, and the son inherited a stronger company.

Similarly, after World War II, Ford Motor Company was floundering. Henry had died, and Ford's rivals had all adopted modern management techniques, while Ford retained the worst features of family management. In addition, towards the end Henry had given major power to Harry Bennett, who was little more than a gangster. The family, sisters of Edsel who had died, saw that young Henry II might be the person to unify behind. But Henry was just out of college, and had shown no aptitude thus far for management. So he was made president with a top manager hired away from rival GM to teach him. Ultimately Henry signalled the end of his apprenticeship by abruptly firing his mentor.

That is why recruiting good non-family top management can be difficult for a family firm. While many people join companies for reasons other than being CEO, top managers want to know where they stand when they enter. They want to know the family rules, expectations, and power structure before they enter. The reasons are obvious. First, they want to know what kind of rules apply to family competitors or coworkers. Can they demand performance from a family member, or would that be insubordination? Are there two company structures, the outside managers and the family managers? The wise outside manager wants to know the rules of the game before entering. That is why many family companies have drawn up rules, and even excluded family members from the company or the top spot. They feel that supporting the power of employees, who are now responsible for the success of the company, is not possible without assuring them that a family member can't jump in and take control. Knowing when to remove the family, or when a family member should step aside for non-family management, is one of the most important strategic decisions a family business can make.

Over time, the symbiosis and balance between ownership, family, and management spheres becomes more defined and codified in a large and evolved family business. The boundaries that a first or second generation family business had to struggle to define are clear, and the rules for moving from one to another have been made explicit.

For its first years, the family can operate its business by itself, with employees in highly subordinate roles. It can also organize the business rather loosely, and act as if the business is an extension of the family. As time goes on, though, the continued success of the business rests not just in the family succession, but in the collaboration that evolves between the family managers inheriting the business and the management team. As we've seen, the development of a strong team means questioning some of the paternalistic elements of the family business, and the creation of new strategies, structures, and styles of family involvement. The business must work with non-family members employees and advisors. Creating a strong non-family team to help run the business, and empowering them with information and responsibility, is the most powerful means to insure a healthy, long-lived family business.

Notes:

1. Hardman, Curtis. "Taking the 'Family' out of Family Business." *Inc.*, September 1986.
2. Adapted from Eric Flamholtz, *How to Make the Transition from An Entrepreneurship to a Professionally Managed Firm.*
4. See Danco, Leon and Jonovic, Donald, *Outside Directors in the Family Owned Business*, and *Family Business Review*, Vol. 1 (3), special issue on outside boards edited by John Ward.

10

Healthy Family, Healthy Business: A Secure Future

"Home is where the heart is. And the heart must come to work, if we are to meet the expectations of the new work force.

"More than ever before, people expect to find their worth affirmed at work. Twenty years ago, not even 5 percent of our population expected to develop their potential and find satisfaction through work. Today, 40 percent of employees believe they have a fundamental right to self-fulfillment, to develop and use their intellectual and creative abilities to the fullest. They believe they are worth as much to the company as their managers. They want to perform meaningful work that brings value to the world, and they have the latent power to insist on being treated as worthy."

-*Kate Ludeman,* The Worth Ethic

As Ludeman suggests, this is an era where the heart is coming into business and the task for the nineties is to create workplaces where people care for one another. My consulting firm, operated with Cynthia Scott, is called The HeartWork Group. We coined the word HeartWork to refer to a special type of work relationship characterized by deep caring for one's self, one's colleagues, and one's work. In a HeartWork workplace, people feel connected to the inner source of their values and the meanings of their lives. They feel cared for by and connected to their co-workers, and feel satisfied, fulfilled and healthy in their work. While many companies are moving to create environments for HeartWork, in my search for places where people can work with heart, the first place I look to is family business.

A family business is formed first because of caring relationships and only secondarily to make profits. A new generation today is entering their families' businesses and forming new ones as an alternative to the depersonalized cultures of many other businesses. They see the family business as a place where managers can be caring, where they can create a business culture that produces profits as well as respecting people. In many ways, family represents the essential qualities of the model for the business environment individuals now seek.

It is ironic that the business challenge of the decade can be answered by family businesses, because until a few years ago, they were widely regarded as dinosaurs, a form of ancient business fast becoming extinct. At the time, most people felt their demise was necessary and good. But family businesses were hardier than the pundits thought and they are having a powerful resurgence.

Family Health Underlies Business Success

There are many lessons and themes that can be drawn from our journey through the world of family business. The most important is that the cornerstone of a healthy family business is a healthy family. While a business can sometimes be financially successful without strong positive family bonds, when the business is a substitute for a vital family, or an escape from, or recapitulation of, family tensions the limitations and difficulties of the family will ultimately sink it. Therefore, you need to build healthy, vital, flexible, supportive, open, and communicative family bonds in order to build a strong family business.

A healthy family is perhaps the greatest resource for current and future business success for it provides a repository of core values, develops committed talent, builds on deep personal connections, and enables the business to maintain a long-term focus on the future. The development of effective governance and communication structures within the family—the Family Council and retreats, for example—will inevitably and positively impact on parallel structures in the business.

A troubled family will also impact the business, albeit negatively. Personal tensions will affect both the owner's ability to maintain a clear focus on the business and will negatively influence the commitment to the future. Bad feelings will promote a me-first attitude towards ownership and management, even if family members are shareholders. A troubled family often denies potential difficulties and crises caused by disgruntled or angry family members. Difficult family patterns are transferred to the business when participants try to use the business to address family hurts. They can frustrate important decisions and muddle the business' goal-directed focus. In addition they can amplify rather than heal the already considerable personal pain that individuals experience due to these issues.

Healthy Family, Healthy Business

My major premise has been that to have a healthy family business you need to have both effective family and business relationships. The underlying characteristics of both relationships contain the same elements:

Caring: Individuals in the family, and in the business, must have a basic respect and caring for one another as people. The business must allow for personal needs, and the business and the family must acknowledge, and strive to accommodate, the needs of family members and employees. People should have a good time together, both at work and at leisure.

Security: Family members and employees work to support themselves and to build a secure future. While job security is becoming a thing of the past, the family business should provide secure employment for employees who are committed to the business, and employees should share in the profits of the business. At the same time, it must maintain strong profitability and effectiveness in order to provide for the future security of the family. A strong business that is run as a business is critical to the future well being of the family members who have a stake in it.

Growth: People in the family need to grow, develop their talents, and realize their unique potential. So do employees—both for their own satisfaction and for the future of the business. A family business that supports personal growth will provide ways for heirs to use the family resources to develop, will allow family members to move appropriately into responsible positions in the business, and will overcome its resistance and fear of change.

Developing caring, security, and growth in the family and in the business, for family members as well as employees, requires a willingness to break with some of the past traditions and habits of the family and the workplace. While paternalism has been the norm of families and family businesses for generations, this book suggests that modern business needs, as well as the emerging values of the new generation in family business demand a new management structure for both the business and for the family, at least insofar as adult children are concerned. There is no more room for "father knows best" in the family or single-person leadership in the modern company. Of course there are still important and powerful representatives of the old style in family business today, but they are moving toward extinction. Neither the family nor the family business, nor any growing business, can be run under one person's exclusive authority.

Bringing it All Together

In summary, as a family business, you have what I have called dual relationships with most family members. You have a personal/family relationship and a work/business relationship. To be successful, you must nurture both.

For a family to develop deep, nurturing, supportive relationships that enable a person to feel connected but also to grow up, it needs to have the following:

1. Clear Sense of Purpose: Knowing what your family stands for and having a vision of the future. Having clear and explicit goals and values.

2. Open, Explicit Communication: Allowing each person to express feelings, needs, issues, desires and aspirations frequently, openly, and immediately.

3. Acceptance of Individual Differences: Resolving conflict, forgiving hurts, and discovering win/win resolutions.

4. Nurturance of Growth and Evolution: Understanding history, able to harmonize individual, family, and business cycles. Expecting change and differences as people mature.

5. Balance: Having a life outside the business and the time as a family to enjoy something other than work.

These qualities are the base upon which you build your family's business relationships. Look at each of these factors and reflect on how your family fosters or inhibits each one. What does your family do to encourage each factor and what does it do to frustrate it? By this time you should not feel helpless if your family makes it difficult for you because you now know many things you can do to change the situation.

Now shifting to your family as a business unit, several elements are important to the effectiveness of your work relationships. To a large extent, these qualities are needed in any work relationship, but, as we have seen, they are sometimes especially difficult to achieve among family members:

1. Future Focus: Planning for business development, career paths, and succession.

2. Clear Roles: Having explicit, clearly defined work roles and differentiated responsibilities.

3. Accountability: Taking responsibility for results and having work evaluated consistently and openly. Rewards for work done, not family membership.

4. Outside Perspectives: Seeking advice from professionals outside the family. Bringing fresh perspectives into the business. Supporting, developing, respecting, and rewarding non-family employees.

5. Business Forum: Formal mechanism for exploring work/family issues and resolving conflicts.

To complete your journey, go back to the **Family Business Assessment Inventory** in Chapter 1, and fill it out again. Have there been changes? What have you learned as a result of your work in this book? Take some time as a family to consider what you have learned about each other, and the effect of opening up to discussion what previously was only assumed.

The family business experience is a container for all of the basic dramas of life and personal development. It expresses what you value most and is your legacy for the future. Working within a business is one of the most powerful and important ways that a family can further the growth and self-expression of its members and create visible, concrete achievements in the community. But many people avoid or withdraw from family business because of conflict or difficulty. My experience and that of many others suggest that the opportunities make it worth braving the difficulties. The results can be yours, not just for a lifetime, but for several lifetimes beyond you. What appear as insurmountable difficulties are usually resolvable. It is worth putting in the "sweat equity" to develop powerful work/family relationships.

I hope you have traveled slowly through this book, stopping to explore your own relationship to your family and its business, and using the book as a jumping-off point for some important self-exploration and family discussions. I have tried to provoke you into your own personal reflections and to prod you into becoming a leader within your family. I have suggested many possibilities for strengthening your business, and avoiding or overcoming the predictable crises and struggles. My hope is that the reflection questions, exercises, and stories have led you to see your family and your business differently. More possibilities and skills should now lie before you for resolving family struggles and for promoting effective business development. If you felt stuck, or caught, between yourself and your family, or between family and business, I hope that you have found some ways to resolve this dichotomy.

I wish you well in your journey toward the best future for you, your family, and your business.

Bibliography

Alcorn, Pat B. *Success and Survival in the Family-Owned Business.* McGraw-Hill, 1982.

Alderfer, Clayton P. "Understanding and Consulting to Family Business Boards." *Family Business Review,* Volume 1(3), Fall 1988.

Aldrich, Nelson W. "Feuding Families." *Inc.,* January 1985.

Appleton, Dr. William S. "Fathers and Daughters." *Savvy,* October, 1981.

Bachrach, Judy. "The Roman Empire." *Savvy,* December 1987.

Bank, Stephen P. and Kahn, Michael D. *The Sibling Bond.* Basic Books, Inc., 1982.

Barach, Jeffrey A. "Is There a Cure for the Paralyzed Family Board?" *Sloan Management Review,* Fall 1984.

Barnes, Louis B. "Incongruent Hierarchies: Daughters and Younger Sons as Company CEOs." *Family Business Review,* Volume 1(1), Spring 1988.

Barnett, Frank and Barnett, Sharan. Working Together: *Entrepreneurial Couples.* Ten Speed Press, 1988.

Barry, Bernard. "The Development of Organization Structure in the Family Firm." *Journal of General Management,* Volume 3(1), Autumn 1975.

Barthel, Diane. "When Husbands and Wives Try Working Together." *Working Woman,* November 1985.

Benedict, Burton. "Family Firms and Economic Development." *Journal of Anthropology,* Volume 24.1, Spring 1968.

Benson, Benjamin. "Do You Keep Too Many Secrets?" *Nation's Business,* August 1989.

Benson, Benjamin, Crego, Edwin, and Drucker, Ronald. *Your Family Business.* Dow Jones Irwin, 1990.

Berger, Peter and Kellner, Hansfried. "Marriage and the Social Construction of Reality." Dreitzel, Hans ed. *Recent Sociology 2.* Macmillan, 1970.

Bernstein, Paula. "Family Ties, Corporate Bonds." *Working Woman,* May 1985.

Blotnick, Srully. "The Case of the Reluctant Heirs." *Forbes,* July 16, 1984.

Bork, David. *Family Business, Risky Business.* AMACOM, 1986.

McLaughlin, Joyce and Byrne, Noel. "Family Business: The Family's View," *Vision/Action*, 7:(4), June 1988.

McWhinney, Will. "Entrepreneurs, Owners and Stewards: The Conduct of a Family Business." *New Management*, July 1988.

McWhinney, Will. "Working with a Family-Managed Business: Elements of the New Practice." *Vision/Action*, Volume 7.(4) June 1988.

Merwin, R.F. "Does Your Firm Need Outsiders on the Inside?" *Nation's Business*, February 1982.

✳Nelton, Sharon. *In Love and in Business*. John Wiley & Sons, 1986.

Nelton, Sharon."Marrying Into a Family Business." *Nation's Business*, April 1989.

Nelton, Sharon."Shaky about Joining the Family Firm?" *Nation's Business*, November, 1983.

Newman, Peter C. "The Promise of Family-Owned Firms." *Macleans*, April 7, 1986.

Novak, Michael. "Family Business and the Business of Families." *Loyola Magazine*, Volume 12(3), Fall 1983.

O'Toole, James. *Vanguard Management*. Doubleday, 1985.

Paisner, Daniel. "The Family Business." *New York Times Magazine*, October 5, 1986.

Paul, Jordan and Margaret. *From Conflict to Caring*. CompCare Press, 1988.

Peiser, Richard B. and Wooten, Leland M. "Life-Cycle Changes in Small Family Businesses." *Business Horizons*, May/June 1983.

Peters, Tom and Waterman, Robert. *In Search of Excellence*. Harper and Row, 1982.

Poe, Randall. "The SOB's." *Across the Board*, May 1980.

Posner, Bruce G. "All My Sons." *Inc.*, January 1987.

Rosenblatt, Paul C., de Mik, Leni, Anderson, Roxanne Marie and Johnson, Patricia A. *The Family in Business*. Jossey-Bass, 1985.

Rottenberg, Dan. "All in the Family: The Top Privately Held Companies in America." *Town & Country*, August 1984.

Rutigliano, Anthony J. "When Worlds Collide." *Management Review*, February 1986.

Ryan, Ann C. "All in the Family." *Minnesota Business Journal*, December 1983.

Schurenberg, Eric. "Family Wealth: A Short Course in Estate Planning." *Money*, Special Report, October 1987.

Sonnenfeld, Jeffrey. *The Hero's Farewell: What Happens When CEOs Retire.* Oxford University Press, 1988.

Stanley, Marcus. *Minding the Store.* Little, Brown, 1974.

Stryker, Perrin. "Would You Hire Your Son?" *Fortune,* March 1957.

Teal, Thomas A. and Willigan, Geraldine E. "The Outstanding Outsider and the Fumbling Family." *Harvard Business Review,* September-October 1989.

Tift, Susan. "Mothers and Daughters." *Savvy,* January 1984.

Titus, Sandra, Rosenblatt, Paul C. and Anderson Roxanne M. "Family Conflict Over Inheritance of Property." *The Family Coordinator,* July 1979.

Topolnicki, Denise M. "Family Firms Can Leave the Feuds Behind." *Money,* July 1983.

Toy, Stewart. "The New Nepotism." *Business Week,* April 4, 1988.

Ward, John L. *Keeping the Family Business Healthy.* Jossey-Bass, 1987.

Ward, John L. "Siblings and the Family Business." *Loyola Business Forum,* Volume 5(1), Fall 1986.

Waterman, Robert, Jr. *The Renewal Factor.* Bantam, 1987.

White, III, Frank. "Widows Who Run the Family Business." *Ebony,* November 1983.

Resources

Seminars and Consulting

The Heartwork Group
Dennis Jaffe, Ph.D.
Cynthia D. Scott, Ph.D.
764 Ashbury Street
San Francisco, CA 94117
Phone: 415-759-9675
Fax: 415-759-7678
Consultation to family businesses on strategic planning, succession, management team and family team development, communication and conflict resolution. Keynote talks, seminars and educational materials based on the material in this book. Consulting to companies about the problems of managing change, growth and creating high commitment, high participation workplaces.

The Bork Institute for Family Business at Aspen
117 Aspen Airport Business Center, Suite 101
Aspen, CO 81611
Phone: 303-925-8555
Fax: 303-925-8557

David Bork, Kathy Wiseman, Leslie Isaacs, Ann Dapice, Sam Lane, Nick Bizony, Elizabeth McGrath, Tom McMurrain and Dennis Jaffe, Associates. Provides consulting and educational resources to family businesses. Sponsors annual Aspen Family Business Conference.

Professional Organizations

The Family Firm Institute
PO Box 476
Johnstown, NY 12095
Phone: 518-762-3853
Professional organization for family business resources, researchers and family business members. Sponsors annual conference, and publishes *Family Buisness Review*, journal of family business.

Newsletters, Magazines

Business Week Newsletter for Family-Owned Business
McGraw-Hill Publishing Company
1221 Avenue of the Americas
New York, NY 10124

Family Business
38 Mahaiwe St.
Great Barrington, MA 01230

Nation's Business
1615 H. St. NW
Washington, DC 20062

Inc.
PO Box 54129
Boulder, CO 80322